THE BITTER END

JUST CAUSE

Selina Rosen

The Bitter End
Selina Rosen
First Edition Copyright © Selina Rosen, 2016

Published under "Just Cause," an imprint of Yard Dog
Press

Print Version ISBN 978-1-937105-86-0
The Bitter End
First Edition Copyright © Selina Rosen, 2016

Yard Dog Press
710 W. Redbud Lane
Alma, AR 72921-7247

http://www.yarddogpress.com

Edited by Tina Black
Copy & Technical Editor Lynn Rosen
Cover art by Melanie Fletcher

First Print Edition June 15, 2016
Printed in the United States of America
0 9 8 7 6 5 4 3 2 1

DEDICATION

Dedicated to Lisa Ann Colton, who gave me the last piece of the puzzle that built the book, and to Knox Inman who asked, "What's with all the bisexual bashing?"

CHAPTER 1

At least narcissists leave you alone until they want something.

It had been a long day, and Ally really just wanted to go home. She slung her tool box in the back of her truck and turned just in time to see Maggie trotting across the parking lot towards her. For a second she started to act like she didn't see her.

"Don't you dare," Maggie said, a hint of laughter in her voice.

Ally sighed and turned to face her.

"Couldn't you call someone else?"

"I get it, I do. I was almost out the door when the damn phone rang...."

"Why didn't you just let it ring?"

Maggie smiled and patted Ally's cheek fondly. "Oh Honey, that is so NOT me. It's an emergency so they would have called you next anyway. The watering system Chuck installed at the Green's is soaking the side of their house."

"If he wasn't Mitch's son...."

"Yes I know but he is and you know damn good and well you'd miss him if he were gone. Sorry, Ally. If it's any consolation this will put you into overtime." Maggie smiled and headed back into the building.

Ally mumbled and went to the supply shed she'd just locked up for the night and unlocked it. She pulled out anything she might need for the job, locked the shed back up, and headed for her truck. Maggie was walking out of the office, her two year old in tow. He waved at Ally and Ally waved back. Mitch was just flat one of the good guys—the proof being that he let Maggie bring her kid to work with her.

Of course it might be nicer if he could pay her enough money to put the kid in day care, but until just the last few months business had been spotty and they'd all had to pull in their belts on occasion. Besides Ally got the impression

Maggie liked having her baby with her, so it was decent of Mitch to let her do it. Maggie walked over holding the toddler's hand and hugged Ally.

"What was that for?" Ally asked with a smile.

"You just looked like you could use a hug," she said stepping back.

Ally smiled. "Thanks." She wondered if Maggie remembered what day it was or if she just sensed that Ally was more twitchy than usual. Maggie was their resident flake; her desk was strewn with crystals, candles and stones of every color and size. She was filled with love and talked of peace and higher consciousness and a bunch of other crap Ally couldn't begin to wrap her head around. Maggie probably knew her better than anyone else, and Ally had so needed that hug.

Tuesday—who'd been born on a Saturday—looked up at Ally and smiled. She sighed, reached in her pocket, pulled out her wallet, and got a dollar bill out. The toddler took it happily, looked up at his mother and said, "Go to the store."

Maggie looked at Ally and smiled. "I asked you to stop giving him money every time you see him."

Ally just shrugged. She'd known this kid all his life—since before he was born—but the truth was that she was only starting to really enjoy him, and she still had no idea what to do with him. When he'd been a tiny baby every time Maggie had tossed him Ally's direction she had been a nervous wreck like she was going to break him or something. Tuesday was really the only baby, or child for that matter, she'd ever been around. He was a good kid; she liked him. He said and did funny things, and he didn't cry and break shit all the time like Ray's kids did. Tuesday seemed really happy when she handed him money, so Maggie wasn't going to win this argument that Ally didn't want to have.

"It will be alright, Ally," Maggie said. She patted Ally on the cheek again and then she and the boy walked back to her old, rattle-trap, almost-green Subaru wagon.

Ally got in the truck shaking her head. She started the engine and headed for the job site. She took a deep breath let it out and said out loud, "My mood must be affecting the ether of the universal chi or something."

Five years. Where did the time go and why hadn't it gone quicker? Five years ago that very day some stupid-assed kid didn't see them and... *Helen's dead five years, and after*

*three surgeries I'm just lucky I can walk at all. Life goes on,
but it really doesn't... at least it isn't the same.*

She shook the thoughts from her head and was almost
glad to see the water shooting across the yard and into the
side of the three-hundred-thousand dollar house. She had
been ready to go home but why? So she could wallow in her
self-pity? Replay the events of that night over and over in her
head, wondering for the hundred thousandth time what she
might have done that would have changed the outcome? So
she could drink a few hard ciders and focus on the emptiness
of her life and her house? It was better to be working.

It was always better to be working.

She had the job finished in a couple of hours but of course
she was now soaking, dripping wet and covered in mud. Still
better than sitting alone at home, and at least it was a fairly
warm day.

As she pulled into her driveway she saw someone sitting
on her door step. She couldn't see who but hoped it wasn't
Laurie. She only ever saw her "friend" when she was drunk
or needed something, usually both. Laurie couldn't go ten
minutes without a woman in her life. Because of this she was
always hooking up with some total skank. Laurie put
everything she had into the relationship—which wasn't
much—then when they had completely used her up and she
was alone she showed up drunk on Ally's doorstep needing
money, help moving, or the ever-popular both.

Ally got out of the truck and tried to wipe all the mud off
her shoes on the concrete surface of her driveway. She looked
towards the doorstep, but without her glasses she couldn't
really make out who it was. She rarely wore her glasses
because the truth was she didn't notice much difference in
the way she saw with or without them. The person looked
too big to be Laurie, so she relaxed a little till she got closer
and could see who it really was and then... well then she
wished it was Laurie.

If you had made a long list of the people she least wanted
to see on this day at this time, he would have been right on
the very top of that list. She walked up and looked down at
the man setting on the porch at the top of the second step.

Before she could stop herself she said with no charity

whatsoever, "What the hell are you doing here?"

The old man looked up at her with a sigh. "I've got no place else to go, Alice."

"Try going home, Dad."

"I can't. I signed the house over to your sister when your mother died. I've been living in an apartment..."

"Then go there." She walked up the stairs past him, sat down on the bench against the wall and took her boots off because they were still covered in thick, red mud. She stood up, pulled her keys out of her pocket and started unlocking the door.

"I can't stay there anymore."

That was when Ally saw the two suitcases on her front porch. She spun on him even as she opened the door, "What's going on?"

"I've got nowhere to go, Alice, nowhere." He started to cry.

She sighed walked over to him put down her hand and helped him to his feet. "Come on in."

His arm lacked any muscle tone at all, and when she helped him inside and flipped on the lights he looked like he'd aged much more than the ten years it had been since she'd last seen him—for the three seconds it took her mother to tell her to leave. He was only sixty-seven, but he looked like he was in his eighties.

"Call Carol and have her come and get you." She wasn't going to leave him outside, but the sooner he was gone the better. *Why tonight of all nights? What in hell's name is going on? Why is he here? Why would he think for one minute that I'd let him stay with me? I'm his demon spawn straight from and going right back to hell where I came from, why would he want to stay here?*

"Carol is the one that dropped me on your door step," he said, using his sleeve for a snot rag.

"What?!"

"Jimmy said it was me or him."

"How is that my problem? It's your house; kick them out. Get on the phone old man. Call them and have them come get you because you are not staying with me!"

"You call her," he said. Now he was mad at her and as far as she was concerned he had no right at all to be in her space much less yell at her.

"She doesn't talk to me for the same reason you don't. Why would I have her number? You call her..."

"I'm your father; you will show me some respect..."

"You know what, fuck stick? I think you're forgetting that you told me I'm not your daughter, and if I'm not then you sure as hell aren't my father. You don't get to play the father card when its convenient for you. I don't respect people who don't respect me. As long as you think you can talk to me like this why on earth would you think I should take you in? You get on the damn phone and call my perfect, perfect sister to which you gave everything while I got a great big nothing and have her get her self-righteous, hypocritical little ass over here and get you. She owes you everything; I don't owe you jack shit. I'm sure she and her husband still go to that fucked-up-the-ass, bible-thumping, moronic, bullshit church you and mother always lived for, so she ought to be all over celebrating Jesus by taking care of you. For that matter pick up your fucking bags and go to the bus station, go home and move in with one of the hundreds of brothers or sisters in your church for whom you have always shoved me aside and dropped everything to go and help."

Without another word he stomped out, slamming the door.

When Ally looked at her hands they were shaking, and she felt like she might throw up. She started to go to the bathroom. He wasn't her problem, and she shouldn't care at all what happened to him, but she went to the door and looked out the peep hole. He was on his cell phone and obviously very upset. Still not her problem. She started back for the bathroom to strip her muddy clothes off and get a shower. She almost had her shirt off when the doorbell rang. She sighed and buttoned her shirt back up.

She looked at the ceiling and shook her head. "You having a good laugh, Helen? This shit isn't funny. Come on, give a girl a break. What should I do?"

She went to the front door and opened it. The old man held the cell phone up nearly in her face. "Your sister wants to talk to you."

Ally took a deep breath knowing she'd be sorry and took the phone anyway. "Come and get him."

"Look Alice I took care of mom and... it's your turn..."

"My turn, Carol?! My turn? Are you fucking kidding me! They kicked me out and have had nothing to do with me since I was seventeen years old because you told them I was queer! They sent you to college, they apparently gave you the house, I'm sure he gave you their business. How do I owe any of you a damn thing? Now you get your worthless, Jesus-jamming ass up and come and get him!"

"Why must you constantly tempt Satan…"

"What's Jesus think of you dumping Dad here with my woman-screwing ass?" There was silence. "Yeah, that's what I thought. Come and get him."

"I can't." Carol started crying then. "Jimmy said he'd leave. He and Dad don't get along, and he said it's him or Dad and he's my husband and the Good Book says…."

"Stuff your *good book*, Carol. It's just an excuse for people to do whatever crappy thing they want to do, always has been always will be. I don't owe this old man a damn thing, and you do. You believe the utter crap he and mother have always spouted and I don't. So… come and get him. Put him in a home; get him back in his apartment. I really don't care what you do with him, but he can't stay here."

"We can't afford to put him in a home and they evicted him from his apartment building because he accidentally started a fire…"

"Started a fire! So you send him to live with me! What happened to Mom and Dad's business why is there no money?"

"No one is fishing. You know how bad the economy has been and if they are fishing they aren't buying expensive gear to do it with. Jimmy's having trouble just staying open. Mom's illness was expensive…."

"None of that crap is my fault."

Carol cried louder. "The Lord works in mysterious ways, Alice. Maybe this is your road to redemption…."

"Fuck you Carol! Fuck you! I'm going to leave him on my porch and you can come and get him or he can live in the street for all I care but he is NOT staying here."

Her sister said she could not come get him, and Ally handed her father his cell phone back and started to push him out the door. "Sorry, but I don't have the money to put you anywhere else and you can't stay here."

"It wouldn't be for long, Alice," he said in a voice tinged with anger. "I've got liver cancer; I'm terminal. They gave me six months, tops."

Ally took a deep breath and let it out then shook her head and refused to cry. She sniffed hard and made herself stop. She looked him right in the eyes and held them. "Five years ago this very night I was nearly killed. Some dumb-ass green kid pulled out of a church parking lot after a youth meeting and hit our car on the passenger's side so hard he left me a cripple and killed the only person who ever loved me. When I called you, when I reached out in my hour of need, my mother answered the phone. When I told her what had happened to me she told me that it was God's way of punishing me for being an evil sinner. So mother died a slow cancer death, Carol has taken and lost everything you ever worked for, and now you're dying a slow cancer death. I'm now apparently the only one you can turn to, so... who is punishing you, Dad?"

She walked in the office and Maggie looked up at her. "Your aura is very dark, are you alright?"

"Honestly no. You would not believe the night I had. Could you maybe talk to the universe and find out what I did to piss them off? I'd really appreciate it."

"What happened?"

"Fourth worst day of my life," Ally said.

Her boss walked out of the office then. Mitch was a big guy, six-five with arms like tree trunks. His black hair had picked up a lot of gray and some of the twinkle had left his blue eyes in the last five years, but he still looked like what he was—a huge, good guy of the white-hat variety. He walked over to her and handed her a paper. "Geez, kid, you look like you didn't sleep."

"I didn't really."

"Leg giving you fits?" He either didn't remember what day yesterday was or he was pretending he didn't for both of their sakes. From the drop of his eyes as he avoided eye contact, she guessed the latter.

"Nope, nothing that minor," Ally said forcing a smile. Mitch was more than just her boss; he was family as far as she was concerned. He was still her boss and she had no trouble at all taking orders from him, and he had no problem telling her if she screwed up. She was a good employee, competent and hardworking, so he didn't ride herd on her or boss her around.

He just did like he had just done—handed her an order and an address and sent her on her way. He trusted her to take the people she needed for the job and to get it done in a timely fashion. She made decent money and she liked what she did. Landscaping hadn't been her dream job. When she had taken it, it was what she could get at the time, but it turned out she loved it, and she had met Helen here.

She'd hated the military, but of course one of the reasons Mitch hired her was because she was a veteran. It gave him some sort of tax cut.

She looked at the order and plans in her hand she wasn't surprised at all they'd gotten the job. It was a big one building a patio, a pergola, and a water feature so it was going to take most of their equipment and half their staff for a whole week. She told Mitch as much, and he just nodded. "Get on it, Ally."

She nodded. As she started to walk out the door Maggie ran up to her and stuck something in her pocket. "It's a stone; it will help balance the negative energy." She smiled. "Come back to the office for lunch and we can talk."

"What are you going to do?" Maggie asked as she handed her son the apple she'd just cut for him.

"I honestly don't know." Ally shrugged. They were in the break room having lunch, but so far Ally hadn't taken one bite of her sandwich. She had no appetite at all. "I put him in my guest room, told him not to use the stove, and to stay out of my face till I found someplace else for him to be. But I can't afford to put him in a home, and if I put him out... well am I legally liable?"

"I don't know; I can look on the internet and see. Is he not eligible for government assistance?" Maggie asked.

"I don't know, but my cunt sister might." Ally sighed. "Sorry Maggie I know you hate that word."

"It's alright. All circumstances taken into account I'd say it fits her—or at least what she is choosing to do."

"The timing couldn't have been worse. Yesterday was the anniversary of Helen's death. Don't think she and I didn't have words last night," Ally said with a smile. The boy reached over and patted her hand, and she got the oddest sensation that he actually cared that she was upset.

"He's very in tune," Maggie explained. She turned to him and said, "Eat your food, Tuesday." Then she continued, "I'm sorry, Ally. I had completely forgotten. I think I did it on purpose. It explains why Mitch was in such a mood yesterday."

"Yeah, he made a point of telling me to drive the truck." Because of course Ally had always driven, but that day her truck had been in the shop and Helen had come to pick her up in the car. Helen had insisted that she could drive the car because after all she had gotten there, and Ally had been just tired enough to let Helen have her way. *He hit my side of the car; it should have been me. I'm the one who should be dead. Helen had lots of people who loved her, but I only had her.* She had her seat belt on. The impact had caused Helen's head to hit the side glass with enough force to shatter both the window and her skull. *She didn't suffer; she was just gone. I'm glad she didn't suffer, but why the hell am I still here?*

"Ally," Maggie said in a gentle voice, "it wasn't your fault."

Ally nodded; she knew that. She knew that because... *I'm the one who should be dead; the car folded up on me like an accordion.*

Tuesday picked up his sandwich and started to eat it. He was humming some song as he chewed, so Ally found herself taking a bite of her sandwich just to see if she could hum and eat at the same time which she should have known she could. Maggie looked at her and smiled, "What?" she said around a mouthful of sandwich.

"That's quite a skill you share with the two-year-old," Maggie said then got serious—metaphysically so. "Your father coming on *that* day... the universe is trying to tell you something."

Ally swallowed then glared at Maggie. "You know what, Maggie? I'm sick to death of the universe's big message to me being that I should just suck it up. In fact I'm tired of sucking it up. I'm like a human vacuum just going through life sucking up any little piece of crap that comes my way. I'm tired of trying to find meaning from garbage I didn't ask for in the first place. It's not *my* fault he has nowhere else to go. It wasn't *my* fault that dumbass kid crippled me and killed Helen. It *was* my fault I joined the national guard, but it certainly wasn't my fault that dumbass Bush decided to start a war and then instead of hanging out here cleaning up storm damage and crap I'm in the big middle of the middle eastern theater. I'm tired of trying to find meaning in the tattered remains of my life, and mostly today I'm just tired!"

She got up and stormed off. Maggie turned to Tuesday and said, "So I'm guessing she's not going to eat her sandwich." She picked it up and started eating it smiling at her son. "Tuna salad, not bad, I hope it's dolphin free."

Sam was surprised he'd slept at all, but the truth was he'd slept better than he had in weeks. When he woke up it was with a throbbing pain in his right side. He got up, opened his suitcase and fumbled through the contents till he found the four bottles of pills. He picked them up in turn till he found the right bottle then poured two into his hand and went off to find the bathroom. When he did he found a stack of paper cups on the back of the sink, so he filled one and swallowed the pills down. They made the pain bearable, but in about an hour he'd be asleep again and then be groggy most of the rest of the day. For the life of him he couldn't understand why his grandson ate the things for fun.

That was what had started the fight that had Carol driving him across half the state yesterday her crying and saying she was sorry every few miles. Sam had gone to get his medicine and noticed half the bottle was empty. He told Carol, Carol confronted Kyle who swore he didn't do it, that he was clean. Carol searched Kyle's room found the pills and by the time Jimmy got done ranting, it was all Sam's fault that Kyle was an addict.

Because of course it was one of the deacons in the church they'd always belonged to who had molested Kyle and at least three other children in the congregation. For the sake of the church the preacher asked them all to let the Lord handle it. To keep it between them and God. Deacon Parish had been tempted by the devil himself, and he had repented. Parish moved away to make it easier on the children.

Jimmy had wanted to go to the police and have the man thrown in jail or worse, but the other children's parents, the preacher, Sam and the other elders of the church had begged Jimmy to keep quiet in order to protect the church and the children from the scandal of it all. They were a very conservative sect which had broken away from the Southern Baptist convention. They were The First Whole Covenant Fundamental Baptist Church of Wicker Falls, and they couldn't afford the bad press. They prayed for everyone involved. Let His will be done. The preacher counseled the victims, explaining that Jesus would wash their sins away and they would be clean again. Though Sam didn't really understand what sin the children had committed by being victims of a pervert, he went along because... frankly because after spending too many years in that church to count, going along was all he knew how to do.

Sam admitted now, and only to himself, that he just didn't want to think about what happened to Kyle at all. Not thinking about it worked for him. Or it did till two years later when Parish was caught doing the same thing in another church in another town and was incarcerated for his crimes. Parish confessed to what he'd done not just there but in Wicker Falls, too. He also told about the cover up the church had orchestrated. Though all involved were questioned, it was their preacher who was fined and put on probation. It was a huge scandal that rocked the town of Wicker Falls and their church to its core and left Sam and Jenny able to attend the church they loved but never again to have the status they once had. Jimmy and Carol had moved to a more liberal Baptist church. They had two younger children who they never let out of their sight and Kyle... He'd never been right since. It turned out that "just not dwelling on it" hadn't really worked for anyone but the pervert.

Sam couldn't really blame Jimmy for wanting him out. Part of the reason he'd given Carol and Jimmy his home and his business was guilt. This thing had screwed up their whole family. They had kicked their teenage daughter out of their house and out of their lives to keep her "sickness" from disgracing them, and what happened? A pervert they trusted ruined their lives.

Alice's words kept ringing in his brain. *Who is punishing you, Dad?*

Nothing, he had nothing. He had an IRA—a whole whopping ten thousand dollars. It wouldn't pay for a nursing home, and no assisted living place would take him now because of the damn fire. He had one child who had tossed him out, and one who hated him because he'd tossed her out. His wife was dead and he was dying and what was the point of their lives? Why had his god abandoned him?

He and his wife had both been raised in the church. But

the truth was he'd gotten way away from it as a young adult. When he went to college he drank and smoked weed, cussed and screwed his share of "loose" women. But when he finished school and moved back home he started dating Jenny and going back to church. He repented of all his sins, fell in love with his wife, and they got married. But he guessed he wasn't done sinning because they stopped going to church. His flesh was weak; he strayed. The only way Jenny would take him back was if they went back to church—and not just *any* church, but one much stricter than the one either of them grew up in. The same church where a deacon molested their grandson.

The truth was that none of it—none of what he'd learned as a child, nothing he'd learned in church in his adult life—had ever rung true with him. He went along out of fear. Fear that to deny these things or to really even think about them would be serving the devil, a one-way ticket to hell. The fact that he didn't truly believe only convinced him that he had to embrace the church doctrine because he was already poised at the gates of damnation for his lack of faith.

But now he was in hell any way. He was dying with cancer stuck in a house with his gay daughter who—right or wrong—hated him.

He was hungry, so he found the kitchen, some box cereal and got some milk out of the fridge. The house was nice, nothing fancy but very clean in good repair and comfortable. The appliances were old and had seen better days but obviously worked well. He wasn't about to try to use the stove even if she hadn't told him not to. He lifted the sleeve of his pajamas and looked at the not-quite-healed burn.

With the drugs I knew I shouldn't drive, but I thought I could still take care of myself, could still cook, but I blacked out and dropped a towel on the stove. I woke up just in time for the firemen to cart me out and why didn't I die right then? That would have been easy, pass out, burn up, dead.

He wandered around the house and saw that there were photos and pictures hanging on the walls everywhere he looked. He smiled when he realized Alice had done most of the paintings. He remembered her as a child always drawing, always painting. She had always been a very good artist, and she'd obviously gotten much better. Most of them were landscapes. There were photos of her in uniform with her unit taken in the Middle East and some in Europe—on leave he guessed. There were lots of pictures of one woman and many of Alice with her.

She was very pretty, black hair, brown eyes and look at that smile. Alice always did look more like a boy than a girl, but this girl was built like a brick shit house. You wouldn't see her in Walmart and think, "Well there's a queer."

Even when Alice was a very young child they would put her in dresses, but as soon as they weren't looking she would change into pants. She was always carting frogs and lizards around in her pockets. Never wanted to play with her sister and any time they went looking they found her with the little boy next door at least as dirty as he was. She wanted to do everything Sam did, so he took her with him. She helped him work on the cars, mow the lawn, she even went fishing with him. She helped in the store and knew more about the gear than he did most of the time.

When they first found out what she was, Jenny had blamed it on him saying it was his fault because he encouraged her to act more like a boy than a girl. They came home from the store one day and Carol—who was two years older than Alice—met them at the door crying even as Alice was yelling at her to shut up. Carol had a bloody lip and a black eye, so obviously her sister had done more than just tell her to keep her mouth shut. With Alice yelling at her to shut up the whole time, Carol told them that she'd come home early from college and caught Alice in her bed doing sexual things with another girl.

Jenny told him to beat the devil out of Alice. There was a minute when it looked like Alice was going to hit him before he could hit her, but when it came down to it she let him beat her. The whole time her mother kept yelling at her, "You weren't born that way! You aren't queer!" And no matter how hard he beat her Alice just yelled back, "Yes I am!" They read scriptures to her and prayed and beat her again and prayed some more, but she wouldn't say she wasn't queer. In fact she told them she hated them and their god. That was when Jenny told her she could repent or she could leave.

Alice had packed up and left.

He'd only seen her once since then. Only once and only for a few minutes. She'd been in uniform, and Jenny wouldn't even let her in the front door.

I can't blame Jenny and I can't blame the church. I followed blindly because I was afraid not to because what if everything I'd ever heard was true and if I didn't do just what I was told I could spend an eternity in hell? It's only now when I reflect on my life, when I look at all the life my daughter has had that I didn't share, that I realize if everything I have been told is wrong and what Alice and others believe is right then I'm going to have to pay for the life I've lived. Maybe the truth is it's stupid to waste the time we have here worrying about what's next at all.

She was exhausted and filthy, and normally this would have been her favorite part of the day, when she walked into her house could get a bath eat some dinner and then sit and watch some TV or read a book. She went and got her mail just to put it off that much longer.

Yesterday her house was a safe haven where she was surrounded by things that comforted her. Today it was a place where a tyrant waited and... what did he expect from her?

She sighed opened the door walked in, and she could smell his cologne in the air. It was the same crap he'd always worn that in her mind she'd always called Conservative Baptist number Five. She locked the door behind her and laid her keys and wallet on the small table just inside the front door. She had found the table upside down in a dumpster and restored it like most of the stuff in her house, not so much because she couldn't afford new stuff as because she liked to take trash and turn it into treasure, to recycle. So had Helen.

Ally looked at the mail in her hand saw what it was and looked at the ceiling. It was a bill from the fertility clinic. "Really, Helen? Your timing could be better." Helen was one of those women whose biological clock had started ticking in her twenties. She wanted a baby right away, but Ally wanted to wait. The next thing she knew Helen had gone and put some of her eggs on ice. It had seemed absurd at the time, and now twice a year Ally had to make a payment to the clinic to keep the eggs. Mitch had been trying to get her to have one implanted for years, but she just wasn't sure it was ever something she wanted to do. She was alone, and how did he expect her to do her job with a little Helen strapped to her back? Yet she couldn't make herself destroy them. She didn't know why really; it wasn't guilt because she hadn't caved to Helen's baby desire. If they'd had a baby it might be as crippled as she was now or as dead as Helen was, and either way that would have made everything that much harder for Ally to just go on.

Her father walked out of the kitchen drying his hands on a towel. He actually smiled at her. "You're filthy; what do you do for a living anyway?"

"I work for a landscaping company." she walked towards the bathroom hoping he wasn't going to talk to her anymore. She supposed after she got out of the shower and got dressed she'd have to make enough dinner for two since she wouldn't let him use the stove.

"How long were you in Iraq?"

"Long enough." She walked quickly into the bathroom and closed the door. She sighed; he'd made a mess. His crap was everywhere, and he'd moved her clothes off the top of the hamper. When she looked for them they were inside it. She wondered if he even realized that she only had the one bathroom. "What a fucking nightmare. He wants to talk like we just do this all the time. Come on, Helen, don't just stand there; do something." She decided to wear the clothes even though they'd been in the hamper because she didn't want to have to go through her bedroom filthy to get clean clothes out of her closet. She stripped, and as she got in the shower realized that she was probably going to have to do his laundry, too.

Because Maggie looked it up and I can be thrown into jail for endangering his old, wrinkled ass if I just put him out. She's going to see if he is eligible for government aid and assisted living, but if not I'm stuck with him. He's dying, though, so it won't be for long... My father is dying. My mother died and I didn't care at all and I still don't. It's not even like you watch the news and some film star has died and you're like, Oh that's too bad. I literally feel nothing because she's dead. He even lowered himself to call me and ask if I wanted to go to the funeral and I told him the truth; I just didn't care. Now he's dying and why does he think I should care?

She sighed as the water ran over her body. She'd come home from the war without a scratch. Three tours of duty she'd done over most of four years, and she'd hurt herself worse cleaning her gun than she'd ever been hurt in the field. Oh, she had scars from the war, but no one could see those. She wasn't home four years when some punk-ass kid with a four-by-four pickup did what snipers and IEDs hadn't been able to. The irony that he was pulling out of a church parking lot when he hit them wasn't lost on her, either. It seemed that churchy-assed people were always to be a giant thorn in her side in one way or other.

It was a good thing the leg brace was washable because unless she wore it she couldn't stand at all without crutches. Her leg was a mangled mass of flesh, metal and bone grafts that hurt every time the weather changed or she bumped or twisted it wrong, and she often wondered if it had been worth the effort to save it at all. The guys at the VA hospital assured her it was, and since most of them were missing something she figured they knew what they were talking about. It was hard to believe that a leg that looked like hers could be the envy of anyone, but it was.

When she walked out her dad was waiting for her just outside the door, and she jumped a little. "So, what's for dinner?"

Oh God he's lonely, so he wants to make small talk. "I'll figure it out when I get to the kitchen. Geez."

He of course followed her into the kitchen and sat at the small dining table there. "It's a nice house."

He just wants to talk as if we have anything to say to each other and without a great big, "I'm sorry I screwed up your whole life beat you and called you names." As far as I'm concerned we have nothing to say to each other, but... if he really has to be here and I really have to put up with him for months maybe small talk is the answer.

"It was such a dump when we first bought it that I couldn't even get a VA loan to carry it, but I had put back a bunch of money when I was in the service and Helen had some. Helen's parents gave us some money, too, so we were able to come up with enough of a down payment that the owners carried the rest just happy to get out from under it. We did a lot of work on it. I still do a lot of work on it. It's not like buying a new house or having one built, old houses have their own set of problems." She could see him physically relax. She went through the cabinets and the fridge. "You're kind of screwed if you don't want spaghetti and salad."

"That sounds fine. I can pay some rent I get an SSI check."

"I'm not going to turn down cash. I work hard I make decent money but certainly could always use more. Like I said it's an old house; there is maintenance."

"Can I stay then?"

"I'm not going to put you out on the street, Dad, but if I can find an alternative I'm not going to do this either." She started cooking mostly so she wouldn't have to look at him while she was talking. "See, because of the way you all treated me, and that stupid-assed church you raised us in, it was a long time before I felt good about myself. There isn't a damn thing wrong with me; I'm good people. I don't want you here feeding me crap again till I can't stand myself."

"I can't make any promises, Alice, because I'm old and set in my ways, but I'm going to try not to do that."

CHAPTER 2

Habitual liars can be great fun at parties because they've just done so much more than the rest of us.

"Why the fuck doesn't she shut up?" Frances whispered in Ally's ear.

"There were three of them," Laurie was saying. She took up a stance making her look like a short, fat dyke trying to do a Bruce Lee imitation, which was about right. "I get like this and I'm all, *Go on take your best shot.* I kick the guy on the right and he folds like a maxi pad in a vending machine. Then these other two assholes they just look at each other and they take off runnin'."

Ally leaned down to whisper in Frances's ear. "I sometimes think Laurie believes she's like that bus in *Speed*, you know if she doesn't tell fifty lies to fifty bimbos before she leaves the club she will explode. Let's face it; she gets a lot more pussy than the rest of us, no doubt because she's just so much more interesting. Come on." Ally waved her hand in the air towards the other side of the room and they got up and moved away from the bar and across the room to an empty table.

"So your dad just showed up?" Frances asked.

Ally filled in all the particulars finishing with, "But I'm not going to tell that story to everyone because it's less believable than the absolute crap that flows from Laurie's mouth. Frankly, I'm mostly just here to get away from him. If I hooked up I couldn't even take her back to my place and let's face it, most of the time when I hook up it's because I have my own house that I don't share with fifteen other dykes."

"I don't want to hear that crap. Look at you and look at me. I'd have trouble getting laid in a monkey whorehouse if I had a sack full of bananas," Frances said. "You with the sad blue eyes, the short black hair, perfect lips, slightly broken nose, a stomach you could bounce quarters off of, and an ass to die for...."

"Frances... are you hitting on me?"

"Would I get anywhere if I was?"

"No."

"Then I'm not."

"Need I remind you that I have a leg that looks like hammered liver?" Ally said.

"That's such a very long way from all the interesting parts," Frances said with a smile. "As they say, chicks dig scars."

She said that because she hadn't seen it; few people had. The doctors, Maggie, and a few women she'd picked up for sex had seen it. Ally wasn't one of those people who said "the love of my life died, I'll never have another." No she wanted very much to fall in love again, to have someone love her, but in the meantime if a woman was interested in a tumble far be it from her to turn it down. However Frances was a friend, and she'd learned the hard way that the best way to stay friends was not to have sex. If you weren't interested in having a relationship with a woman, it just made things weird when they wanted something you didn't know was even on the table.

"How long is your dad staying?"

"Not more than six months. He's dying, and that's how long they gave him."

"Damn, Ally, I'm sorry."

"Don't be. I can't look at you and say I honestly care whether he dies or not. If he has to live with me, sooner is sooo much better than later."

"That's horrible."

"It's true, Frances. You know... I told you how they treated me. He hasn't apologized. Hasn't even tried. He just wants to talk about inane things as long as we don't discus at all my queerness. I never dreamed I could be so uncomfortable in my own home, and I once dated a huge girl who rolled over and nearly smothered me in my sleep."

It was a Friday night and she didn't have to work the next day but, by nine she was most of the way home. Her cell phone rang and she answered it. "Hello."

"Ally, this is Maggie. I know it's late...."

"It's not that late." Ally laughed. "You spend too much time with that baby."

"Yeah, that's the thing see... could you watch Tuesday for me?"

It was the tone of her voice. "What's wrong?"

"Mona's sick; they have to do surgery."

Maggie had looked troubled most of the day. When Ally asked her about it she said she had a bad feeling she couldn't quiet, and she didn't want to talk about it. For the hundredth time Ally wondered what it must be like to be so connected to the "universe" that you knew something horrid was about to happen but not really what much less how to stop it. "Is she going to be alright?"

"I don't know." Maggie's voice cracked a bit. "I don't want to have Tuesday up at the hospital."

"Isn't there anyone else, Maggie? I mean, seriously, you could write everything I know about kids on the back of a tic-tac box and have room left over."

"My sister Mona is the one he usually stays with, and my brother is at the hospital, too. He won't stay with just anyone, and I don't want to leave him with just anyone. I trust you, Ally, and he likes you."

"He does?" Alley asked.

"Of course he does; you give him money all the time. Look he's potty trained and he sleeps by himself. Please, Ally...."

"Of course." She sighed; she was such a huge sap. "You want me to come over there and get him?"

"I'm half way to your house."

"Do you remember where I live?" Because as far as she could remember Maggie hadn't been to the house since Helen died.

"Yes."

They got to the driveway at exactly the same time, so she pulled in and Maggie pulled in behind her. "He's already asleep," Maggie said, opening the back door. "He's allergic to strawberries so check the packages on anything you give him to make sure there aren't any in it." Maggie pointed at him, "Could you?"

"Ah, yeah sure." Ally had a brief but hot argument with the car seat belts before she finally freed him. When she did he was like trying to handle a piece of cooked pasta. She sort of laid him on her shoulder like she would a sack of soil. Maggie smiled at her.

"You really don't know what you're doing, do you?"

"That's what I said."

Maggie walked over and rearranged the baby so that his

head was resting on Ally's shoulder and her forearm was under his butt. Ally started carrying him towards the house as Maggie grabbed about a hundred pounds of crap out of the back. Maggie walked in front of her and held her hand out expectantly. Ally moved to try to get in her pocket, but Maggie just reached in and fished the keys out, the rock she'd given Ally came out with them, and Maggie smiled.

Ally just shrugged. "I need all the help I can get right now. It's the red key. So what's wrong with Mona, or is it none of my business?"

"Seriously they don't know. Something to do with her heart. She's fifteen years older than I am, and about a hundred pounds overweight. She lives in an aura of stress. They say she hasn't had a heart attack, but she's going to if they don't do the surgery." She opened the door. "His binky is in the outside pocket of his diaper bag. Don't give it to him unless he just won't calm down."

Alley nodded as if she had a foggy idea what Maggie was talking about.

"I have no idea when I'll be back, but if he needs to talk to me you can call me. Don't give him beer, and don't feed him a bunch of crap. If you have any questions please call and...."

"Alice is that you?" Her dad yelled, walking into the hall from the kitchen. Tuesday jumped at the sound of his voice.

"Quiet, Dad, you're going to wake the baby," Alley whispered. "Maggie this is my dad, Dad this is Maggie. Little guy is Tuesday." Her dad made a face when he heard the boy's name, and Ally hoped he was going to keep his Bible-thumping mouth shut.

"He has very negative energy," Maggie whispered to Ally, as if you had to be a voodoo practitioner to know that.

"Of course he does; he's a conservative Southern Baptist," Ally whispered back.

Maggie nodded as if that made perfect sense. "I've... I've never been away from Tuesday overnight before...."

"If you get out of there—no matter what the time—you can come and get him."

"Thanks, Ally, you're the best." She kissed the top of the boy's head set all the stuff she was carrying on the floor and took off. She had no sooner run out the door than she came back and put Ally's keys right on the table Ally always put them on. Then ran out again, locking the door.

Ally looked at the keys and whispered to the sleeping baby. "Your mama is just plain weird."

"So is that your lover and this is your kid?" her dad asked, obviously pissed off at the prospect by his tone and his volume.

"Not that it's any of your damn business," Ally whispered, "but Maggie is one of my co-workers. She's a friend and this is her kid who was built the good old fashioned way by two heterosexuals humping each other's brains out, so it's all good. If your yelling wakes him up, you can deal with him. And for the record if I had a lover and we wanted a baby there wouldn't be a damn thing wrong with that."

Which, if she didn't want her dad to scream and wake up the baby, she probably shouldn't have said.

"I am trying to understand, trying to wrap my head around all of this, but bringing children into a house with two women is not just against god it is against nature itself. What sort of child would they raise?"

Tuesday woke all the way up which allowed Ally to yell back at her father, "I don't know, Dad maybe a straight one since my super-gay ass was raised by two uptight fundamental homo-hating Baptists. Now since you are in my house you can shut your mother-fucking, holy-roller mouth or get the hell out."

Tuesday started to cry.

"How about I just get a belt and beat the hell out of you because you have cancer? How about I beat the living shit out of you over something you can't do anything about?" She grabbed the bag Maggie had said held the binky—whatever the hell that was—and walked with the boy to her room. He stopped crying as soon as she left her father standing with his jaw hanging open in her hallway, so she guessed maybe Tuesday could feel the same bad energy his mom could. She shut the door.

"Where's my mom?" Tuesday asked.

"She had to go stay with your Aunt Mona. You and me are going to hang out here."

She noticed then that Maggie had already put him in his pajamas. She set him down in the middle of the bed. How little was he, could he be trusted in the middle of the bed? Would he roll off and hit his head?

"Do you need to take a leak?"

He shrugged his little shoulders, a look of confusion on

his face.

"Do you have to pee?"

He shook his head no.

"Your mom said you sleep alone, so... I'll just make you a palette on the floor."

He shook his head no.

"No? Why not?"

"Sleep with you, Ally," he said.

"But your mom said you sleep by yourself."

He shook his head.

She sighed. "Are you going to fall off the bed?"

He laughed. "I'm not a baby."

"You aren't?"

"No I'm two..." He held up two fingers. "...and half."

"But you don't sleep in your own bed," she said.

"Not a grown up, Ally."

"Ah, can you stay here while I go to the bathroom?" She really didn't have any idea.

He shook his head no, so he followed her to the bathroom. She had him turn his face to the wall while she took a leak. Then they started back towards the bedroom.

Her father stepped from the guest room into the hall.

"Alice?"

"What?"

"I'm sorry for what I said."

She just nodded and quickly brought the boy into her room, closing and locking the door behind her. That's how uncomfortable her father made her; she was locking her bedroom door to protect not herself but the boy.

She was suddenly exhausted. She picked Tuesday up and set him on the bed. He started to move to the other side, and she said, "No that's my side you sleep on Helen's side."

He nodded as if that made sense.

"Here watch some TV while I change into my bed clothes." But of course when she turned on the TV there was porn on a DVD playing, and she wound up standing in front of the screen doing a dance that would kill a more limber person as she tried to get it turned off. She pulled the DVD out and found something more suitable which was... Basically anything that was on TV. Figuring he would focus on Sponge Bob dumbass, she changed then she sat down on the edge of the bed, made sure her arm band crutches were where she could reach them, and started to take the brace off her leg. She was just about finished when she realized the boy was sitting nearly on top of her looking over her shoulder watching what she was doing. She looked at him and he had a pained expression on his face.

Great. As if it wasn't enough to turn Maggie's kid onto lesbian porn now he's seeing something that is sure to give him nightmares.

She put the brace away and pulled her pajama pants leg down. "How'd you break your leg?" he asked.

"A dumbass hit me with his fucking car," Ally said.

"Why?"

"Because he was a dumbass. I thought we covered that." She smiled at him and turned off the TV. "Why don't you lie down and go to sleep?"

He nodded and lay down. She covered him up and then got in bed and turned out the light.

"I have to have the light on."

"Are you fucking kidding me?"

"Nope."

She turned the light back on.

"Does it hurt?"

"My leg?" she asked, hoping he wasn't talking about the porn because face it if you didn't know what you were seeing, you might think you were looking at a bad wound. She didn't really start to breathe again till he nodded. "Sometimes."

"What's that thing?"

"It's a brace it keeps my leg from folding when I don't want it to. It helps me walk."

"Oh." This time he nodded really big. "That's why you walk funny."

"Exactly." She laughed and rubbed his head. "Now can we go to sleep? I'm really tired."

"My mom tells me a story."

"I don't have any kid's books, dude, and I'm afraid your mother would get really pissed if I read to you from *The Naughty Stewardess That Would.*"

"My mom makes up stories."

"Dude, I can't just make up a story."

"Please."

"Once upon a time there were three little girls who went to the police academy...."

When she woke up the light was still on and there was a little boy sleeping on her head. At least mostly. She moved him and lay him beside her then moved to turn the light off, but of course now she was up so she had to piss. She sat up, grabbed her crutches, and made her way to the bathroom. She took a leak then noticed that the TV was still on in the living room. She went in to turn it off and found her dad asleep on the recliner. In his hands was a photo album. It was open to pictures of him and her fishing on White Horse Lake. She was maybe all of six. She shut the album and set it on the table. He had brought it with him because it certainly wasn't hers. She thought briefly about waking him up to go to bed and decided it was foolish since she often slept in the recliner. Besides, he was a mean old son of a bitch who was fixating on who he wanted her to be not who she was.

She went back to her room and found that the boy had moved to her side of the bed. She turned the light off and crawled into Helen's side. They'd been together just under three years when Helen died. She'd now been gone much longer than they'd been together, but Ally could still feel her presence... at least she wanted to think she could.

Nothing was the same now that Helen was gone. Nothing except the way she'd made Ally feel: whole, complete, wanting for nothing. Even the leg didn't take that away. Helen had made her feel good about herself. Ally never had before, and even though Helen was gone it was a gift she'd given Ally that hadn't gone away. Her dad could say all the ugly shit he wanted to and it wouldn't change the way she felt about herself because for one bright, shining moment the most wonderful person in the world had loved her.

Her cell phone rang and she answered it, looking at the time it was nearly nine. Beside her the boy was still asleep. "Hello."

"Did I wake you?"

"Yeah. It's alright; I've slept half the day away. How is your sister?"

"I still don't know. They didn't take Mona back for the surgery until five this morning. She had a quadruple bypass and there were some complications. I'm too tired to remember or really understand what they were. They still have her in recovery. They let Mom go back—you know because she put on a huge show like she cared. If she comes back and everything's alright... I have another favor to ask."

"Sure. I mean you lied to me; your son doesn't sleep by himself. In fact, he used my head not so much for a pillow as a bed. He may have seen some porn; I'm not sure. I told him an inappropriate bedtime story till he went to sleep asking twenty questions about my creepy metal leg. I'm not sure that in the long run you're going to see what I've done as a favor, but hell, go ahead ask for more. Knock yourself out."

Maggie laughed. "Alrighty then. I need some sleep. could I maybe crash there just a couple of hours and then I can take my son and go home if my sister's alright? In other words can you watch him while I sleep?"

"Sure no problem, so far he's still alive, in one piece and everything."

Maggie rang the doorbell and Ally's father answered it. "Come on in she took the boy and they're in the back yard doing something."

"Thanks." Maggie nodded and started through the house.

She was exhausted, but not so much so that she couldn't feel Helen's presence as she walked through the kitchen. She stopped for a minute and took a deep breath. Maggie was so raw from all she'd been through with her sister, and with no sleep, that she felt Helen's loss completely as if it were brand new. Helen had been her best friend since high school. She'd loved Helen like no one else in her life. Maggie's tears started to fall. She went to the kitchen sink and washed her face quickly, groping blindly until she found the roll of paper towels on the counter. She dried her face but found that she couldn't quit crying, so she sat down on a chair at the table put her face in her hands and just sobbed. She'd lost Helen she couldn't lose Mona, too.

Ally walked in the back door towing Maggie's son behind her, obviously not understanding that he took five steps for every one she took.

"What do you mean you don't want another bowl of cereal?" Ally asked.

"I want something else," Tuesday said.

"Like what?" Ally asked, as if she couldn't imagine that

there was any other sort of food on the planet. They were all the way in the house when Ally saw Maggie and the state she was in. "Maggie, is Mona...."

"She's fine; she's going to be fine I'm just exhausted."

Her son ran to her and hugged her neck. She hugged him back feeling better about nearly everything. She looked at Ally and shook her head sadly. "Honey, you have got to let Helen go; she can't just stay here."

"Yeah... we aren't having this conversation, my psychic friend. Let me get you something to eat and then you go take a nap."

The back door in the kitchen had a window in the top part of it and Sam looked out it. There was a small shed in the back, and it looked like Alice had hauled out a bunch of her fishing tackle and was going through it. It was that time of year. Spring, a great time for bass fishing; this time of year the store would fill with tourists heading for White Horse Lake to angle. He wondered where Alice fished around here. She was showing the boy all the different things and obviously telling him what they were for and how you used them. He remembered doing the same thing with her.

There was never anything wrong with her she was just different and we couldn't have that. And she's right; we raised her. We did everything in our power to break her and break her spirit, and we couldn't do it. I don't have enough time to do things like I did last night. It would be easier if my body wasn't riddled with cancer and my brain wasn't filled with all the damn dope. I'm just going to have to try harder not to purposely antagonize her. Try harder to really understand.

He swallowed hard and opened the door. He walked across the deck and down the steps. Alice looked up and saw him and went right back to talking to the boy, ignoring Sam.

"You put your thumb on the button, pull back and then sling forward and let go of the button." She was helping him practice casting, and the boy seemed delighted. He noticed she had taken any hooks off the line and just had a small lead sinker on it which is what he'd done for her.

"A Zebco® that's what I taught you to fish with," Sam said.

"I thought that's what I remembered. I can't lie; I don't really know much about kids," Alice said.

And where would she have learned? When she was a

teenager I had her working the shop with me. She was never around any of her sister's kids because we were so afraid she was a bad influence. All this pain, all this unnecessary pain, how could any of that serve God, and how could I ever have thought that it would?

"It looks to me like you're doing fine. Kids aren't so different from adults, plus well you were a kid once; what did you want most?"

"To be an adult."

"Exactly. Then once we're adults we really just want to be kids again." He moved to sit in a lawn chair in the shade, remembering that one of his medications said to avoid sunlight.

Alice helped the boy again then as he was reeling the weight back in said, "Now don't let the bastard get away, show him who's boss."

"Ah Alice, at the risk of starting another fight, you might want to ask the boy's mother how she feels about the boy cussing...."

"Yes, Dad, because violence and intolerance are fine, but cussing is evil...."

"Looking at his mother I imagine she doesn't allow a lot of violence or intolerance. You just might want to see if she wants her son to cuss like a sailor."

"He's not going to cuss just because I do."

Sam laughed and smiled at her. "You're right; you don't know anything about kids."

CHAPTER 3

You can always get a hypochondriac to leave by reminding them that, as sick as they are, they should really be home in bed.

Maggie definitely needed this. She'd spent the week working all day and then going over to her sister's house to help her out, all with Tuesday hanging on her leg. Her brother was coming to help their mother do it over the weekend to give Maggie some relief. She really just needed to go take a nice yoga class, immerse herself in the calm, find her center again, restore her chi, before she ripped someone's face off and ate their brain.

She was both glad and a little sad when Tuesday was more than happy to leave from work with Ally. When she'd asked if Ally would mind watching him for a few hours Ally had asked if he could spend the night so she could maybe take him fishing Saturday morning.

"Not on a boat; just down off the bank at the lake," Ally said. "My dad's a prick, but he loves to fish, and he's dying so I guess I should take him and...."

"If Tuesday is with you he is less likely to show his ass?"

"Exactly."

"I don't know, Ally. The lake that can be dangerous..."

"But *Nature*, my crunchy granola friend, lots and lots of fresh air and sunlight."

But now Maggie was wondering if she liked Tuesday being gone over night two weeks in a row. Besides, for three days after he'd stayed with Ally last time everyone and everything had been a dumbass. *But... I haven't been laid in forever and my tubes are tied, so if I should meet a man at yoga class whose spirit is in tune with mine....*

Tuesday had spent the night again and had again slept mostly on her head because he would neither sleep by himself, nor would he let her turn the light out.

Now they were sitting under the shade of a tree with their lines in the water. She had brought folding chairs mostly because she guessed her father would need one, which he proved he did when he sat down to fish—something she had never seen him do. Her dad just kept looking over at her and smiling. She couldn't imagine why. She tried to just ignore him. Of course she couldn't catch a damn thing because Tuesday didn't want to fish so much as he wanted to reel. So she was forced to cast his line every few minutes even though each time she told him to let it set or to reel slower, it didn't work.

Finally she got a strike, popped it just right and reeled in a nice-sized bass. She had just landed it when her dad had one.

"Fish on!" he cried and stood up.

She had strung her fish when she saw something playing with Tuesday's bait. She quickly grabbed hold of the end of his pole, gave a yank and hooked the fish. Tuesday just sat there. "Now reel, Tuesday, now reel dammit!"

The boy started reeling fast as he could, but he'd hooked a fair-sized fish and it was putting up a bit more fight than the boy could handle. "Come on, Tuesday, man up! Reel that bastard in." She stood behind him and started helping him even as she saw her dad pull his fish out of the water. "Come on, you son of a bitch." She saw her dad shake his head as he put his own fish on the stringer, but he was still smiling and he didn't say anything.

They finally pulled the fish on the bank and Ally went to get it off the hook even as the boy slung the pole from side to side yelling, "I got one! I got a big one!"

"Be still, dammit Tuesday." Ally laughed and finally got the fish off without getting a hook stuck in her cheek or the pole in her eye—which was a small miracle.

For the next half hour they were getting hits pretty heavy, and then nothing.

"Well we caught everything out of this hole," her dad said.

Ally didn't know who looked more tired, the old man or the toddler. Either way she decided it was as good a time as any to pack up and go to the house.

If Maggie believed in the walk of shame that would have been what she was doing. She didn't believe in being ashamed, so instead she was doing the walk of *that was some pretty disappointing sex.* She walked in her house and went straight in to get a shower. Pete wanted to see her again and she decided she would. He was a nice guy and easy on the eyes. Lots of times the first time you had sex with someone it was just sort of flat.

The big problem with pursuing a relationship—and it's what she told him—was that she neither wanted to bring him around her child nor spend a lot of time away from her son. She didn't give him her number but said that she would call him.

The simple truth was that unless the sex was much better next time she couldn't afford to waste her time because frankly she didn't really need anyone for anything else. She was perfectly happy it being just her and Tuesday. She'd been perfectly happy alone till birth control failure happened, so now she had Tuesday she sure as hell didn't need anyone else unless they actually enhanced her life.

She liked to have good sex every once in a while, but getting good sex could be like finding hens' teeth. It needed to be better than she could give herself or it wasn't worth the time or effort it took.

When she got cleaned up and changed she headed for Ally's to pick up her son. She smiled as she pulled into the driveway. It wasn't hard to guess what Ally did for a living; the yard and flower beds were beautiful. The house was immaculate inside and out. She had once told Helen it should be in one of the dozens of lawn and garden magazines Ally subscribed to that Maggie got when Ally was finished with them.

She found all three of them in the back yard grilling. Maggie looked at the herb garden. *Helen wanted it so she could walk out of the kitchen and pick fresh herbs. Ally made it for her and even though Helen has been dead for years she keeps it just the way Helen did… the Rosemary is bigger.*

Tuesday was running around and around playing with bubbles that Ally must have bought him because he didn't bring them with him from home. The old man was lying on one of the chase lounges on the deck in the shade asleep.

Tuesday saw her first. He looked up at her and waved. "Mom! I caught some fish. We cut off their heads and now were cooking them and then we're going to eat them."

"There is enough for everyone. We were catching those bastards like crazy," Ally said.

"Some dumbass ran right in front of us," Tuesday said excitedly.

"Tuesday, come on, son, don't say dumbass. I told you that's not nice," Maggie said with a sigh.

"See? I told you Alice," the old man said not opening his eyes.

Ally walked over to get something out of the cooler, and it was obvious both from the way she was moving and the expression on her face that she was hurting.

Maggie walked over and opened the cooler. "What are you after?"

"A hard cider."

"What happened to you?"

"When the lovely gentleman ran in front of us I had to slam my brakes, and since it's my right leg that's a mangled piece of meat it hurt like a dog of the female persuasion. How's that, Dad?" she hissed towards him.

"Better," the old man said with a laugh.

"What a dumbass," Maggie whispered in her ear. She dug the bottle out of the cooler and handed it to Ally, got one for herself and shut the cooler. "Do you need to go to the doctor?"

"No, but I wouldn't say no to you working on it."

Because of course while Ally—like most people—made a face every time she said anything the least bit metaphysical, Ally knew some energy work and a message would help her. "I can work on it after we eat. Thanks so much for watching Tuesday."

"You know what? I sort of like taking care of him."

Maggie laughed. "You sound surprised."

Ally shrugged. "Kids have always made me kind of nervous I guess. I mean how the hell do you know what they want?"

"They just want to be loved. They want attention, to be respected, to be accepted," Maggie said.

"Kumbaya and all." Ally grinned as she opened the bottle with a bottle opener that was attached to the side of her grill, handed the open bottle to Maggie and took the other bottle from Maggie opened it and took a drink.

"Can I have one of those?" Ally's father asked from the deck.

"They're alcoholic, Dad, you want a root beer?"

"No, I want one of those; they smell good."

Maggie got one out of the cooler, opened it and brought it to him.

He opened his eyes and smiled at her. Not a bad smile, and today his energy wasn't bad either. "Your boy is a natural fisherman like Alice." He took the bottle from her, took a swallow and smiled. "This is really good."

"Really, Dad? And lightning isn't striking us dead or anything," Ally said.

Maggie shook her head and went to join her son playing with the bubbles. "Did you have a good time?"

"Yes, Mom. I felt a little sorry for the fish, but Ally said it's the same for the fish whether you catch them or buy them in a can. Either way they wind up just as dead." He shrugged.

Maggie worked at blowing a huge bubble and Tuesday laughed and clapped. "Ally look."

Ally looked over and smiled. "That's quite the skill that you share with the two-year-old."

Ally watched as Maggie rubbed the ugliness which was her lower right leg. Occasionally she would stop, hold her hands close but not touching Ally's skin, and that was where the weirdness came from because Ally swore she could feel warmth flowing from Maggie's hands through her leg.

"He can sit in a room alone for a minute." Maggie laughed. "I don't let him go in a public restroom by himself or leave him alone while I do, but I can't believe you let him go to the bathroom with you in your own house."

"He said he couldn't be alone."

"He doesn't *want* to be alone, there is a difference."

"So what did you do? Did you find the balance you were looking for?"

Maggie smiled looking up from Ally's leg only briefly. "Yes and no. The yoga class was very nice. The guy I spent the night with was sort of the sexual equivalent of a brick of tofu, and I don't mean in that he was really filling way. He was pretty and nice enough but if he doesn't do a lot better next time then I'm done with him. So, what's wrong with you?"

"Nothing's wrong with me. What do you mean?" Ally was more than a little unnerved.

"I'm doing energy work on you; you can't really lie to me so?"

Ally took in a deep breath and let it out. "That dumbass ran in front of us. I nowhere near hit him but... It twisted the shit out of that mess but worse than that it took me right back to that night. I shook it out of my head because your son and my dad were in the truck with me. Then I got home and we were all sitting on the back deck eating when I realized that I haven't cooked out or eaten back there with anyone since Helen died. I maintain it. Hell, I'll even make myself a meal and eat out there by myself. I've brought women back here and I fucked them in the guest room, but I still fucked them here, but I haven't purposely had anyone over to just hang out in years."

"Why not?" Maggie asked in a quiet voice. "It's a beautiful place."

"Because that was what Helen did, you know that Maggie. Helen was all about having theme parties and barbeques and fish fries. She loved to spend time with our friends and her family. She loved to host gatherings. I never did it before Helen and I haven't done it since, but... I like having people over, turns out it wasn't just her thing. I think I'm doing really good. Most of the time I feel like I'm handling it really well, that I've moved on, but I haven't really. I'm sort of in a holding pattern. You weren't in the house ten minutes when you said it—I have to let her go."

"Well she can't stay here; it isn't good for either of you," Maggie said.

"Having my dad here is like just ripping the scab off a wound that was nearly healed. Were you able to find out anything about getting him someplace besides here to stay?" Ally quickly changed the subject because she wasn't big on crying in front of anyone, and she felt if she kept talking about Helen she was going to cry.

Maggie was silent but not because she had to be to do the work even though that's what she was pretending.

"Well?"

"I did, but you aren't going to like it. He doesn't qualify for any government assistance other than his Social Security because he still technically owns the hardware store..."

"It's a fish and tackle store."

"The government thinks it's a hardware store. Anyway, as long as he still owns that he has too many assets for the government to pay for any kind of nursing home. They will pay for hospice care when the time comes, but basically he'll have to be bed ridden before they will do that." Maggie was silent and didn't look at her when she said. "Do you still want him out?"

"I think my stupid sister and her jerk husband should let Dad sell the store, pay for his nursing home, and let me have my pathetic life back. But I don't know, Maggie, I think he's actually trying. I mean today, fishing with him and Tuesday, it actually brought back some good memories. The shittiest thing he said all day was that I might ought to watch my mouth around your kid—which I'm guessing you sort of wish I would too, so.... what did you say? The universe is trying to teach me something. As long as he's not spouting his hateful religious crap I think I can put up with him till he has to go to hospice. Hell, I did three tours in Iraq. I can do six months standing on my head right but.... I'm thirty-seven years old, Maggie. Till this I hadn't spent even a minute with him in twenty years. The fact that he doesn't think anything they did to me was wrong is what makes me want to kick him out on his ass."

"Just because he hasn't apologized doesn't mean he isn't actually sorry," Maggie said. "Some people don't know how to admit they're wrong about anything. They are afraid to show any weakness. He's dying, Ally. He's dying in pieces, and he may not apologize to you before he goes. You have to be alright with that." Maggie did something quick then, there was a slight clicking noise, a sharp pain, and then her leg just didn't hurt.

Ally let out a sigh of sure bliss.

"How's that?"

"Better than sex."

"Well it was for sure better than the sex I got last night."

She walked Maggie and Tuesday out and started the egregious process of taking the car seat from her truck to Maggie's car. "Why don't they make these damn things easier to use?" Ally asked when her fourth attempt to put it in the car failed. "Kids are going to get hurt because the seats aren't in right because you have to be a fucking engineer to get them in."

Maggie laughed, gently pushed her out of the way and put the car seat in. Then she buckled the boy into the seat.

Tuesday smiled at Ally and said, "Fucking engineer." At which point Maggie turned to her and glared even as Ally was cracking up.

"It's not funny," Maggie said, looking first at her son and then at Ally and back. "Do not say fucking."

"Can I say engineer?"

"Yes."

So the boy started yelling it over and over again.

"Thanks a lot, Ally!" Maggie yelled out the window as she backed out of the driveway

Ally laughed and went back in the house. She looked in the living room and saw her dad was asleep on the couch. The TV was on, so she went in found the remote and flopped in her recliner. She put her legs up, marveling at the fact that her leg didn't hurt at all. She looked for something to watch, and her dad didn't so much as stir.

And then for reasons known only to her libido she was horny. She got up, got cleaned up, changed her clothes and went to the club.

Sam woke up. He had no idea what time it was. The drugs often left his mouth feeling dry and his mind foggy. He sat up and looked over at the TV. Some late show bore was talking, so it was probably around midnight. He went to the bathroom then decided to turn off the TV and head for his room and an actual bed. As he walked past Alice's door he could see the light on and heard what he assumed was the TV going. He decided to say good night and thank her for taking him fishing. He was well aware that she didn't have to be nice to him at all and certainly she didn't have to go out of her way to do so. He opened the door, realized exactly what he was seeing, and quickly closed it but not before exclaiming. "Dear God!"

"Christ on a crutch!" Ally yelled, looking at the girl. "Fuck!"

"It's alright, baby," the girl said. She was a little hotty, but about as sharp as a stick of butter. "He's gone. Lay back down and I'll finish."

"So not in the mood anymore, Trish." She ran her hands down her face and started dressing. She fumbled around looking for her brace and trying to get it on. "I'm really sorry."

Trish laughed, stood up, and started dressing, "Don't be. I already had my turn. Even better this time."

"Why didn't I lock the fucking door? Why didn't I think to lock the fucking door?" *I'm in bed with a three-year-old who's sleeping on my head and I lock the door. I'm having sex with some girl I hardly know but have screwed twice before and what I do know is that she's a bit kinky, and I don't lock the door. What the hell is wrong with me?*

"You had other things on your mind, and your hands were sort of busy."

It was true. She'd had her hand in Trish's pants and her finger on her clit the minute the front door closed. *So it could have been worse; he might have stumbled into the hall and caught us... No it could not have been worse.*

"Let me talk to my dad real quick, and then I'll take you home."

"I'll just call Rachel and have her pick me up."

"Rachel?"

"My girlfriend, silly."

And now it's worse. "You have a girl friend?"

She laughed. "I've had the girl friend every time we've done it. I thought you knew. Don't worry she doesn't get jealous. We're not exclusive. She sort of likes to do me right after someone else did; you know when I'm already wet."

"So much more than I wanted to know, Trish." Ally finished dressing even as the girl called her lover to come pick her up.

"She's on her way, thanks." She kissed Ally on the cheek and left.

I'm being punished for bringing a slut into mine and Helen's bed. Ally looked up at the ceiling, "You having a good laugh, Helen? This shit is not funny." She washed her face and hands and brushed her teeth before she went to try to talk to her father. She found him in the guest room pacing back and forth. "I'm sorry, Dad..."

"Sorry, why are you sorry, Alice? You're a lesbian right? You aren't ashamed of that or so you told me, so why are you sorry? If it's not wrong why are you sorry?" His tone was impossible to read.

"I'm sorry because I didn't lock the door, and no one should ever have to walk in on any one—and maybe especially their kid—having sex." And she thought, *especially not with some slutty twit she picked up in a bar.*

"Your leg is a mess, Alice. I didn't know... I wouldn't have guessed it was that bad."

Ally laughed. "You catch me having sex with some trollup and you're pacing back and forth like a mad man and... it's about my leg? The leg isn't my fault; there is nothing I can do about the leg."

He stopped and turned to face her and there were tears in his too-shiny eyes. "You really did almost die?"

Ally nodded. "Yes." She reached down and pulled up her pants leg. "I can only walk on crutches or with the brace." She put her pants leg back down. "I lost a lot of blood. I was stuck in the car and they had to use the Jaws of Life to get me out. I knew Helen was dead and the whole time I prayed to die. I passed out long before they pulled me from the car. When I woke up after the first of three surgeries and I wasn't dead, I was really pissed off. Three surgeries and a year of physical therapy, my leg hurts all the time, it barely works, and after five years the leg wasn't even close to the worse thing that happened to me that night."

"And we weren't there for you. I wasn't there because you like girls." He started crying then and flopped down on the bed. "And I just saw you with a girl and the worst thing I saw was your leg."

Ally fought her own tears. "Dad you're tired, and I can tell by the glassy look in your eyes that your drugs are working overtime. Why don't you get some sleep?" He didn't fight her as she helped him into bed and covered him up. "Dad, what did you want anyway?"

"I wanted to thank you for today. I haven't had that much fun in years."

"I had a good time, too."

"That little boy loves you, Alice."

"You think so, huh?"

"Yes, and I love you, too."

So she went to bed thinking maybe she and her dad had turned a huge corner and woke up Sunday morning to him banging on her door demanding to be taken to church. When she told him she didn't know where a Baptist church was, he wanted to know why she didn't go to church and things sort of went downhill from there. She got the phone book, found a Southern Baptist church and drove him there, happy to get rid of him for a few hours. She was hardly home when he called her to come get him. Apparently their preacher knew nothing about the true word of God. He was probably too liberal for him, like the preacher didn't believe in public stonings and such.

She brought him home and then pretended like she got a call and told him she had to go to work. She left, drove out to the lake and did some more fishing. She let everything she caught go because she didn't want to explain where all the fish came from. Besides she still had a bunch in the freezer from what they'd caught the day before.

"Hey, I thought that was you." She turned and saw Ray from work walking down the bank, his tackle in hand. When he saw her let the fish go he yelled, "What are you doin'!"

"My religious fanatic father caught me having sex with a whack-job girl from the club and he had to go to church today to wash my sins in the blood of Jesus. Then I had to go back and get him probably because they weren't nearly hateful enough for him. I just really don't want to hear any of the crap that might come out of his head. For one thing the girl I brought home..."

"Yeah?"

"Well I did her but she'd only started to do me when dad walked in which is a mood killer. So I didn't even get my rocks off. I told him I had to work so I can't come home with fish."

"Well don't throw them back; give them to me. Kathy is on the rag and her kids are bouncing off the wall so I told her I was going fishing but I spent most of the day swilling beer and watching porn at Billy Bob's, so I had by God better bring home some fish."

"And balance is restored." Ally laughed and cast.

"Better watch it; you're starting to sound like Maggie."

It was a normal Monday morning; it was bright and early she was loading the truck with Ray and Chuck. "Every ten minutes from the time I got home till I went to bed last night he was like, 'Why don't you go to church?' and no matter how many times I tell him I don't want to talk about it he just keeps asking till I just give up and go to bed at like eight, so then I was wide awake at five, so I went to the diner had breakfast and drank about seventy-five cups of coffee till it was time to come to work and that, Chuck, is why I'm in such a big-assed hurry."

"Well I just can't keep up. I don't feel so hot," Chuck said.

He was a big guy like his dad, but not as good looking and certainly he wasn't as smart. But he was Helen's brother, so Ally loved him even though he got on her last nerve. "My stomach kind of hurts."

Ray looked at Ally and smiled, and Ally nodded.

"You don't look so good either, Chuck," Ray said.

"Really?" Chuck asked.

"Yeah. I didn't want to say anything, but you're kind of gray around the gills," Ally said.

"Am I?" Chuck asked. "You know I do feel warm like I might have a fever."

"I hope you aren't contagious," Ally said.

"Do you maybe need to lie down, Chuck?" Ray asked.

Chuck mumbled something about needing to go home for the day and started back to the office. When he was well out of sight and hearing range, Ray and Ally high-fived each other.

"Works every time," Ally said with a laugh.

Turned out the last laugh was on them, though, because Mitch made them take the new guy with them, and they needed him about as much as they needed a turd on a sandwich. Ally actually hated to train new guys anyway, and this douche had made it clear from day one that he didn't think Ally should be in charge of anything but maybe baking him a pie. She'd dealt with enough of that shit as a child and in the military to last her a lifetime. She was tired of having to prove or explain herself to anyone about anything.

She was good at her job and she knew it. When new guys found out—and they always did because the old guys told them—a lot of them assumed she was in charge of the crews because Helen had been Mitch's daughter. But she'd already been working for Mitch a couple of years when Helen came in the office to talk to her father one day and they met. The truth was the only time it had ever been clear that Mitch was not happy with Ally was when he found out she was sleeping with his daughter. As mad as Mitch had been if he didn't really need Ally and she wasn't damn good at her job, he would have fired her for sure.

Of course it wasn't like Mitch didn't already know Helen was gay. He did, and he'd already come to terms with it, but having one of his employees diddling his little girl had pissed him right completely off. As soon as Mitch realized Ally wasn't just using his daughter for sex, that she really loved her, Mitch had gone right back to treating Ally like the son he never had because... well, Chuck.

New guys came in she had to train them, and every single one of them—even Ray and Billy Bob who she now counted among her closest friends—just had to test her metal. Business was picking up, which was good, but this douche was the third new guy she'd been asked to train in the last three months, and she was tired of being tested.

She was especially tired of it today. When she had to call the office because the posthole auger she told the new guy to load didn't make it onto the truck, it was all she could do to stop herself from throwing a living fit.

Maggie pulled up in one of the work trucks and Ally went to get the equipment out of the bed herself just to keep from having to ask the dumbass to get it. If he once again gave her that look that near screamed it was beneath him to take orders from her she was going to plant her boot in his ass. She dropped the tail gate and got the auger out of the truck. From his perch in the back seat of the truck Tuesday waved at her, and was obviously shouting her name. So she walked over and opened the door.

"What?" she asked with a smile.

"Can I stay with you?"

"When?" Ally asked.

Maggie had gotten out of the car and was standing at her shoulder she sighed. "Ally, he's two and a half. He means now. Right now."

Ally laughed. "No you can't stay with me; I'm working." She rubbed the boy's head.

"I already told him that."

"Mom's working and I stay with her," he said.

"And that's what he told me."

Ally held the auger up. "Alright, but your mom doesn't work with stuff like this that could rip a little boy's arms and legs off. Why just last week a kid walked up and..."

"Ally for God's sake." Maggie shook her head. "Do not traumatize my baby. Just tell him no he can't stay."

"Sorry, bud, your Mom said you can't stay," Ally said and smiled.

"Chicken shit," Maggie whispered in her ear. "So what happened? You don't forget stuff. Are you okay, is it your dad?"

"Oh my dad's driving me bat shit crazy, but I didn't forget anything. It's that new guy. I told him to get it; he 'forgot.' I think he wants to make me look bad because he doesn't like working under a woman. Since I'm a top, too...."

"It's not funny, Ally, that's bull shit. Tell Mitch. That's sexual harassment..."

"I got this shit, Maggie. No sense in bothering Mitch. If he doesn't quit his shit then I'll go to Mitch. Thanks for bringing this." She started to walk away.

"Ally," Tuesday said.

"What?"

"At least kiss me goodbye," he said, holding up his arms. Ally looked at Maggie.

Maggie shrugged and smiled. "It wouldn't kill you to be more demonstrative."

Ally looked to make sure the guys weren't watching, and then she kissed the boy on the cheek. He of course grabbed her neck, hugged her and planted a sloppy kiss on her cheek.

She mumbled something and took the auger to where they were working. She set the tool down. They didn't need it yet, but it was stupid to wait till they did because that slowed everything down.

Maggie started backing down the driveway.

"The new age hippie flake has a killer ass and rack," the new guy said. It took Ally a minute to realize who he was talking about, but she did and was already pissed off before he said, "Is anybody tappin' that ass?"

"Watch your fucking mouth, new guy," Ally said. She purposely put down the hammer she'd been getting ready to use because she knew herself. She watched as Maggie drove away, Tuesday waved at her, and she waved back.

"I mean come on it's pretty obvious which side your bread is buttered on, Butch. Don't tell me you haven't noticed that she is really built and with just enough extra cushion for the pushin' if you know what I mean." She turned just in time to see him make an obscene movement with his hips.

"Dude, that's not cool," Ray said, as much as a warning as anything else.

Ally stood to her full five-foot nine-inch height and glared at the dumbass. "I told you to watch your mother fucking mouth."

"That's the problem with chicks on a job like this one, lighten the fuck up," he said. "You want to do a man's job but you hate men and you want us to act like women."

"What she wants is for you not to act like a rutting pig. Maggie is our friend. I don't appreciate your crap, either," Ray said.

"You don't have to kiss her ass; she ain't the boss...."

"I *am* his boss, but he doesn't have to kiss my ass because he's my friend. *You* have to kiss my ass because I *am* your boss and you *aren't* my friend."

"So..." He took in a deep breath and seemed to make a decision. "Does she bat for your team and the little bastard came from a sperm bank? Or maybe she just screws everything that moves so no one knows who the baby daddy is, and if so can I get me some?"

Ally punched him in the face, he punched her back. She didn't block fast enough and he blooded her lip which did nothing but piss her off even more. She brought a spinning kick into his gut that nearly creamed her leg and sent them both crashing to the ground. Ally got up before he did as if she hadn't just completely fucked her leg up and yelled at the pecker head as he staggered to his feet. "You limp-dicked little bastard. You're fired!"

"You can't fire me, dyke."

"Yes I can, prick!"

Ray had to separate them more than once.

Maggie carried her sleeping baby in and lay him down in the closet. It was a big closet which housed most of their hard files, and she'd put a tot bed in it because she could close the door and it was quiet enough that Tuesday could actually take a nap. Mitch came out of his office obviously a little hot under the collar, and at first she was sure she had done something wrong. "Did you see it?"

"See what?"

Mitch sighed. "I guess that's a no. I'm not sure because he was hard to understand, but I think Ray said Ally kicked the crap out of the new guy and fired him. They're on their way back here now and the only reason I can think of for them to come back here is that the new guy wants to press charges."

"I didn't see anything and.... I was just there. Is Ally

alright?" The new guy had a couple of inches and a good twenty pounds on Ally.

"No idea, but it had to happen right after you left. Maggie, can I count on you to...."

"I don't believe in lying, but I really didn't see or hear anything. You know I've got your back Mitch, Ally's, too."

She was glad Tuesday was taking a nap because when they walked in the new guy had a bloody nose and a black eye, Ally had a bloody lip and Ray was helping her walk. They were all three splattered with blood.

"What the fuck is wrong with you chuckle heads?" Mitch boomed.

Maggie cringed and hoped Tuesday was going to be able to sleep through this.

"He/she started it," they both accused at once, and it looked like Ray was going to have to separate them. From the blood splattered all over his work shirt it looked like he already had at least once.

"He was running his mouth. I fired him. For some reason he thinks I need your permission to fire him. Get this; he wants to file an incidence report, but I'm the one who acts like a girl," Ally hissed.

"What is wrong with people? Why does it have to come to blows? Why can people not just talk things out?" Maggie said. Then she went over and took Ally from Ray and helped her into the break room. "What a dumb ass dyke thing to do, Ally. Of all the stupid shit! You won't go to Mitch and tell him this guy disrespects you because that might cost you butch points so you just decide to kick the guy's ass. I'm going to get the first aid kit. Stay right here and try not to be a violent idiot for a minute." Maggie started down the hall for the shop because of course that was where they kept the first aid kit. She made a mental note to get another one for the break room. When she came even Mitch's closed office door she would have had to have been deaf not to hear them because they were all yelling instead of talking.

"What the hell happened?" Mitch asked.

"She went nuts and hit me," the new guy said.

"Shut up new guy. I'm not talking to you, and if Ally says you're fired you're fired. Ray, what the hell, man?"

"New guy was talking smack about Maggie. Ally asked him nicely to shut the fuck up but he just kept right on running his mouth."

"What sort of shit?" Now Mitch sounded as mad as she'd ever heard him.

So Ray gave him a blow-by-blow account, and by the time he was done even Maggie wanted to hit the guy.

When Mitch started yelling at the guy he hadn't gotten past, "Think that's cute to call someone a dyke!" when Maggie quit listening, remembering that Ally was bleeding all over the break room and rushed to get the first aid kit. As she was nearly running past Mitch's door back from the shop he was still yelling. "Ain't no one here gonna back up yer story, pecker head. You're fired. I can replace any one of the men who work for this company and run things just fine or fire them all and hire a whole new bunch, but I can't run this business without either one of those girls, so get yer shit and get off my lot."

Maggie smiled as she ran on into the break room. She got out some gauze and wet it and started to clean Ally's lip. She looked into Ally's blue eyes and could see so much rage there, the effect of a whole lifetime of bullies. "I'm sorry I snapped at you, Ally."

Ally just shrugged and smiled. "It's alright I heard the love behind the words *what a stupid-ass dyke thing to do.*" She wasn't mad at Maggie. "Maggie." She took the gauze from Maggie's hand and held it to her own lip. "My lip doesn't really hurt. I blocked most of the punch and it cut on my teeth. No real impact. But in order to keep from kicking him with my brace I kicked him with my good leg which was actually a lot worse for my bad leg. Can you please try to fix my leg because if you can't I need to go to the hospital. I'm about to pass out."

She noticed then that Ally had already taken her brace off. She pushed Ally's pants leg up till she could actually work on the leg. "This would be easier if we could just take your pants off. You've popped it out of place again...." she sighed "...so soon after doing it before. You're going to have to take it easy for a couple of days, Ally."

"Don't you dare say I'll have to stay home because if I have to spend two days cooped up in my house with that old Bible-thumping moron I'm going to blow my...."

"Don't say it even in jest, Ally. At the very least you are going to have to let the other guys do more. You know, do what your job really is, and do less of the heavy lifting or you're going to screw this shit completely up, and I'm telling Mitch as much...."

"Dammit, Maggie..."

"Don't you dammit Maggie me." Maggie started to cry. "Someone has to look out for you, Ally."

"Hey, it's alright Maggie. I'm alright."

"No, but you will be." Maggie pulled on the leg. She knew it was going to hurt like a bitch; that was why she was crying. What Ally had done *was* a stupid butch thing to do but... honestly it was kind of nice to have someone stand up for her honor. She started rubbing Ally's leg, kneading the pain out.

"Thanks, Maggie," Ally sighed with relief.

Tuesday came running in from Maggie's office and was obviously excited to see Ally till he saw Maggie working on her leg. He walked over close and watched her for a minute. He made a pained expression, and Ally laughed reached out and rubbed his head. If she kept doing that the poor kid wouldn't be able to walk past metal without getting a shock. Maggie smiled and shook her head.

"Did the machine hurt you?" he asked, his eyes big.

Maggie could see the mischievous glow in Ally's eyes, so she leaned forward and whispered, "If you tell him yes I will snap your leg back out of place. Nor do I want him to know what happened. He idolizes you. I don't want him to be like every other man and dyke on the planet and think violence is the answer to everything."

"I fell," Ally said, and then whispered leaning forward till her face was almost in Maggie's, "I thought you didn't like lying."

Maggie looked up at her and their eyes met. It almost happened right then. "You could have just said you hurt it."

"But I did fall..." Ally whispered and smiled "...when I kicked the fucker in his stomach I fell right over with him."

"Lovely." Maggie mumbled as they both sat back up. Tuesday was still sleepy, no doubt because while she couldn't tell what he was saying anymore she could still hear Mitch bellowing. Tuesday walked over and held his hands up to Ally. "Honey, Ally is hurt."

"It's alright, Maggie, you're fixing me right up." Ally took the gauze away from her lip. It appeared to have stopped bleeding, so she put the gauze down on the table top, reached

over picked Tuesday up and sat him on her lap. All her rage
was just gone.

In that moment Maggie realized that Ally loved her son,
and she had the strangest feeling and again it almost
happened, but what almost happened she couldn't quite put
her finger on. She took in a deep, shuddering breath and for
a second stopped working on Ally's leg.

"You alright, Maggie?"

"Yeah, I'm fine." She looked at Ally. "I think I'm fine."

"What happened to him?" Tuesday asked, his eyes huge.

Maggie looked up and saw the new guy walking by, a
check in his hand, and a snarl on his face.

Ally smiled hugely and told Tuesday, "He fell, too."

"Oh… was it because of that machine?" he asked. Maggie
cut Ally a look.

"No… but it is a really dangerous machine," Ally said.

Mitch walked in closely followed by Ray. Mitch looked at
Ally. "You alright to work? No, screw that; you'll just lie.
Maggie, is Ally alright to go back to work?"

"She can go back to work, but she needs to take it easy.
This is the second time I've had to do this in less than three
days. If she doesn't take it easy it's just going to pop out
again and then she's going to need some serious down time."

"Should she go home for a couple of days?"

Maggie looked from Ally to Mitch and back. "If she won't
do something stupid, she'll be better off working because her
dad is still at her house."

"That's seriously fucked up," Mitch said. "I'm really sorry
about this crap today, Ally. You tried to tell me not to hire
him, and I didn't listen. We need another guy, and this time
I'll let you pick him. And now I hate to say this but I need you
both back on that job and… I'm going to get Chuck off his
death bed to help you." To answer the look on Ray's face he
said, "That's what you assholes get for fighting."

"I wasn't fighting," Ray said.

"No but I'd be willing to bet money that you helped Ally
convince Chuck he was sick, and if Chuck had been with you
instead of that prick none of this would have happened."

"You were fighting Ally?" Tuesday asked.

Maggie sighed and glared at Ally.

"Ah… fighting is bad?" Ally said.

Sam sat and looked at the TV. He had spent the early
morning drinking coffee in the back yard and watching the
birds come into the feeder just off the back deck. Alice was at
work, and he was all alone without enough energy to do
anything he would have liked to do like fiddle with her plants,
sweep the deck or maybe walk around the neighborhood.
Anything but just sit.

But just sitting was soon too hard. He was afraid if he lay
down on the chase lounge he'd go to sleep and then when it
went from shade to sun he'd fry. So he'd gone back in the
empty house and sat in the recliner put his legs up and tried
to find something worthwhile to watch on TV which... he
didn't have much longer to live, and he was just going to get
progressively worse till he died, and watching mindless drivel
on TV was how he was spending what little time he had left
on earth.

He had accomplished nothing with his life. His business
was barely open, his children hated him—for different reasons
but they did—even though Carol would never admit it she
did. The church he'd poured so much into... serving Christ
had cost him everything he had been promised it would give
him.

Alice was a lesbian. She had always been his favorite and
he'd had to cut her out of his life. At least he thought he did.
For years that was the worst thing that ever happened to
him. Then his wife got cancer, and now he had it from smoking
the cigarettes both of his children had begged them to stop
smoking, but since the Baptists found smoking to be an
acceptable sin they just kept doing it. Carol smoked but Alice
didn't. He also knew Alice did no sort of drugs because when
she'd been called into work on Sunday afternoon he had
turned her house upside down looking for a cigarette. He
hadn't smoked since his wife had been diagnosed. The
cigarettes were what had killed her and what were now killing
him, but yesterday he'd just wanted a cigarette. Since he
was dying anyway what was the point?

Alice was a queer and he was only beginning to understand
that it wasn't something that happened to *him.* It wasn't
even something that *happened* to her it simply *was,* and that
being the case who was to blame? If God made us in his
image and Alice was queer who made her that way? He chose

to smoke; no one made him do that. Alice didn't choose to be gay; she just was. Parents were supposed to love their children unconditionally, but they hadn't. At least he and Jenny hadn't—not Alice—they demanded she be something she wasn't or they just couldn't love her.

He was dying, he couldn't find a cigarette, and his daughter didn't go to church anymore. Not any church, and why not? He wanted to know but was afraid to find out. He had gone yesterday hoping that the preacher would say something that would shine a light that would tell him just exactly what to think. That's what his parents had taught him and Jenny and his church friends had reinforced it. When you had a problem you looked for words of wisdom in the preacher's sermon or you opened the Bible, read a passage and twisted it till it told you what you wanted to believe in the first place and acted like the very hand of God had lead you.

And what happened in church yesterday? The preacher started his sermon telling them to call their senators and governor and plead with them to pass the freedom of religion bill. *He said "As God-fearing Christians we have the right to hire or fire people whose lifestyle goes against the will of God. Homosexuality is a grave sin, and to allow those people to have rights is a slap in God's face. When did it become alright to take away our rights to support these godless pedophiles?" I didn't hear him after that because I walked out. He would have people believe that Alice is a sinner that she's the one we have to protect our children from, but it was a man I trusted who spouted the very same stuff who ruined Kyle. So what's the lesson? That Alice is really going to burn in hell or that everything I have ever believed is crap and... Why doesn't Alice go to church... any church?*

The doorbell rang and he struggled to get out of his chair. It rang again. "I'm coming," he snapped. When he finally made it to the door he was winded. The doorbell rang yet again, and he jerked the door open and snapped, "I said I'm coming." Then he looked at the huge, dark-headed man standing there. Sam struggled to catch his breath. "I'm sorry. Can I help you?"

The man seemed to look him over, judge him, and in an instant find him wanting. "What's it going to cost to get you the hell out of here?" He walked in the door like he owned the place, pulling his wallet out of his pocket.

"Excuse me?"

"Look man I ain't no big public speaker. I'm Ally's boss. She just came back all beat up and had beat the crap out of one of the new guys. The guy was a prick, and he more than had it coming, but it's not really like Ally to go off like that. I know having you here is stressing her right out, so... what's it going to cost me to get you out of here?"

"I... I have nowhere else to go," he said. He looked at the man's wallet. "I don't want your charity."

"But you'll take the charity of a kid you beat and threw out of your house. Look, I need Ally or I have no business, but beyond that," the man was visibly choked up but cleared his throat and went on, "Ally is family to me. I had two kids— a son who is possibly the biggest disappointment of my life, and the jewel in my crown." He pointed to a picture on the wall. "That little girl right there. She loved Ally and Ally loved her, and there isn't anything wrong with that, and I'll beat the dog shit out of any man who says there was. Ally's all that I have left of Helen, so... you can't be up in here screwing with her head. Ain't no one any better than Ally. The fact she'd let you stay here after everything you did to her ought to be all the proof you need of that."

"I... I'm sorry for your loss," Sam stammered out, not really knowing what else to say.

The big man laughed, not a pleasant sound. "Really? Because Ally called you when Helen died and you told her some bullshit about how it was God's will."

This man knew the whole story, but then Sam guessed it made sense that he would and... *he's Alice's father now. I kicked her out of my life and he took my place.* "I wish I could go back and fix things, undo things I did. I can't. I'm dying, and maybe I deserve having nowhere to go and she doesn't deserve it but... I only have a short window of time in which to try to make peace with Alice before I die."

The big man nodded his head then, resigned that he wasn't going to get Sam to leave Ally's he put his wallet away. "You're going to have to unlearn all the hateful crap you've been taught if there is any chance that you can do that. I know because that's what I had to do when Helen told us. My wife just took it in stride but it took me some time to wrap my head around it because even though I'd walked away from all that garbage it was still there. I was raised in the same sort of church you were raised in. If you had seen those kids together you would have known there wasn't anything wrong with them. This is their house. Ally shouldn't feel uncomfortable in her own house. If you can't let her be herself here, then you need to get the fuck out and I'll pay for you to go someplace else."

Sam nodded, watched him leave, then went to the bathroom and threw up. He wound up having to cradle the toilet. He finally gave up, lying on the bathroom floor sick and crying.

Ally sat in the driveway looking at the two steps to the front door. At that moment they might as well have been Mount Everest. She wished now she had taken Maggie's offer to drive her home. Driving the truck had hurt worse than anything else that day. Except maybe Maggie putting her leg bone back in place. Swallowing whatever pride she had left she pulled a shovel out of the bed of her truck and used it as a crutch to get up the walkway then she looked at the two steps, took a deep breath, and using the rail in one hand and the shovel in the other hoisted herself up them.

She heard a noise and wished she could have acted surprised that Maggie had followed her home. As Maggie got out of the car she started to insist that she didn't need her and that she should go on home, but that would have been a lot of trouble to go to just to tell a huge lie.

Sam woke to the sound of people talking and he felt better. After he threw up he realized he had taken the wrong amount of one pill and not enough of another, and since he had puked them all up he had retaken his medication in the proper amounts and felt nearly—but not quite—human again.

He sat up on the couch and listened. He smiled when he heard the little boy's voice. Then he remembered the visit from Alice's boss and he stood up realizing he had no idea how badly Alice was hurt. He got up and went in the direction of the voices. He cringed when he realized they were in Alice's room remembering what he'd just seen in there. The door wasn't closed but he knocked on it anyway.

"Come in, Dad. I'm not having sex this time."

"That's not funny. You shouldn't purposely torment him," he heard Maggie whisper.

"Oh, I don't think he thought it was funny either. Suffice it to say it was the weekend for bad sex."

When he walked in Alice was laying down wearing shorts and Maggie was rubbing her leg. When Alice turned to look at him she had a fat lip but otherwise seemed to be fine.

The boy was sitting on her stomach. He looked up at Sam. "Fighting is bad."

"Yes it is," he said, smiling at the boy. "Are you alright Alice?"

"I'm fine."

"At least you didn't dislocate it this time, Ally, but you aren't fine. You should take a couple of days off," Maggie said.

"Should she go to a real doctor... no offense."

"None taken. If you can talk her into it you're a better man than I am," Maggie said with a laugh. She grabbed a bottle of something, put some in her hands and started rubbing it into Alice's leg. "Tuesday, quit wallowing Ally now. I told you she's hurt."

"He's alright, Maggie. I have abs of steel."

Maggie giggled. "Well that's what Helen always said."

The boy moved anyway. He lay down beside Alice and put his arm around her, and she put her arm around him. "You be alright, Ally."

"I know that, bud."

"That's about all I can do with it. Use your crutches, hard head, and stay off it as much as possible. Keep it up. Think about taking a couple of days off or... at least let me drive you to and from work." Maggie put the bottle of oil into her purse. "Come on, Tuesday, we need to go home get something to eat then go take care of Aunt Mona."

"Can I stay with Ally?"

"Honey, Ally needs to rest, and there is the driving back and forth and...."

"Why don't you eat here then go take care of your sister then come stay the night and you can take Ally to work in the morning? That would be a lot less driving." Sam smiled when they all looked at him like he'd lost his mind. He shrugged. "I could sleep on the couch. You could have my bed."

"That's actually not a bad idea, Maggie," Ally said. "You've been running like a crazy person and most nights Dad sleeps on the couch or the recliner anyway. It will save you some running."

"But you can't… shouldn't… be running after Tuesday."

"Oh, I'm not going to; he's going to take care of me." Ally dug in her pocket and pulled out her phone. "Asian food or pizza?"

"Asian," Maggie said.

"Pizza," Tuesday said.

"Pizza it is," Ally said, smiling at Maggie. "So?"

"Okay, it's a plan," Maggie said. "I'm assuming you have the stuff for a salad in the fridge since it's what you live on."

"I do."

When Maggie went to the kitchen Sam followed her. "Is she really alright?"

"No. She will be, but she's not right now. That leg's a mess; there are seven pins in her foot, a plate with six screws in her tibia, and two different bone grafts made out of calcium carbonate on her knee. There are pieces of muscle and ligament that are missing. I sometimes think she would have been better off if they had just cut it off. It dislocates easily and it hurts all the time."

"Do you go to church, Maggie?"

She got really busy pulling stuff out of the refrigerator.

"You seem very religious."

Maggie sighed and made herself even busier but spoke, "I'm not religious; I don't go to church. I'm spiritual, which means I try to live and do no harm, to love, to have no fear, and to make peace where there is strife." She laughed and added, "And then some silly butch takes offense at what someone says about me and my son and gets herself hurt fighting for my honor." She started getting things out of the cabinets. It was clear she knew right where everything was. "I pray, I meditate, I believe everything is—for lack of a better word God—and God is everything."

"That sounds religious," Sam said with a smile.

"Religion says, 'Here's a box. Get in it, do what you are told to do when you are told to do it, and you will be righteous.' Spirituality says, 'You are righteous because you exist. You know what is right, do that.' That's the difference."

"Do you know why Ally doesn't go to church?"

Maggie sighed. "You know what, Sam? I think you should ask Ally."

"I have till I'm sure she wants to hit me," Sam said. "She

won't answer."

"Then quit asking," Maggie said with a laugh.

"You must be here a lot," Sam said.

"Why do you say that?"

"You know where everything is."

And she did, too. "Till Mona had to go to the hospital I hadn't been here since Helen died." Maggie's voice wavered. How could she know where everything was? "It's like the herb garden."

"What?" the old man asked.

"I know where everything is because Ally hasn't moved a single thing since Helen died. Everything is exactly the way she left it. Excuse me." She put down the knife she'd been using to cut the tomato and walked back to the bedroom. Ally was laying in the bed with Tuesday beside her watching TV some show Maggie normally would not have let him watch.

"Something wrong?"

"That rather depends on what I'm going to find in your closet." She went over to the closet, opened the door, walked in and sighed. She ran her hands down her face, grabbed a dress on a hanger and walked out with it. "You wear this a lot?" Ally looked away. "Why Ally? You know this isn't what Helen would want for you." She hung the dress back up right where she had found it—which she only realized later was sort of hypocritical. She walked to the foot of the bed and looked at Ally. "You have to let her go, Ally." Tears were running down her face and she wiped them away.

Ally nodded at her. "I know, Maggie, I know. I should get rid of her things. I will."

"I could pack them for you."

"Yes, because looking at you I can see that it wouldn't bother you at all." Ally smiled. "I'll hire someone to do it. I mean it won't be hard. All her stuff is on the left and all mine is on the right."

"Don't make Mom sad; give her the dress if she wants it that bad," Tuesday said.

Ally laughed and shook her head. "Helen would have loved him, Maggie."

Maggie nodded wiped her eyes and went back to the kitchen. The old man was now sitting at the table. "Everything alright?"

Maggie nodded silently and went back to work. *I thought I was over missing Helen and I'm obviously not and your daughter's house is a shrine to a dead woman but everything is great.*

"I met the girl's father today," Ally's father said.

"Mitch came here?" Maggie was shocked. When Maggie had told him that she hadn't been to Ally's house since Helen died he had said he hadn't either, that he just couldn't make himself go there. Why on earth would he come here today of all days?

"Yes, he wanted me out of Alice's house. He blamed me being here for her fight. He seems to really care about Alice."

"You're still here?"

He avoided her unasked question. "What was the girl like?"

"Her name was Helen," Maggie said.

"What was Helen like?"

Maggie's mother was always moving them from one town to another as the "spirit" guided her. Agnes Muntz's spirit however was unfortunately guided at least in part by severe manic depression. Agnes had three children, each with different fathers. Of the three fathers only Mona's had kept in touch with his child. Chad was two years older than Maggie. Maggie was the youngest, and the sad truth was that she and Chad had been mostly raised by poor Mona. Mona was twenty-five, Chad was twelve, and she was ten when the spirit moved their mother to Flint Town right next door to Helen and her family. They were the same age, liked all the same things, and were instant friends.

Maggie loved Helen and Flint Town on sight, so when two years later the spirits wanted Agnes to move again, Mona put her foot down. Agnes moved anyway. Nothing really changed because Mona was really the only mother they had ever known. Agnes would drop in periodically to check on them and give them some money—never more than enough for her to feel like she had the right to tell them what they were doing wrong. Mona worked, and when things got tight Mona's dad would send her some cash, always enough to remind them that Mona had a dad who really cared about her.

Mitch knew things were tough, so he was always giving her and Chad one odd job or another and paying them way more than it was worth just to help out.

Helen had always been there for her, and she'd always been there for Helen, and they had never really been out of each other's pockets. Maggie had worked hard to get the grades and she was able to get scholarships to go to Flint Town University, which was just fine. Of course Helen applied to and got into a far better college in another state. They kept in touch but only really saw each other over the summer and breaks for four years.

Helen had taken landscape design in college and went into the family business. Maggie went into physical therapy to use her natural gift for healing. She got a job in another city and saw Helen even less though they talked on the phone two and three times a week.

Maggie made the mistake of treating one of her patients with reiki. The patient didn't complain, quite the opposite, but word got out and the next thing she knew she was being sued by the hospital she worked for and the state yanked her license to practice. She was about to counter sue to get her license back when the hospital promised to drop their law suit if she would agree to drop hers. The problem was she couldn't get her license back without winning her lawsuit. Her lawyer assured her this was probably the only way that she was going to get out of paying more money than she could ever make because there was no way she could win her case.

She lost her license to practice PT, her apartment, her car, everything, and had to come back to Flint Town with nothing and move in with Mona. And Helen was right there in an instant with encouraging words, insight and love, and then she took her and got her the job she still had. Now Helen was gone and most days it still didn't feel real and Ally... Ally had a closet full of clothes that wouldn't fit her even if she would ever wear them in a million years.

She realized she'd been silent too long because she'd made the whole salad. She looked at Ally's dad. "Helen wasn't like anyone. She was Helen. If you weren't trapped in religious dogma, if you were open to spirit, then you'd look at this home, at the pictures on the walls and you'd know her."

The doorbell rang. "Don't you dare get up, Ally Taggert!" She ran in and went to Ally's night stand and grabbed her wallet.

"Why do you know where all my shit is?" Ally asked with

a laugh.

"Because I have a really good memory and you haven't moved a thing, not a thing." She looked with meaning at the closet. She took the wallet and headed for the door. Ally made a lot more money than she did, and she was the one who ordered the pizzas, so Maggie wasn't paying for it. She opened the door, took the two pizzas and paid the guy. "Two ginormous pizzas to feed two women, a two-year-old, and a cancer patient, what the hell was that woman thinking?"

She stopped at Ally's bedroom door. "Get your crutches hard head and come on. I need to eat and get out of here."

Ally mumbled something to Tuesday and he giggled, so Maggie knew she really didn't want to know what.

As she walked in the kitchen and set the boxes down the old man looked at her and said, "Her name isn't Taggert."

"It is now, Dad, so drop it. If I had married a man my name would have changed. For all intent and purposes I married a woman, and I legally took her name," Ally said, as she walked into the room using the hated crutches.

Maggie could tell the old man was fighting not to say anything, and she could have kicked herself. Of course they didn't call her Full-disclosure Maggie for nothing. She tended to say what she thought and what she felt, but she wasn't mean and she didn't like to hurt people's feelings or make them mad. She liked to help keep the peace not break it. "Why did you buy enough pizza for an army?"

Ally shrugged. "I was hungry, there's four of us, I figured a half a large pizza apiece."

Maggie smiled silently put some salad on her plate and reached for a piece of pizza.

"What?" Ally asked.

"I find it hard to believe that you with the rock-hard abs can eat a half a pizza. I know I can't, and the baby might make it through a half a slice."

"So, we'll take the left overs to work with us in the morning," Ally said.

Maggie nodded; that would work.

"I can eat a whole piece," Tuesday told Ally then glared at Maggie as if she had embarrassed him horribly in front of his friend.

"Can you eat a half a pizza?" Ally asked him.

He looked at her and shook his head.

"Well you should have told me before I ordered so much pizza. What the hell were you thinking?"

He took a bite of pizza and said around it, "Ally, you do know I can't count."

"You can't?" she asked as if it were unbelievable.

"No." He laughed.

"What about you, Dad, can you eat a half a pizza?"

"Not anymore, but back in the day I could eat three or four pizzas and finish off with a whole cake," he said, even as he took a half a piece out of the box.

With a bit of shock Maggie realized this was where Ally got her sense of humor from.

He smiled and shook his head.

"What, Dad?"

He looked up at Ally smiled and shrugged. "I'm happy."

The funny thing was to Maggie's ears he sounded shocked.

CHAPTER 4

If someone tells you they hate you, you no longer have to worry whether they like you or not.

When Maggie got back to Ally's with an overnight bag, Ally's father was asleep in the guest room and she didn't feel like sleeping on the couch with no bedding or bumping around looking for it. When she walked into Ally's bedroom the light was on and Tuesday was asleep on Ally's head. It was a good thing Ally slept on her side or he would have smothered her. Maggie didn't think about it; she changed into her nightgown, removed her son from Ally's head, turned off the light and purposely got between Ally and Tuesday. Ally needed some sleep, so if Tuesday was going to sleep on anyone's head it would be Maggie's. It was a huge king-sized bed, so there was plenty of room.

When she woke up in the morning she had more than the usual disorientation that you had from sleeping in a strange house because Tuesday was sleeping with his feet pressed into her stomach and Ally was wrapped all around her. She opened her eyes and the light was barely coming in the windows which meant it was probably nearly time to get up anyway. But the alarm wasn't going off so it was probably Tuesday kicking her in her stomach which had awakened her. After all there was a reason she'd moved him to his own bed. She started to just go right back to sleep and then suddenly she became very aware of the fact that she was sleeping in Helen's bed with Helen's partner and far from feeling weird she felt strangely comfortable.

Helen always said sleeping with Ally was like sleeping with an octopus. I don't think I could get away from her right now if I tried, and I certainly couldn't do it without waking her up.

She felt Ally's breath against her neck, and it almost happened right then, but Tuesday picked that moment to kick her in the stomach again. She reached to grab his feet, but Ally had a death grip on her arm and she just pulled her back to her and then she kissed the back of her neck.

Damned alarm. Ally didn't want to get up. She was perfectly comfortable. She kissed Helen's neck again and heard Maggie saying. "Ally, you need to wake up and quit doing that."

Ally was up, but it took her a second to let go of Maggie. "What the hell!"

"Your dad forgot and went to sleep in the guest room. I didn't want to sleep on the couch. I thought I was doing you a favor by putting the head-sleeping boy on the other side of me. I'm ashamed to say that's the best night's sleep I've had in a couple of weeks, and I didn't mind the kiss at all." She grinned wildly at Ally. "You have very soft lips."

Ally mumbled things even she didn't understand reached over and shut off the alarm clock then got up grabbed her crutches and started for the bathroom. She had that dream all the time, but when she woke up her arms were empty and she felt horrible. Waking up and being wrapped around Maggie had not felt awful at all—weird, but not awful. And what she wasn't about to tell Maggie was that was the best night's sleep she'd had in years.

By the time she got showered and dressed Maggie had already set out the cereal and milk and Tuesday was dressed and eating. Ally sat down. "Thanks for everything, Maggie, my leg feels so much better this morning."

"You're welcome, but I swear Ally if you do any stupid shit and screw it up again today I will have Mitch send you right home."

"It's a deal." Ally didn't want to hurt it again. She was pretty tough, but she didn't think anyone realized how much the damn thing hurt.

"Your lip looks pretty good this morning. If I didn't know I couldn't tell," Maggie said.

"I'm... I'm sorry about...."

"Hey, I got into your bed. You didn't do anything wrong. I don't feel weird about it, and I'm sorry if you do."

Ally nodded relaxing a little. She looked at Tuesday; he had milk all over his face and way too much cereal in his mouth. Ally smiled.

"I thought you were just kidding, but when I got here last night bigger than shit he was sleeping on your head," Maggie said. "I moved him. He kicks, he wallows, he woke me up this morning kicking me in the stomach because he'd turned sideways in the bed, but he's never climbed on my head."

"Well he's done it every time he's slept with me."

Tuesday seemed to realize they were talking about him then, and he looked from his mother to Ally, "Are you my dad?"

"What!" Ally and Maggie gasped at the same time.

"Are... you... my... dad?" He asked slowly because they were obviously imbeciles.

Ally cracked up laughing. Then stopped when she saw the look on Maggie's face.

"Ally isn't your father," Maggie said carefully.

The boy looked disappointed, and Ally guessed from the look on Maggie's face she was afraid next he would ask who his father was. The boy's father had been an absolute douche bag. He had beaten Maggie nearly to death when she told him she was pregnant. It hadn't hurt the baby at all, just Maggie.

What Maggie didn't know and had better not ever find out was the reason she'd never seen or heard from him since was because Mitch and Ally had gone out looking for him, found him alone, and accidently killed him. Then they had carefully, meticulously, run every bit of him through their industrial chipper-shredder, composted him, and then spread him in gardens all over a tri-state area. She had killed men for less, so she, for one, didn't have any guilt at all about it. She and Mitch had never said one word about it since, not even to each other.

Ally had a little guilt when, on occasion, Maggie would worry about him showing up and trying to have anything at all to do with her son. Ally assured her that wasn't ever going to happen. Peace and love Maggie sure as hell wasn't going to understand what she and Mitch had done, even though the actual killing had been an accident. Maggie would say they should have let the cops handle it, but what the hell had the cops done? Nothing.

"Are you sure?" Tuesday asked her.

"I think I'd know," Ally said.

"Can I tell people you're my dad?"

"Knock yourself out, kid," Ally said with a laugh.

"No you may not because it's a lie," Maggie said, and she

shot Ally a look that would peel paint.

This made Tuesday cry.

"Now see what you did," Ally said in an accusing tone

Ally was actually mad. No, Ally was furious. She was going out of her way to confuse Maggie's baby, and she was mad at Maggie. Ally got up walked over picked him up and held him, letting him spill a mouth full of cereal all down her clean work shirt. "It's alright baby," she patted his back.

Maggie was at a loss; she had hoped to put this off. She didn't know what to say or do.

Ally walked over, sat him down on the counter, got a wash rag and wet it. She wiped off her shirt then wiped his face off. "You're okay, Tuesday."

She looked at Maggie. "Can we talk for a minute?"

Maggie nodded. Ally brought Tuesday back to his chair and sat him down. "Everything will be fine. Now finish your breakfast," she ordered.

He sniffed nodded and started eating again.

Maggie followed Ally into the hallway, "Why are you so mad at me?"

"Seriously? What's wrong with me?"

"What?"

"I care about him, I've been around him all his life, I could be his dad. He calls Mitch grandpa; Mitch and I have the same last name."

"And... Why does that make sense?" Maggie laughed and shook her head. "You can't be his dad Ally, you don't have a penis."

"Now you sound like my fucking father. I'm the closest thing to a dad he has."

"I don't understand why you're so upset. I just need to answer his questions honestly."

"Really? Because as you keep reminding me, he's two and a half. Do you really think he's going to understand things like you were having trouble getting over Helen's death so you were smoking weed all the time dropping a little acid and you went out with a string of dick heads and then you met their king, or what he did to you? Why he did it? How he just disappeared to escape prosecution?"

Maggie took a deep breath and let it out. She felt sick to her stomach. "I hate that I did this to myself and to him and...."

"You keep telling me everything happens for a reason. You helped save me, Maggie and that kid saved you. He's not going to ask questions you don't know how to answer if you give him what he wants. I can do this; I can be his almost, sort-of, pseudo daddy. Look, you know Helen wanted a kid, wanted one so badly that I still have the frozen eggs to prove it. We were going to have a kid, and I still wouldn't have a penis. That kid would have had two mothers. What makes your kid any better than the one Helen never got to have? Would it be so horrible for your kid to have two mothers? I can be like a weekend dad except for the whole lack of a penis thing."

Maggie thought about it for just a second which was wrong because this was actually a huge decision that affected them all. "Alright. It's completely crazy, and I'm sure I'm just being a huge chicken shit, but everyone screws up their kids, right?"

"Yeah, I mean look at us," Ally said with a shrug.

They walked back in the room and Tuesday who had finished all his breakfast and was completely over crying looked at them expectantly.

"Ally can be your other parent."

Tuesday jumped down ran over and hugged Ally around the knees so hard he damn near took her down. Ally picked him up and hugged him. He kissed her cheek and said, "I'm going to call you Allybaba."

Ally looked at Maggie and smiled. "There you go, then. Now let's load up our illegitimate love child, check to make sure my Dad's still breathing, and go to work."

"Now see, Ally, you can't be saying crap like that." Maggie sighed and followed her down the hall.

As they were getting in the car and Ally was once again having a fight with the car seat, Maggie had a strong memory of the feel of Ally's lips on the back of her neck that sent a shiver up her spine. Ally got in the passenger's seat and dragged her crutches in with her.

"Allybaba, can I have a puppy?"

"No you can't have a puppy," Ally said.

"But you have a yard, Allybaba."

Maggie looked at Ally. "You do have a yard, Allybaba."

"I don't want my yard all torn to shit, and we all know who will get stuck picking up dog crap." She turned around to look at Tuesday. "You can have a bird."

"Can it be blue, and can we name it Jack?"

"Of course," Ally said.

"You do realize he will not forget about the bird," Maggie whispered at her.

"Why do you think I said bird? I don't want a damn dog, but I've always wanted a bird. The only reason I don't have one already is because Helen didn't want a bird because of the noise and the mess, and as you said I have to let her go."

Ally, Billy Bob and Chuck were laying in the last of the plumbing for a sixteen-thousand dollar waterfall and pond system that she was super proud of. Chuck had gone off to get something they needed from the truck and it was a sure bet he wouldn't be back for twenty minutes.

"Having him in the house is dredging up so much shit. I told Maggie when we were driving into work that I feel like I'm about three seconds from anger-induced turrets where he's just sitting there and I yell out, 'I hate you!' You know what Maggie said?"

"God alone knows with spacy Maggie," Billy Bob laughed.

"Maggie said, 'Well at least then he won't have to wonder whether you like him or not'."

Billy Bob looked over at her and smiled.

"What?" she asked.

"Nothing."

"Don't nothing me. What are you grinning like an idiot about?" She hated working around the crutches, but was glad she was using them because they kept her from abusing her leg and it was healing faster than it normally did. Mostly as long as she had them her crew didn't mind at all doing more than they had to, so in other words the parts of their jobs she normally did. If she didn't have them they could see her drag that leg all over the place and not lift a finger to do one extra thing. When she was using the crutches they automatically took up her slack. She guessed because when she had them it was obvious that something was wrong with her.

Humanity was pretty superficial on most days.

"You know when you beat the crap out of Tucker...."

"Who the hell is Tucker?"

"The new guy. When you kicked his ass because he talked

smack about Maggie I thought *what's that all about* but then when I saw you guys come into work this morning... When did you and Maggie hook up?"

"Is that what everyone is whispering about? What a bunch of old women you are. Christ, Mitch pays you assholes way too much if all you do is sit around and talk about my nonexistent love life. Maggie has been taking me back and forth to work all week because my leg got screwed up in that fight."

"Why'd you kick Tucker's ass then?"

"Because he was talking crap about Maggie and Tuesday."

"Was it the kind of crap that if one of us said it about some fine bitch walking down the street you would have kicked our ass?"

"Shut up, Billy Bob, and hand me a pipe wrench. While you're at it could you at least pretend to be working?"

He handed her the wrench. "Well was it?"

Ally thought about it a minute. "Probably not, but he wasn't saying it about some bimbo none of us knew; he was saying it about Maggie."

"But you and Maggie aren't an item?"

"Billy Bob, Maggie is straight."

Billy Bob laughed. "You silly bitch, Maggie's not straight."

"She is, too."

"No she's not. She may not be banging your stupid ass, but she isn't straight."

"And how the hell would you know that?"

"Dorthia..." Billy Bob's sister, "...went to school with Maggie and Helen."

"Yes and high school kids never make anything up just to use it to bug the living shit out of each other." Ally sighed and went right back to work.

"She told Dorthia she slept with a bunch of women in high school and college."

"Lots of girls experiment in high school and college. It doesn't mean they're gay."

"A woman sleeps with another woman, she's gay or bisexual. Dorthia said Maggie is bisexual."

"Come on, Full-discloser Maggie is bisexual—and by the way stop looking like that—only straight guys think bisexual women are sexy. It's sort of a turn off for a gay woman." Billy Bob was full of shit. Maggie believed in open honesty. Besides, she couldn't keep a secret—any secret. Maggie was Helen's best friend; if she was bisexual Helen would have known and if Helen knew she would have told Ally. "We are not sleeping together, so you can tell all the guys at work and then you'll have to find something else to gossip about."

The news started with violence at a site where protesters had attacked a crew of work men building a mosque in a major city. She didn't notice which one and didn't care. As far as she was concerned there was hate speech on both sides. Ally didn't watch the news for a reason.

Her dad had turned this shit on and she was about to change the channel when her dad said, "Damned ragheads. Am I right?"

Ally took a deep breath and let it out. She really wanted to just say nothing, but her mouth got in the way. "If we think all Muslims are evil why are we over there fighting in the first place?"

"They worship a strange god...."

"Oddly enough they think they worship the same god you do. Most of you have no idea why we're over there. It really is because of the oil, but the excuse we use is that we are trying to free the repressed. It's a civil war between two different factions of the same stupid-assed religion, and whoever is in charge represses the other one so you can never free the repressed just change whose being repressed. We take this one out of power and put this one in and then in a few years we have to go back and change it back and... we shouldn't be there at all. I met lots of those people you call 'ragheads' and I won't say they are no different from me because they are, but they certainly are no different from you. They believe all the same stupid crap, all the same hateful 'We're better than you' shit. Just like you and your church friends they think it represses them for anyone to do anything they don't like, they think they only have rights if they are allowed to persecute others.

"Don't you get it, Dad? I basically didn't have a lot of choices because you kicked me out of the house; I had no money and nowhere to go. I didn't join the National Guard because I wanted to serve. I joined because it was going to help me get an education, give me much-needed cash, and I wasn't supposed to have to go to war. I was supposed to be here cleaning up storm damage and maybe busting up riots. But, no, a president you no doubt voted for started a stupid-assed war and I got deployed. I had a girlfriend at the time who begged me to tell them I was gay. After all at that time the rule was 'Don't ask; don't tell'. But I literally couldn't have stayed in school or paid my rent without it. So I went.

"I did three tours. After the first one the girlfriend was gone, which was good because then I didn't have to pay to keep an apartment. Sending women into combat was strictly experimental, and I had to sign a bunch of papers to do it. But I did because it's really just as dangerous to just be there as it is to fight. And when you fight you get combat pay. They put you someplace you're more likely to get killed and they give you more money. How cool is that? I went again and again. The men I served with blamed me that we didn't get sent to really dangerous areas. The ones who were happy about it figured I was good luck, but the ones who really thought it was going to grow their dicks if they got to kill someone called me Affirmative Action and a lot of other stuff that wasn't so nice. Three tours and my troop had never seen any real action. We were three weeks from being sent home. Three weeks! We're doing a sweep in what's left of a town—which was always creepy anyway because you're walking along and you see a kid's toy and you realize this was somebodies yard. We know there are insurgents so we're on high alert and I know, I just get this feeling in my gut that this time things are going to be different I tell the lieutenant that we should pull back, but he tells me to shut my Affirmative Action mouth and do what I'm told. He was nice that way. Three seconds later he blows up basically all over me, and I start shooting. I know I killed at least three of them, probably more, but I know I killed three of them because I saw them before I shot them. I aimed at them and killed them. All but three of us got out. I was covered in blood and gore from head to toe, but none of it was mine. I didn't have a scratch.

Do you know what I was thinking when I was in the troop carrier heading back to base with my lieutenant splattered all over me?"

"No." Her father was crying but she wasn't.

"I wondered if those men I killed cared more about their lives than I cared about mine. They were at least fighting for something they believed in. Not me, I was just killing to keep from being killed, to keep the guys with me from being killed. Because we were on one side and they were on the other. They told us we were fighting for freedom, but that's bullshit. I was fighting for a country in which I didn't have any rights and then they give us some rights and what do you Bible-thumping morons do? You run as fast as you can to have them yanked away. Give us the right to marry and then pass laws so that we can legally be discriminated against. Give with one hand and take away with the other. Helen and I wanted to get married. Five years ago we couldn't and now we could, but the hate hasn't stopped. If anything it's gotten worse. I fought for a country that didn't want people like me. I was killing people just like you."

As if to prove her point, the news story on the TV now was about another state trying to pass a Freedom of Religion act. Ally pointed at the TV, "Ragheads, Dad? What makes you think I see them any differently than I see you? I came home a killer Dad, a trained killer with blood on my hands. I needed to know that what I had fought for was worth it, so I came home and my parents wouldn't even let me in the house. You... didn't even come to the door."

Ally got up grabbed her crutches and went to the kitchen. She went to the fridge and pulled out one of the hard ciders opened it and took a long drink. When she looked up her dad had followed her to the kitchen. "Dad, I really need to be alone a minute."

Sam was remembering what the big guy had said about not making Alice uncomfortable in her own home. "I'm sorry, Alice."

"For what Dad, for what? You ought to be sorry for a lot of things, but I don't think you are." Alice was obviously mad. "You want to hear some crap? They gave me an award for sharp shooting and one for courage. The colonel who gave it to me gave a speech. He said if it wasn't for me my whole unit might have been killed. Those men I 'saved'—except for a handful of them—they had all made it clear they saw me as a liability, Affirmative Action bullshit. You kill a bunch of people and they reward you. They kill us because they're afraid of us and then we kill them because we're afraid of them and it never ends and none of it makes any sense because at the end of the day all the assholes who want the wars on both sides believe the same, damn, hateful religious crap."

"Is that why you don't go to church, Alice?"

Alice laughed, shook her head and took another drink. "It's one of the reasons, but mostly it's because that pervert Deacon Parish did me the biggest favor when I was ten years old."

"Laban Parish." Sam walked over and sat down hard in a chair across from her, his hands balled into fists and he swallowed hard. "What did he do to you?"

"What do you think he did to me? The same thing he's locked up for now. At least he tried to, but he hardly did more than touch me and make me touch him because you see the whole time he was telling me that Jesus wanted me to let him put his steeple into my heavenly gates I knew that was bullshit. He put my hand in his pants and told me to grab his pillar, and I did, and I dug my nails in deep and ran them down the length of his cock. Then while he was rolling around on the floor bleeding I got away."

"Why didn't you tell anyone?"

"I did tell someone. I told mother who slapped me for lying and grounded me for a week."

Sam broke down. He put his head down on the table and sobbed.

"It's alright, Dad. He gave me the biggest gift because from then on I didn't believe a fucking thing any of you said. Have you got any idea what it's like to be a gay kid and sit in a place like that listening to all the hateful crap that gets spewed about people just like you? The way I felt about myself, all the self-loathing. I never had as much trouble with that once I knew it was all a bunch of lies. How many nights did I lie in bed and pray, *Dear God what is wrong with me? Please fix me.* But after Parish touched me, tried to talk me into letting him fuck me, I knew I wasn't the problem. I wasn't the one who was sick. When my own mother called me a liar and punished me for something I knew had really happened I never again doubted myself. I never again believed there was anything wrong with me. The service damn near broke me again, but gardening, designing landscapes, and then building them... being with Helen, having friends like the guys I work with, Mitch, Karen, Maggie... I don't doubt myself now, not ever. I lost Helen, and I fought for my life, and none of you can hurt me again because I still have me."

"That bastard, that horrible bastard." Sam mumbled into the table. He forced himself to pick his head up and wiped his face on his shirt sleeve. "Do you really want to know what I'm sorry for, Alice? I'm sorry for everything. Everything! Mostly I'm sorry that I was so pussy-whipped that I never had the balls to stand up to your mother and tell her to back the fuck off me and my damn kids. I didn't know, Alice. She never told me that he touched you what he tried to do. If I had known... maybe Kyle...." He just trailed off.

"Dad, who's Kyle?"

"Your sister's oldest son. It doesn't matter; that doesn't matter, not now. I'm so, so sorry, Alice, for beating you, for kicking you out, for not letting you in, for not talking to you on the phone when Hellen died and you were injured. Maggie told me that a spiritual person would look at the pictures on the wall and at this house and know everything they needed to know about Helen, and so I spent most of this week wandering from picture to picture from photo to photo, and I think I know her. She was a beautiful, vibrant woman, full of life, who loved with her whole heart. She loved music and art and gardening. She liked to entertain, to bring her friends and family together, she loved to dance and sing, and above all of that she loved you, and clearly you loved her.

"I've been trying to think of what to say to you, how to make it right between us. Some grand speech, and I've got nothing except... when Carol left me here I was sure I had wasted my whole life. I'm sorry that I wasn't the father you needed me to be, but my life has not been wasted because you are my daughter and you..." Sam could no longer stop his tears. "...you, my dear Alice, are the most amazing person I have ever known. You came from me, and while I can't take any credit for the person you are, you wouldn't be here without me and so... my life wasn't a waste at all."

"Dammit dad," she got up walked over and hugged him and just bawled, "Now it's going to make me sad when you die."

"Wow," Maggie said, "he apologized. That's huge."

"Yeah, right? I mean it was the emotional equivalent of spring cleaning," Ally said. She shifted in the car seat trying to get comfortable.

"Is the leg really better, Ally?"

"Yeah this is the crap it always does, but to make you happy I will carry these fucking crutches around today because I've found that the dick heads who will normally stand and watch me run circles around them all day or wait for me to tell them what to do as if they don't know will jump through hoops to beat me to stuff as long as I'm on crutches. I'll get through today, take it easy over the weekend, and by Monday I'll be as good as... well, what I normally am."

"Allybaba," Tuesday said from the back seat.

"What son, what?"

Maggie smiled, but didn't say anything. It was sort of cute how quickly Ally had adopted the role of Tuesday's other parent. Weird but cute. She still wasn't sure it was a good idea, but Ally was right. Tuesday hadn't asked even one more question about his father for which she was glad because she still didn't have any idea how she would explain him in a way that Tuesday would understand and that wouldn't mean years of therapy.

"Is today the day we're going to get the bird?"

"Yes, Tuesday, yes. For the love of God we will go get the bird as soon as we get off work."

"And it will be blue and we'll call it Jack?"

"Yes."

"Can we go for ice-cream?"

"Sure."

"No we can't. You have fed him quite enough crap this week," Maggie said.

"A frozen yogurt then?" Ally asked.

"Well alright, but you don't have to buy him stuff all the time."

"Yes I do." Ally looked at her like she had just gone criminally insane.

Maggie laughed and shook her head. "If you really feel better, Ally, I have a huge favor to ask...."

"Yes, he can stay overnight while you go on a date." She made air quotes.

Maggie hadn't given Pete a thought since their date. "I'm not going on a *date*, Ally, I just realized I didn't even call him back. I'm not sad, but relieved, so my guess is that was a dead end. I have way too much on my plate with Mona...."

"And having to cart my crippled ass around," Ally said with a sigh.

"You know what, Ally? I think this was good for you-know-who, and thanks. This is actually working out really well. So I have another huge favor..." she grinned, reached over and patted Ally's leg. "As you know, Chad is basically worthless; my mother has gone back to Dallas, thank you universe: Mona cannot nor should she try to do her yard work, but you know how she is and if her yard gets any worse she's going to."

"I can do it tomorrow."

"I don't want you to do it, Ally; I want you to help *me* do it."

"Of course I can." She was sort of quiet then she said, "Why don't you and Tuesday spend the night tonight and then we can get up in the morning, come to the shop and grab one of the trucks and everything we need."

"And I can play with my bird all night," Tuesday said.

"You know that bird's going to bite him," Maggie said with a sigh.

"Probably."

Maggie had gone to pick up their plant order and she was now heading to the building site. From the backseat of the truck Tuesday was making sure she didn't have even a minute to have a single thought of her own by bombarding her with a never-ending stream of questions.

"Can we stay the night at Allybaba's, Mom?"

"Yes, I suppose so." Maggie sighed, wondering briefly if it was such a good idea for either of them to spend so much time with Ally.

"Why did we have to pick up plants?"

"Because it's part of my job."

"They're pretty. Do you think they are pretty?"

"I do."

"Why don't we have a yard?"

"Because we live in an apartment, Honey."

"So?"

"So no one has a yard in an apartment building."

"Why not?"

And it went on and ever on until she couldn't have been happier to pull onto the job site. Until she looked up and saw Ally going over the plans with the client.

She got Tuesday out of the truck, watching the woman with more than normal interest.

"Can I go see what Ray is doing?"

Maggie looked to see that what Ray was doing wasn't dangerous. It wasn't; he was just laying in some watering tubing. "Yes, but don't get in his way."

She looked back to where Ally was talking to the homeowner. The client was a beautiful little blonde-headed woman with a great ass, and her body language was all wrong for a straight woman or even a gay woman who wasn't interested in being all over Ally Taggart. As Maggie started to unload the plants from the trailer something altogether ugly started to gnaw at her gut. She stopped briefly to address her emotions and realized she was jealous. She looked quickly at Ally and realized that Ally was completely unaware she was being flirted with; she was all business. Maggie started to relax and then... why was she jealous? *Because I'm as bad as Ally is with her closet full of Helen's clothes. In my mind Ally is still Helen's wife and I don't like someone else flirting with her which is just ridiculous, so that's all of that. Who knows? This woman might be perfectly lovely and just what Ally needs.* She went back to unloading the truck, but she couldn't quit watching the woman, and when the bitch reached over and fixed Ally's collar... that was when it happened. *Oh my God! I'm not jealous for Helen; I've screwed around and fallen in love with Ally and... that blonde bitch needs to check herself.*

Before she could stop and think about it, Maggie was walking over to where Ally was. She realized she needed a reason to interrupt them, so she came up with a lame one. "I brought the plants."

Ally stopped talking and looked at her, a confused expression on her face. "Yeah, thanks."

Maggie looked at the other woman, actually frowned, then turned caught Ally's eyes and held them. "I was thinking we could stop by the store on the way home, pick up some things, and I could make dinner tonight."

"All right," Ally said, and an air of *what the fuck is wrong* entered her voice.

Maggie really wasn't good at hiding her feelings when she knew she had them. She put her arms around Ally's neck and hugged her, then kissed her cheek, glared at the bitch, then walked back to the truck and started unloading it, noticing Ray and Chuck and Billy Bob were all suddenly both really busy and grinning like idiots. Tuesday ran over and wanted to help her, so she put him to unloading some of the smaller plants.

"Ah," Ally looked at the client. "That's about all really." She folded the plans and looked back over to where Maggie was unloading the truck. "I have to go check on the plant order. If you have any more questions...."

The woman smiled a knowing smile. "She's very pretty, but a little jealous."

"Ah... I'm not sure what she is. If you'll excuse me."

Ally walked straight over to where Maggie was.

Tuesday ran over and Ally picked him up. He put his head on her shoulder.

"Maggie what the hell was that?"

"That woman was flirting with you. You didn't notice, but she was and when I saw it..." Maggie put down the plant walked over and looked up at her. "...I just saw red and I realized that I love you."

"What?"

"I said I love you."

"Then Billy Bob isn't full of shit. You are bisexual."

"Billy Bob *is* full of shit, but yes I'm bisexual."

"What's that mean?" Tuesday asked.

"It means your mother *can* keep a secret when she really wants to. Go to sleep... or something," Ally ordered. "What the hell, Maggie? You normally can't keep a secret for longer than it takes to go in your ear and come out your mouth. What happened to Full-discloser Maggie?" And then she knew. She sighed and patted the boy's back, at least in part to keep him from hearing the whole of their conversation. "Helen told you not to tell me because I was always super jealous of her and she thought if I knew I wouldn't ever let you do anything together without me. But, Maggie, I never would have been jealous of you. Helen was a fem. She liked butch women. Besides, Helen has been dead for five years. You could have told me at any time in that five years." And then she knew why she hadn't. "Maggie, you fucking hypocrite."

Maggie actually cringed.

"You didn't tell me because Helen made you promise you wouldn't, you get all over me because I have a closet full of her clothes yet you couldn't tell me... *this*... because you told her you wouldn't."

"I told you now. I didn't say I didn't need to let her go, too." Maggie smiled. She walked over, got on her tip toes, and kissed Ally on the lips. Ally kissed her back.

It was really nice. She sighed. "So am I freaking you out a little?"

"No you're freaking me out a lot," Ally said with a laugh.

Ray and Billy Bob walked over and started unloading the plants; mostly she was sure so they could spy on them. "What a bunch of assholes," Ally mumbled. "I've got to get back to work."

"Me too. Where are your crutches, hardhead?"

Ally looked around. She hadn't remembered taking them off, and it took her a minute to find them. She nodded her head towards them, and when she did so realized Tuesday had nodded off. "Our son is asleep."

Maggie nodded, went and opened the truck door so that Ally could put him in his car seat and then fight with the buckle. When she stood up Maggie wrapped her arms around Ally's neck and this time when she kissed her Ally didn't hold anything back. There was that little spark that had been gone from her ever since Helen had died. It was just back. She pulled Maggie more tightly to her and kissed her again, and that was when her crew started their crap—the hooting and the wolf whistling—and she just couldn't begin to care. Remembering they both really did have to go back to work, she pushed Maggie to arm's length.

She brushed a strand of red hair out of Maggie's face and smiled at her. "So... I'll see you after work." The crew had finished unloading the trailer, so had no reason to stand around and try to hear what they were saying and pretend that wasn't what they were doing.

Maggie nodded silently. Ally closed the door then walked with Maggie to the other side of the truck and opened the door for her. "You know I can open the door myself right?"

"I do, but then I would have had no excuse to follow you over here would I?"

Maggie got in the truck.

"You know Maggie when I woke up the other day with you in my arms... it felt right. This could work."

"I think so, too."

"We should probably not rush into anything."

Maggie smiled at her. "I can wait if you can."

"We don't have to take it too slow." Ally kissed her on the cheek and moved to close the truck door. She watched as Maggie drove away. Immediately they started in on her.

"Geez, Ally, I thought Maggie wasn't a bisexual," Billy Bob said.

"She was all over you like white on rice," Chuck laughed.

"Shut up, ass holes!" Ally yelled but laughed. "Get back to work."

They went back to work but of course they didn't stop teasing her for a good fifteen or twenty minutes. Finally she and Ray were working on the filtration system and away from the other guys. "So how long have you and Maggie been an item?"

Ally looked at her watch. "About thirty minutes now. Maggie said the client was flirting with me...."

"She was, and in a way that made me wonder if you had just gone dead below the waist," Ray laughed.

Ally shrugged. "Apparently seeing it made Maggie decide she's in love with me."

"So what now, dude?"

"Seriously? Just now, kissing Maggie, that's absolutely the most turned on I've been since Helen died. I'm sure Maggie will ask the stones and crystals whether we are supposed to be together or not, but I... well I think Maggie can make me really feel again."

After work they went to the pet store. There were baby rabbits on display as you walked in the door, and Maggie wasn't too surprised when her son's bird obsession became a rabbit obsession. She was even less surprised when Ally caved in. As they were loading the unassembled free-standing hutch into the back of Maggie's car, Ally looked at her and smiled. "Looks like I'm never getting a bird."

Maggie laughed and held the hatch down while Ally tied it so that it wouldn't fly open, not because the box wasn't completely inside but because the latch didn't work. "Five trucks at the yard, and I have a truck, and we're loading this huge thing in the back of your Subaru."

"Well in our defense we went after a bird."

Tuesday was sitting in the back seat holding the rabbit very carefully. Maggie couldn't say she was sorry they got the rabbit instead of a bird. The rabbit was something he could more easily interact with.

Look at her. She's beautiful, and she's perfect for Tuesday. I think she's perfect for me, too, and I don't want to wait. I don't want to take it slow; I want to get naked with her and see what happens. But she's got so much on her plate: her father's living with her, and he's dying, and there is still the closet full of Helen's things.

"You alright, Maggie?" Ally asked.

Maggie looked at her and nodded. "This may sound crazy, but I'm a little nervous. I just really want this to work out with us."

Ally took in a deep breath and let it out. "Me, too. I had no idea you were even attracted to women, and it's a lot to digest in an afternoon, but I can't lie and say I never thought about you. You know I love you, and I love that kid."

"But?" She could hear the hesitation in Ally's voice.

"I can't say I'm *in love* with you, Maggie, but I have no doubt in my mind that I could fall hard for you given more than an afternoon to process it."

Maggie laughed, and Tuesday screamed from the back seat. "Mom, Jack pooped on me!"

She watched as Ally found a wet wipe and cleaned him off.

All the way home her son monopolized the conversation with questions about rabbits. She wound up having to take them back to Ally's before she could go grocery shopping because they had to drop off the rabbit and hutch in the alley and carry it into the back yard.

Maggie started to just get in the car and go, but then she walked back in the gate and over to Ally who turned to face her, going for her wallet. Maggie wrapped her arms around Ally's neck, "It's not your money I want."

Ally wrapped her arms around her waist, pulled her to her and kissed her, and Maggie's knees went weak.

"Mom," Tuesday protested. "We're trying to work here."

"Yeah, Mom," Ally said when she finally stopped kissing her.

Maggie nodded breathlessly, got in her car and left.

Sam watched as the car drove away and smiled. He walked out the kitchen door onto the deck, then out to where his daughter was assembling some sort of cage against her shop. The boy ran up to him. "Ally's dad, look what we got! His name is Jack."

Sam reached out and petted the rabbit, and he smiled at the boy. "He's a humdinger."

"Is that good?"

"Yes." Sam laughed as he watched where his daughter had thrown the instructions to the side and was working on assembling the cage herself.

"It would be easier to just build something from scratch," Alice mumbled.

"That's what I always think," Sam said.

Sam found a chair, sat down, and the boy walked over with the rabbit.

"You want to hold him?"

"Yeah sure." Sam took the tiny rabbit. If it was scared at all by the boy carting it around, it wasn't showing in its behavior, and it seemed content to just sit in his hands and let the boy talk to him.

"Why did she name him Tuesday?" Sam asked Alice.

"Because it's her favorite day of the week," the boy not Alice answered. So Sam got the idea that the boy was asked this question all the time.

"Why?"

"It's the day of the week she moved to Flint Town and met Helen and the day that she started working at Taggert's Landscaping and the day she found out she was pregnant with him—though he was born on a Saturday," Alice said. "Apparently that's only part of the list of good things that happened to her on a Tuesday."

Sam still thought it was a dumbass thing to name a kid. He saw how quiet Alice got. "What is it Alice?"

"Ah nothing," Ally said except when she thought about it the first time she had held and kissed Maggie had also been on a Tuesday, and she hadn't meant to but she still had and what was it with Maggie and Tuesdays?

She got the cage put together while her Dad held the rabbit and Tuesday gave her way too much help.

Maggie came out on the deck. "Dinner won't be long. Tuesday come in here and leave Ally alone."

He took the rabbit from her father and started inside.

Her father looked at her and grinned a huge grin, but didn't say a thing.

"What?"

"Well you said she wasn't your girlfriend and that wasn't your kid."

She looked at him to see if he had reverted to form, but he was still just grinning.

"At the beginning of this week I didn't have a father or a kid or a girlfriend. As of this morning I now have all three, so suffice it to say it's been a busy week for me." She smiled and kept working. She was done and had Jack in his cage before Maggie finished dinner.

She had made some fish cakes, some mashed potatoes, and a big salad. Ally couldn't say she didn't like having a woman cook for her because that would be a lie. Helen was an awful cook, but she still liked to eat her cooking just because she cooked for her. *The only thing that is really giving me pause is the bi-sexual thing. Not because I think Maggie would cheat; I know she wouldn't—at least not without asking permission first—but because I just really don't like going where a penis has been, but I know damn good and well I have been before. So I just won't think about it. My dad's here, Tuesday's here, we probably shouldn't be all over each other right away. We should take it slow. It would be easier if she would quit looking at me like that.*

"Mona told me not to bother coming over tonight since we're coming in the morning to work on her yard," Maggie said. She was sitting to Ally's right and Ally wasn't surprised at all when Maggie's hand moved to her thigh or when she started to gently kneed the flesh there until Ally put her hand under the table and made her stop. Maggie put on a fake pout then shrugged and went back to eating her dinner.

"This is really good, Maggie, thank you," Ally said.

"You're welcome." And it was the way she said it.

Is she doing it on purpose or is it all in my head? Every move she makes everything she says is suddenly the most sensuous thing I've ever encountered. How soon can we put that kid to bed? Where are we going to put him? When's my dad going to crash? Can we really do this, and if we do should we just do it or should we move a little slower? Helen's dead, my dad's dying, and life is short. If we should be together we've already wasted so much time.

"It is good, Maggie. Really hits the spot." Her dad pushed away from the table. "I'm going to get a shower and go to bed." He looked with meaning from Maggie to Ally, and Ally actually blushed. He winked at her then walked over and kissed her on the top of her head. "Sleep well."

"Ah... You, too, Dad."

After dinner, Tuesday played in the kitchen floor with some toy cars Maggie had brought for him when she went by her apartment to get clothes for her and Tuesday. Ally was helping her do the dishes and was pretty quiet.

All this time I've purposely never brought anyone around him. I hardly dated at all and never even let a man pick me up from Mona's. Now Tuesday is totally attached to Ally, and she to him. What if it doesn't work out between us and... I know it will. This morning I had no idea how I felt about her and tonight I'm completely in love with her. Am I fucking crazy or has this been going on for a while and I just didn't realize it? And I don't care; right now I just want to be with her.

"Allybaba can you play with me?" Tuesday asked.

"I'm kind of helping your mom right now and," She looked at where he was playing and frowned. "I really can't get down in the floor right now, baby."

"We could play on the table."

"Alright when I get done."

"I've got it; go on," Maggie said and kissed Ally on the cheek.

Ally looked at her, caught her eyes, and whispered, "Maggie, everything you are doing is driving me nuts."

"Good," Maggie smiled. "I'm playing for keeps, Ally, not just playing."

"What if I disappoint you sexually?" Ally whispered, because of course Ally knew exactly how Maggie felt about sex.

"That could never happen, Ally."

"And see? Now you're just making me really nervous. It's a lot of pressure." Ally sighed and went off to play with Tuesday.

Maggie finished up and turned the dish washer on. She sat down at the table and watched them play.

Just a week ago if you had asked me if there was anything except someone to have decent sex with missing from my life

I would have said no and now... How could I not have seen how my feelings have changed towards her in the last five years?

"Allybaba, are you sure Jack will be alright outside by himself all night?"

"Of course he will; he's not some pussy...."

"Come on, Ally," Maggie said disapprovingly.

"Geez, Maggie, I just meant cats are always yowling to come in and crap," Ally said with a smile. "He'll be fine. We got him a nice home and he's in the yard, so no dogs can mess with him. He needs to sleep; we all need some sleep. Don't you feel tired?"

Maggie laughed. "It's only seven, Ally."

"What a good time to go to bed! I know I'm sleepy," Ally made a huge fake yawn.

"If he goes to bed before eight, he'll get us up at about six."

"Why?" she said, looking at Tuesday in mock despair. "Why would you do that, and on a Saturday?"

He laughed got out of his chair and walked over to crawl up in Ally's lap. "You're funny Allybaba." He started petting her head.

"Why don't we go watch some TV?"

"Alright, but I pick." Maggie watched as Ally and Tuesday exchanged a look. "And you will not gang up on me."

She noticed her Dad went to bed in the guest room and wondered where he thought Maggie was going to sleep or if he knew and figured he might as well be comfortable.

Maggie found a show about whales which was actually pretty interesting. When she sat down in her recliner Tuesday started to crawl up in her lap, but Maggie snagged him, kissed him on the top of his head, and steered him over to the couch. Ally thought it was because of her leg, but then she wound up with Maggie in her lap. Not too surprisingly Maggie managed to sit on her in such a way that she didn't hurt her leg at all and seemed to have barely any of her weight on Ally. She wrapped her arms around Ally's neck and rested her head on Ally's shoulder. Ally put her arms around Maggie, turned and kissed Maggie on the neck. Maggie whispered in her ear. "I'm not sleeping on that couch, but Tuesday could. I don't care if it's crazy, Ally, I don't want to wait."

"Well we have to because he can't go to bed before eight, so be a good girl watch and learn about whales, the sea's gentle giants."

"Allybaba?"

"Yes son," Ally said.

"How sick is your Dad?"

"Very sick," Ally said, feeling a little sad.

"That's what I thought." He looked over at them and frowned. "I don't see why I can't sit on her and you can."

"You can," Maggie said. "It's just my turn."

"Oh," he said, as if that made perfect sense.

Tuesday became engrossed with the whales, and Maggie became all about getting into Ally's work shirt. She unbuttoned it and then she put her hand inside and started rubbing Ally's stomach. Ally didn't want to make her stop, but she wasn't really comfortable with where things were heading with Tuesday sitting right there.

"Get up, Maggie, I'm going to go get a shower."

Maggie got up and then helped her up.

"You do know I can get out of my chair myself."

"Yes, but then I wouldn't have an excuse to touch you," Maggie said.

Maggie watched as Ally left the room. *I'm being way too aggressive but dammit I'm not good at pretending.* She sat down in Ally's recliner and started to watch the show. Tuesday got up off the couch and came and crawled into her lap. she hugged him and kissed the top of his head.

"Are you sure Jack's alright?"

"Yes, Honey."

"We can share Allybaba."

Maggie chuckled. "We can?"

"Yes, she needs a little boy and a woman. That's what her dad said."

"Her dad said that?" Maggie asked in shock.

"Yes, he said he wants Ally to be happy because he doesn't have long."

Maggie wondered if the old man had slept in the wrong place by accident either time.

Ally walked in wearing her robe carrying some sheets and blankets and made a bed up on the couch for Tuesday. Maggie took him in got him a bath and dressed him for bed. He started to bitch that he wanted to sleep with Ally, but Maggie just sat down with him told him a story rocked him and he went right to sleep. Ally took him from her and laid him down on the couch and covered him up.

Maggie started for the shower, and Ally followed her. "If he wakes up in the middle of the night is he going to get scared?"

"The light is on and he knows the house, he'll just come find us."

"But if we lock the door—and I'm not doing anything at all if we don't—then he might get scared."

Maggie stopped turned around and looked up at her. "You aren't trying to back out of this are you?" She grabbed the belt on Ally's robe and jerked her against her. Ally took her in her arms and kissed her good and long and hard. When they parted Maggie caught her breath and said, "We can unlock the door after we get done. Tuesday's going to be fine. You're worse than he is about the rabbit."

"I should probably tell you that our son is more important than a rabbit, and… I've already checked on that rabbit twice since we put it in the cage."

Ally wondered what—if anything—she should wear to bed. She finally just took off her robe and her leg brace, crawled under the sheet and damn near got up again because suddenly this seemed like it was the most insane thing she'd ever done and was just a really bad idea. Now she just couldn't stop thinking about the bisexual thing. Ally had always been pretty vanilla; was she going to have to get toys, a strap on? That wasn't appealing to her in the slightest. Was Maggie going to be ogling men all the time, wanting them? That was just gross.

And hadn't she just agreed to be Tuesday's parent and how responsible was it for her to be even thinking about having sex with his mother when until that morning she hadn't even known sex with Maggie was a remote possibility? She looked at the ceiling and snarled. "This is a hell of a week for you isn't it, Helen? Well don't just stand there! What do you think? Should I play house with your best friend or not? Fine, be that way. You lied to me. Alright you didn't lie but you didn't tell me the truth and neither did she. You might have told me and trusted that I wasn't such a jealous asshole that I would try to drive a wedge between you and your friend."

The door opened and Maggie walked in wearing a blue and green robe with some swirly pattern on it. The robe barely covered her tits or her ass. It accented her curly red hair and brought up her green eyes not to mention what it did for her figure. Maggie was smoking hot, always had been, but you didn't check your partner's best friend out, or even the straight girl who works in the office the way Ally was checking Maggie out now. *My God she's gorgeous, way out of my league, but then so was Helen.*

Ally watched as Maggie closed and locked the door. Maggie walked to the end of the bed and looked down at Ally, and suddenly Ally was really aware that she was naked under the sheet. Maggie smiled at her, "So... what did Helen say?"

"The same unhelpful nothing she always says," Ally said nervously.

Maggie started to remove her robe so slowly that Ally watched, occasionally having to remind herself to breathe. When Maggie was finally naked she reached down and just jerked the sheet right off Ally.

Maggie crawled across the bed and right up Ally's body. Ally grabbed hold of her and pulled their bodies together and then they were kissing, and any doubts Ally had were just gone. She let her tongue roam around the inside of Maggie's mouth and Maggie started sucking on it. Ally came, not a lot but a little. She slammed Maggie back onto the bed and climbed on top of her. She wrestled her tongue away from Maggie, moved to take one of Maggie's nipples in her mouth, and felt Maggie's fingers dig into the flesh of her back.

Maggie wanted her, really wanted her, and that got rid of any remaining nervousness Ally had. There was something damn near intoxicating about knowing that someone wanted you as much as you wanted them.

Maggie made it clear that she was not going to find Ally an unsatisfactory sexual partner—not worth her time—when during climax Maggie came so hard Ally wound up with cum in her nose. Ally had to move quickly to keep Maggie from snapping her neck, reminding Ally that you really had to make sure you put your shoulders in the right spot to protect your head.

Maggie had barely stopped gasping and Ally had hardly

cleared her nose so that she could breathe when Maggie was all over her. Maggie was by far the most aggressive lover she'd ever had, but as she came so hard she nearly passed out, she decided that wasn't a bad thing at all.

They'd cleaned up, put on pajamas, unlocked the door, and now Maggie was lying in her arms her back to her and all she could think was that they had wasted so much time.

She was almost asleep when Maggie turned in her arms and kissed her gently on the lips. Maggie's lips were trembling slightly, and for a minute Ally thought she had done something wrong. "I love you, Ally."

"And I am crazy—because let's face it this really is crazy—in love with you." Maggie turned around again and Ally pulled her tightly to her. "Maggie, you rocked my world."

Maggie laughed and patted her arm. "Oh baby you only got as good as you gave."

Maggie woke up and didn't have even one moment when she didn't know where she was. Ally was wrapped all around her, her breath on the back of Maggie's neck, and she had been wrong.... She *could* get out of Ally's arms and she could do it without waking Ally up—which she did.

CHAPTER 5

If people in your life find a way to use up all your spare time you never have to sit and wonder what you're going to do on your day off.

Ally woke up and instantly realized there was no woman in her arms where there should be, and she wondered if maybe she had dreamt the whole thing. Then she sat up and she could smell Maggie's perfume—patchouli, possibly Ally's favorite scent—so she knew it had been real. Besides she could feel the dopamine rush still running through her system.

So where the hell is she? Did she have a change of heart? Did I do or say something wrong?

The door opened and Maggie walked in and locked it. she looked at Ally with urgency. "Your dad and Tuesday are still sound asleep." She threw off her robe and crawled right into bed with Ally.

Ally smiled and grabbed her. "I thought you left."

"Ally, you couldn't scrape me off with a shovel." Maggie started to kiss her, and Ally pulled back.

"At least let me brush my teeth."

"I brushed mine; that's good enough for both of us." Maggie kissed her and she kissed her back. Maggie grabbed Ally's hand and stuck it between her legs. She was already wet, so Ally didn't have to wonder what Maggie wanted at all.

Sam had woken up to the sounds of someone having a really good time. He smiled, shook his head, and made his way to the bathroom. As he was washing his hands he realized he actually felt nearly human.

The girl was calling out, "Oh God!" but Sam was pretty sure Maggie wasn't praying.

"Well good for them," he said to his reflection in the mirror. "Tell me, what sort of god would give her all that love and…" there was another load moan "…energy, and then tell them they had to do something, anything else? I don't have time to get used to it or to accept it; I have to be alright with it right now."

He brushed his teeth and left the bathroom just as the boy was walking out of the living room rubbing his eyes. "Hey there, Sport," he whispered. "Do you have to pee?" he asked, knowing. The boy nodded and Sam went and got him, took him by the hand and led him to the bathroom and over to the toilet then walked outside and waited for him.

The boy walked out and looked up at Sam. "Where's my Mom?"

"She and Ally are sleeping," he said. "Come on, I'll get you breakfast."

He nodded and followed Sam towards the kitchen. He was glad the racket from Ally's room had died down. He got some cereal down and poured a couple of bowls full then got the milk. "Ally's Dad, can you go get my rabbit for me?"

"As soon as we finish eating, Sport."

The boy made a face and looked at him, munching on cereal. "My name's not Sport," he said, milk and cereal running down his pajama shirt.

"And my name's not Ally's Dad." Sam laughed. "My name is Sam."

The boy nodded, kept eating and Sam realized the boy was eating as fast as he could because he wanted to go play with the rabbit.

"Slow down, Spo... he'll still be there when you get done eating." And then the noise from Ally's room started again. This time it was his daughter, and he neither felt like he was alright with it enough for that, nor did he want to answer any questions the boy might have. "Let's take our cereal and eat on the deck. That way you can see your rabbit."

He unlocked the back door and grabbed both of their bowls. The boy opened the door and beat him through it. Sam went out, quickly closing the door behind him.

Tuesday ran right off the back deck and went to check on the rabbit. "Jack is alright!" he said as if surprised, and he started to get in the cage.

"Tuesday, come up here and finish your breakfast then you can play with him," Sam said. Suddenly he was filled with the most amazing sensation like his soul was free. Like it was no longer in that box Maggie had told him about. Like he was really seeing the world for the first time, and where was he? He was with his daughter and her family. He was living the last of his life with his favorite child and her new family and it didn't matter at all that it wasn't the picture he'd drawn for her. She was happy.

The boy sat down across the picnic table from him and started eating his cereal. "I like eating outside."

"You know what?" Sam said, "So do I."

"I like you, Sam."

"I like you, too, Tuesday."

"I'm sorry you're so sick."

Sam reached over and rubbed the boy's head. "You know what, Tuesday? I'd rather be sick then to never know what I know right now."

"What?"

"That all that really matters is love, and to shut the door on love—that's the biggest sin of all."

Tuesday laughed, "You sound like my mom."

"They're in the back yard," Ally said, sighing with relief.

"Calm down, Allybaba. I told you he was fine," Maggie said, walking up behind her and wrapping her arms around Ally's waist. She rested her head on Ally's back and just sighed. Ally grabbed Maggie's hands and held them as much to keep them out of her pants as because she wanted to hold Maggie's hands.

"When I saw Dad was gone, too... I don't want him taking Tuesday anywhere. He's taking a lot of very high-powered drugs."

"He knows that, and he wouldn't take Tuesday any further than the back yard," Maggie said. "His energy has changed, he's shifted, and Tuesday's safe with him." She let go of her and walked over to the counter. "So you want cereal right?"

"Yes."

"You want to eat on the deck?"

"Yes." Ally moved to turn the coffee pot on; she always set it up the night before. "You were amazing, Maggie." For some reason she couldn't look at her.

"You weren't so bad yourself," Maggie said. She walked over till Ally had to look at her. "Are you alright? Feeling a little guilty?"

"I'm more than alright, Maggie. Yes I feel a little guilty

and... you know what, Maggie? It's a little disconcerting that you always seem to know what I'm thinking."

"Disconcerting—my that's a big word to come from such a beautiful mouth." Then Maggie was kissing her and she was kissing Maggie. Maggie moved away from her. "Don't feel guilty. Guilt is a wasted emotion."

"I've had sex since Helen died. I didn't have any guilt because it didn't mean a damn thing. But the way I feel about you...."

"Neither of us is ever going to forget Helen, Ally. You weren't the only one who loved her. You know as well as I do that Helen is just fine with us together."

Ally did know that. She didn't know how, but she did.

When they walked out on the deck the air was clean, the sun was shining, birds were singing, Tuesday was running around the yard chasing the rabbit who wasn't really running from him, and Maggie's heart felt so full that she thought it just might bust. She sat down at the picnic table with a sigh.

"Allybaba, Jack got out of my arms."

"He dropped him," Ally's dad supplied.

"He won't let me catch him," Tuesday said.

"Stop chasing him, son." Ally walked down the steps, went to the herb garden and picked something. "Come sit on the step. Be very still and see if he'll come for this fennel."

He came over and she hugged him, handed him the piece of plant and walked back up and sat down next to Maggie.

"You aren't afraid he'll get out of the yard?" Maggie asked in a whisper.

"No, the back yard has a rabbit-proof fence plus the rabbit's not really running from him. I think if he stops moving the rabbit will come right to him. Jack was right in the front door of the pet shop which means he's been manhandled by kids most of his short life. I picked him because he was the least afraid. He likes Tuesday."

Maggie nodded and kissed Ally's cheek. Ally looked at her dad, but neither of them said anything, and Maggie wasn't about to put this genie back in the bottle just because anyone might be uncomfortable or annoyed. Ally started eating so Maggie did, too.

"Look Allybaba look!" Tuesday yelled, and bigger than shit that rabbit was chewing on the fennel.

"Now very carefully reach out and pick him up," Ally coached.

Maggie couldn't believe it when Tuesday picked the rabbit up and then he was holding it and feeding it the fennel and Maggie grabbed her phone and took a picture.

"You… You took most of the pictures in the house," Ally's dad said.

"Yes I did."

"Maggie has always taken really good photos. How did you know?"

He shrugged and smiled. "She isn't in many of them."

Maggie nodded, so he really had looked at all the pictures. He knew Maggie was Helen's best friend, so if Maggie wasn't in that many pictures it meant Maggie was taking them. He had learned to see with his soul instead of his mind.

"Could we go fishing today, Alice?" the old man asked.

"Yes, can we, Allybaba?" Tuesday asked, jumping around till he dumped the poor rabbit on the ground but this time he picked it right back up again.

As if reading her mind Ally bent down and whispered in Maggie's ear. "If something happens to it I will just get another one."

Maggie looked up at her in disbelief. "Ally, that is a living, breathing thing not a toy, and he needs to learn to handle it responsibly."

Maggie got up and took the rabbit from her son and stuck it back in its hutch. When her son started to protest she said, "No, now you have to be more careful. You can't just be dropping him all the time."

Immediately, without saying a word, Tuesday turned to look at Ally.

Great! She hasn't been playing this role for a week and already he's going to look to her to see if what I say still goes.

She was greatly relieved when Ally said, "Your mother is right, Tuesday. Leave him alone for a while. He's not a toy; he's a living, breathing thing."

She smiled broadly at Maggie and Maggie just grinned back.

Then Ally turned to her Dad. "I can't go fishing today, Dad. Remember I have to go take care of Maggie's sister's yard. She just had heart surgery."

"If you just haul the equipment over there I can do her yard," Maggie said.

"No, Maggie we'll do it together. We can go fishing tomorrow, Dad," Ally said.

"But it's Sun... Tomorrow would be great. We can all go," he said.

"Maggie doesn't like to fish," Ally said.

"But I love to go to the lake." The main thing right then was that she didn't want to be separated from Ally for even a few hours. They'd have to go to work on Monday and then she wouldn't see her most of the day and then if they weren't living together—and as long as Ally's dad was living there she probably shouldn't even think about living there which meant she was going to have to go back to the apartment. That being the case, she at least wanted to spend every minute she could with Ally. "I'd love to go to the lake. I haven't been in ages, and you guys could all fish and then we could come back and I could fry up a huge batch of fish and make some hush puppies."

"You are a lovely girl," Ally's dad said.

"Yes you are." Ally smiled at her, and all she wanted to do was grab Ally and take her back to bed. How lovely was that?

"So, what are you doing with that?" Mona said, pointing at where Ally was riding around on the mower with Tuesday. "Or am I wasting my air even asking?" Maggie got really busy pulling weeds out of her sister's flower beds. "That's what I thought. What happened to Pete?"

"Who?" Maggie asked with a smile.

"Is that safe?" Mona asked pointing once again at Ally and Tuesday.

"She's finished mowing; the mower deck isn't on, so yes."

"I'm pretty sure you know that's not what I meant. Look me in the eyes, Maggie."

Maggie took a deep breath. She didn't really want to. Mona was more like her mother than her mother was, and she cared more about what Mona thought, but she was going to do what she wanted to do regardless of what Mona thought. So finally she looked up and made a big deal out of looking her in the eyes, which made Mona laugh.

Mona shook her head and sighed. "I knew when every other word out of your mouth was Ally that you were falling hard, so spill it. Tell me how you wound up with Helen's widow." And so Maggie told her, and when she finished Mona sighed. "So let me get this straight. Till yesterday morning you didn't know you were in love with her and till that time she had no idea at all that your *love gate* swung both ways, and now you guys are in love. I wish I could say I was shocked, Maggie, or that I could even work up surprised, but this is the sort of crap you've always done—except this time you're really in love and every day she's becoming a bigger part of Tuesday's life. I'd bet money you still haven't told her everything."

"I'm happy, Mona, just be happy for me."

"Can I also be super jealous because I've never had a man, any man, look at me the way that woman is looking at you." Mona sighed. "You know what? I don't want you to get hurt, but what I know about Ally—and it's a lot because she was all Helen ever talked about the whole time they were together and all you've talked about for most of the last three years—is that she isn't going to hurt you. That if she says she loves you she means it even if it is crazy fast."

"I haven't been talking about Ally for three years!"

"Yes, Maggie, yes you have, nonstop. Ally this, and Ally that, till I'm surprised she doesn't sweat honey and fart rainbows. What do the spirits tell you?" she teased.

"That it's time; that it's right," Maggie said, and went back to work.

"And you're sure that at least in part this isn't because she's your hero? That you think you owe her something?" Mona asked carefully.

Maggie took a deep breath and let it out. She tried not to think about it; it was in the past and she tried to live in the present. She had told the bastard she was pregnant. They didn't have anything approaching a relationship. She didn't love him, he certainly didn't love her, and by then she knew he was a prick, but never in a million years did she expect that he was capable of what he did.

Maggie had always been a good judge of character, but she'd been high the whole time they'd been together—most of the time since Helen had died. Just pot mostly, an occasional hit of acid, or snort of coke. She was just numbing herself, and it was the only way she could explain that she was so wrong about anyone. She didn't know, hadn't guessed, he would try to beat her to death so that she wouldn't try to get child support from him. He'd kicked her so hard that he'd actually broken her ribs. She had internal bleeding, but though it had been his intention to kill the baby, Tuesday's health hadn't ever been in question; he was fine. And here was the real kicker: when she'd gone to talk to Doug she hadn't been sure she was going to keep the baby, but after Doug beat her and the baby was fine, she knew she had to.

And they were both alive only because of Ally. She had called Ally earlier in the day crying and telling her that she was pregnant. When Ally called later to check on her and Maggie didn't answer her phone, Ally kicked the door down found Maggie unconscious and rushed her to the hospital.

"No, Mona, I am not with Ally out of a sense of gratitude. I know it sounds crazy, but I love Ally. I don't have any doubts at all about that."

"And how was the sex?"

"If I tell you about that, you really will be jealous."

"Tell me anyway. I haven't had sex in so long that even vicarious lesbian sex sounds good to me right now."

"I can do the weed eating Ally," Maggie said, trying to take it out of Ally's hands. Ally looked at her and grinned.

"I'll do it. Just go inside with your sister and Tuesday and put him down for that nap you said he needs."

"He does need a nap, but Mona can do that easier than I can," Maggie whispered. She didn't let go of the weed eater. "You could go put him down for a nap and I'll do the weed eating. For very selfish reasons I don't want you to bugger your leg up again."

"I'm fine." Ally kissed her on the forehead. "My leg is fine, and I'll be super careful."

"I know how to run a weed eater, Ally."

"I know you do, but for very selfish reasons I don't want you to be tired 'cause you know when my dad crashes and the kid goes to sleep we will spontaneously erupt in passion."

"You smell good," Maggie said, taking in a deep breath.

"I'm filthy sweaty." Ally laughed.

"You always smell good." Maggie breathed again, and then Ally was kissing her and the only thing between them was the stupid weed eater—which neither one of them was letting go of.

"Christ!" Mona yelled from the back porch. "Is that a pheromone-powered weed eater?"

"Is she mad? You know, about us?" Ally asked in a whisper.

"No, but she does think we're crazy, and she's surprised you don't sweat honey and fart rainbows," Maggie said with a laugh.

"Did you explain that I can't be held accountable for a strange medical condition?" She looked down at Maggie's hands on the weed eater. "Let go of my weed eater, woman. If you must weed eat then get one of the others—and goggles and ear protection. Mona can put our son down for a nap."

With both of them working they finished quickly and packed all the gear back on the truck. Mona still lived next door to Mitch and his wife, and Ally was kind of glad they hadn't been home all day. Not because she was using the company equipment, she had permission to do that, but because she didn't want Mitch and Karen to see her and Maggie together. She knew they were going to find out—probably already knew because those assholes she worked with were nearly as bad as Maggie was at keeping their mouths shut—but Ally didn't want Mitch and Karen to see them together. It might be hard for them, and she didn't want that. Losing Helen had damn near killed Mitch, but he'd gotten past it. Karen hadn't been right since. She went from one anti-depressant to another and one therapist to another, and there had never been anywhere for her to put her pain. Karen purposely went out of her way not to see Ally, so the last thing Ally wanted was for Karen to see her and Maggie all over each other and Maggie had agreed. But Mitch and Karen weren't home, so....

Pulling on the damn starter cord had hurt her leg and why confounded her almost as much as the fact Maggie knew it would. Mona had cooked a big dinner for them and it wasn't hard to figure out why Mona had a heart condition. A huge lasagna, garlic bread dripping with butter, and the vegetable was broccoli in cheese sauce—which was mostly just cheese sauce.

They had no sooner sat down to eat than Maggie glared across the table at her sister and said, "Mona, you can't eat like this. You have to stay on the diet the doctor gave you."

"I have been. I cooked this for you guys."

"I'm not sure we need to eat the big stroke dinner either,

Mona."

"What is it you always say, Maggie? Moderation in all things, even moderation."

Ally smiled. It was a Maya Angelou quote, at least that was who Ally had heard say it. The food was good, and she was super hungry.

"Allybaba," Tuesday started around a mouthful of lasagna.

"Tuesday, don't talk with your mouth full," Maggie said.

Mona looked shocked and said in mock horror, "Aren't you afraid you are going to crush his tiny psyche by using such negativity?"

Ally grinned and kept eating; she knew what this was all about. For three months when he got old enough to start talking, Maggie had decided that she didn't want anyone to say anything remotely negative to Tuesday. They were all supposed to phrase everything in such a way that they didn't say anything negative so that something as simple as "Don't talk with your mouth full" became "Tuesday, when you talk with your mouth full, people might have trouble understanding you, and you aren't fully realizing your food." Then it was to be his decision whether he talked with his mouth full or not. They were all about to strangle Maggie before the experiment stopped. Mitch even went so far as to tell Maggie she was a new age moron, and that Tuesday was going to grow up with more ticks than Ally had.

"I said I was sorry and that I was wrong," Maggie reminded.

Tuesday had swallowed and he turned to Ally, "Allybaba?"

"Yes, Tuesday,"

"When we go fishing tomorrow can I bring Jack?"

"No," Ally said.

"Oh, another no!" Mona took in a deep, shuddering breath. "You let him go fishing? Was he completely traumatized by the murdering of aquatic life to provide sustenance for us filthy humans?"

And that of course was all about the time both Maggie and Helen had gone totally vegan for about two months. Ally liked to think of that as her two months in food hell.

"You can just can all that crap at any moment, Mona," Maggie said with a frown. "Ally knows my entire life's history, so you're just wasting your time doing bear tricks."

"So who is Jack?" Mona asked Tuesday.

"He's my rabbit."

"Maggie, a rabbit in an apartment?" Mona made a face.

"He lives in Allybaba's back yard," Tuesday said.

"Well of course he does." Mona looked at Maggie and just shook her head. Then she looked at Ally. "So Allybaba, some people think a long time before they get a pet, but you just run right out and get one." Her meaning wasn't lost on Ally. Maggie shot Mona a look that would have burnt toast.

Ally took a deep breath and let it out. "When you lose a pet suddenly and go through a long period of pet mourning... five years is a long time to think about what you really want, and if you find it you just grab it and hold on tight. When I woke up this morning all I could think was that we had wasted a lot of time... you know, not having a pet."

Oh my God he's going to put her eye out," Maggie said, and she ran down towards the lake to help Ally get the fish off the boy's line. A few minutes later Maggie was holding the end of the pole still while Ally pulled the fish off. Sam smiled as he watched the girl cringe and look away as Ally put the fish on the stringer. She had a kind heart.

He had fished for a while and now he needed a break, so he was sitting up the bank at a picnic table with Maggie's sister Mona. She was a big gal, pretty but nothing at all like her sister. In fact, if he didn't know they were sisters he never would have guessed it looking at them.

"Being sick sucks," Mona said.

"I couldn't agree more."

"I'm sorry; I forgot. I've got a lot of nerve bitching to you."

Sam smiled at her. "I'm sixty-seven, young by today's standards true, but still an old man. You... You're just a kid. To have to have a quadruple bypass... that's pretty earth shaking."

"Maggie said you're terminal. Is it too forward of me to ask what you have?"

"Fourth stage liver cancer, and before you ask, it's from smoking."

Mona sighed no doubt because she knew what that meant. There wasn't going to be a miracle; he really was going to die. "So, we both did it to ourselves, me from eating the wrong things and like a pig, and you from smoking, but it wasn't our intention to kill ourselves, so it seems a little extreme for the universe to choose death and near death to teach us a lesson.

You want to hear the real twist?" She didn't wait for him to answer. "I'm a cardiac care nurse, so I knew. I knew I was playing with death. My father—not the same as Maggie's father—died of a heart attack two years ago. I eat all wrong. I don't exercise. I have nothing but stress at work. I don't have a personal life. I've been on high blood pressure meds for years. You think I'm fat now? You should have seen me when I had the heart attack; I was at least twenty pounds heavier."

"You need to take care of yourself," Sam said. He looked at Maggie. "Your sister really loves you."

"I know, and do you know why? Because our mother is a crazy-ass bitch," Mona hissed, and in her voice Sam could hear a lifetime of pain. "Our mother is bipolar and has never tried medication or anything else to control her mood swings. How does she deal with her multitude of mental problems? By just doing whatever she wants, whatever she feels like doing. She moved me every few months and always away from my dad, who was a great guy and really wanted to be a dad when she never wanted to be a mother. She was always getting evicted, losing jobs and…. She's your age and she's still doing the same crap. I was fifteen when Maggie was born. I don't think Mom really knows who her father is, but the guy she pinned it on didn't want anything to do with Maggie. Two years before that she had Chad—more or less the same story. Maggie is always reading some book and trying to do everything right with Tuesday because I raised them. I was a fifteen-year-old kid. I didn't know what I was doing, and our mother sure as hell didn't. People always thought Maggie and Chad were mine, that we were lying by saying they were mom's.

"We landed here. I liked it; the kids liked it, and none of us wanted to leave. So she just left us here and then they were completely my responsibility."

"So… you never really had time to have a family of your own."

"And I didn't want one, Sam. I never had a childhood. I have no life why do you think I tagged along with you all today? I'm fed up with being responsible for anyone but me. I'm forty-nine years old. You say I'm a kid, but I'm not. And our lives were so screwed when we were kids that I have used my siblings and my stupid-assed mother as an excuse to just not get involved with anything or anyone else. I love Maggie and I love Chad. I especially love Maggie, and I can always count on her. But... I just want to do what I want to do and not have to worry about anything or anyone anymore, and if that..." she pointed to where Ally was helping Maggie cast "...works out, then I don't have to worry about Maggie and Tuesday anymore because Ally will take good care of them."

"I think you can stop worrying. I think that is going to work out just fine," Sam said. He smiled as Ally helped Maggie reel in a fish. Then laughed as Maggie made Ally let the fish go. "I think that is just about perfect."

It was her favorite kind of job. The home owner had more money than sense, and he wanted something in a particular spot but didn't really know what. Maggie had gone out and taken pictures of the site, and Ally had sketched up four or five things taking the lay of the land into consideration and she'd run the sketches by Mitch. He picked one, and now she was doing her favorite part of the job. She was doing a water color of the design.

Long ago she had made Tuesday an easel, and when she painted he would sit beside her and paint, so that wasn't new. Neither was Maggie or several of the guys standing around and watching her. When she was painting like this she didn't notice what any of them were doing; she was completely in the zone.

Mitch walked into the shop. "You assholes do know the only one working right now is Ally—that you aren't actually helping."

Ally smiled and kept working as the guys mumbled and went to find something productive to do.

Maggie started to go back to her office and Mitch walked over and clamped one of his huge hands on her shoulder. "You can stay, Maggie." He let go of her and walked around till he could see the painting. He nodded appreciatively; he knew that the paintings were what had their customers shelling out top dollar for their work. The fact that they were able to make something at least as pretty as the picture was why they had a good reputation.

Ally and Helen used to design them together, but Ally had always done the painting. When Helen had done it herself she'd used a computer program; she couldn't really draw. "It's sort of like magic," Mitch said. He let go of Maggie. "How it starts as an idea in this hard ass thing..." he poked Ally in the head with his finger and she laughed. "...and comes out there." He pointed to her brush.

"I'm painting, too, grandpa," Tuesday said.

"So I see." He was quiet for a minute then sighed and said, "So what are you assholes doing?"

"I was working, Mitch, you know how I get. If I had noticed them all standing around I would have told them to get to work," Ally said. "They couldn't have been standing there long."

"I wasn't talking about *all* you assholes, I was talking about *you* assholes, specifically you and Maggie."

Ally jerked and flinched, and wound up putting a long strip of green where she didn't intend to. She put the brush down.

Behind her Mitch took in a deep breath and let it out slowly. "That's what I thought. Maggie, you can quit cringing; I'm not going to hit anyone."

Ally stood up and turned around to face him.

"Ally why do you always have to sleep with *my* girls?"

"They're very pretty? It's never been a plan, Mitch, it just happens. In my defense, neither time did I make the first move."

He looked at Maggie and she smiled weakly and shrugged, "She's hot."

"That's what Helen said. Girls, I'm trying to run a business here. Things are just starting to pick up again after the recession. I can't afford to lose either one of you, not for the company and not for myself. And," he nodded his head towards Tuesday, "there is someone else to consider here. If you're just screwing around and wind up having some stupid fight...."

"We aren't just screwing around," Ally assured him quickly.

Mitch nodded looked down at Tuesday and watched him paint for a minute then looked at Maggie. "I knew. I knew when you started standing around watching her paint with that moon-eyed expression on your face, when she was finding excuses to drive all the way across town just to have lunch with you and the boy; I knew it was only a matter of time." He took his finger and pounded it into Ally's shoulder, and now she cringed. "I'm going to tell you just what I told you before. Don't you break this girl's heart, and I mean this, and I don't care how crazy it sounds. You *always* drive if you're both in a car, *always*. I don't care if your leg is fucked five ways from Sunday. And..." His voice caught in his throat "...I'm really not ready to see you guys...."

"We won't even hold hands," Maggie assured him.

Ally nodded.

Mitch turned and went back to his office.

Ally looked at Maggie. "Well that went better than I expected."

Maggie just nodded.

CHAPTER 6

If you expect nothing of someone, they never disappoint you.

Maggie had just walked into her apartment, Tuesday in tow, when her smart phone rang. She fumbled around and finally got it out of her purse. She answered it with a smile, "Hello Ally."

"Come on, Maggie. I don't see why you have to go home. I miss you already. I'm lonely."

"Spend some one-on-one time with your dad."

"Ah come on, Maggie, you know we can only continue to get along if we converse as little as possible."

"I just think... I think we need to have a night apart, a little return to normalcy. For one thing I'm going to have to clean all the rancid stuff out of my fridge and do some laundry because I haven't really been home in..." She counted on her hand. "...seven days. And before that I was hardly home because I was basically leaving from work and going to Mona's. Tuesday hasn't been in his own bed...."

"I like the couch," Tuesday said, but in the meantime he had pulled out several toys he hadn't seen in at least a week.

"See, he likes the couch, Maggie," Ally said.

"It's one night, Ally."

"I'll probably cry myself to sleep."

"I'm sure that you won't."

"I... I've forgotten how to masturbate."

Maggie laughed. "In seven days? I seriously doubt that."

"You could do your laundry here. We could make dad sleep on the couch and Tuesday could have the bed, and...."

"Ally I haven't been home in a week I have a billion things to do, I'm sure you do too. If I'm there we will only get the one thing done."

"But... It will be done so well."

"Mom. I'm hungry," Tuesday said.

"I have to go. I have to feed my son."

"Our son," Ally corrected. "Did I do something wrong?"

"No, baby, you didn't do anything wrong. It's no wonder you're always so twitchy. Relax. You have done everything right." Maggie laughed. "We're dating, and people who are dating don't normally spend a week at a time together. It's sort of stupid to pay rent on an apartment I'm never in."

"Then don't. Why don't you guys move in with me? I could clear my studio. We could put Tuesday in there; I never use it anymore anyway."

"I'd sort of like you to start using it again."

"I want you to live with me, Maggie."

"We've only been dating for a week; it's crazy."

"Maggie who the fuck are you kidding? We aren't dating; we are in a committed relationship. I have a fucking stupid house, and we should all live in it. I know it will be tight until my dad dies, but he's not going to live much longer and..."

"What a terrible thing to say, Ally."

"But it's true, Maggie. Come on, I love you guys, I miss you."

"It's crazy, Ally. Right now we're like the hugest lesbian stereo type."

"No we are not because I didn't just pick you up in a bar last night. We have known each other for years. We have already wasted so much time we should have been together."

Maggie laughed, "Can you let me go so that I can get things done and we can talk about it tomorrow?"

"Can I call you later?"

"Yes," Maggie chuckled, "Please."

After they wasted several minutes trying to get the other one to hang up first Maggie was finally off the phone and had no idea who had actually hung up first.

Her refrigerator smelled like ass, and she wound up throwing nearly everything into a bag that she would bring with her to work in the morning and throw into the composter. It was the only way she could get over the waste. She made some turkey burgers she pulled out of the freezer for the two of them. Tuesday was so busy playing in the land of forgotten toys she had trouble getting him to sit down to eat.

He looked at her and frowned as he started to eat. She was pretty sure she knew why as he had thrown himself a pretty nifty little fit when he realized they weren't going home with Ally. No sense in asking him what he wanted to do; she knew. This was a tiny no bedroom apartment. It had a small bathroom and a kitchen nearly as small. Both her bed and Tuesday's and the dining table were all in the main room with the only other furniture being a bedside table, a coffee table, and an ancient couch she had draped in tapestries just to make it presentable. She'd have to go on a search for quarters so she could take their laundry to the laundromat in the basement to do it, and.... *I was perfectly happy with this place and now it seems empty and depressing and Ally has a perfectly good washer and dryer that I wouldn't have to find quarters for. She's right; who am I kidding?*

She dragged a couple of boxes out of the closet.

"What are you doing, Mom?" Tuesday asked.

When she turned he had most of his dinner on his face and shirt. She picked him up, took him to the bathroom and washed him up. "What are you doing, Mom?"

"Washing you up," she said, kissing his nose,

He giggled.

When she came home and Tuesday and Maggie weren't either with her or right behind her, Ally didn't know who was more disappointed, her or her father.

When she couldn't get Maggie to say she was going to move in immediately if not sooner, she just had the most awful, sinking feeling. Like Ally must have done or said something that made Maggie rethink a life with her. That maybe having more than ten minutes to think about a long-term relationship with twitchy Ally, Maggie had decided she didn't want to.

Ally had made dinner for her dad and this time he ate more than she did, and it wasn't because his appetite had improved.

She was fresh out of the shower and half way through getting her work clothes set out for the next day when she noticed it. All of Helen's things were gone. The whole left side of the closet was just empty. She took in a deep shuddering breath and let it out. Then she ran out of the closet and out of her room. She found her dad in the living room.

"Dad what happened? Where are Helen's things?"

"I put them in bags and had Good Will come and get them," he said in a quiet voice, as if he didn't know how she might react. And for a second she didn't know herself. Then she walked over to him, hugged his neck, and started crying.

He patted her back. "I'm sorry, Alice."

"No, Dad, thank you. Thank you so much. I couldn't do it, and it needed to be done."

"I know. I heard you and Maggie talking about it. I can't do much, but putting clothes in bags and making a couple of phone calls I can do. Honey, why are you crying?" He patted her back reassuringly.

"Because she's gone Dad, Helen's gone. I let her go, and now she's just gone."

Maggie looked at the clock. It was nearly nine she had already put Tuesday to bed, and Ally hadn't called back. She was getting super nervous when the doorbell rang. When she looked out her peephole it was Ally, and when she opened the door there was a huge stack of boxes at Ally's feet. Maggie smiled then walked into Ally's waiting arms and received her kiss. When their lips parted Maggie said, "I've already started packing."

"So what goes?" Ally said, bringing in the stack of boxes.

"Most of this crap can just go into a yard sale," Maggie said. "You know how I feel about stuff. We need our clothes. I've got some personal stuff, and all my stones, books and herbs are already packed"

"I put all my stuff on one side of my studio, and I figured we could put our son in there now like it is and later on I'll move my crap."

"Is this crazy, Ally? I mean really maybe we should stop and talk at least think about it for a minute," Maggie said.

"Think about what, Maggie? You always say listen to the universe, and it will talk to you. I came over here with boxes, you were already packing, and... today my Dad packed all Helen's things and gave them to Good Will."

Maggie sat down on the end of her bed and started crying. Ally didn't ask why, so maybe she knew.

She sat down beside Maggie and drew her into her arms. "I'm tired of waiting to have a life, Maggie," Ally whispered to her. "I want to live with you and Tuesday. I'm ready to move on. Are you?"

Maggie nodded silently and Ally picked up her chin and dried the tears off Maggie's cheeks with her thumb.

"Then let's get what you already packed and Tuesday's

toy box and some clothes and take our sleeping baby home."

Of course they didn't get to Ally's till nearly eleven. Ally had insisted on bringing Tuesday's bed because Maggie had made the mistake of saying he hadn't slept in it in a week. And when they got to the house Ally insisted on bringing in all the boxes in case it rained and then she just had to set Tuesday's room up and move him from the couch to his own bed, so it was midnight before they got to bed. But that didn't stop Ally from crawling all over her until they were having what was perhaps their most energetic sexual encounter yet. Then Ally promptly passed out wrapped all around her in a way that already felt wonderfully familiar.

This is crazy, Maggie thought, *and I know I should be worried, but right now I feel like I'm really home for the first time in my life. Every place I've ever lived before has always seemed like just a place to sleep and keep my shit. This is where I belong.*

When Ally woke up the alarm sounded like a bomb exploding. And she just wanted to lay there hold Maggie and sleep.

Maggie stretched in her arms.

"I could sleep at least another hour," Maggie said.

"Me too and then…."

"Yes, I would imagine the, 'and then' is why we're both so tired right now." Maggie laughed and rolled in her arms. "That's not a complaint. I'll take tired over frustrated any day."

Ally kissed her on the forehead then got up before she got hot because there was something worse than tired or frustrated, and that was tired *and* frustrated.

She headed for the bathroom and found Tuesday wandering around in the hall. She went over, grabbed his hand, and walked him to the bathroom. "Allybaba, how did I get here?" he asked in wonder as he managed to pee everywhere but in the toilet. Ally got a wash cloth wet and started to clean up the pee.

"Son, lift the lid and watch where you aim that thing." Ally laughed as she rinsed the wash cloth then wrung it out and threw it in the hamper.

"How did I get to your house?"

"I wanted you to be here, and so then you were."

"Where is my mom?"

"In my bed where she belongs."

"How did my bed get here?"

"We live here now, Tuesday," Maggie said from the door.

"Is that my room?" he asked, his eyes big.

"Yes, Tuesday, yes it's your room," Ally said. "Just stay out of my crap till I find a better place for it."

"I have a room!" he yelled, and went running out of the bathroom and down the hall.

"Ah the pitter-patter, clomping, banging, of little feet," Ally said, smiling at Maggie.

"Are you sure you're ready for all this, Ally? It's a lot of change all at once."

"But it's all change I want to make, Maggie."

Maggie didn't have to wonder what she meant. Ally's life had been filled with moments where everything had changed and none of it was what she wanted.

Ally's dad walked in to have breakfast and he smiled when he saw Maggie, but sat down at the table without a word. Not too surprisingly they were once again having cold cereal. Maggie decided she needed to do the shopping.

"Tuesday, come and eat," Ally ordered. Tuesday ran in and climbed up in the chair next to Ally where Maggie had been sitting before she got up to get the coffee. He started eating her cereal, so she passed out the cups of coffee and sat down in the place she'd set for him and ate his.

"I live here now," Tuesday told Ally's dad.

"Now?" Sam laughed. "I think you've been living here for a while." He actually winked at Maggie.

"But I have a room now. My own room." He looked at Ally. "Allybaba, can I play with Jack before we go to work?"

"Sure, baby."

"Can we move his cage into my room?"

"No, we cannot," Ally said.

The house phone rang, and Maggie—being the most ambulatory—waved Ally back into her chair and got up and answered it, "Hello."

"Alice."

"No, this is Maggie, can I ask whose calling?" Because of course some strange woman calling Ally's house had suddenly become her business and when had she become such a jealous, jealous bitch?

"I'm Sam's daughter," she said. "Could you please put him on the phone?"

Maggie was instantly pissed as hell for two reasons. She knew the old man had a cell phone, and if he wanted to take her calls he would have, and second would it have killed the bitch to say Ally was her sister? "Sam, it's your other daughter, do you want to talk to her?" Maggie asked very purposefully.

"No, I do not. I thought I made that clear," he said.

"Give me the phone," Ally said. Then smiled up at Maggie and added, "Please."

Maggie handed Ally the phone and sat back down at the table. "What do you want Carol?.... We're having breakfast.... Yes that was my 'lover'.... Since you've left him here he's been exposed to all sorts of horrible things, Carol.... fishing.... and rabbits, Carol, rabbits!"

Sam laughed and shook his head.

"Dad, it's about your doctor appointment. She says you have one today."

Sam grudgingly took the phone from Alice's outstretched hand.

"What, Carol, what do you want?"

"I just realized that you have an oncology appointment today."

He had noticed he was running low on a couple of his prescriptions.

"Can you not have my records transferred to a doctor here?"

"Not on such short notice, Dad. I'm sorry; I just... I forgot all about it."

"Well thanks a lot for that, Carol."

"I'm nearly there now, I figured Alice wouldn't be able to get off work on such short notice..."

"And she wouldn't because she practically runs the company she works for," he said proudly.

"I'm going to come and get you. Dad, the kids miss you. I miss you. Why don't you pack and plan to stay the weekend? I can bring you back to Alice's Sunday afternoon."

He missed his grandkids; he'd like to see them. It would probably be the last time because he *would* have his records transferred to a doctor nearby. It wouldn't hurt to let Alice and Maggie have some time... well, not alone because they'd still have the boy, but without him around to worry about. "Jimmy going to be alright with that?"

"Yes, Dad."

"Alright then, but you bring me right back Sunday afternoon. I like it here with Alice and her family."

"Dad... Alice doesn't...."

"Don't you say it, Carol. I don't want to hear it."

Ally was driving because it was what Mitch ordered, but since everyone in a tristate area now knew they were a couple Maggie said it was bad for the environment and made no sense for them to take two vehicles when they worked at the same place.

"Your dad didn't seem very happy to be going," Maggie said.

"He told me he wanted to see his grandkids but that he doesn't give a damn about anything else there." Ally looked over at Maggie. "We will be almost alone for the first time."

"Yes, because it has so repressed us to have him there." Maggie laughed. "Although..." She lowered her voice. "If Mona was in better shape we'd leave Tuesday with her so that we could actually be really alone."

"You know what, Maggie? When we lock the door I don't feel like there is anyone else in the world, just you and me." She looked out the windshield at a bank of clouds. "I don't like the look of that. Could you turn on the radio and find the weather report?"

Maggie shook her head and did it. "So Mitch said what he did and now all you can think is that when you are driving you are responsible for not just me but Tuesday."

That was of course precisely why she didn't want to play with the radio herself. With Maggie and Tuesday in the car she didn't want to focus on anything but the road. In short, it now made her a nervous wreck. Maggie found the weather and they were expecting thunder storms late that night. Ally half wished it would rain so she couldn't work and she could finish moving Maggie and just have an entire Dad-free weekend. He had been pretty good, but he still occasionally had moments of Baptist turrets, and if nothing else things were good enough between them that she was super nervous around him because she didn't want things to go back to where they had been. Part of her wondered if he was going to come back from Carol's the way Ray's step kids came back from their bio daddy's house, having unlearned everything Ray had taught them and just going out of their way to be obnoxious.

Sam so didn't want to talk to Carol that he pretended to sleep. But apparently she either wasn't buying it, or more likely she didn't care if he just needed to sleep because of course she wanted to know all about Alice but didn't have the balls to just ask.

"So, what have you been doing?" she asked. He kept trying to pretend to be asleep, so then she yelled. "So what have you been doing!"

He looked at her and sighed. "There isn't much I can do. I sleep a lot. I watch a lot of TV. Alice has taken me fishing a couple of times. There is a beautiful little lake not fifteen minutes from her house, and the bass have been biting like crazy. I spend a lot of time in the yard and on the deck. She has a beautiful place." And then he tried to fake sleep again.

"Has she been taking you to church?"

Yes because that's so damn important. I'd be better off watching the boob tube all day as wasting one more minute in church. I'm dying of cancer, but beyond that knowing what I know now, why would I ever go back there?

"I asked has she taken you to church."

I know how to shut her up; I'll tell her the stinking truth. "She took me once, but the preacher was spewing a bunch of homophobic crap. I'd rather spend my time playing with my nearly three-year-old grandson and his pet rabbit. Your sister has absolutely the cutest, most well-behaved little boy and a stunning very gentle, sweet wife. She has a lovely family."

"Dad, Alice doesn't have a family ..."

"Stop right there, Carol. You have no idea what you're talking about. I'm still your father, and your religion says you have to honor me."

"*My* religion, Dad?"

"Yes, *your* religion. I am no longer religious; I am spiritual. I won't stay in the box anymore and do what I'm told. I know what is right and that is what I will do with whatever time I have left. I won't waste another minute in stinking church."

The rest of the trip was mostly wonderfully silent.

The oncologist took some blood, told him he'd call with the results in a few days, gave him new prescriptions, assured him he would transfer his files to an oncologist in Flint Town, and sent him on his way. He didn't give a damn about Sam. Sam was dying, he had declined chemo treatments because they would have made him sick and there was only a small chance they would even prolong the inevitable. He might have lived a little longer, but he would not have lived as well. He knew this because they'd talked Jenny into chemo. It had been easy to do because she was convinced Jesus was going to cure her, that he just needed time and apparently a little medical help to do it.

But Jesus didn't save her; she died a slow and painful death. So what was the point?

Since Sam wouldn't take the very expensive, unnecessary chemo treatments, he was worth nothing to greedy doctors who got rich off the misery of patients. So the doctor wrote him his prescriptions for mind-numbing drugs and sent him on his way.

Back at Carol's he visited with Amy and Alex. At six and ten they were still full of joy. Kyle said he was glad to see him and he hugged his neck, but Kyle was in trouble; Sam could see it in his too-shiny eyes.

Dinner was quiet, and the conversation boring, not like Ally's house at all. Jimmy barely said hello to him. Halfway through dinner Sam was full and suddenly realized what he was seeing propped up in the corner of the room. Picket signs. Picket signs asking congress to pass the Freedom of Religion bill. And that, as they say, was the last straw. Sam stood up, walked over and grabbed a sign that said, "Homo's rights don't come first; vote for the Freedom of Religion act."

"What's this?" Sam demanded.

"A bunch of us are going to the capital tomorrow to fight for the Freedom of Religion act," Carol said.

Sam counted the signs. "Even Amy and Alex, even Kyle?" He looked at Kyle, and Kyle looked at the table top. "Is that how you want to spend your Saturday, Kyle?" Kyle didn't say anything.

"The children are learning a valuable lesson about standing up for what they believe."

"No!" Sam yelled. "They are learning a valuable lesson

about standing up for what other people believe instead of using their own minds and deciding what's right. This hateful crap has got to stop."

"Watch your mouth in my house, old man," Jimmy said.

"This is only your house because I gave it to you and what could you possibly do to me that isn't happening already? I am tired of being blamed for what happened to Kyle. What happened to Kyle was no more my fault than it was either of yours. We let that bastard go and what he did to those other kids.... That I own a piece of, but...." He looked at Kyle. "I am so sorry for what you went through. You need real help, not some church asshole who is not unlike the one who abused you in the first place, but an actual therapist, real rehab, not a prayer circle." He turned to face Carol then and she cringed, "You know who is to blame? Your mother. Because that same sick pervert molested your sister. He molested her and she told your mother and your mother beat her and punished her... and from the look on your face right now, Carol, I'm guessing that I was the only one who didn't know that. You knew, and you let your son be alone with him so... It's your fault. *Yours.*"

"I didn't know he was a homosexual..."

"Parish isn't a *homosexual,* Carol, he's a *pervert* who preys on kids. This picket line you want to go march in, it won't stop people like him. He's not gay; he's a pedophile, and no matter what you've been told they aren't the same thing."

Kyle was crying, and so was Carol. Jimmy looked like you could have knocked him over with a feather. The two little ones obviously had no idea what they were talking about just that their grandfather was yelling and their parents were upset. "Get this boy some real help. If Jesus was going to save us all where was he when that pervert was molesting my daughter or your son? Just praying isn't going to fix him. Kyle, none of it was ever your fault, none of it. There is absolutely nothing at all wrong with you. You didn't want it; you didn't ask for it.

"Jimmy, Carol, instead of going to the capital and marching to make your sister and the lives of people like her harder, why don't you sit down as a family and make a plan to fix all of this? Now Carol get up and take me home, right now!"

When they got in the car he didn't have to pretend to be asleep because that had just emptied him of any energy he had left, and he more passed out than fell asleep

After work they loaded exactly one more truckload of stuff out of Maggie's apartment when Maggie announced she literally couldn't care less about anything else. Since the watches and warnings were starting to come in faster and more furiously for later that night, Ally was happy to get back to the house. They had just brought in the last box when it started to rain, and their area got its own severe thunderstorm and tornado watches.

"Allybaba..."

"Yes, I will go get Jack." Ally walked out to the back yard. The wind was starting to blow pretty hard, and the rain was coming down. She got the rabbit and ran back in with it under her shirt. She handed him to Tuesday and went to towel dry her head and put on dry clothes.

Now the truth was that Ally was not really afraid of storms and never had been, but Helen had been petrified. The way Maggie had been acting all evening, Ally assumed Maggie had a fear of storms, too. When she asked Maggie about it, though, Maggie said she didn't have a fear of storms in general, she had a fear of *this* storm. Ever since then Ally'd been at least as jumpy as Maggie was, because Maggie's predictions were right way too many times to just ignore her.

When Ally came out of the bedroom towel-drying her hair and wearing dry clothes, Maggie was on the phone with Mona telling her to go to Mitch's—of course Mitch had a state of the art storm shelter because he had a little girl who had been deathly afraid of storms, and there was nothing Mitch wouldn't have done for Helen.

"Do it, Mona. You know Mitch and Karen won't mind. Just go, and do it now," Maggie said. "Well do." She hung up and put her phone in her pocket.

Ally opened the trap door in the middle of the hall that led down to *her* state of the art storm shelter. She was glad to see the lights were on. She had set up a small solar panel that charged a battery bank that gave power to the storm shelter. Not a lot, but enough to keep a cell phone charged, run a couple of fans, a radio and the lights. The lights were on; that meant the battery was fully charged because when you opened the door the lights automatically came on. When you closed the door, you had to use a switch to turn them back on, but by then you were already in the hole.

And this thing which had been a huge pain in the ass to build under an existing house was only here because Helen had been so petrified of storms and Mitch had helped Ally—both physically and financially—to build it.

Maggie was wigging out, and it wasn't hard to talk Tuesday into taking the box Ally had put Jack in down into the "underground fortress" and going to sleep there which he did as soon as Ally had read to him from one of his books and before Ally even finished the story. She covered him up, pushed the box holding the rabbit under one of the benches, and crawled out of the hole to find that Maggie had stopped unpacking her things and was glued to the weather running on the TV.

"He's out." Ally sat down in the recliner and looked expectantly at Maggie who was sitting on the couch. "Baby I'm sitting here, and my lap is getting cold." Maggie got up, never turning away from the TV, walked over and sat in her lap. Ally wrapped her arms around her. "Maggie, we'll be alright. The baby is already in the storm shelter. If they change us to a warning, we hear hail, or you say go, we will crawl in with him."

Maggie nodded but didn't say anything. It looked like all the storms were actually going south and north of Flint Town. The thunder was loud; one blast shook the whole house, and it was raining so hard they could hear it. It was really hairy for about ten minutes and Ally was about to insist they go underground herself when it was calm and the watch in their area ran out its time.

Maggie didn't seem to calm down, and Ally decided she knew just exactly how to make Maggie relax. She undid the button on the top of Maggie's jeans. Maggie snickered, "Now what are you up to? We aren't out of the woods yet."

Ally undid Maggie's zipper and stuck her hand into her pants and then... Her dad ran in the front door quickly followed by her ultra-tight-assed Baptist sister.

"Dad, you have the worst timing!" She quickly took her hand out of Maggie's pants, and Maggie got off of her zipping her pants which turned out to be a good thing because the next thing she knew her father had shut and locked the front door and was yelling.

"There is a twister headed this way!" Then the TV said

the same thing, then they could hear the hail, and then the tornado siren went off.

"Storm shelter." Ally grabbed Maggie and didn't really notice that she was dragging her till she was doing everything but pushing her down the stairs. "Come on; let's go. Move it!" Carol didn't have to be told twice, but her dad looked from her to the hole.

"Alice, you know how I am about tight places, and... I'm going to die anyway."

"Not tonight, Dad, not tonight. Now get in the fucking hole!"

"Please, Sam," Maggie cried. "Please I need Ally in the storm shelter, and you know she won't go without you."

Her dad sighed but started down the stairs, and Ally was right behind him. She slammed the lid shut and locked it. She flipped on the light switch and the fans started and the radio came on. Maggie grabbed her and held her, and she held Maggie. Maggie was just sobbing.

"We're all going to be alright, Maggie," Ally assured her.

That was when it hit. It sounded like the house was coming apart on top of them. The storm shelter was tight and mostly sound proof, and Ally suddenly wasn't sure at all that they were safe, and Tuesday didn't so much as roll over. Her father sat on one of the benches and Carol sat beside him crying just as hard as Maggie was.

Maggie said something in her ear that she couldn't hear. "What!"

"I slept with Helen." Maggie said.

Ally was sure the shock on her face would have stopped that tornado dead in its tracks if it could have seen it. "What?" she asked hoping she had misheard.

"I slept with Helen."

"While we were together!?"

"No of course not. When we were in high school."

A wave of relief washed over her. "Then I don't care, Honey. Why would I care?"

"I was in love with her. Till you she was the only person I ever loved."

"Oh, baby." Ally kissed the tears off Maggie's face. "That's alright. And your confession is a waste because we aren't about to die." Then Ally said loudly enough that everyone but the sleeping boy could hear. "Everybody calm down. None of us is going to die. Mitch and I built this to withstand an F5 tornado if it was standing on the ground outside. Instead it's under the house and mostly in the ground. We have enough food and water for a month stored here."

Maggie was calming down.

Ally smiled down at her. "So the only secrets you can't keep are other people's."

Maggie could feel the death in the storm hours before it hit. Then when she was actually putting her things in Helen's closet she realized she had to tell Ally the whole truth. So when it had sounded like they were all going to die she couldn't let them all die without ever telling Ally everything, and Ally... Well Ally acted like Maggie told her they had driven the same car. The only time it looked like she might come undone was in the three seconds that it took Maggie to tell her that she had never slept with Helen while Helen had been with Ally.

Ally just kept holding her and reassuring her till the storm passed and there was quiet, an all-wrong quiet. They could hear the radio again, but obviously the reporters didn't have a clear idea of what had just happened, and how would they? Ally kissed her and she kissed her back.

"See? We're all okay."

"You aren't mad, Ally?"

Ally smiled at her and kissed her again. "Why would I be?" she whispered. "Who that knew her didn't want to sleep with her, and once you had how could you not love her? She was right, though, if I had known I never would have let the two of you continue to be friends, and that would have been something I would have had to live with forever. Now go check on our son."

Maggie nodded, dried her face on her sleeve and went and sat down by Tuesday. He was sleeping soundly; she rubbed his back just because she needed to touch him.

Ally looked at her dad. "Dad, I'm sorry I ever said you have shitty timing."

Ally waited for several minutes until the reporter on the radio was apologizing for the short notice. Apparently this had just fallen right of the sky on them. They were saying all the major storms had left their area now, and that there were none behind it. She took the keys out of her pocket because any time there was inclement weather she put her work clothes and work boots on and put her keys and her cell phone in her pocket. She opened the safe in the wall and pulled out her gun and holster, checked the clip, and loaded the gun then put it on under her arm.

"Why do you need that, Ally?" Maggie asked. No big surprise that Maggie didn't like guns. Helen hadn't, either, which was why her service revolver was locked up down here.

"Maggie, you know that if I can get out of the area I will have to go to work. After a tornado dogs are loose. They're all freaked out, and some of them are attack dogs. There could be looters. This is SOP." She grabbed both head lamps, stuck one in her pocket and put the other one on. She grabbed a dust mask

"I'm going with you," Maggie said. "I can help you find people."

"Let me check our house first. You know… if we still have one. Get the gas off, stuff like that, and then if I think I need you I'll come right back and get you."

"Promise?"

"I promise."

Maggie nodded. "Ally, please be careful."

"Yes, Alice be careful," her father echoed.

Ally nodded and opened the door, and from what she was seeing her house was fine. Of course tornados were tricky; the whole back wall might be gone. "I'm closing the door behind me. There is a lot of dust, but I think the house took little to no damage." She put the dust mask on and shut the door.

Her phone rang and she answered it. "I'm fine, Mitch, but we got hit. How are you guys?"

"It missed us completely. Please tell me that Maggie and the boy…"

"They're here," Ally said. "We're all alright. Hell, Tuesday slept through the whole thing."

Then Mitch was crying and he said, obviously not to her, "They're alright, and they are all together." Mitch seemed to take a second to calm himself and then said, "Ally we just saw some news feed. Maggie's apartment house is gone. For a second I was afraid Mona was going to have another heart attack, and then I reminded her that they were probably with you, but I couldn't be sure. Is there any way Mona can talk to Maggie? She's a mess, Ally."

"Yeah, sure, but Mitch tell her not to tell Maggie about her apartment building. Not now please, she's a wreck as it is."

"Yeah, I'll bet."

"Wait a second." Ally opened the door to the shelter again.

"Maggie could you come up here? Mona wants to talk to you, and I'm pretty sure cell phones won't work in there."

Maggie nearly ran up the stairs, sat on the top step, and took the phone from Ally's hand. "Mona, are you alright?"

"I'm fine, so is Chad. All we got was a little wind and some hail here. How about you and the baby?"

"We're all fine. We were in the storm shelter, but it looks like the house is alright, too."

"Maggie... I was wrong. This thing with Ally, it's not too quick. Not too quick at all."

"Maggie, give me my phone back, Honey. I've got to check things out. I'll come back when I'm sure we're safe." Maggie handed the phone back to Ally and when she walked back down the stairs Ally closed the door.

"Thanks for not telling her, Mona."

"You're right, Ally, there is no sense in telling her right now. And Ally..." She started to cry. "Thank you for having them with you. Thank God they were with you."

"Yeah, I'm not going to think about it right now or I'm going to start bawling, and I have to check shit out. Good bye, Mona."

Ally went to the kitchen, grabbed a zip lock bag, put her phone in it and put it in her pocket. Then she grabbed an adjustable wrench out of the tool box she kept under the kitchen sink. She walked out the back door and turned off the gas to the house just to be on the safe side and put the wrench in her pocket. A quick look around showed no obvious damage to the back of the house or her shop. And when she checked the inside of the house the only damage she found was that the bathroom window was broken. But this was scary because there was a four-foot piece of metal pipe sticking through it. Ally grabbed the pipe and it came free, knocking the rest of the glass from the window into the tub.

When she walked out the front door her house looked fine. She'd know more in the daylight. She could see tree limbs and debris in her yard, but nothing either front or back that looked really bad. All three cars were completely untouched. She began to wonder where all the noise had come from, there was a lot of marble-sized hail on the ground, but surely that wasn't all of it. Looking around more she finally realized what she was seeing—the house to her right was gone and so were all the houses across the street. All the electricity was off, and it was pitch dark outside as far as she could see. The only light was coming from her head lamp.

Sam watched as Maggie cradled her son. He was asleep and hadn't woken up, so he guessed she just needed to hold him. As far as he was concerned, he'd been way too long in that hole and Alice had been way too long out of it. He got up and started looking around. "What you looking for, Sam?" Maggie asked.

"A flashlight. I'm going to go check on Alice, and before either of you try to stop me, remember that unlike Alice— who has everything to live for—I have nothing to lose and I'm going to go check on my child."

From the look on Maggie's face she knew just exactly why he needed to go. She understood that there was nothing you wouldn't do for your child. Carol of course had to be Carol.

"Dad, Alice can take care of herself."

"Yes because she's always had to. Well not today, Carol, not today."

"Go Dad," Maggie said, and she put her baby down and started to help Sam look for a flashlight. She found a cache of six of them, and handed him one. "Be careful."

Maggie watched as Carol tried to find service on her phone for the fifth time. "I need to tell my husband that I'm alright, if he even cares."

"Well if he doesn't he won't care if you call, will he?" Maggie said coolly. "Ally said she didn't think the cell phones would work in here. If you walk into the house, I think you can probably get cell service, and it should be safe enough." Maggie handed her one of the flashlights and stuck another one in her own pocket. Carol gave her a "go to hell" look and then started up the stairs. She had some trouble opening the door. When she walked through she didn't close it, and since the air in the hole was being filtered Maggie walked up and closed it for her.

All right I shouldn't have said that bitchy thing to her; that wasn't helpful. The problem is I know more than I need to know about that bitch, not because Ally told me but because Helen did. She treated Ally like crap her whole childhood and I know her kind. It wasn't enough to have all their mother's attention; she wanted all their father's as well. So she did everything in her power to punish Ally for being born. And then she dumped the old man on Ally and it must be chapping her ass that they have found a way to mend their relationship and she's back on the outside.

Carol wasn't gone long when the door opened and she came back coughing and sputtering. She had put her cell phone in her pocket. She sat down and was silent. Maggie had just decided that she was going to do her best to be pleasant when the bitch looked at her with contempt and said, "Homosexuality is a sin against God."

Maggie smiled sweetly. "Really? Then why does it exist? Why would a loving god make someone like me love a woman and then say, 'but not too much.' When God makes a homosexual do you suppose he means them to act like a straight, or do you suppose they are only following the will of God when they are their authentic selves?"

"God doesn't make homosexuals."

"Then who does? You know what? I don't want to listen to your negativity. Outside people are dead, and Ally is out there seeing what needs to be done. I'm worried about her. Life is short, and I don't have time for this continued pissing contest you've got going on with your sister. You might as well save your breath. I've done sick before and *nothing* I do with Ally is sick."

It was still raining, and the rain was quickly settling the dust. Ally stepped back onto the porch and out of the rain as her dad walked out of the house with a flashlight. "Dad, what the hell are you doing?"

"I'm checking on my child," he said.

"I'm fine, Dad let's go back inside." The air inside the house was still dusty, so she opened the front and back doors to air things out. "I was just starting to see other flashlights as I came in. I can't see city lights in any direction, and I can't really tell where the road is. There are downed power lines everywhere, but fortunately at least here they all seem to be dead."

"How can you tell, Alice?" her dad asked, as if he knew what she was getting ready to do.

"Well they aren't whipping around in the air throwing sparks like in the movies," Ally said. She smiled and shrugged. She closed the kitchen door, but left the front door open. "Dad, what are you doing here anyway? I thought you were staying the weekend at Carol's."

"There was crap," he said simply and shrugged.

She nodded and opened the door to the storm shelter in time to hear her stupid-assed sister praying for God to remove the demon from Maggie. Ally all but jumped into the storm shelter. Maggie was grinning like she was amused by Carol's stupidity. Ally grabbed her sister by the front of her blouse, jerked her to her feet, and shook her till her teeth rattled. "How fucking stupid are you? You will shut your evil-spewing mouth in our home right now, or I will throw your ass into the street with the rubble. If you ever talk to Maggie like that again I will rip your head off and shit in the hole." She threw her back on the bench, and Carol looked like she was going to say something else. "I mean it. I will put your ass out in the rain in what's left of this town. This is our house, *ours*, and you *will* respect us here."

She listened to the radio, and hearing that they were once again giving them an all clear she took off her wet shirt and handed it to Maggie then walked over and picked Tuesday up. "Honey, could you," she pointed at the box under the bench, and Maggie grabbed the rabbit and followed her up the stairs to Tuesday's room. Ally lay him down.

"Do you want a dry shirt, baby?" Maggie asked.

"No, it will just get wet again." She took the box with the rabbit in it and stuck it under Tuesday's bed then took the shirt from Maggie and put it back on. "We need to clean up the glass off the bathroom floor and out of the tub so Dad or Tuesday doesn't get cut, then you need to come with me and help." She handed Maggie the head lamp out of her pocket, and Maggie put it on and switched it on, turning the flashlight off and sticking it back in her pocket. "Everything out there is a mess." Maggie started to go, and Ally grabbed her arm. "I don't want you to look for dead people, Maggie. Just the living. Neither you or I need to deal with the dead."

Maggie nodded and went to get the broom, dust pan and the trash can. She didn't want to look for the dead, either. People would laugh at and make fun of her—though she didn't really care—then come to her any time there were people missing in the national forest or the lake area and ask for her help. Usually by the time they came to get her it was too late, and mostly she helped them find bodies. Ever since she had Tuesday, though, she had declined to help unless she knew the person was alive. The dead didn't care where their bodies were. And people always thought they wanted the closure of finding the body, but it never brought anything but pain. The tornado had killed people; she knew it. Ally was right. They needed to focus on the living.

By the time she got to the bathroom Ally had already gotten a battery-powered lantern and put it inside and had picked up all the bigger shards of glass. She slipped them into the garbage can. She looked at Maggie. "If you aren't up to this…"

"Don't even say it, Ally. What good is being able to do something if you won't do it? I wouldn't want you out there by yourself anyway. Nothing I could say or do could make you stay, so don't ask me to." Ally took the broom and started sweeping up the mess. "I don't mind looking for people who can be helped; I'm just over looking for dead people."

"So what did you say that tipped my stupid-assed sister off that you're a psychic?"

"Nothing, that's not what she was going on about. All of that praying the demon out of me was apparently because I'm a non-repentant queer."

Ally turned to her and grinned. "Well, you are pretty non repentant. Do you think it's safe to let Tuesday stay with my dad and twatzilla?"

"I don't think your dad would let anything happen to Tuesday. Tuesday's asleep, so he isn't going to hear any of the ugliness that comes from her mouth."

"Dad!" Ally hollered, dumping the glass in the trash. Ally's dad showed up in the doorway looking rather funny with his *I'm ready for action* face on. "Dad, Maggie and I have to go look for survivors. Can you keep an eye on Tuesday?"

"Of course, but Ally shouldn't you wait for emergency crews?"

"Dad, I am down as a first responder. I'm one of the people

who would normally be called to work something like this. I have no idea if anyone else can get to us, and if they can how long it would take. Maggie's had medical training, I've been trained in reconnaissance, and I have the tools. Don't let Carol anywhere near our son."

"I won't, Ally. Please be careful. Both of you be very careful."

Maggie followed Ally out to the shed; it was still raining. Ally took the head lamp off Maggie's head, put a hard hat on it, then slipped the light onto the hat and then fixed her own hard hat. She grabbed her chain saw and a pry bar then she looked at Maggie expectantly. Maggie concentrated just a second and then she started walking with Ally right behind her. It wasn't easy. The minute they stepped through their gate into the alley there was debris everywhere. The house to the south of them looked like someone had picked it up, twisted it, and thrown it back down. Maggie pointed towards a pile that used to be the middle of the house.

Ally nodded and moved to go ahead of her. She handed the chain saw and pry bar to Maggie and started picking up boards and tree limbs and throwing them out of the way.

"Hey, is there anyone in there?"

"Yes! We're alright, but we're stuck, and I'm not sure how long it's going to hold or how much is over us. It keeps shifting and popping."

"Where were you when it hit, Fred?" Ally asked, hoping it would give her a little better idea how to find them and get them out.

"In the closet under the stairs."

It took her a second, but she got her bearings. A tree top had landed in front of the door with pieces of house. "Maggie, shine a light." She showed where with her head lamp. Maggie nodded. Ally started up the chain saw and started cutting while Maggie gave her light, and it was Maggie, so she just put the light right where it needed to be without directions. When they got Fred and his wife and kid out, they headed back towards their house. They left Fred's wife—Ally never did know her name—and the five-year-old in the living room with her dad and the gaping, soul-sucking void which was her sister. Fred grabbed a hammer Ally offered him and went with them to help look for other survivors. Fred looked at Maggie as if he was surprised she didn't stay back at the house with the old man and the women folk. He was a nice enough guy, but sort of a misogynist—the funniest part of that being that he obviously didn't see Ally as female.

The next person Maggie found was an elderly woman under a stack of debris and in pretty bad shape. By then emergency response teams had made it to the scene and were setting up floodlights. They took over from them and started rushing the old woman on a litter over the debris field where four blocks away there were ambulances. Four blocks was as close as they could get. It was hard to know how bad the road was under stacks of rubble which used to be people's lives.

Over the next two hours Ally and Maggie and their ever-growing number of debris movers pulled eight more people from the wreckage. Happily, none of them had more than a few minor scrapes, and all of them along with Fred and his family moved to a shelter that had been set up at one of the high schools where there was water and power.

Ally and Maggie went home. Crews would work through the night, but all they would find was bodies. They'd gotten everyone living out.

Ally and Maggie put her hard hats and tools away and went in the house, closing and locking the door behind them, physically and metaphorically locking all the chaos outside. Maggie insisted Ally go right to the basement and lock her gun back up, so she did, taking the clip out of it and drying it off and oiling it before she locked it back in the safe.

They brought their robes with them to the bathroom, took their wet clothes off and threw them in the bathtub. Ally looked at Maggie; she looked a little beaten and sad.

"It will be alright, Maggie. We did what we could do," Ally said.

Maggie nodded and finished towel-drying her hair. In the morning it would be a mass of tight ringlets that Maggie would bitch she couldn't get a brush through, and look just the way Ally liked it. Ally pulled a wet wipe out of the box on the back of the toilet and used it to wipe Maggie's face off, and Maggie smiled.

"You do realize that..." She took the head lamp off and set it down on the sink. "That with these things on any time we have looked at each other all night we have blinded one another."

She was right; Ally took hers off and set it on the back of

the toilet. She went back to wiping Maggie's face off.

"What are you doing, Ally?"

"I don't know, trying to take care of you I guess. I know how much that sort of thing takes out of you." She stopped and kissed Maggie gently on the lips then took the towel from Maggie and started to dry her own head. "In the morning I'll hook up the generator and the water system."

Maggie put on her robe and looked at the floor. "You really aren't mad?"

It took Ally a second to realize what she was talking about. "No, Maggie, no. I'm fine with it." Ally laughed. "Is that what you're all messed up about? For the love of God, Maggie, there was a tornado, my sister showed her whole entire huge ass, we've been dragging people out of what is left of their homes for hours, and I know you have been ignoring the dead...."

"There are three here and more across town," she said.

But if she knew it was her apartment building she wasn't saying, and if she didn't know Ally wasn't going to tell her. That's what she learned in the military.

"My point is... Aren't you the one who always says live in the now and not in the past? You loved Helen. I loved Helen. She loved us. She's gone, and we're still here."

When she went to check on everyone her sister was in the guest room and her dad had taken the cushions off the couch and was sleeping in the floor next to Tuesday's bed.

Maggie looked over Ally's shoulder and whispered in her ear. "That is the cutest thing ever."

It sort of was.

Ally's cell phone was ringing, so she let go of Maggie and reached over and grabbed it. "Hello, Mitch."

"Hey big hero, you and Maggie were all over the news this morning. We're going to come clear your road first mostly because I need you in the cherry picker with the chain saw."

Maggie rolled over and hugged her, but she didn't wake up.

Ally smiled and started rubbing her hand over Maggie's back.

"Can you hear me Ally?"

"Yes, me in the cherry picker..." That woke Maggie right up.

"With the saw? I hate that, Ally," Maggie said, her voice heavy with sleep.

Mitch laughed. "So can I talk to your better half?"

Ally handed Maggie the phone and she took it. "We saw what you were doing and I know what you were doing even if most people don't. And even though I make fun of you I know your gift is real, Maggie. So how are you, really?"

"Alright, a little tired. I'd rather you didn't stick Ally in the cherry picker with a chainsaw working around electrical lines, but I didn't like that before I was sleeping with her, and it isn't because I'm a wreck from the storm. I'm... I'm fine." And she was, too. All of that, all of it, and she was just fine. *Because I didn't need her; I was perfectly alright alone. I don't need her, I want her, and so all she has done is enhance my life. I didn't need anyone to complete me because I was already a whole person. With Ally I have more than I could ever need, and so all of this... and I'm fine.*

"I need you in the office on the phones, Maggie. If we can get you both out, can you come in? If not, I can get Karen to do it."

Karen couldn't do it; she'd have a nervous breakdown. Most of the crew would be clearing power lines for the next few days if not weeks, and all of their customers with storm damage were going to be calling. She was going to have to do landscaping triage, deciding what was the most urgent. She was going to be shuffling crews here and there and dealing with irate customers who thought their need outweighed everyone else's. "If you can get us out, I can come in."

"Great." He sighed with relief. "Can I talk to Ally again?"

Ally took the phone from Maggie. "What?" Ally asked as she played with the tendrils of Maggie's hair.

Mitch laughed, and then got serious, "Ally... I hope what I said the other day... Well, I don't disapprove of you and Maggie. I don't want you to think I want you to be alone forever. You and Maggie are both adults, and it's really none of my business what you guys do." And in the background Ally could hear Karen—of all people—prompting him. "I'm alright with seeing you together. I love you both, and I'm just so glad you're all okay."

"I love you Mitch... thanks."

"Hopefully we'll see you in a while."

She shut the phone off and set it down.

"So what was all that?" Maggie asked.

"We have Mitch's blessing."

"I thought we already did."

"Get this, I could hear Karen in the back ground prompting him, so apparently she's alright with us, too."

"And…" Maggie took a deep breath and held it "…you're alright?"

"Maggie, if I can deal with you having slept with men… a vision of you and Helen doing it is not necessarily a turn off."

"But the bisexual thing is?"

"No… not really."

"But you wonder if I'm going to eventually make you wear a strap on or I'm going to want a man again?"

Wow it really was eerie the way Maggie just knew things. From Maggie's tone Ally couldn't tell if she was mad, hurt, or just a little put out, but she guessed it might be all three which certainly that wasn't Ally's intent, but since she was asking. "Yes, sort of."

Maggie looked up at her and caught her eyes. "I'm bisexual because I can become physically attracted to either sex, but when I'm with someone I'm not wishing I was with anyone else. I dated men for so long because then it didn't feel like I was lying to anyone, but the truth is I have always preferred women. I am completely, unbelievably, satisfied with you sexually, and wouldn't have you make any changes. I am madly in love with you and don't want anyone else, ever."

Ally grabbed Maggie and threw her on her back and then she was just all over her.

Sam woke up with the boy shaking him.

"Sam, what are you doing in my room?" He laughed.

Sam looked at him and smiled. "I was afraid of the storm."

Tuesday nodded and padded off towards the bathroom. Sam had a little trouble getting out of the floor. He started after the boy who was already getting the lay of the land because he got there just fine all by himself. He waited for him outside the bathroom door and when he walked out Sam went in.

By the time Sam realized he couldn't brush his teeth or flush the toilet, Tuesday had already taken his rabbit out of the box and was sitting in the kitchen floor holding him. "Look how much he pooped," the boy said, making a face and pointing at the box.

"Yep that's a lot of poop." Sam picked the box up and put it out on the deck.

The milk in the fridge was still cold, so he got it out and closed the door. He wondered for a minute what Ally was going to do without her coffee. He had just gotten a bowl of cereal for himself and the boy and sat down when Carol walked in looking like something the cat dragged in and the dog wouldn't eat. Sam took the rabbit from the boy.

"Tuesday, sit down and eat your breakfast." The boy got up and got into the chair. Carol made a face, and Sam answered, "It's Maggie's favorite day of the week."

Sam took the rabbit outside and put it in his cage. Alice's house and the houses north of it were all fine, but the houses on the south side of hers were gone as far as he could see, and he knew everything across the street was gone.

It was horrible, and he quickly went back inside.

"I'm Carol."

"But who are you?" Tuesday asked.

Sam gave Carol a hard look and said, "Don't you dare say anything hateful to this boy."

"I wouldn't, Dad, he's just a child. It isn't his fault..."

"There is no fault here," Sam looked at her sternly. "And while you are in Alice's house, you will remember that."

Tuesday looked confused. "Who are you?"

"I'm your mother's sister."

"No my mother's sister is aunt Mona."

"She is Allybaba's sister," Sam said and told Carol, "He calls Alice Allybaba."

The boy shook his head and obviously wasn't buying any of it, but he just ate his breakfast and didn't say anymore.

The racket started up in Alice's bedroom and Sam grinned and started eating, pretending not to hear.

"What on earth are they doing?" Carol asked, her eyes wide.

Sam looked at her and grinned. "Well let's see. There was a tornado and they spent most of the night saving people buried in rubble, and yet—though occasionally it may sound that way—they are not praying. However, I wouldn't be at all surprised if they weren't talking in tongues."

Carol gasped and started to have a meltdown, and he

held up his hand. "Not in your sister's house in front of her son. Oh, and I just remembered... I'm so sorry. What a shame it is you will miss the family day of hatemongering."

Ally walked into the kitchen, fully dressed in her work uniform and boots. She bent down and kissed Tuesday on the head, snarled at her sister, and turned to her dad. "Dad, do you feel up to coming out with me for a minute?"

He nodded and stood up.

Ally turned to her sister. "Carol, if you can't say anything nice, say nothing at all to either my partner or my son. Come on, Dad." He followed her onto the deck. "Maggie and I are both going to have to go to work, but there is no reason for you to have to rough it or for everything to go bad in the fridge." She walked over and opened the trap door in the deck and there was her generator. "You flip this switch off and that keeps our electricity from going into the electric company lines and electrocuting anyone working on them. If the power comes back on, flip the switch back on, and flip the switch off on the generator here. Once I crank the generator over everything in the house should run within reason. Don't use the stove; don't use the clothes dryer."

He smiled at her. "I don't anyway."

"Well don't. I turn this spigot, and now our water won't run into the water company lines. When I start the generator it will activate the pump and there will be running water in the bathroom but nowhere else. Use the 'If it's yellow, it's mellow' rule. I have no idea how long we're going to be without utilities..."

"If it's yellow it's mellow?"

"Only flush shit, Dad we don't have an unlimited water supply," Ally said. He nodded and she cranked on the generator until it started. "It should run till... At least until Maggie gets home. I'll probably have to work till midnight."

"Why?" he yelled, trying to be heard over the motor, and Ally ushered him back inside and shut the door before she answered.

"I wasn't just talking shit. I really am a first responder because Mitch has a contract with the electric company and we have to clear the power lines. Mitch will clear the roads because he has the equipment, and that's the kind of guy Mitch is."

Sam nodded. Inside the kitchen the refrigerator was humming, but more importantly the coffee maker was going. Maggie walked in wearing tight jeans and a loose T-shirt. She had been unable to tame her hair, and she looked amazing. She looked at Ally and smiled, and Ally smiled back.

"Allybaba," Tuesday said, and pointed at the chair next to him so she sat down. "Did you see how much Jack pooped?"

"No, was it a lot?"

He nodded and made a face.

"And see, that's why he can't stay in your room."

Tuesday nodded as if it all finally made sense to him now.

"Eat, son."

Carol made an unhappy noise and that was all the reason Ally needed. "Dammit, Carol..."

"Ally," Maggie said calmly, and cut her eyes towards Tuesday.

Ally got up from the table with an effort. "Carol, kindly meet me on the porch," Ally said, and her sister took off towards the front of the house.

Maggie gently took hold of Ally's arm, got on her tip toes and whispered in her ear. "Don't take it personally, Ally. This is her problem; don't make it yours, and don't beat her to a bloody pulp. That won't fix anything and it will only make you feel better for a minute."

"Are you sure, Maggie?"

Maggie nodded and kissed her on the cheek.

Ally found her sister standing on the porch looking at the absolute destruction all around them. She had of course already lit up a cigarette. Before Ally started to unload the tirade she had carefully composed on her walk to the front of the house she heard something Helen had always said and Maggie still said. *The universe will talk to you if you are open enough to listen.*

Ally took in a deep breath, let it out slowly, and listened then said in a voice nowhere near a scream, "And my house is fine, Carol. My family and my house are fine. Three people died here last night and more died in an apartment house across town, but me and my family are fine. Our house was hardly touched, and our fence took only minor damage. Our son literally slept through the whole thing; even our stinking rabbit is alright. The middle-aged Church of Christ couple that lived two doors down are dead. They hated me. When

Helen and I first moved here they went to city hall and tried to have the neighborhood zoned non-gay. They couldn't, but they tried. They're dead, Carol. We're fine; our home is fine." She laughed then. "Hell, I'll tell you better than that, and you can believe it or not. We just last night moved the last of Maggie's stuff out of the apartment building that blew to pieces last night. But you know what? None of that matters. I'm proud of myself, Carol. I *like* myself. Hell, you dumped Dad on me, and he's dying and... My life is perfect. I'm happy, so you can condemn me and call me names all you like. Go ahead and picket to have my rights taken away, vote against me, say hateful things to the woman I love whom you don't even know. Nothing you can do will ever hurt me because *I don't care what you think*. I expect nothing but crap from you, so... you never disappoint me."

Maggie walked out then, mostly Ally was sure to make certain Ally wasn't pummeling Carol, but her lame-assed excuse was, "Honey is it alright to brush my teeth?"

"Yeah, let's go I'm done here." Ally followed Maggie back into the house and to the bathroom where Tuesday was already brushing his teeth, thus proving that Maggie just wanted to check on her. Ally grinned at her as she put the toothpaste on her brush.

"What?" Maggie asked, toothpaste foam coming from her mouth.

"Could you not just use your psychic powers to see if I had become violent?"

"No," Maggie said then spit and started brushing some more.

"Son," Ally reached over and caught the toothpaste that was getting ready to fall off his chin into the floor. "You can spit any time you like."

He spit. "Mom said to remember we don't have much water," he said, shrugging.

"How does spitting use water?"

Tuesday shrugged.

She washed her hand.

"Alice." Her sister was standing in the open bathroom door. "A news crew is at the door they want to talk to you both."

"Dammit," Ally said, looking at Maggie. "Rock, paper, scissors for who runs out the back door." Because of course neither of them wanted to talk to the press. They'd both done it before for different reasons, but they had no desire to do it ever again.

Then her Dad was at the bathroom door. "Alice, there are some people…"

Ally sighed because what she knew was that they weren't going to go away till they talked to someone, and they wouldn't give her nearly the shit they would give Maggie. "You owe me," she said to Maggie.

"Make a list; I'll work it off. I don't mind at all." Maggie kissed her cheek.

Ally walked between her dad and Carol and through the house to the open front door. Not one, not two, but three news crews.

"We wanted to talk to Maggie Muntz, too," one of the reporters said.

"We are kind of busy. I need to gear up and get to work clearing the road. Maggie doesn't want to talk to you, because you guys always make her look like a new-age flake. I don't have time to answer a bunch of silly-assed questions. We found twelve people. With the help of our neighbors we pulled them out. It's not brave or extraordinary; it's just what people do. Now… there are a lot of people who would be happy to talk to you; go talk to them, please, and let me get back to work."

And they left, which showed they were at least as rattled as everyone else about a giant twister tearing chunks out of their town. When she walked back in the house she closed the door behind her and was sorry to see that her sister was back in her house again. "Chicken shit," Ally said to Maggie, who just shrugged.

"They would have asked me a bunch of ridiculous questions," Maggie said.

"I didn't know… I didn't know that you were out there in all that… saving people," Carol said in shock.

"What did you think they were doing, Carol, looting? I told you what they were doing, so what? Am I a liar now?" her dad asked in disbelief. "They brought three of the people they pulled out back here."

"I… I thought they just came here."

"Alice and Maggie are heroes, not just last night or today but every day," her dad said. "In a world full of bigots and haters they get up every morning and they live in truth."

Ally was surprised at how actually touched she was. "Thanks, Dad. Maggie, follow me." She walked down the hall, stopped and turned to face Maggie. "So... I see you've been talking to my Dad a lot."

"He has questions; I answer him." Maggie grinned back with a shrug.

"I'm going to go get my chain saw and meet Mitch and the crew somewhere in the middle. The sooner we can get twatzilla out of here..."

"Twatzilla!" Tuesday shouted as he followed them.

Both he and Ally cracked up.

"Ally," Maggie protested. "Don't teach him terrible things like that."

"Twatzilla!" Tuesday shouted again, just because he'd gotten such a good response the first time and Ally laughed more.

"Tuesday, please son, don't say that," Maggie pleaded.

"Twatzilla!"

Ally cleared her throat and made herself quit laughing. "Now, son, don't say that again; it's not nice."

"You said it."

"But it wasn't a nice thing to say,"

"Then why did you say it?"

"Because..."

"Ally Taggart," Maggie warned.

"I shouldn't have, I was just mad."

"Because she's a bitch?" Tuesday said with a grin.

"Yes," Ally started laughing again.

Maggie looked from Ally to her son and back again. "When we get the calls from the kindergarten teacher, *you* can go to the school and tell her why our son talks... well just like you." She stomped past her towards the kitchen, and Ally followed.

"Ah come on, Maggie."

Ally looked down at Tuesday who was following her. "Now look what you did; you got me in trouble."

"I'm sorry, Allybaba."

When she reached the kitchen Maggie turned on her and there was fire in her green eyes. "I'm sorry, baby," Ally said.

"Me too," Tuesday said.

"I don't want you to say mean things, Tuesday," Maggie

said, and it was clear she was talking to Ally as much as her son.

"Which is another reason I need to get to work clearing that road, remove the toad, spray for warts."

Sam ignored Carol, seeing her only reminded him of what he had let himself become, of all the time he had wasted that he could have spent with Alice. Carol epitomized his wasted life. He had given her everything he had to give; she was a huge nothing. He had done nothing at all for Alice; Alice was amazing. He had an idea. He could hear not just Alice's chainsaw but others going as well. He walked into the bathroom where Maggie was doing the dishes in the bathroom sink. He smiled. This girl was the whole package, beautiful and warm and resourceful.

"Maggie, I noticed there is a plug in on the front porch. I'm not good for much, but if we could move the coffee maker to the porch I could make coffee for everyone working out there."

"That's a great idea," Maggie said.

Sam noticed Tuesday was sitting on the side of the tub looking like someone had stepped on his rabbit.

"What's wrong?" Sam asked him.

"Allybaba and I got in trouble."

Sam grinned. "What for?"

"Talking mean. It's that girl's fault," Tuesday said.

"No one can make you talk mean, Tuesday," Maggie said.

"Well if anyone could, it would be Carol." Sam chuckled and shook his head.

Maggie helped him move the coffee table onto the porch and then the coffee maker and all the creamer and sugar and coffee he'd need for the day. She even found disposable cups and made a sign that said free coffee.

Carol just sat in the living room and watched TV. She didn't lift a finger to help. She started to light a cigarette and Maggie said, "No smoking in the house; go to the back deck." As Carol went to the back deck Sam gave her an odd look. Maggie grinned the most impish grin and said, "Well I don't want the shame of the neighbors seeing Ally's sister smoking."

Maggie busied herself cleaning the house and putting her things away. Sam sat on the porch making, pouring and handing out coffee and felt useful for the first time in years.

Neighbors were helping neighbors. They'd lost everything but themselves and each other, and they were so happy to be alive that even sifting through the remains of their homes looking for the things they most cherished, the photos, the mementos, while there were momentary tears most of the time they were talking even laughing, and he was part of it. They would come, get coffee, thank him and talk to him. They would tell him all that Ally and Maggie had done the night before, and his feelings of pride were only marred by the two-hundred-twenty pound blotch sitting on Ally's couch wasting air.

The chain saw Ally was wielding looked way too big for her, and he realized early on why Maggie chose to stay in the house. She didn't want to watch Ally run the saw; it made her nervous. He knew it must because it made him nervous. By noon Ally had met Mitch and the crew in the middle. Maggie had made them a bunch of sandwiches, and this gave him another idea. He would make sandwiches for the people working. When he told Maggie she told him she would stop at a store and buy what he needed to do it on her way home from work that night.

As she and Mitch were walking up on the porch, Carol walked out of the house. "Can I get my car out now?"

Ally looked at Mitch and he nodded. "It's not quite clear yet, but you should be able to get back to the main road and then it's mostly safe from there to the freeway."

Carol rushed past them towards the driveway.

"I already got my bag from your car; thanks for asking. I'm not going to see you again, Carol," her dad said at her sister's departing back. Carol stopped and turned around slowly. "I hope you fix yourself."

"Me? What? Dad I.... I love you. I hope you see the light before you die, that you embrace Jesus again and...."

Ally walked back down the steps turned her sister around and started pushing her towards her car. "So nice of you to drop by, twenty years is too long. Never, ever come back again."

"Dad wants to be buried with Mom," Carol said. Five seconds ago she'd been ready to leave, and now she was digging her heels in. So it really was all about nothing more than making Ally uncomfortable in her own space.

"Then you can come get him when he dies. Now go."

"No, I don't want to be buried with that bitch. Cremate me and throw me anyplace else, Ally," her dad said, and Ally smiled because that was the first time he hadn't called her Alice. "Just go, Carol! Leave us alone!" Her dad stood up then and pointed at her sister. "How dare you judge anyone after all that you have done?"

Maggie walked out of the house just as Ally was about to forcibly shove Carol into the car. Maggie lifted her palms skyward and intoned strange words and then pointed both her index fingers at Carol and shook, the strange words growing more intense. Carol ran to her car, got in and took off screaming, "Save me Jesus, save me!"

Maggie turned to face Ally and said, "Come on there are sandwiches on the back deck and you know if you don't hurry the rest of the crew will eat them all."

Ally and her dad and Mitch all looked at Maggie in amazement.

Maggie laughed at them. "Seriously, guys? That was all just for show. I made it up on the spot. I didn't want Ally to beat the living crap out of her sister, and I wanted the harpy gone. I don't have dark, magic powers," she started into the house, quickly turned and looked at all of them and said, "Or do I?"

"Not funny, Maggie," Mitch said following her inside. "Not funny."

CHAPTER 7

*If you are always broke, eventually people stop hitting you
up for money.*

They worked through the weekend, and then Maggie was
working a regular work day, but Ally was working twelve-
hour days. People were still sifting through the rubble, and
Maggie had no idea what they'd spent on sandwich and coffee
stuff. She was happy to do it, but it was a lot. The activity,
instead of making the old man sicker, actually seemed to
have put a bit of spring back into his step. He had made a
bunch of new friends, he was performing a needed service,
and he felt useful.

When Ally got home in the evenings she was beat. She
would get a shower and Maggie would get her something to
eat. Ally would spend time with Tuesday for no more than an
hour till he had to go to bed.

Tuesday had gotten used to spending lots of time with
Ally, and he was really missing her. So badly in fact that one
day when she didn't get back to the shop for lunch he actually
cried. Maggie was well aware of how lucky they were. If they
hadn't decided to live together she might have been in the
apartment building. Five people had died in that building,
and there was not a brick left standing. Still, she was sick to
death of Ally working all the time and way ready for them to
find out what their lives together were really going to be like.

Hell, foreplay had become fifteen minutes of Maggie
working on Ally's leg and her back so that Ally could move
well enough that they could have sex.

Maggie had just taken the last of five phone calls that had
all come in at once when Mitch came into the office and
grabbed her shoulder, making her jump. "Come on." He half
dragged her towards the shop.

"Mitch, what the..."

"Shush, Maggie." He opened the door to the shop. "Listen."
She did, and then she looked at Mitch with astonishment.

"Ally's singing."

He nodded, and she could see the tears in his eyes.

"The guys on her crew, not even Ray worked with her before Helen died; they didn't know. I heard her and asked Ray about it. He said she started doing it about three days ago."

When Helen was alive, Ally whistled or sang most of the time, often the same song over and over for days. But since Helen had died not a note, not a whistle, not even so much as a hum. Nothing. She had just stopped. Mitch had noticed it before Maggie did. When Maggie asked Ally about it she had said she just didn't feel like singing, that she couldn't even make herself do it, it was just gone. Ally was a fantastic whistler, but she had an amazing voice, and they had all missed what Mitch had called their little walking radio. Chuck would have known, but of course Chuck had been out sick for the last four days.

And here they were, everything was a mess, Ally was working all the time and in a world of pain, and yet she was singing again.

Mitch gave Maggie a huge bear hug. "Thank you, Maggie."

"Me why me?"

"Listen to what she's singing, Maggie."

She did and smiled. Ally was singing Witchy Woman.

"Go on in there and give her a hug. I'll keep an eye on Tuesday," Mitch said, and went back to her office.

Maggie walked over to where Ally was sharpening a chain saw and singing up a storm, her ass shaking all over the place to the music coming out of her mouth and in her own head. Maggie stood on her tip toes and kissed the side of Ally's neck, and she was almost sorry when Ally stopped singing and turned around to face her until Ally wrapped her arms around her and hugged her. They kissed, and a couple of the guys who were also working in the shop started to make smooching sounds because they were oh so very mature. She didn't care, and neither did Ally. When she stopped kissing her, Ally moved her head back but didn't let Maggie go.

"Mitch said I could have weekends off again starting this weekend. I was thinking... you know I've never even taken you out."

"Oh Honey, we're both so tired and we haven't been home

and I just want to be home with you. We can go out some other time. I just want you to myself."

"With my dad the sandwich, coffee man, all his followers, and our two-and-a-half-year-old. It sounds like heaven. I'll tell you what I'm not doing; I'm not cleaning up any storm wrack... except maybe our own. And I need to fix our bathroom window, and...."

"You're already filling the whole day with work. Honey, I'm fine with the garbage bag taped over the window. Nothing is urgent, why don't you actually just rest? Spend some time with me. I don't need or really want to go out, but I would love to just relax with you." She smiled at Ally, pulled her head down to her and kissed her again. "Thank you."

"For what?"

"Just thank you." The phone was ringing again, and having Mitch answer it was about as helpful as if Tuesday answered it. "I have to go."

Ally released her and she started back for her office. The fact that Ally was singing again put a spring in Maggie's own step because to Maggie it meant Ally really loved her. She wasn't about to say anything about the singing to Ally for fear she might stop.

She walked in and answered the phone. Noticing that Mitch was all about helping Tuesday build a Lincoln log home and was purposely ignoring the ringing phone. "Hello, Taggart's Landscaping."

"Maggie, this is Mona. Listen, we've got Ally's dad in the emergency room...."

"What's wrong with him?" Maggie asked.

"He has cancer," Mona said with a laugh. "He just blacked out and he seems to be awake and alert now. The doctor thinks it's anemia, most likely caused by the cancer. They're going to give him an iron infusion. He didn't want me to call you guys, but I thought Ally would want to know what's going on."

"Is it bad? Does Ally need to come down there right now?"

"No, I suggest that when I get off shift I just take him home. He really doesn't want to be a problem. Honey, don't get attached to him.... He's dying. He's not going to die today, but he's going to die."

Maggie knew that. "I'll tell Ally what's going on and try to get her not to come down there...."

"She can go if she needs to go," Mitch said.

"He's alright, Mitch," Maggie said. "If you could bring him home, Mona, that would be great. Thanks."

"You're more than welcome. I love you, Maggie."

"I love you, Mona. If there is any change...."

"I'll call you. Bye."

"Bye." Maggie hung up the phone, took a deep breath and looked at Mitch. "He just blacked out but.... It's going to be mostly downhill from here on."

Mitch nodded and smiled up at her from where he was sitting on the floor. "You guys sure picked a hell of a time to start a new relationship."

"Do you think so?" Maggie grinned and walked out to the shop. Ally was singing again, the same song, and still sharpening a chainsaw, but one look told her it was a different one. When she got Ally's attention and told her about her dad she didn't know what she was expecting but it wasn't....

"That's awful nice of Mona. Let's pick up some steaks on the way home and I'll grill them. Dad obviously needs some red meat; do you want fish or chicken?"

"I don't eat much red meat, but I'd happily eat a steak tonight."

"Really?" Ally said, as if it was the most shocking thing she'd ever heard.

"Yes, really." Maggie started to go back to her office, but she stopped and turned before opening the door. "Ally.... Are you alright?"

Ally didn't have to ask why Maggie asked, she knew. "Mona said it wasn't that bad, right?"

Maggie nodded.

"Honey, we all know he's dying. He didn't want me down there he doesn't want to hear that he shouldn't have been making sandwiches and coffee for everyone. The truth is I'm all about him doing whatever he wants that doesn't have him burning our house down or shoving his holy roller crap down our throats. I know I'll be sad when he goes Maggie, but right now, with you and Tuesday even with all this crap I'm happy. I'm not going to let Dad's illness or anything else steal that away from me." She walked over and hugged Maggie. "I love you, Maggie!" she yelled loud enough that everyone in the shop could hear it.

Maggie laughed and hugged her back. "And I love you!"

Maggie yelled back.

"I love watching!" Ray yelled from across the shop where he was working on the cherry picker.

Maggie doubted many people realized the amount of time they had to spend working on the equipment after something like a tornado. They were running everything hard for long days on end. Maintenance and repairs that they might otherwise do every three to six months they had to do every two or three days.

"Such jackasses," Ally mumbled.

"You know they all think they want to see us do it, and you know none of them could watch for ten minutes without their heads exploding."

"Or something."

Sam felt pretty rough, and he had a weird, metal taste in his mouth. He looked across the cab at where Mona was driving. "This is a really nice car."

"Thanks, I get a new one every two years." She laughed, and when she did she sounded so much like her sister it made Sam smile. "To tell the truth, I'm not the kind of person who gives a crap what I drive, but.… Maggie and I have a brother who is sort of a leech on our asses. He can't keep a job for more than ten minutes, and he is always a day late and a dollar short. He isn't as dysfunctional as mother, but he's running a close second. Chad could never get more than a few bucks from Maggie because she has always needed every penny she made just to pay the bills since she lost her license to practice medicine.…"

"Maggie's a doctor?"

"No, she's a physical therapist." Mona then returned to her story, without answering any of the questions now swirling around in Sam's head. "Anyway, he couldn't get money from Maggie so he was just nickel and diming me to death, and then I realized he can't get money from me if I don't have it, so every two years I buy a new car and when he asks for money I just look at my car sigh and tell him I'm broke. He hasn't asked me for a dime in nearly a year now."

"How did Maggie lose her license?"

"She used her powers for good corporate medicine can't have anyone doing something that actually works that they can't figure out how to charge for. They threatened to sue her unless she quit practicing. It really sucked, too, because Maggie loved what she did, she made really good money, and she is really, really good at it. The proof is that Ally walks at all."

"Maggie helped Ally with her leg?"

"Oh, hell yes. God knows the VA didn't give a damn about what happened to Ally. Oh they'll give her braces and crutches all day, but the PT she was getting through them was laughable. The injury wasn't service related, so they cared even less than they normally do." Mona grinned and shook her head. "I guess when I think about it it's kind of surprising they didn't end up together years ago. When Helen died and Ally was all boogered up she was ready to curl up her toes and die, and Maggie wasn't far behind her. Maggie trying to 'save' Ally is really the only thing that kept Maggie sane.... at least as sane as she was. For a while she was pretty crazy on good days. Maggie did some seriously stupid crap, but that was mostly after she got Ally up and walking. It was like she knew they couldn't both be self-destructive at the same time, so she got Ally over the hump and then she fell apart. Then Maggie got pregnant with Tuesday and Ally saved her and all the self-destructive stuff just stopped with both of them."

"Ally saved Maggie?"

"Yep, Tuesday, too, really."

"What about the boy's father?" Sam asked. He couldn't say he hadn't been worried about him showing up and causing problems. Ally and Maggie were both women, and a lot of people felt the same way he had just a few weeks ago when he first just contemplated the idea that Ally might be raising a child with a woman. If the father showed up that could mean big problems for Ally and Tuesday.

"He isn't coming back," Mona said.

"How do you know that?"

Mona was silent for a moment then she said, "Because he nearly beat Maggie to death when he found out she was pregnant. Ally found her and took her to the hospital. If he shows up he goes to jail."

"But when the statute of limitations..."

"Then he'd have to pay a butt-load of back child support, and believe me he doesn't want anything to do with Tuesday. So don't worry about that." Mona smiled at him. "You know

I have to say I expected you to be a total shmuck, but you're actually a decent guy."

Sam laughed. "Gee, thanks."

"Sorry, I tend to say whatever I'm thinking. At work I'm always getting in trouble for my lack of filter."

"I find the honesty with which both you and your sister approach the world to be refreshing," Sam said honestly. "To tell the truth a few weeks ago I was probably every bit as big a shmuck as you expected me to be."

"Seeing mortality up close and personal has a way of making you take an inventory of your life. I know I'm rethinking everything..."

"You need to live, Mona. Go after exactly what you want; don't wait till it's nearly too late." Sam started to cry. He couldn't help himself. He felt like crap, and he'd thought he was going to die when they rushed him to the hospital. In that moment he couldn't tell even himself whether he was happy or sad that he hadn't.

Mona pulled into the parking lot of a park and stopped the car. She reached across the car and hugged him.

"Oh my God, Mona. I wasted my life. I threw Alice into the world to do or die when she wasn't more than a child. So many times she needed me and I wasn't there. I wasn't. I missed nearly everything. I had nowhere to go, and who took me in even when she didn't want to? This time with Alice and your sister and that little boy have been some of the happiest days of my life. This last week I helped people, sick and weak, I feel like I did more good in this last week than I have done in the rest of my life. And Alice? She and your sister, they were the heroes of the day, and I got to see them on TV and hear people talking about what good people they are. I don't deserve to be with them or to have any of this. I deserve to be stuck with Carol and her awful family in that horrid town rotting a little more every day as the people I went to church with tell me it's all God's will."

"I'm not good with this kind of crap, Sam, that's Maggie. But everyone has a story, and if you didn't deserve this, you wouldn't be here now to enjoy it. You know what, Sam, it's not just the heart attack or the surgery that's made me take a good look at my life. Maybe you're here now for me because what I've learned from you is that it's never too late to change."

They sat there, talked, and had a good cry.

"Ally!" Maggie grabbed the box out of the cart and read the ingredients then put it back on the shelf. "Just let me shop, Ally. You push the cart." She pulled another box off the shelf, read the ingredients and put it in the cart.

Ally bent down till her face was even with Tuesday's. "This is going to take forever."

"It always does," Tuesday said with a sigh.

Ally laughed and kissed his cheek.

"When did you stop doing a set of Chi Gung in the morning?" Maggie asked.

"When you stopped asking me every day if I was doing it," Ally said with a smile, pushing the cart behind Maggie and enjoying the view.

"So.... Nearly three years ago."

"I blame you," Ally said.

Maggie laughed and put yet some other mostly inedible health food in the cart. Ally didn't care. Maggie was a good cook and she made stuff Helen would have turned into something only slightly more palatable than cat litter taste good. Flipping it around Ally asked, "Why don't you do a Chi Gung set every morning?"

"I was until some over-sexed woman was spending every morning crawling all over me," Maggie whispered, turning to look at her with a smile.

That smile, it could light up a whole room.

Maggie turned back around. "We will start doing Chi Gung again in the morning."

Ally rolled her eyes and Tuesday giggled.

"I don't know what you did, Ally Taggart, but I know it was bad."

"I will do whatever you ask of me, but I have to tell you that I prefer my workout."

"I didn't say we had to stop that. It's adding, not taking anything away."

They turned a corner to come to the much-needed alcoholic beverages aisle, and there were Frances and Laurie fighting over what kind of cheap beer to buy. They looked up saw her, got an eye full of Maggie and the boy, and drew all the right conclusions. They looked at each other, grinned, and Ally wondered which of them had lost the bet. Frances and Laurie had both called to check on her right after they saw her on TV and realized her house was in the tornado zone. They were her friends, and Maggie was Helen's friend, so they'd all met each other... where else? At her house at the many parties Helen used to throw.

"Hey look! It's the town heroes," Frances said.

"You know, I got caught in a tornado once...."

"Yes, of course you did Laurie, and was there a witch and a dog caught in it with you," Maggie said, rolling her eyes. If Ally didn't already think Maggie was the most amazing woman on the planet, that would have clinched the deal.

Frances cracked up and the look on Laurie's face was priceless. "Do you guys need any help?"

"Great timing," Ally said with a laugh. "We got our water back yesterday, and the electric is back on today. We didn't get hit; it was way too close for comfort, though."

"We?" Frances asked with a knowing smile.

"Yes, *we* jackass," Ally said, and started pushing the cart again. She stopped and got a couple of six packs of the hard cider. She caught Laurie checking Maggie out, and Ally reached out and took Maggie's hand, looked at her friends and said, "Mine." Then she started walking, dragging Maggie after her and pushing the cart she turned and shouted over her shoulder, "All mine!"

"Selfish!" Frances shouted at her departing back.

"Please tell me you didn't sleep with either of those assholes," Ally said.

"Please. If I had, do you really think either of them could have kept their mouths shut about it? If Laurie didn't lie and tell you that she had done me, you can bet your sweet—and it is sweet—ass that she didn't know or even have an inkling that I was batting for both teams."

Tuesday looked at Ally smiled and said, "Sweet ass."

Ally cracked up, then stopped laughing, looked at Maggie indignantly and said, "Now see what you've done."

An elderly woman walked up to them deliberately, and Ally was sure she was about to get a supermarket sermonette, which was only confirmed when the woman started with, "Bless you children."

Ally's blood started to pump hard and fast, and her stomach rolled, and she realized that she had a visceral fear of fundamental religion that she probably needed to address in therapy. After all, this old woman was no threat to her.

Maggie put a hand on her shoulder, so she must have sensed the change in Ally.

"I want to thank you both. You pulled my sister out of the rubble after the storm. It isn't often you find good people like you. You put yourselves in harm's way to help others with no reward for yourselves. Bless you."

"You're very welcome," Ally stammered. She took in a deep breath and let it out.

"How is she doing?" Maggie asked the old woman.

"Very well, thank you. She is staying with me right now, and just so happy to be alive. I'll let you get back to your shopping." She started to walk away then turned around, "You have a beautiful family."

"Tha... thanks," Ally said, and realized that the glow she was feeling inside was what it felt like to have acceptance and respect from a stranger. To have someone know you were gay and have respect for you accept you even though there was nothing in it for them. She almost chased the old woman down and thanked her again.

Her Dad and Mona beat them both home, and when they drove into the driveway Maggie had to park behind Mona. Her dad was already back to making coffee and sandwiches for the neighbors who were still working on sifting through the rubble for their things. She wasn't about to bitch at him about it. What was the worst that was going to happen? He was going to die pouring someone coffee? The truth was Red Cross had yet to make it to their street, so it didn't just seem like he was doing something worthwhile, he actually was.

Her neighbors only had a couple of more days to salvage what they could, and then the city was going to come in with front-end loaders and dump trucks and haul the rest off. After that they'd see who decided to build back and who was leaving. This was a poorer section of town, and property values had gone steadily down for years. The tornado had hit here and wiped out a few blocks, and then it had jumped over and taken out a few blocks around Maggie's old apartment complex, but the bulk of the damage to property—though no deaths— had happened on the south side of town where all the upper-middle-class lived, and of course that was where the Red Cross was.

She and Maggie unloaded the groceries from Maggie's car

and Tuesday from her truck and started for the house. Tuesday looked at her dad and asked, "Do you feel better?"

"Yes."

"But do you need a little boy's help?" Ally asked her dad with a wink.

"I sure do."

He smiled at her and he must have read the look on her face because he said, "I'm alright Ally, but I sure could use some help."

"I can help!" Tuesday was excited.

He had asked her what her dad was doing, and when she told him how much it was helping people Tuesday decided he wanted to help, too. So all the way home he kept saying how he knew how to make a sandwich, and then he went through all the steps over and over and over again.

So he stayed there with her dad while they brought the groceries back to the kitchen. Maggie started to unpack the groceries while Ally went to light the grill. Mona was in the back yard and she already had the grill going. She smiled at Ally. "I'm hungry, and I figured I'd get a jump on the fire."

"Thanks." Ally of course walked over and took over the fire-building chore. "How bad is my dad?"

"For a terminal cancer patient he's doing pretty good. It's not bad yet, Ally, but it's going to get there pretty quick now."

Ally nodded. She knew that because Maggie had already told her. She played with the fire a little then added some wood she'd cut for the purpose.

"I haven't been here since Helen died and.... Ally nothing has changed. My sister and her son are living with you now and there are still pictures of Helen everywhere and not a single thing has been moved inside or out. The plants have grown some; that's about it."

"Mona... the day Maggie moved in a tornado tore up our neighborhood. All we have done is work; this is the first time I've been home before dark since it happened."

"Are you going to let Maggie make this house hers, or are you just going to keep it as a shrine to Helen forever? Because frankly, Ally, I don't think that's fair to Maggie. You know to live in you and Helen's house instead of you and Maggie's house," Mona said, and Ally noticed Mona was drinking what had probably been the last of her hard cider supply, so it was a good thing she'd bought more.

"All of Helen's things are out of the closet," Ally defended. "Maggie's stuff is in there."

"And... when did Helen's stuff leave?"

Ally got very busy with the coals in the fire.

"When Ally?"

"Last week."

"And who got rid of them?"

"My dad."

"Are you going to let Maggie make this her home, too?"

Ally hadn't thought about moving stuff or changing stuff around. She found when she thought about it, it did make her a little nervous, but Mona was right. Maggie needed to be able to move stuff and put her own stuff up. "Maggie can do whatever she likes."

"And you aren't going to have a nervous breakdown?"

"I never said that," Ally laughed. She turned and faced Mona. "I'll be alright with it because it doesn't make sense to get all worked up over it. I'm the one who asked Maggie to live with me; it's stupid to think she wouldn't want to change anything. I love Maggie and I want her to be happy. If she's happy; I'm happy."

Maggie walked out with the steaks. When Ally looked at the fire it was just about perfect.

Mona took in a dramatic gasp. "My God, Maggie, are you now carting around the flesh of something that once had a nose?"

"Stop it now or you know I won't be able to eat," Maggie said, and handed the bowl to Ally.

"You aren't just carrying it you're going to eat it too?" Mona teased.

Ally put the grill on the fire then stuck the steaks on and closed the top. She walked over to the hose, turned it on and washed her hands and the bowl. When she turned the water off and turned around. Maggie was looking at her, a seductive twist to her lips, and Ally realized with a moment of shock that Maggie had been checking out her ass. *Wow, I'm a sex object! I don't know if I'm annoyed or turned on. Most probably turned on, after all everything she does is a turn on and now.... The hunter becomes the hunted.*

She ran over, grabbed Maggie, picked her up and spun around with her then put her down and kissed her. She just meant to give her a minor kiss, but when Maggie kissed her back it was clear that wasn't going to do it.

When Maggie finally let her have her mouth back, she moved to whisper in her ear, "The things I am going to do to you." Maggie's hands moved to grab the waist band on Ally's pants and she dragged her against her.

Maggie was normally really sexually aggressive, but not in the yard in broad daylight, in front of... well her sister and when Ally's dad and Tuesday were both still awake and.... *What did I do to get her all worked up? It can't just be because I ran and grabbed her.*

Maggie started working the snap on Ally's pants and Ally grabbed her hands.

"Honey, we have company, the baby's on the porch with dad, your sister is standing right there, and there are steaks on the grill," Ally said in a quick panic.

Maggie looked at her sister expectantly, and Mona laughed and said, "I'll watch the steaks and check on the baby, but make it quick."

And the next thing Ally knew she was being dragged by the front of her pants across the yard through the house and all the way to their bedroom. The minute she slid the lock closed Maggie was all over her.

"Maggie what the hell." Ally laughed.

"I need you, I need you." Maggie breathed against her lips, and then she pushed Ally against the door, Ally's pants fell to her ankles, and then Maggie was touching her and she still had no idea what had so turned Maggie on—which was a shame because she would have liked to be able to do it again.

"Your grandson's a nice-looking boy," George said as he took the sandwich and the coffee Sam handed him. Tuesday had gotten bored "helping." When no one had come for a while he'd gone to his room, grabbed a couple of trucks and a stuffed animal, and was playing on the front lawn where apparently a downed limb was something else altogether in his little mind.

"He's a humdinger," Sam said with a smile.

George was a middle-aged man Sam had seen at least three times a day for the last week. He was on his own out trying to save his house. It was badly damaged, not gone, and he was trying his best to repair it. His kids lived out of state, and his wife had been trying to have a nervous breakdown ever since Ally and Maggie had pulled her and George out of their storm shelter. It was in the ground and they had been safe, but part of the back wall of their house had landed on top of the shelter door and in the two hours that they'd been stuck in there unable to get anyone to hear them, George's wife—in his words—"lost her tiny little fucking mind."

So George was mostly on his own trying to gather what he could of their things, put them in the living room, and tarp them until a crew could come in to repair his house. He was staying in his bedroom to make sure people didn't rob him blind. His wife was apparently staying with her mother across state, and George had laughed one day and told Sam it was the best vacation he'd had in years.

"Jason said you blacked out on him and had to be taken to the hospital. You alright, Sam?"

"Nope," Sam said, but he managed a smile. "I'm dying of cancer, but not today."

"I'm awful sorry to hear that, Sam." And Sam could tell he was, too. "You sure have been a life saver for all of us this week, between feeding us and letting us use your bathroom."

"Ahh... This isn't my house, and I'd appreciate it if you didn't tell my daughter that I let everyone use her bathroom especially since she was trying to conserve the water." Sam smiled at all the times he'd repeated "If it's yellow; it's mellow."

George nodded then looked troubled and said, "I wasn't like those dumbass Suttons, but I have to tell you the truth. I wasn't too thrilled when your daughter and the Taggart girl moved in here. But they were always good neighbors. Our dog got loose one day and Myrtle was wigging out, well here comes Ally and Helen and they've caught the dog. We thanked them, got to talking to them, and realized they were just like everyone else. Everyone in the neighborhood—except maybe the Suttons, may they rest in peace—were just torn up when Helen got killed. Helen was a beautiful, wonderful girl, just a real doll. Since then Ally has still been a good neighbor, but obviously just sort of going through the paces if you know what I mean. The other night when I heard her chain saw and then when she pried that door open I was never so happy in my life to see two people as I was your kid and her new girlfriend, and when I saw the new girlfriend...." He rolled his eyes. "Well, it was obvious why Ally's smile is right back to what it used to be. Helen was a looker, but this new girl…." He rolled his eyes again and Sam laughed. "I owe them big time. Be sure to tell them how much we appreciate them. Let them know they ever need anything all they have to do is call."

"I will," Sam said.

Tuesday came trotting up with the stuffed animal. He looked up at George, apparently just noticing he was there. "Want some coffee?"

"I have some, thank you."

Tuesday frowned and looked at Sam. "I was supposed to help."

"I could use some sugar," George said.

Tuesday picked up one of the cubes in fingers that could have been cleaner. He had been fascinated with the cubes the minute Sam showed them to him. "One lump or two?" Tuesday said, just like Sam had taught him.

"One." George smiled and let him drop it into his cup sweat, grass stains and all. "Thank you very much."

"It was nothing," Tuesday said, and got off the porch and went back to playing.

Sam chuckled and shook his head.

George went back to work and Sam watched the boy play. It was about time for him to call it a night, but he was tired and sitting there was as good as sitting anywhere else. He was enjoying watching the boy obviously spinning a whole story about his toys and the tree limb.

Mona came out on the porch and sat in the other chair they had brought out there. "Steaks are done and I whipped up a salad if you're ready to eat. No sense waiting for Maggie and Ally; I have no idea when they'll be ready for dinner."

"Where are they?" Sam said looking at all three vehicles in the driveway.

"I'll give you one guess," Maggie said, cocking her eyes at him.

Sam chuckled. "I can wait to eat if you can."

Mona smiled a knowing smile. "If we eat on the back deck we probably won't be able to hear them."

"Ha, ha, Mona," Maggie said, walking out the front door pulling her hair back with a hair band. No doubt about it, Maggie was a beautiful, sensuous woman. Since Ally liked girls, who could blame her for wanting to be with her... well, all of the time?

As if reading his mind Mona turned to him and said, "It wasn't Ally; it was all her. Poor Ally never had a chance once Maggie decided she wanted her, and I'm not just talking about twenty minutes ago."

Maggie smiled unashamed, and said as if it explained everything, "Ally was singing today."

She walked down in the yard and started talking to her son listening intently as he explained to her what he was playing.

"Well," Sam said smiling at Mona. "Ally has always had a beautiful voice."

They ate dinner on the back deck. When the mosquitoes decided to come out Sam went to the living room as the women gathered everything up and brought it inside. He didn't have much of an appetite, but it was still a lot more than Jenny had on the chemo, and food still tasted like food to him most days.

He sat down and turned on the TV; he had just missed the news. Ally didn't watch the news, at least not on purpose. She said it depressed her. But since she'd been working so late all week and Maggie was usually in the kitchen cooking dinner when it was on, he'd been able to watch it. He still wanted to know what was going on in the world. *Why? Why do I care what's happening across the street much less across the world? It's not like I'm going to live to even vote in the next election and now.... I wouldn't have any idea how to vote. I guess I'd have to vote for whoever I thought was going to make Ally and Maggie's lives easier.* He did want to know what was going on, but he wouldn't even ask to make Ally suffer through the news. This was her house. She didn't have to take him in, had no reason to, but she had and he wanted to be as little trouble as he could be. He decided he would check into getting a short-term subscription to the local paper. He could probably get it on line and just read it off his computer screen.

Mona walked in then, closely followed by Maggie. Mona walked over and hugged him, making him feel warm. Like her sister she was extremely kind hearted. "Take care of yourself, there's no sense dying till you have to."

"I will, and thanks for everything, Mona," Sam said.

"Sam, do you have a penny?" Maggie asked. "I lost mine."

Mona laughed. "You need a new car, Maggie."

Maggie smiled at her. "Why? Chad knows I don't have any extra money."

"I think you're forgetting that you have two incomes now."

"Hum, you may have a point."

Sam was sure he couldn't guess how a penny was going to get Maggie a new car. He looked in his pocket, pulled a penny out, and handed it to her anyway, but couldn't help asking, "What do you need it for?"

"I broke the key off in the ignition switch about a month ago," Maggie said with a smile. She held the penny up, "But on the plus side I can now start it with a penny."

"You need a new car," Mona said again, following Maggie out of the house.

"My car is fine," Maggie said.

Sam knew what they were doing. Maggie had to move her car so that Mona could get out. When Maggie walked back in she locked the front door and then walked over and tried to give him his penny back.

He smiled up at her. "Oh, it's your car key now, dear."

"There's really nothing wrong with my car," she said. She walked over and dropped it on the table by the door. "I'll just put my key here with Ally's."

"I'm just saying you can do whatever you like to the house," Ally said. She was lying in bed holding Maggie.

"I'm not in any big hurry to change things, and I can't believe Mona was meddling…. You know, again," Maggie said.

"In the morning why don't we clean the rest of my crap out of Tuesday's room and stick it in the shop? Then we can go to the hardware store and get a new window for the bathroom and a bundle of shingles because I'm going to have to replace a bunch of them on the roof. Let's get paint for Tuesday's room and…"

"Honey, what happened to resting this weekend?" Maggie asked with a sigh.

"If we did all of the stuff I just said, it would still be like a vacation after the last few weeks I've put in."

"Can we just play it by ear, baby, see how you feel in the morning? I feel like we've been running for weeks, and I just

want to spend time with you. Tuesday has missed you and....
Ally you know your dad doesn't have much longer. You might
want to actually spend some time with him."

"Alright.... But I'm still moving my junk and fixing the
window, and before you bitch even with a trip to the lumber
yard it's probably only going to take me a couple of hours,"
Ally said. "Maggie, what would you like?"

"You know what I like."

"I suppose I do." She kissed the back of Maggie's neck.
"But I mean... you know if you could have your dream home....
Okay, maybe not your dream home because I'm an okay
carpenter, but not the best. What would you like in the yard?"

"An organic vegetable garden, an orchard, and hens so
we could have our own eggs," she said in one breath, and
then she was wiggling out of Ally's arms. She turned the
bedside lamp on and went to the closet. She came out after
a few minutes with a spiral notebook which had so much
stuff glued to the pages that it was bulging. Ally sat up in bed
and Maggie crawled up beside her and opened the book and
then she was just showing her what had to be years of
dreaming of having her own yard and garden. She was rattling
a mile a minute, and Ally got caught up in her excitement
because after all she loved to design landscapes and some of
the ideas Maggie had or had cut out of magazines and
catalogued looked like a lot of fun. About half way through
the book Ally laughed.

"What?" Maggie asked with a grin.

"We'd need about twice as much yard to do everything
you want to do."

"Oh, come on, I've seen you accommodate the customers
by sticking more than this into a smaller space."

"Yes and it's always my favorite thing to pull a rabbit right
out of my ass," Ally grumbled.

Maggie laughed and kissed Ally's cheek. "I know we can't
do it all. This was just my wish book for if I ever had a yard."

"Honey, are you only with me to get my yard?"

"Well it is one of your more attractive features."

It took considerably more than a couple of hours to get all
the stuff out of Tuesday's room and take it to the shop and
fix the window, mostly because getting the old frame out
turned into a major fiasco. Ally wasn't surprised at all that

Maggie was good help. After all she'd worked with Maggie for years. Maggie mostly worked in the office, but if Ally needed an extra hand or someone called in sick, Maggie often took up the slack.

The whole time she was on the ladder trying to fix the window her Dad stood on the ground at the foot of it and tried to tell her what to do. She was getting madder and madder. Just before she told him to leave her the fuck alone she took a deep breath and actually listened to him.

"Ally, just cut through the old frame with your saws-all in several places and then yank out the pieces. After all, you aren't going to use the window again." She realized that was what he'd been trying to get her to do for the last thirty minutes and that it made perfect sense. Before she had time to come down to get the saw Maggie had already handed it up to her.

Of course the old window frame was out in less than ten minutes, and she was putting the new window back in. But of course him being right only further aggravated her. She was glad when he took Tuesday and went back to the porch to continue to feed the masses coffee and sandwiches, so maybe he knew he was getting on her last nerve.

She moved the ladder from the side of the house to the back so that she could get on the roof to fix the shingles, and that was when she and Maggie had the first real fight they'd had since Maggie had stopped doing her PT after the accident.

"Come on, Ally, let's just take the rest of the day…"

"It's supposed to rain tonight and I'm not sure the roof won't leak. It will only take me maybe an hour," Ally said, grabbed the bundle of shingles and started up.

"No, Ally," Maggie said firmly then she sighed. "At least bust the bundle in half, that's too heavy for you to carry up the ladder."

"I can carry a full bundle of shingles up a ladder."

"You can, but you shouldn't, and you know it."

But of course Maggie saying that just made Ally that much more determined to do it. She started up the ladder with the bundle, and Maggie was silent but she held the ladder for Ally anyway, and of course about half way up Ally realized that Maggie—like her dad had been earlier—was one hundred percent right. The bundle was way too heavy for her road-kill leg on the ladder. But then she *had* to do it. By the time she made it to the roof her leg was throbbing. She dropped the bundle and then sat down beside it.

Maggie had moved away from the ladder so she could see Ally on the roof. "Ally, are you alright?"

She wasn't but of course she couldn't tell Maggie that, so instead she shouted back at her. "I'm fine! Would everyone just leave me the fuck alone! I'm fine. I existed for five years just fine without everyone telling me what to do!"

"Don't you yell at me, Ally Taggart!" Maggie shouted, and then she walked around to the front of the house. Ally pulled up her pants leg and readjusted the straps on her brace as if trying to convince herself that was all that was wrong.

"Stupid leg," she whispered in disgust. "I hate this stupid, fucking leg, and why am I so pissed off today, why?" In her head she started counting days. *No, I'm weeks away from my period, and I only ever have one day of PMS anyway.*

She might have figured it out right then and quit being such a bitch, but Maggie showed up to watch her no doubt because she was worried about her because.... It had been a stupid butch thing to do. Maggie could tell she was hurt because it was Maggie, and even though Maggie was now obviously every bit as mad as Ally was, Maggie was going to come and keep an eye on her *because she loves me and she's afraid I'm going to get hurt acting like an ass.*

And this really pissed Ally off, so she got right up and started pulling the damaged shingles off and putting the new ones on. She was finishing the last one when she realized two things. First, it was more than stupid to have brought the whole thing up there because she'd used less than half the bundle and her leg was hurting so bad and was so weak that she'd had to crawl to do the last three shingles. And second, now she had no idea how she was going to get off the God damned roof because there was no way she could get down that ladder.

Maggie appeared seemingly out of thin air. She picked up what was left of the bundle of shingles, walked over and dropped it off the roof onto the back deck, then she walked over to Ally and looked down at her. "So hard head, how bad are you hurt?"

"I'm not," Ally hissed.

"You're a fucking liar!" Maggie yelled, then lowered her voice. "Would it have killed you to listen to me?"

"I'm not a fucking invalid, Maggie!"

"No, but if you keep pushing yourself to do shit you shouldn't you will be," and it was clear Maggie was working on her calm. Because the truth was—and Ally knew it—that Maggie worked so hard at creating inner peace and balancing her energy because Maggie was a hot head. "Are you going to let me work on your leg so you can get off the roof?"

"I'm fine."

"Alright then," Maggie turned and started down the roof towards the ladder. Half way there she turned around, and that was when Maggie lost it. "You stupid-assed butch, if I leave you on this fucking roof I'm going to go right down and call Mitch to come get you with the cherry picker. Now what's more embarrassing, admitting that you screwed yourself completely up because you wouldn't listen to me, listen to me now and let me fix it, or having Mitch and a crew come to save your ass because we both know you can't get off this roof by yourself right now."

"Is everything alright?" her dad yelled up at them.

"Everything is fine!" Ally glared at Maggie as if everything was Maggie's fault.

Maggie turned around and started for the ladder.

Sam walked back up on the porch and sat down.

Tuesday looked at him.

"They're fine," he said.

"They don't sound fine; they sound mad," Tuesday said.

"They might be, but they're still fine, Tuesday. People can get mad at each other. It doesn't mean they no longer love each other. They won't *stay* mad at each other."

"But I don't want them to be mad," Tuesday said with a frown.

"You know, Sport, by the time they come down I doubt they'll be mad anymore."

Tuesday sighed, "You forgot my name again, didn't you?"

Ally looked from Maggie's departing back to her leg and back again. Maggie was right. She couldn't get off the roof without help, and Ally would almost bet money that Maggie would call Mitch the minute she got to a phone. "Maggie, wait."

Maggie turned and looked at her expectantly. "You're right.

You were right about everything. I should have stopped for the day, I shouldn't have tried to carry a whole bundle, and my leg is so completely fucked up right now that if you can't fix it Mitch will have to come and get me, and yes that would be more embarrassing."

Maggie walked up the roof and sat beside her. She took her hand and held it, and Ally started to cry. She just didn't do that, so she wondered if maybe she'd done the math wrong and she did have PMS.

"Oh baby, it's alright. I'll fix it and we'll get you off the roof."

"I'm sorry, Maggie."

"I'm sorry, too. I knew you were in a mood. I should have been less bossy and more persuasive." She kissed Ally's cheek.

"But why am I in such a mood? I was in such a good mood this morning." Ally sniffled and dried her face on her shirt sleeve.

"Honey, you were trying to fix the window and your dad was telling you what to do the whole time because he couldn't really help."

"I didn't want his help because I do that kind of shit all the time and I didn't need his help. He was just making me a nervous wreck, and when his idea made it much easier than anything I would have done, it just made me even madder. I just needed to do something to prove to him and to you that I didn't need his help…"

"I'm sorry because I know now that when I told you that you shouldn't do this, it just made it that much worse. But Ally, you ought to know that I don't think there is anything you can't do. I just didn't want you to get hurt, and selfishly I wanted you to get some actual rest and spend some time with me not working." Maggie let go of her hand and moved to help Ally pull her pants leg up. Maggie took the brace off and looked up at Ally with tears in her eyes. Ally knew what that meant, that meant her leg was about to hurt like a bitch.

"But it will feel better after you do it, Maggie," Ally reminded. She went ahead and lay down on the roof in case she might do something as wimpy as pass out. "I don't like it when anyone does what he did, Maggie, but I just realized why it made me so mad when *he* did it. Where was he when I really needed him? He was passing judgement on me, leaving me to fend for myself. I don't need him now, my life is great, and I just wanted him to leave me alone and let me do it my way even if it was wrong. So then I thought I needed to do this to prove some point and what did I prove? That I can be a stupid asshole, and we already knew that."

Maggie smiled and kept massaging her leg.

"I shouldn't have taken my shit out on you, Maggie, not at all. I know, have always known, that you are in my corner, you've always had my back."

"And you've always had mine. Because of that we have always been able to yell at each other and know all will be forgiven. Mostly you shouldn't take your shit out on yourself," and that was when she snapped Ally's leg back into place and Ally was glad she was lying down because she didn't black out, but if she'd been sitting up she probably would have. Maggie lay down on the roof on her side beside Ally and put her arm around her. "I got so mad at you because I knew you were going to hurt yourself just to make a stupid point."

"I'm such a fuck up; I'm so sorry, baby." Ally wrapped her arms around her.

"It's a lot, Ally. Me and Tuesday would be enough, but then there is your dad, and he's trying so hard to fix things with you before he dies, and then the whole town gets blown to pieces."

"Jesus, what are you two over-sexed morons doing now?" Mona called from the ground with a laugh.

"Wouldn't you like to know?" Ally yelled back.

CHAPTER 8

*If you aren't sure why you're feeling inadequate, find a
passive aggressive; they'll tell you.*

Maggie wouldn't have minded at all if Mona had been alone
or with anyone else, but she was with their mother, Agnes,
who had never met Ally, and who Ally only knew from what
Helen, Mona, and Maggie had told her. None of which was
good, and all of which was unfortunately true.

Maggie really just wanted to spend some time working on
Ally's leg and then actually get to the resting part of the day,
but in true Agnes fashion she was bound and determined to
make the storm that had killed twelve people and trashed
their neighborhood all about her.

As Maggie helped Ally down the ladder and off the roof,
she whispered in Ally's ear, "Do yourself a favor; go to our
room and stay there. I'll tell her you're hurt and...."

"I have to meet her sooner or later, but we will stop and
get my crutches. That way she will believe it if I say I have to
go lay down."

"Just remember everything I told you about her. She's
bipolar, but that's the good news. She's also a classic
narcissist, so she's never ever wrong, and everything that
happens to her is someone else's fault. She's passive-
aggressive, so she's never really happy unless she can make
other people feel like total crap." Maggie frankly couldn't think
of a worse time for her mother to show up except that was
the only thing her mother was really good at, finding the
moment when you least wanted to see anyone and especially
didn't want to see her and then.... There she was. It was like
her super power.

By the time they were walking out the front door, Agnes
had Tuesday in a bear hug and was crying all over him. "Oh
my poor children, when I think of how close I came to losing
you all." Maggie walked over to Mona and pulled her to the
side of the yard.

"What the hell, Mona? Why did you bring her here?" Maggie hissed. "What did I ever do to you?"

"Let me guess the timing couldn't have been worse," Mona said, knowing. "I actually had a date. He had just come to pick me up and Mom showed up a few minutes later. It's a good thing I didn't think he was my soul mate because I doubt I'll ever see him again."

"Ally and I just had our first fight.... Since we've been together, that is." Right after Helen died when she was forcing Ally to do PT they had gotten into fights that made the one they just had seem like not much more than a nasty disagreement.

"And you were what, going to have make-up sex on the roof?"

"No." Maggie laughed. "It's a long story, but Mother.... None of us needs Mother, and I hope she doesn't make me have to tell her that yet again." Maggie was glad when she saw her mother put Tuesday down. He immediately went to Ally and wanted to be picked up no doubt because her mother had traumatized him.

Ally wrestled with her crutches and then picked Tuesday up. Before Maggie knew it her mom was hugging her. Maggie reluctantly hugged her back and immediately the crap started as her mother whispered in her ear, "Really, Maggie, couldn't you do better than your dead friend's crippled girlfriend?"

"Mother, don't start," Maggie said, pushing away from her. Of course she never should have said that because it was like issuing a challenge.

Ally felt like a huge, raw nerve. She was twitching more than normal, her leg hurt, and she felt like a heel for fighting with Maggie when she wasn't really mad at Maggie at all. She was working hard at not being pissed at her dad, and any other day would have been a better time to meet Maggie's mother than today was.

Chickening completely out she decided she wanted to put off the inevitable meeting at least a little longer. "I have to go put my tools away," Ally said. Tuesday wanted to go with her, so she put him down took his hand and started in the house.

"I better help you," Maggie said, and in seconds she was with them. To the look on Ally's face as they walked through the front door Maggie whispered. "Hey, I don't want to talk to her either. I know you can do it yourself but...."

"You know what, Maggie? The truth is right now I would kind of like the help," Ally said. "I know I deserve it on more than one level, but my leg is still killing me."

"You don't deserve it, and I need to do a bunch more work on it," Maggie said. "We can do it after we put all the tools up."

"How long do you think we can avoid your mother?" Ally asked with a laugh.

"She'll probably come in there while I'm trying to work on you, and I know you don't like people to see your leg, and I'm not going to be able to do the voodoo that I do so well with her around sucking all the life out of all living things."

Tuesday turned and looked up at Maggie. "Are you talking about Grand Sugar?"

"Grand Sugar." Ally made a face.

"Oh yes, because my unplanned pregnancy was such a bother to her, don't you know, what with her being *way* too young to be a grandmother. She has him call her that," Maggie whispered in Ally's ear.

"Seems to me that if your youngest child is old enough to have a child, you're old enough to be a friggin' grandmother." They were on the back deck and she pulled the ladder down and started carrying it to the shop as Maggie picked up the stack of new shingles and followed her. Tuesday ran around picking up the busted shingles she'd thrown off the roof haphazardly into the yard. "Grand Sugar, bluck," Ally grumbled. There were things that when she heard them set her teeth on edge. This made-up, cutesy fucking name for an obvious bitch was one of them. They had put all the tools away and now she and Maggie were helping Tuesday pick up the broken shingles. When she and Maggie got to the trash can at the same time Ally asked, "Baby, what's your mother's name?"

"Agnes," Maggie said.

"Well I like that better than Grand Sugar." She made a face and Maggie laughed. Tuesday forgot he was "helping" and went to get his bunny out of the cage.

"Allybaba, can I take Jack to meet Grand Sugar?"

"Bluck." Ally shuddered. "Sure, Honey."

Tuesday got his rabbit and took off.

Sam knew it was his fault the kids had a fight, but by the time he realized he was pissing his daughter completely off the damage was already done. And here was the thing. His father had always done the same thing to him, so he should have known how irritating it was except that now he knew exactly why his father had done it. Because Sam was now in the same place his father had been. He couldn't really help physically anymore, but he had a lifetime of experience that Ally didn't have, and he just wanted so badly to help her. But she didn't care what he knew, she just wanted to do it herself and impress him and her woman, to show them that she knew what she was doing, too.

If there was an afterlife where you saw your dead loved ones, he was going to have to look his dad up and apologize for all the times he yelled at him to, "Just get off my back I know what I'm doing." Because five seconds watching his daughter do something he could have done easily just ten years ago and he was standing their telling her every move to make and getting agitated when she didn't listen and when she did and it worked.... *Well then it was all I could do to keep from yelling out I told you to do that an hour ago if you'd only listened to me and.... Well that was exactly the kind of shit my dad used to do to me that got on my last nerve.*

And because of the way Ally lived in the world if they'd been in each other's lives the last twenty years and he had let her be herself they would have had more a father-son relationship than a father-daughter one. Then he realized something else. *Even in my own head I no longer call her Alice because she's not that little girl anymore, she's a completely different person. She's Ally. Ally killed and buried Alice a long time ago, and now I have a different child.*

Maggie's mother was standing in the middle of the lawn looking out in all directions at the devastation around them. Mona walked up to Sam and seeing his smile said in a whisper, "She's crazier than a shit house rat."

"That's what you and Maggie already told me, and yet I think I would have guessed," Sam said. "But that's not what I was smiling about. I just realized that Ally is my son."

"You do know not to tell her that, right? Gay people can get all sorts of weird about gender crap."

He nodded and asked in a whisper, motioning to the woman

in the middle of the yard, "What is she doing?"

"Working herself into a frenzy so that she can pretend to be as touched by this disaster as the people Ally and Maggie pulled out of the rubble. She's a piece of work; I shouldn't have brought her over here. She just kept demanding I do so, saying she had to see them to make sure they were really alright. Here's what sucks; no matter how shitty your parents are you still feel like you have to do what they tell you."

"As far as I know she hasn't even called and it's been...." He tried but couldn't remember exactly how long, the days all ran together for him now. "...a while."

"Thank you, Sam, that's what I said." Mona flopped in the chair beside him looking at her mother's back. "It's simple. She was super busy doing something she thought was oh so important and completely missed the fact that her children and grandchild lived in the town decimated by the tornado till her best friend of the week pointed out that she should be some concerned that her children and her grandson were in the middle of a disaster."

"My wife was like that, everything for show. I don't think she ever had a real emotion.... No, that's not true. When I first met her she was wonderful, but after we got married she turned into her mother."

"Let's pray for Ally's sake that Maggie doesn't turn into our mother. Let's just say the most interesting thing about mother is that she's a total bitch. Her hobby is training new friends to be enemies."

"Yep, that sounds like the girls' mother. Jenny changed as soon as we got married, but the real changes didn't happen till she had Carol. In those days you didn't hear about postpartum depression. She got over it pretty quick and she just loved Carol, but when Ally was born Jenny was worse, and she never really wanted anything to do with Ally. After Ally was born she didn't want anything to do with me, either. Someone ignores you long enough it doesn't take much to turn your head, and Dedra actually wanted me." He looked quickly around to make sure no one was in hearing range then asked, "Have you ever experienced passion, Mona?"

"I have.... It's been a while, but I remember it."

"When I was with Dedra I felt alive really alive for the first time in years. I should have fought for that, but I didn't. All I could think was that I was committing a horrible sin for which I'd have to pay. But that didn't stop me just kept me from fully enjoying it; do you know what I mean?"

Mona nodded. "It feels too good to quit, but you know eventually you'll have to pay for it."

"And of course I did. Jenny found out and she brought the hammer down. If I didn't do things her way she'd make sure I never saw my kids again. That would have killed me, and she loved Carol so Carol would have been fine, but Ally... She would have killed Ally just to hurt me because you see I love Carol, but she never had my heart the way Ally did. I figured Jenny's garbage was the good Lord's way of telling me I had taken a wrong path; it was my cross to bear. So I just gave up, kissed that bitch's ass, and let her drag us to that hateful church where that pervert put his filthy hands...."

"What, Sam?" Mona prompted when he stopped talking.

He needed to talk to someone because it was eating him up. "He molested Ally, and she told her stinking mother, but I never knew. Fifteen years later he molested my grandson, Kyle. Jenny told me to beat my child because she was queer, and I did, and she told me to put my child out, and I did that, too, but everything looked fine to those idiots at that church. We had us a jet plane, first class ticket to heaven in their minds because we put our child out because she was an abomination before God. We were the pillars of that church, and there was a cancer there that ate our souls, and no one cared till the monster did it again in another town to a bunch of other kids and the chickens, as they say, came home to roost."

"Who molested Ally?"

"Labon Parish did, the same creep they locked up down in Monroe two years ago, and until Ally told me I never knew because my wife—who never grew tired of rubbing my infidelity in my face—never said a word about it. She and Carol both knew. They knew what he did to Ally and they let Kyle be alone with him, and do you know why?"

Mona shook her head.

"Because they thought Ally lied; they thought she made it up. She was ten years old. I should have taken her and Dedra and run off as far as I could from that place and those people. Instead I just immersed myself in their lies and crap and became part of it, because I was a damn coward. Afraid to try something different because what if it was as bad, or worse than what I already had? I let myself be as blind, as ignorant, and as hateful as they were because it made the bitter pill I had to swallow easier if there was no choice—and with my religion there wasn't. I'm not to blame for what happened to Kyle, but what happened to those kids in that other town? That's my fault. And what happened to Ally, that's my fault, too, because I never should have made her grow up in that house with that hateful bitch."

Agnes walked up on the porch then, and Sam fell silent. "I must go talk to your sister; she simply cannot live here in the middle of this debris field. The energy is much too negative. She needs to move back in with you till she can find someplace safe for her and her son. She doesn't need to carry this girlfriend of hers around."

She looked at Sam. "No offense."

Sam looked at Mona then he sat his jaw and stood up. He caught and held Agnes's gaze. "Don't you dare start any crap for my girl, she's been through enough. Don't come up in here under the guise of caring about Maggie and Tuesday, and try to ruin what they have with Ally. Why don't you make like a baby and go?"

Mona actually giggled, and when her mother cut her a look she just shrugged and said, "Don't start shit if you don't want stink, Mother."

"Now see here, old man, I don't know who you think you are…"

"I think I'm Ally's dad, and that I'm way behind on acting like a father to her. I'm not going to live much longer, but while I'm alive no one, not you or any other asshole, is going to come up in here and try to start shit for her and Maggie and the boy. If you're smart, you'll try to learn something from my mistakes and not waste what time you have running from being a parent to your children."

They were almost to the front door when Ally put up a hand and stopped Maggie.

She had hold of Tuesday's hand, so she put a finger over his lips and said, "Go play in your room for a minute."

He nodded, thinking it was a game and took off.

Through the half-opened door Maggie could hear her mother. "You've got a lot of nerve. I've been worried sick about my kids and Tuesday."

"Really? Then why when this one has heart surgery is it her brother and sister that take care of her, and why when that one is in the middle of a tornado does it take you this long to come and check on her? Why didn't you call? This is a perfectly nice home, and my daughter isn't a cripple that Maggie has to care for. She hurt her leg fixing the roof because you see Ally takes good care of them, a lot better care than say you ever have. This girl here, she raised herself and then she raised your other two kids. Your kind of help those kids in there don't need. Ally and Maggie have a whole world of people telling them they shouldn't be together; they don't need you. What's your reason for trying to cause trouble? You just want to make drama."

"That was never my intension. I just want something better for my kids."

"That's such crap, Mom. Maggie and Tuesday were living in an efficiency apartment in a building that is now completely gone. Ally *is* the 'something better' you should want for Maggie. It's always the same old thing. You start something trying to get a rise out of someone, and then when you do it's like a lovely field trip to victim land for you. You came, you saw, you picked a fight you, go home and tell all your friends how everyone abuses you. Then you don't have to lift a finger to actually help anyone. If Maggie and Tuesday hadn't been with Ally they'd be dead right now. That's what any other mother on planet earth would be thinking; she wouldn't be bitching about where they are, she'd just be thanking God that they weren't dead."

"I don't have to stand here and be insulted like this."

"No, because you could get on your broom stick and go," Sam said.

Maggie actually laughed and she slapped her hand over her mouth.

Ally moved over to her and whispered in her ear, "Should we try to stop them?"

"Why? If Mother said something that stirred both Sam and Mona up this much, it had to be bad. It may be chicken shit, but I'd just as soon let them fight with her. Come on, let's go to Tuesday's room and he can play while I work on your leg a bit. Suddenly the energy doesn't feel bad at all."

"But what color, Tuesday, what color?" Ally asked from

where she lay on his little bed.

"Green... or blue... or yellow," Tuesday said, Maggie and Ally laughed.

"Pick a color, one color to paint your room, Tuesday," Maggie said.

"Yellow... or blue... or green... maybe green... or yellow... or blue."

This time Maggie and Ally cracked up.

He looked at them with total disgust. "You aren't helping. It's hard to decide. Why can't I have all three?"

"Because paint is expensive, son," Maggie said.

"It's probably going to take nearly three gallons to paint it anyway. We could do all three colors, Maggie," Ally said, and then Maggie could see the wheels turning. "We could do stripes."

"Yeah!" Tuesday said.

"I could paint a mural."

"Yeah!" Tuesday said, then shook his head. "I don't know what that is."

"It's a lot of work is what it is, and unnecessary," Maggie said.

"Why ya gottah be like that, Maggie, all stifling my creativity?"

"You're the one who moved all your painting stuff out to the shop building," Maggie said.

"What would you paint, Allybaba?" And for a second Maggie was just impressed that at under three Tuesday could figure out that if Ally needed painting supplies, a mural must be a painting.

"What do you want me to paint, Tuesday?"

"You're going to make *me* a painting?"

"Yes, right on the wall, any wall in your room what do you want."

"A tree."

"A tree?"

"Yes, I like trees, Allybaba."

"Is that it?"

"A river with a boat... no a pirate ship, and a rocket in the sky, and the moon, and a Taggart's gnome. That's all; nothing else."

Ally smiled and looked at Maggie.

"What?"

"Well, he's kind of like you; he wants to cram everything into a very small space." Then seeing the look Maggie gave her, she quickly added as she turned red. "Like with the yard. I was talking about the yard."

Mona walked in and Maggie turned to face her. Mona grinned, knowing. "So are you guys hiding in here so that you didn't have to be part of the 'Oh, goody, Mommy's come to visit' fight?"

"Yes," Maggie said.

"Why is everyone so mad today?" Tuesday asked, shaking his head.

"Because darkness has fallen on our town, you know mother," Mona said, shrugging. "Listen, in true mother fashion, realizing that she is on the verge of losing any connection with her kids—which of course she is going to need when she gets old, she has apologized to me and Sam and wants to take everyone to dinner."

"Why God, why," Maggie said, shaking her fist at the universe in general. She looked at the confused look on Ally's face. "Mother treats restaurants like Switzerland; they are neutral territory, and she knows we won't show our asses in public. However be warned it won't stop her showing hers if the mood strikes her."

"Is she paying?" Ally asked Mona.

"Hells yes, or I ain't going," Mona said.

"Okay, let's go," Ally said.

"Mona, remember your diet."

"I'll let you order for me, Maggie."

Sam put his coffee and sandwich stuff away for the night with some help from Maggie and Mona then said he wasn't feeling well and wanted to stay home. Mostly he didn't want to be around that woman at all, but then neither did her own kids, so he didn't feel bad about it. He did feel sorry for the kids, though.

He got on his lap top, got online, found the local paper, paid for it with his credit card and started to read it on his screen. Though now they had all left he supposed he could have watched the news on TV. He shrugged and kept reading. He had shocked Ally when she realized he was better with a computer than she was. He reminded her that he had always loved technical gizmos and gadgets.

He had read through most of that day's paper when a byline caught his eye and held it. His blood ran cold. What the hell kind of world did they live in? The Freedom of Religion act was still front page news; they expected the legislature to pass it later that month. This article would have been hidden nearly in the back of the paper. Convicted child molester Parish slated for possible early release because of hardship. Parish claimed he had been gang raped by the other prisoners and since he was diabetic he was having trouble healing from his injuries. His attorney said he would not be a danger to the community. If they released him he would be put on probation and be registered as a sex offender. He wouldn't be allowed around kids at all. Monroe's prosecuting attorney said Parish's accusations of brutality and hardship were unwarranted, that he was a dangerous criminal that they planned to work to keep behind bars, but Sam got a bad feeling in his gut.

He wondered how lawyers slept at night. Parish's attorney went on and on about the brutality of Parish's treatment with no thought at all to the hell Parish had inflicted on his victims. On families that were ruined and lives tainted by his horror. No, Parish's lawyer was all worried about his client's rights. It made Sam wonder what sort of man the lawyer was, if maybe he didn't also secretly molest children for a hobby.

Sam needed to go to that hearing. He needed to tell the court what sort of monster Parish was. Tell them what his actions did to those kids and their families. How nothing was ever the same.

And he would if he lived that long and was well enough to do so.

Agnes took them to an Asian restaurant. "I thought about this nice little Middle Eastern place, but then I remembered you were in the war," Maggie's mother said to Ally as the waitress brought the menus to their table.

"You were in the war?" Tuesday asked Ally eyes big.

"Thanks, Mom, thanks a lot," Maggie said with a sigh.

"Yes I was, Tuesday," Ally said to him, and then to Maggie's mother, "But I don't have a PTSD episode if I eat Middle Eastern food."

"Allybaba..." He handed her the menu he'd been looking at. "...order me something I like. You know I can't read."

"Why doesn't he just call you Ally?" Agnes asked.

Mona cut her mother a look. "Gee, I don't know Mom, why doesn't he call you Agnes, or I don't know, grandmother? Grand Sugar makes me want to take a shot of insulin every time I hear it. Oh but wait, Tuesday decided to call her Allybaba, and you told him he had to call you Grand Sugar, so only one of those can be blamed on the baby," Mona said, and Ally decided she liked Mona more and more all the time.

The waitress came and they all ordered, with Agnes doing that thing that in Ally's mind meant you were bound to be eating human spit. She could order nothing right off the menu. No, it was "do you have this" and "could I get it without this, that and the other thing?" "Could I get this instead of that, and could you add something else, and if you don't have that could you substitute this for that and could it be served in a blue glass vase with a sprig of mint and a red rose?" It was ridiculous.

There was literally nothing the woman did that wasn't either to draw attention to herself or that wasn't all to serve her. Yet as far as Ally could see, absolutely the only thing the least bit interesting about her was that she was a total bitch.

Agnes said she had COPD. To hear her talk it was a horrible affliction she didn't ask for, and the universe had made her life hard with it. Half way through dinner she ran outside to smoke a cigarette because apparently it was bullshit that smoking caused her disease and in her words she loved everything about smoking.

All of her children's lives she did whatever the hell she wanted, and thought of them really not at all until it was time to put on a show others could see. She would go to every event they had at school then let them get off the bus and go to an empty house. She left them with whoever would watch them, fed them when she felt like it if she did. She put on a play for the world of being super mom, but anyone who knew her knew that her children had never ever come first. Yet now she expected them to drop everything because she wanted to pretend to be concerned. She seemed completely oblivious as to why they had zero respect for her.

And she just kept taking pictures. No doubt so she could show all her friends and make them believe that she gave a diddly shit about her kids.

Ally had been so busy that she didn't know till she, Maggie, and Tuesday were driving to the restaurant in her truck that the bitch not only had never called Maggie to check on her since the tornado, but she hadn't bothered to call either Mona or Maggie and tell them she was coming.

And she knew more about Agnes from what Helen had told her than she did because of anything Maggie had said. When she thought back on it she should have known by the reams of personal information Helen had about Maggie that they had at one time been more than just friends.

Chad had met them there, and for his part he was trying to just be invisible. He knew that Ally and Maggie were together, but hadn't really seen them "together" till then, and it was clear that he wasn't entirely comfortable with them. Not because he was a homophobe, but because he'd had a huge crush on Helen and had always resented that she wound up with Ally. Ally found herself wondering if Chad knew Helen had also slept with his sister. And then she knew, *For all his faults he's very loyal to his sisters. He never had a crush on Helen; he knew his sister loved her, that's why he couldn't stand that I was with Helen because he knew Maggie loved her. Dammit, that's what Maggie meant. That's why she expected me to be more upset. She never got over Helen. She was still in love with Helen when she died. That's why she fell completely apart, and that's why she only dated men, because if she couldn't have Helen she just wasn't interested in any other woman. And now that I know that... am I mad? No, but I feel bad that I took Helen away from Maggie. But I didn't. They hadn't been together since high school. Helen wasn't in love with Maggie, but that didn't stop Maggie from loving Helen and... we should be on Jerry Springer for God's sake!*

The fact that Ally got through the entire meal without telling the old bitch to eat shit and die was nothing short of a miracle. Her leg hurt and driving was a bitch, but she was so happy to escape Agnes she hardly noticed the pain.

"She asked if she could come help us tomorrow, and I told her I'd rather eat broken glass," Maggie said. "I... Would it be too much to ask that we just have a day where nothing weird or stupid happens and we don't have to deal with any shit?"

"Apparently yes. You know what would be great? If we could just put your mom and my sister Carol in a cage, give them hedge trimmers, and let them fight to the death."

Maggie looked back to make sure Tuesday was asleep, which he was. Then she looked at Ally. "You know what? All things considered I guess we were due for a big fight. I mean you and me baby, we've been munching on a big, dry stress sandwich our thirst quenched only by the most awesome sex for weeks now."

"But awesome sex makes damn near anything bearable. And the fight was all my fault and it wouldn't have happened if I had tied up my inner asshole a bit more tightly." Ally took a deep breath then let it out and then *she* made a quick check to see if the baby was really asleep before she said. "I'm not really very bright, Maggie. Until tonight I didn't understand what you meant when you said you loved Helen that you were always in love with her. You never got over Helen, did you?"

"Well she didn't give either of us a lot of choice, did she?" Maggie said with a sad smile. "She was never as into me as I was her, baby, and the first time I saw her with you I knew why. I flat wasn't her type and I never, not for one minute, resented you. A couple of times I wanted to be you, but I never blamed you for Helen not wanting me. Now I love you, and I realized I hung onto the idea that I loved Helen because it stopped me from getting attached to anyone else. But what I feel for you Ally, it's so the same, but so different."

Ally laughed. "What the hell is that supposed to mean?"

"It's pretty obvious, Ally Taggart. The love you have for me is the same as what I have for you, and that's what makes it the same but different."

"How did you get to be the amazing person you are with a mother like Agnes?"

"First off, you're amazing, and your mother was also a bottomless pit of dread. Second off, Mona raised me, and she's pretty awesome. But also with Mom's help when the therapist wanted to know what was wrong with me, I always knew just what to tell him."

Sam was kind of sad when the front-end loaders and dump trucks came in to clean up the mess because all of his friends stopped coming for coffee and sandwiches. They had put all the stuff away, but he found he still liked to sit on the front porch, and some of the neighbors still came by to see him but now they were bringing him a coffee or a doughnut. Ally and

Maggie were working regular hours again, so he was getting to spend more time with them. Maggie had talked him into taking fewer pain pills, and she had put him on a bunch of vitamins and herbal supplements. At first he had done it just to humor her, but a week and half after taking her advice and the fistful of pills she handed him twice a day, he was feeling better instead of worse for the first time since they told him he had cancer.

Ally had started painting the boy's bedroom, and Sam felt good enough that he had to stop himself from doing it for her when they were all at work. Ally was a perfectionist, and she was painting three of the walls in blue, green and yellow diagonal stripes. The fourth wall she said she was going to paint a mural on, and while he could have painted the stripes he knew Ally wanted to do it in a particular way and he needed to keep his hands out of her project. They had moved Tuesday's tot bed and toys into the living room, and he was sleeping there till his room was finished. Ally had come home one day with a used TV and hooked it up in the guest room so that Sam could still watch TV after they lay the boy down for the night.

Yet he still wasn't watching the news anymore. Ally was right; it was depressing. However he was still reading the paper everyday on line. It just didn't twist his gut the way watching it did. Maybe it was the lack of sound and moving images. Sam suspected it probably had a lot more to do with being able to glance and pick what he did or didn't want to know about and read the articles without the theme music for this or that disaster or the reporter's inflection.

Fred from next door parked in the driveway and came walking up. "Hey, Sam, is Ally around?"

"Nope." Sam looked at his watch. "They should be home any minute though."

"Mind if I wait for her here?"

"Not at all, take a load off. Would you like some coffee?"

"You know Sam I think I've drank enough of your coffee to last me a lifetime, thanks."

Ally pulled in the driveway. Ally and Maggie got out of the truck and Maggie opened the back door and released the boy. He immediately ran into the yard and got on the big wheel they had bought him the day before.

Ally looked tired like she'd put in a hard day, yet there

was a huge smile on her face that Sam knew really belonged to the stunning red head who walked over and took Ally's hand. What sort of jerk would want to crush that kind of love? *A jerk like I was who doesn't understand that love is love. That it's just that simple. I stayed in a loveless marriage I believed it was sanctioned by God and condemned people like my daughter because who she loved made me uncomfortable, and now seeing them together seems completely natural.*

"Hey, Fred. How's it going?" Ally said, waving.

"Better, but not great. Can I talk to you for a minute?"

Maggie was pretty sure Fred meant he wanted to talk to Ally alone, but Ally just drug her along with her till they were over by the fence that bordered Fred's yard. At least what used to be Fred's yard.

He looked at Maggie only for a moment, then shrugged and started talking. "The insurance company gave me fifty thousand for my house, which is crap. I don't really want to move, but Bev says she wants to move someplace where they don't have tornados. After we were all nearly killed I can't really blame her. Our kid is still having nightmares." He half smiled. "At least we'll finally be away from her mother. My company will pay to move me to their Denver office, but they want me to leave in the next two weeks. If I could get another fifteen thousand for my lot I'd feel like I wasn't getting completely screwed on what I paid for my house in the first place. I'm told that's a really good price, but that no one's going to want to buy it any time soon because of the tornado. I would be willing to owner finance it for nothing down. I mean seriously what could you do to it that would make it worth less money? I'd carry it for eight percent interest, five hundred a month. I thought I'd ask you first."

"That would give us enough room to do whatever we wanted," Maggie said in Ally's ear.

"I'd love to but I think that's a little over what I can afford right now." Ally was obviously doing the math in her head. She'd just pulled all kinds of overtime, and Maggie knew Ally was expecting a big check, but a week of rain could eat any extra up quick. Maggie knew Ally made more than she did, but also knew she still had a house payment and a truck payment and she had no idea what the utilities cost. Ally would never overextend herself financially, and she knew what she could and couldn't afford. Maggie sighed she looked over to check that Tuesday was alright, which he was. Then she saw her car and she remembered something Mona had said. She grabbed hold of Ally's arm and shook her.

"Ally, we have two incomes now. I'm not paying rent. We could do this."

Ally nodded. "Give us a minute Fred."

She pulled Maggie back across the lawn. "It's a lot of money. I mean it's a good deal, but still a lot of money, and…"

"Are you afraid to buy property with me, Ally?" Maggie asked, a look of mock hurt on her face.

Ally laughed. "No, if you really want it let's get it."

Maggie nodded and they walked back over to Fred. "Let's draw up the paperwork; you've got a deal."

At dinner Ally and Maggie were excited, and Sam found that he was excited for them. They had big plans: they wanted to build a garden and an orchard and maybe a grape arbor, and they wondered if they could legally have bee hives. Ally wanted to build a waterfall and a swimming pool.

"A swimming pool!" the boy exclaimed.

"A swimming pool is so dangerous," Maggie said, shaking her head.

"It doesn't have to be deep or big, Maggie… I mean I don't know how to build a swimming pool, so it would mostly just be like a big fish pond… that we could play in."

"I don't know," Maggie said.

"Mom, Mom…" The boy stood in his chair and threw his hands up. "…you worry too much."

Sam laughed and so did Ally. Maggie took a deep breath looked at the boy and said calmly, "Tuesday, sit down and eat your dinner."

He nodded and sat down. He picked up his fork and looked at Ally. "She does worry too much."

"You don't even know how to swim," Maggie told Tuesday.

"My Allybaba will teach me," Tuesday said around a mouthful of food.

And Sam remembered teaching Ally to swim mostly by accident. He smiled at the memory.

"What is it Sam?" Maggie asked. She did seem to have the most uncanny knack for reading people.

Sam looked at Ally. "Do you remember how you learned to swim?"

Ally shook her head.

"I had taken you to the lake to fish. You weren't much older than your boy here and not as big. We were down on the dock on White Horse where I had taken you dozens of times, but I never gave you a real hook—it was one of those hooks like you use on Christmas tree bulbs—so you'd never caught anything. You didn't mind. You just liked to cast and reel it back in, and you were pretty good at it. You were happy if you brought in strings of algae on your line back then. So we're sitting there 'fishing,' and you actually catch a fish on that damn ornament hook. It's a *big* fish, and you won't let go; you're reeling and tugging on your rod and reeling some more. Long story short, that fish drags you right off the dock and I dive in after you because you couldn't swim. For a second I can't find you; the water is murky. I just panic. Then there you are, kicking and flailing and you still have your pole in your hand. I grab you and pull you out of the water. I sit you down, but you take off running. I figure you're scared, but then I realize you were trying to drag that huge fish onto land—which you did."

He looked at Maggie. "I'm shaking like a leaf and my heart is pounding and I'm just so glad she isn't dead, and this one...." He pointed at Ally. "She runs down, grabs that fish by the gills, picks it up, turns to me and says, 'Anyone can catch any fish if they have the right bait'." Sam cracked up and Maggie smiled but looked some confused by how funny Sam thought it was.

"Dad owned a fish and tackle store; I used to go to work with him," Ally started to explain. "I must have heard him tell fishermen that a thousand times."

"After that I let her use real hooks and we couldn't keep her out of the water, any water. She would break the ice off the lake to go swimming," he said.

Maggie looked from her son to Ally. "Alright, we can have a swimming pool but it has to have a fence with a gate that locks."

Sam wondered where that memory had been hiding. *I put it away with all my other memories of Ally. Locked it all away and didn't think about it because Ally didn't turn into who I thought I wanted her to be. She was a huge disappointment. I was ashamed of her. I let other people's opinions shape the way I saw her. She changed so much so quickly; she went from a happy, playful, loving child to a surly, quiet angry....* All these years he had thought it was puberty and her *deciding* she was queer. *She changed because he touched her. She changed because he made her distrust everyone and everything. It wasn't because of what she was. She always knew what she was. We didn't, but she did. No, she changed because that pervert put his filthy hands on her. She didn't kiss my cheek anymore or hug me or even tell me she loved me. Why? Because I was a deacon just like Parish, we believed the same things and how did she know I didn't have that in me?*

"You alright, Sam?" Maggie asked.

He nodded. "I'm just suddenly very tired. I'm going to go lay down." He wasn't tired. He felt sick and not because he was dying. He got up and went to his room where he lay down on the bed and looked at the ceiling. "I let fear rule my life."

She was helping Maggie clean up after dinner. Tuesday came rolling in the kitchen on his big wheel. Maggie looked at her and shook her head.

"What?" Ally asked.

"It was a mistake to bring that thing in the house," Maggie said.

"He couldn't get any traction on the grass, Honey, and I didn't want him on the sidewalk it's too close to the road," Ally said. *You don't understand anything* was implied.

"Tuesday, if you break anything, that thing goes right back outside," Maggie warned.

"Allybaba already told me that." He drove around the table and then started back down the hall. He really was being careful; he wasn't going fast and seemed to actually be able to steer it.

"If you've got this, Maggie, I'm going to go finish painting the last of the yellow in Tuesday's room. Then tomorrow I can start on the mural."

"It's a little boy's room, Ally, not the Sistine Chapel."

"I'm not painting naked angels and people; that would be wrong," Ally defended.

"Yes, but I've seen the drawing and it's beautiful, but way

too much work."

Ally walked up behind her, grabbed her, hugged her and whispered in her ear, "Nothing I do for you or for him could ever be enough."

Maggie turned in her arms and kissed her.

"I don't think you have any idea how the things you say and do make me feel. I think that's the most amazing thing about them," Maggie said. "I've got this if you want to go paint."

"Well I sort of just want to hold you now," Ally said, reluctantly letting her go.

She started out of the room and was almost run over by Tuesday. She made a big deal out of jumping out of his way and he laughed. "Hey! Watch where you're going."

"Ally, why don't you check on your dad before you go to work? He sounded a little out of sorts."

"Craaap," Ally said, but she started down the hall with Tuesday big wheeling behind her. She stopped at her dad's door. It was closed, so she knocked.

"Come in," he said. So she did, Tuesday right behind her.

"You alright, Dad?" Ally asked.

Her dad moved to sit up on the side of the bed and looked at Tuesday with meaning.

"Son, go ride in the kitchen." Ally picked him up, wheeler and all, and turned him around.

He laughed and took off back down the hall. She closed the door. "What's up?"

"What exactly did she say to you, Ally?" he asked quietly.

"Who Dad? When?"

"Your mother when you told her. What exactly did she say?"

Ally took a deep breath and let it out. "I shouldn't have said anything. I don't talk about it to anyone but the therapist. It happened, it's in the past. I like to keep it there."

"But... we were close then, Ally. Why didn't you come to me? When she didn't believe you, why didn't you come to me? What exactly did your mother say to you?" He was shaking and near tears.

Ally took a deep breath. He obviously at least thought he needed to know. "I told her what happened. She asked Carol if he'd ever tried to touch her, and Carol said no. So she said I was lying. I said I wasn't lying and that I had his blood under my fingernails to prove it. Then she said if I wasn't lying then I must have asked for it because that's what girls like me did. We asked for it."

Her father took a deep breath and ran his fingers through his hair. "You should have known, Ally. You should have known that I would have believed you that I never would have thought it was your fault."

"But I didn't know that, because you never disagreed with her. You always just did whatever she told you to do. It's not a big deal, Dad," Ally said. "It's not my favorite memory, but it certainly isn't the worst thing that's ever happened to me. It could have been worse. I've never had sex with a man, and if he had penetrated me I think it would have left a much deeper scar on my psyche. Dad, no one I know knows, and I don't want them to. I don't want Maggie to know because if she does she's going to want to talk to me about it. I've already dealt with it in therapy, and I don't want to talk about it again. Please, Dad."

He nodded. "I'm sorry, Ally."

"You know what? Right now I'm happy and I wouldn't trade my happiness now to have had an uncomplicated, less traumatic life in the past."

She walked over and kissed him on the top of his head then went off to work on Tuesday's room. She could hear Maggie talking to Tuesday in the kitchen even as she pried the lid off the paint can. She couldn't hear everything they were saying, but apparently Maggie had put the big wheel on the back deck and he was riding it out there which… well there was a light on the back deck and a lot less crap to run into, so it was a good idea.

Parish. She hadn't given the bastard a moment's thought in years, but he was all over the news right now. Even though she didn't read or watch it, the guys she worked with mostly kept her up on current events. She had just blurted out what Parish did to her, and now her Dad had questions that she couldn't really blame him for having.

They should hang that bastard by his balls because the truth is I did get off easy. He raped a dozen kids that they know of. Why didn't he try anything with Carol? Because at twelve she was too old for him; most of his victims were younger than I was.

Then she started painting. As she was painting she

thought about building a waterfall and a pool and maybe a playhouse and a swing set for Tuesday. She thought about building all of the wonderful things Maggie wanted to build in her garden and completely forgot that there was ever any ugliness in her life because the truth was when she weighed the good with the bad there had really been a lot more good. She thought a lot of people lost sight of that, that the traumatic events were usually there and gone.

She had to make herself paint the yellow stripes and not start the mural because that was what she really wanted to do, and except for work.... *I haven't done a painting in years. Helen died and except for work none of my painting supplies were even touched. They just sat here. Now this is a little boy's room and I have the property to make a separate studio for painting if I want to. Maggie has made me remember what it means to love. What an amazing feeling it is to love and to be loved. How empty my life was when I didn't have that.*

Sam was lying on his bed having himself a nice little pity party when he heard something wonderful. He got up walked over and opened his door. Ally was singing. It was a song he remembered from his youth. The title of the song and the artist eluded him, but the chorus proclaimed that if you wanted to get to heaven you had to raise a little hell. And she wasn't just singing, she was tapping her feet and occasionally slapping something, all in perfect rhythm and with such joy that he finally heard what Ally had said. *She's happy now, so the past doesn't matter to her.*

He stood outside the door to Tuesday's room just listening and watching. She kept singing the same song over and over, and he realized the thing she was occasionally slapping was a plastic bucket. She was still painting stripes with a precision that was baffling considering all the jumping around she was doing.

Maggie walked in the back door into the kitchen, Tuesday's hand in hers. Sam watched down the hallway as she slid the lock closed on the door then reached down and picked her son up as if he were incapable of walking.

She walked up to him in the hall listening to Ally and smiled. The boy whispered something in Maggie's ear and she whispered something in his. He nodded and she set him down. He crept around the corner and looked into his room.

When he turned back around, he was obviously so excited he could hardly contain himself, but he took his mother's hand and let her start leading him towards the bathroom.

Maggie stopped just long enough to whisper in Sam's ear. "I'm half afraid if she realizes she's singing again that she will quit."

"Singing again?"

"Until a couple of weeks ago she hadn't sung a note since Helen died."

"My dear girl, you would make anyone sing."

CHAPTER 9

If someone you hate dies, you never have to remember them fondly.

They had finished all the paperwork on the lot next door and it was theirs. It was a large lot, three-quarters of an acre like Ally's. Just like that, Maggie owned property—and not just the new lot because Ally had insisted on putting Maggie's name on her house as well.

Less than six weeks ago she was a single mother living in an efficiency apartment. Now she was part of a family with a nice home and a huge yard. Though she was sure she should be, Maggie wasn't panicked at all.

She walked from the kitchen down the hall and peeked in. Tuesday and Sam were sitting in folding chairs watching Ally paint. The tree and the river were done, and now Ally was painting the pirate ship. Mitch had pegged it; watching Ally paint was like seeing magic performed. There was nothing, and then there was art.

How did I stand at her shoulder all those years and not know I was falling in love with her? And how on earth could I not fall in love with her? Look at her; she is perfect.

She got caught up and nearly burnt what she was cooking. Luckily she got back to the kitchen just in time to save it. She was about to go get everyone for dinner when the doorbell rang. "I've got it," she started for the door, stopping at Tuesday's room, "Dinner's ready."

"Thanks." Ally got up from where she'd been sitting on the bottom of a plastic bucket and set her pallet and paintbrush on top of it. Ally stretched picked Tuesday up and started for the bathroom with him to wash their hands. Maggie forgot she'd been headed for the door and actually jumped when it rang again.

"I'm coming!" She double timed it to the door and opened it. "Sorry I was.... Karen?"

Karen looked nearly as shocked as Maggie was, and Maggie

knew damn good and well that Karen knew she was living with Ally now. "Can I come in?"

"Yes of course, Karen, come on in. We were just getting ready to eat. You're welcome to join us." Karen walked in and Maggie shut the door behind her.

Ally walked out of the bathroom pushing Tuesday in front of her. "Who was at the door...." and then Ally stopped and looked at Karen. "Karen, is everything alright?" Because of course Karen had avoided Ally like the plague ever since Helen died, and she sure as hell had never been to the house since.

"Yes. I'm sorry I should have called first."

"You're family, Karen. You don't have to call first," Ally said. She walked over and hugged Karen, who fell completely to pieces. She hung on Ally's neck, sobbing. Maggie wasn't sure her presence in Ally and Helen's house wasn't the problem, so she started for the kitchen with Tuesday.

"Maggie, I wanted to talk to you too, please," Karen cried.

Maggie really wished she didn't, but Maggie turned to Sam who had just walked out of the bathroom.

"Sam, dinner is ready. Could you take Tuesday and...."

"Sure," he said, looking at where Ally was holding the crying woman.

Maggie leaned into him and whispered, "Helen's mother."

He nodded, took Tuesday's hand and started for the kitchen.

"I don't like it when people are sad," Tuesday told Sam.

"Neither do I, Sport." Sam led him to the kitchen.

Maggie swallowed and walked over to where Ally and Karen were. Maggie was silent. She caught Ally's eye, but Ally looked as confused as she was and shrugged.

"I'm sorry, I'm so sorry, Ally. I just abandoned you," Karen said.

"It's fine, Karen. I get it; I'm not upset with you," Ally assured her.

"I've actually been doing so much better the last few months. You two together has actually made me feel even better, because as odd as it may sound I think the two of you being happy is going to give Helen some peace."

It didn't sound odd to Maggie. Helen had moved on; she wasn't stuck here anymore.

"Poor Mitch, he's been a rock and he's stood by me when

I've been basically useless. I was doing better and feeling better, and then today...."

She started crying harder, so Ally held her tighter and Maggie asked carefully, "What happened today, Karen?"

"I saw him. I saw the bastard who killed Helen and nearly killed Ally. He's in his early twenties now. I was at the store and he was there with his mother and he was smiling and laughing, Ally. He was laughing!"

Maggie watched as Ally took a deep breath and held it then slowly released it. Now Maggie knew exactly why Karen had come there—because Ally understood completely why Karen was so destroyed that he was laughing and happy— and so did Maggie.

He had taken Helen away from them and mangled Ally's leg so that none of them could ever forget it. It was why Karen avoided Ally. Her limp was a constant reminder that Helen was gone. The logical part of Maggie's mind told her he'd been a kid, it was just a tragic accident, and that he deserved to have a chance to have a life. But the part of her that had nearly died with Helen, the part that had watched how Helen's death affected everyone she loved; wasn't as forgiving. So she completely related to how Karen was feeling.

"I lost it, Ally...." Karen cried. "...in the middle of the supermarket. I walked right up to them and I just lost it. I yelled at him and his mother for about five minutes. How dare he laugh and be happy I said. I've spent five years in hell. I told her that she gets to spend time with her son but I don't have my daughter because her son killed my child. And the whole time the mother was screaming that it was an accident and her son had been through enough and the boy was apologizing over and over. Store security shows up and asks if there's a problem. Is there a problem?"

Ally shuffled over to the couch with Karen and sat down with her as Maggie found a box of tissues, took one for herself, and then handed the box to Karen who took it and started drying her nose and her face.

"And of course the real problem is that yelling at that kid didn't make Helen magically come back to life. He made a stupid ass mistake. It could have happened to any one of us. He's not some criminal mastermind or a junkie or a drunk who just didn't give a shit. He was a stupid kid who had way too big a truck and pulled into a car he didn't see. There's no place to put it, there's no one to blame; it just is. I was just starting to feel like myself again, and now I'm afraid this is going to send me crashing right back to the bowels of my personal hell."

"It doesn't have to; you don't have to let it." Maggie sat down on the other side of Karen and put her hand on her back. "It's not going to, and do you know why? You just said it—there is no one to blame; it just is. Allowing yourself to be yourself is how you can best be with Helen. Helen was always Helen."

Karen nodded, managed a smile and dried her face again. She'd made quite a pile of spent tissues on their coffee table. "Your dinner is getting cold," Karen said. "I should go."

"Why?" Ally asked. "Stay and have dinner with us."

"Mitch will wonder where I am."

"Then Ally will call and tell him," Maggie said.

Karen looked around the room as if wondering if being there was such a good idea, then she nodded and Ally called Mitch, who said he was coming over and they could feed him, too.

After dinner her dad went to his room saying he was tired. Karen was helping Maggie with the dishes and stuff, so Ally want back to paint some more. Tuesday and Mitch went with her.

"Wow, Tuesday, this is great," Mitch said, sitting down on the folding chair her dad had been sitting on earlier.

"There is going to be a Taggart gnome on the ship," Tuesday said.

"Taggart gnome?" Mitch asked.

"He's got a story for the concrete gnome that sits with all the other display items at Taggart's," Ally said with a grin and started to paint.

"He protects the shop, Grandpa," Tuesday told Mitch. "At night he fixes things."

"That's good to know. We should put him to work on Uncle Chuck's lead ass." Mitch laughed.

"It's going to be a huge picture," Tuesday told him then went running out of the room for reasons known only to him.

Mitch looked at what Ally was painting. "Life's strange isn't it?"

"You mean because there is a kid in the room Helen wanted

to use for a nursery?" Ally asked carefully.

"And because of who that kid is... Speaking of strange, what's my wife doing here?" So Ally told him. "You know, Ally, in some ways I think she's doing better than me because if I'd seen that fucking punk and he had so much as grinned I would have had to beat his ass, and being in this house is still really hard for me."

"I know."

"How did you do it, Ally? How did you stay here?"

"How could I leave? At least being here I could remember that I was once happy, that I could *be* happy. I never would have known that without Helen." Tuesday came running back into the room with the drawing Ally had made him of what she was painting. "Now I'm happy here again."

Tuesday walked over to Mitch expectantly. Mitch picked him up, sat him in his lap, and Tuesday showed Mitch the picture, telling him all about it. Then he told Mitch about what they were going to build on the lot next door.

"So... you're going to be busy for a while, Allybaba," Mitch said.

Ally laughed. "Yeah, it looks that way."

"Maggie loves you, Ally...." Mitch said, "...at least as much as Helen did, and you love her every bit as much as you loved Helen. I can see it in your eyes when you look at her. At first it just about killed me to think of you together, like you were both cheating on her but... I'm glad you're happy, and I'm glad it's with Maggie."

She heard it in his voice. She turned to him, her eyes narrowing to slits. "You.... You knew about Helen and Maggie," she accused.

He got really interested in what Tuesday was telling him then—the same stuff he'd been mostly ignoring only seconds ago.

"So you knew all along that Maggie was bisexual."

"In my defense Helen told me not to tell and you know damn good and well that I know how to keep a secret." Mitch laughed. "So when did Maggie come clean about her and Helen?"

"During the tornado when she thought we were all going to die. I think she was disappointed that I wasn't more upset. She told me I acted like we'd accidently drank from the same glass."

They had just closed the dishwasher and sat down at the table with herb tea when Tuesday came running in and wanted to go to the back porch and ride his big wheel, so Maggie opened the door and turned the light on.

"Mitch tells me Ally's really good with Tuesday," Karen said.

"Amazing actually."

"I can't believe Ally's letting her dad live here." Because of course Karen knew just exactly how Ally's parents had treated her.

"He's dying, and he's working extra hard to try to fix things with Ally. I'm actually going to miss him when he's gone. He's a pleasant fellow and he told my mother off, so he's kind of my hero now. Ally still doesn't really know what to do with him."

Karen sipped at the tea in front of her. "You know what turned things around for me?"

Maggie shook her head silently.

"Mitch said he thought the drugs were doing more harm than good. He said every time they put me on a new antidepressant I felt better for about ten minutes and then I was worse. I found an herbalist...."

"Why didn't you come to me?"

"Honestly, Maggie, seeing you since Helen died hasn't been much easier for me than seeing Ally. When I saw either of you and she wasn't with you it just made it so much more obvious that she was gone. The herbalist weaned me off the antidepressant and put me on a bunch of supplements. No longer in a drug induced haze I really dealt with the depth of my grief for the first time. Then gradually the light started to filter back into my life. You know how you said that maybe I needed to see that kid today? Well I think maybe I needed to come to this house and see you both today, too. I'm glad you asked me to stay and glad that Mitch came. I was afraid I'd feel worse, but I think I'm finally ready to take my life back."

Tuesday rode in the house then stopped got up and pushed the big wheel back on the porch remembering that Maggie asked him not to bring it in the house. He almost got the door closed then walked over to her, stopped and made a face.

"What baby?"

"I fagget."

"*Forgot*, Tuesday, you *forgot*," Maggie said.

"That's what I said." He walked towards the hall, no doubt to go to his room to see what Ally was doing. Maggie got up, shut the door the rest of the way and locked it then turned the lights off on the deck.

Karen looked at all of Maggie's jars of herbs stacked on one corner of the cabinets. "I'm glad it's not just like it was. That would have been too hard I think."

And for the first time Maggie felt good about moving Helen's stuff out to make room for her things. She wasn't about to tell Karen that if she'd been there a month ago everything would have been just the way Helen left it or that till then Helen's spirit had hung out mostly in the kitchen they were sitting in.

Tuesday came trotting back into the kitchen. "I went and asked Sam what I fagget…"

"*Forgot* or at this point I'd even take *forget*. I don't want us to be the only lesbian couple in the world that has a child who says faggot," Maggie said with a sigh as Karen laughed. "Honey. Sam went to bed."

"He said I could come in. He's just watching TV," Tuesday said. Then he frowned hard at her. "Mom! You made me fagget again." He stomped back out of the room.

"*Forget*, Tuesday!" Maggie yelled after him.

Karen laughed. "They grow up so fast. How old is he now?"

"He's about to be three," Maggie said.

"That's right his birthday is what…."

"Three days after Ally's."

Tuesday ran in then and said, "Sam wants to know what we're doing for Allybaba's birthday."

"You should throw her a party. Their birthdays are close enough together you should have a party for both Ally and Tuesday," Karen told Maggie. "You could have it here at the house, and I'd be happy to help you."

"We're having a party!" Tuesday yelled and took off down the hall.

Maggie looked at Karen and shrugged. "I guess we're having a party."

There was still a lot of storm damage, and every day it seemed like at least one of their jobs was cutting a tree off of or moving debris off of something she'd built that she'd been really proud of that now had to be fixed. No matter how good a repair they did, Ally could always see where they had repaired it, and she was never quite as happy with it.

They had moved and ground up all the storm wrack and now she had to chip out a two-foot by four-foot section of the patio around the pond because the massive tree that had landed on it had cracked the crap out of the patio and crushed the side of the fish pond. They had more than enough work—which was good for business—but Ally wasn't really happy with the reason they had all the business. Tearing up crap that she and her crew had built was always hard because by God when they built something, they built it right.

So she already wasn't in the best of moods when Billy Bob said to Ray, "I still can't believe they are even thinking of letting that baby raper go."

"Me, either, what a load of crap, and it looks like it's a done deal," Ray said, taking the rock she handed him that she'd just pried out and slinging it in the wheel barrow. "All worried about his rights and his pain. I say if he really is getting raped by the other inmates he's got it coming and good riddance."

"They're going to let him go because they don't want to get sued. The ACLU is threatening to represent him."

Ally's heart actually seemed to slow and she got a sick feeling in her stomach when she realized who they were probably talking about. She stopped working and looked up at Ray. "Who, who are they probably going to let out?"

"Laban Parish," Ray said.

"They should hang him up by his balls," Billy Bob hissed.

Ally quickly went right back to work. It didn't matter. Why should it matter? She was a grown woman and she'd been able to stop him when she was only a kid and he was nearly as old as her father now and in bad health. He wasn't out yet, and if and when he got out he'd be on the sex offenders register, so he wouldn't be able to hurt anyone else.

But dammit he deserves to rot in jail, and if he's really getting raped he deserves that, too. But it doesn't matter. It shouldn't matter. I just need to put it out of my head. I did for all the years I thought I was the only one he messed with. It doesn't matter.

"Fuck, Ally!" Billy Bob said, and he was suddenly kneeling

on the ground beside her.

He grabbed her hand and it was only than that she realized she was bleeding. A sliver of rock or concrete must have hit the back of her hand and opened a wound. It wasn't a bad cut. Still, if she hadn't been distracted it wouldn't have happened or at the very least she would have noticed. So she blamed her crew and was instantly pissed off at them.

She pulled her hand away from Billy Bob's got up and headed for the truck. Half way there she realized she had no reason to be mad at them. She hollered back towards them, "It's not bad; just bleeding like a stuck pig. I take way too much ibuprophin, so my blood is like water."

In spite of her announcement Ray nearly beat her to the truck. He started taking care of her hand. "You okay, Ally?"

"I'm fine Ray!" she snapped.

"Alrighty then." He put gauze on the cut then wrapped it with duct tape and they went back to work. They weren't back at it ten minutes when they started talking about Parish again, so Ally put her ear buds in and put her music on high and carefully put it out of her mind.

It was Ally's birthday, but Sam really felt like it was his party. In the last few weeks he could feel his health slowly fading. He knew he wouldn't live much longer, but he felt like he could tie up all the loose ends in his life with a neat little bow and die in peace.

And this was a real party. There was live music, a keg of beer, barbeque, and food everywhere. People were dancing on the deck and in the yard, and he didn't even care that he didn't know most of the people there because everyone talked to everyone and he didn't feel left out at all.

This was something like he'd never been to before. Church parties were a joke with everyone afraid to smile too much or have too good a time. Their idea of jokes were lame ass at best. They drank red Kool-Aid® and ate chips and different salads that different ladies from the church had made but that always tasted just the same.

In college it had been all about drinking as much as you could till you puked, screwing anything that moved, and doing insanely stupid and even dangerous things to impress people just as stupid as you were that you'd—likely as not—never see again once you graduated.

Because he'd gone right from college back to church as his only social outlet, he'd missed... this.

These were responsible people who weren't religious fanatics. They were enjoying each other's company and having a good time. The band played a steady stream of classic rock with a few new tunes and they were just the right amount of loud. The lead singer and the guitarist were a gay couple Ally knew from one of the clubs. She had built their flower garden and fish ponds. They were playing at her party, and in return she was going to build them something called a pergola, which Sam didn't really know what the hell that was but he hoped she built them a nice one.

The jokes they told were sometimes rank but always funny. Most everyone was having a few drinks, but no one was getting slobbering drunk. The people who had kids had brought them with them. They were having Tuesday's birthday, too, and Karen had rented some big balloon-jumping-in castle that they had set up on their new lot for the kids to play on. Without making any real plans the parents sort of took turns watching the kids play. And never, not for one second, did he think the kids were in any danger from a pervert.

There were gay people, there were straight people, hippies and business people, black, yellow and red people, there was even a girl with green hair. The longer Sam sat there sipping his hard cider and watching them all, the more he realized that they were really all different but the same. They all stood around and talked or danced or sang along with the music, and it was an actual, honest-to-God celebration. Not something pretending to be fun or a bunch of people all trying to get drunker or more stoned than anyone else so they'd have an excuse to do things they knew they probably shouldn't do in the first place.

Mona sat down by him on the glider and he looked at her and smiled. She had been dancing for about twenty minutes, and he'd enjoyed watching her. She had really good rhythm, and her boobs had just the right amount of bounce when she danced. She'd already worked up a sweat. "My brother and sister hit me about a minute apart and informed me that I needed to take it easy."

"Well you did just have heart surgery. How much weight have you lost, Mona?"

"Forty-five pounds now and I've had all those bypasses so exercise is good for me. I also know when I should listen, you know, so Chad tells me and I blow him off, but Maggie tells me and I'm all about going and sitting down for a minute because as you know she's a witch," Mona said, laughing.

Ally walked by carrying Tuesday who was crying, huge tears rolling down his cheeks.

"What's wrong with Aunt Mona's baby?" Mona asked.

"Big boy hit me," Tuesday cried.

"It was an accident," Maggie said, running up behind Ally. "He's a little tired."

"But I don't want a nap, Mom, not at my party." Tuesday just cried.

"Why don't you put him here, Ally?" Mona said, slapping her knees. "Maybe all he needs is a rest."

Ally looked at Maggie and Maggie nodded her head, so Ally sat Tuesday on Mona's lap and he cuddled up to her as she held him.

"Would that be alright, Tuesday? Would you just sit here with Sam and Aunt Mona for a minute?"

He nodded

Sam reached over and patted his back. "You're alright, Sport."

"Tuesday," he said slowly, sniffling as he looked at Sam. "My name is Tuesday."

Sam and Mona both laughed. Tuesday laid his head on Mona's ample bosom, and it was pretty obvious that Maggie was right; the boy was tired.

Maggie had dragged Ally off to dance with her, and Sam was pleasantly surprised to see that Ally could dance.

As if reading his mind, thus proving Maggie wasn't the only one in which the force was strong in their family, Mona said, "You should have seen her before. Ally used to be a hell of a dancer."

"She dances better than I ever could now," Sam said.

"You danced? I thought you were a Baptist."

One of the guys Ally worked with walked over and said, "Baptist. Do you know why Baptists don't make love standing up?"

"Ray, that is like the oldest joke in the world." Mona laughed.

"Well I haven't heard it," Sam said with a grin and a shrug.

"They don't want people to think they're dancing," Ray said and then he took off.

Mona shook her head and said, "A drive-by joking."

Sam laughed. "It was pretty funny and unfortunately true. When I was in college I danced. When I was in college I did all sorts of 'evil' vile things.... You know; I had fun." Sam noticed Tuesday was just about out.

Maggie and Ally walked up to where her sister and Sam were sitting and Tuesday was asleep. "See I told you Ally, Mona can always get him to go to sleep and without the crying." Maggie scooped him out of her sister's arms and said to Mona, "Come on open the doors for me."

"I could...." Ally started.

"Ally, you stay here and talk to your dad for a minute," Maggie said, looking at her sister with meaning. Mona glared back at her but got up.

The house was mostly empty because everything was going on outside. Mona closed the door to the house. "Which door is the baby's?" Mona couldn't remember.

"First door on the left right across from ours," Maggie said. Mona opened the door, gasped, and Maggie smiled. Mona hadn't seen the room since Ally finished painting it.

"Oh, Maggie, this is amazing," Mona said, stepping back from the mural for a better look.

Maggie lay Tuesday down on his bed and took his pants and shoes off. He was out and probably wouldn't wake up till morning. He'd played really hard all day and without a nap.

Maggie walked up next to her sister and looked at the painting. "Only Ally could take the list of weirdo stuff Tuesday rattled off and make a cohesive painting out of it."

"What does Tuesday think of it?"

"He loves it, but I think even at his age the thing he loves most about it is that Ally would do it for him."

"He's three years old, Maggie. That's what *you* love most about it, and I have to tell you I would have been impressed just with the stripes."

"She's going to paint one in our room. She said anything I want."

"So... are you going to do like your son and pick fifty things that don't go together just to challenge her gift?" Mona asked.

"I have no idea, just that I want one. When I asked her if I could have one she said she would paint whatever I wanted."

"Maggie, that twitchy, twitchy girl loves you," Mona said.

"And I love that twitchy, twitchy girl." Maggie started out of the room and without turning to look at her sister asked, "Mona, are you doing what I think you're doing?"

"So what if I am?"

"*You* told *me* not to get attached," Maggie reminded.

Ally sat down next to her dad. "You having a good time?" he asked her.

"Yes, what about you?"

"An absolute blast."

Ally laughed. "But Dad, all you're doing is sitting here."

"No I'm sitting here on the wonderful deck built by my beautiful, resourceful, successful daughter while we celebrate her thirty-eighth and my grandson's third birthday. And there are lights and music, and people laughing and having a good time, and no one is putting up a front, and no one is here who would rather be someplace else. I'm right in the big middle of it and I never thought I'd even get to see you again. The universe has been awfully good to me right here at the end, Ally, and so have you and Maggie. I got you a birthday present, but I ordered it on line. It has to be custom made, so it won't get here for months. When it gets here I want you to remember all the good times we had there."

"What is it, Dad, a vacation?"

"Wait and see, Ally. Just wait and see."

Maggie and Mona came back out and Maggie pulled Ally to her feet to dance. Mona sat back down by Sam.

It was a slow song and Ally was glad because she'd danced too much. She pulled Maggie to her and they started to dance. In the background she could hear Laurie chatting up—or at least trying to—one of Maggie's yoga friends.

"I just kept digging through the rubble and the whole time all I can hear is this little dog barking, but finally I pull her free...."

"Well, that's new," Maggie whispered in Ally's ear. "You know, tornado lies."

"She asked me to help her move on Thursday."

"What did you tell her?"

"That you wouldn't let me; that you insist I spend all of

my time with you."

"Wow, I'm kind of a bitch," Maggie said. "So was this alright? Did Karen and I do too much?"

"This was perfect, but..." She leaned in closer and whispered in Maggie's ear. "...I'll be glad when they all leave and it's just me and you."

"And what will you do when it's just me and you?"

"What do you want me to do?"

"That thing you do where you stick two fingers in and take your tongue...."

"Geez, Maggie!" Ally kissed her just to shut her up.

When she stopped kissing her Maggie looked at her with a devilish grin. "Don't ask if you don't want me to tell you." She looked at her expectantly, "So?"

"So.... What?" Ally asked not understanding.

"Will you do that thing with two fingers and your...." Ally covered Maggie's mouth with her hand, and Maggie laughed. Ally took her hand away. "Well will you?"

"You know I will." Ally grinned down at her.

At nine-thirty the band stopped playing. By ten everyone was gone, and Maggie had dragged Ally off to bed. Sam was still sitting on the deck with Mona talking about everything and nothing.

"Where did everyone go?" Sam asked with a laugh.

"This is a residential neighborhood and lots of these people like your friend George are still trying to make their homes livable. When Maggie invited everyone she asked them to please be gone by ten. Plus there is the whole not being able to go more than twelve hours without having sex with Ally."

"I'm pretty sure that street runs both ways. You know what shocks me? There were at least sixty people here today, counting kids, and it's not some horrible, trashy mess."

"No smokers, not back here anyway. They put the smokers on the front porch and wouldn't let them smoke anywhere else. Smokers trash shit out. Nonsmokers don't. Of course not all smokers trash crap out and not all nonsmokers put their trash where it goes, but as a general rule smokers make a huge mess. Plus most of Ally and Maggie's friends are as green as they are. Notice the trash cans have all been split into recyclables and non-recyclables."

"I was a smoker; I don't think I was a slob," Sam mumbled,

trying to remember.

Mona chuckled. "Well, I guess I should get up and go home." She must have seen the disappointed look in his eyes. "Aren't you normally in bed by now?"

"In bed, yes, but not normally asleep. They're in a new relationship and they have a kid already. I try to go to bed early enough that they can have some time alone."

"So you just go to bed when Tuesday does." Sam nodded. "But you aren't really tired."

"Nope, I just watch TV."

"So...." She smiled at him. "You want to fool around?"

Sam laughed.

"Old man, I'm serious as a heart attack, and I've nearly had one of those. I like you; you like me, I could use a tumble, and I bet you could, too."

"I... I don't even know if I can still get it up."

"But it couldn't hurt to try, could it?"

"Not too shabby old man, not too shabby." Mona laughed. She kissed him gently on the lips and then rolled out of bed and started to get dressed.

"Mona.... I don't know what to say. You were amazing."

"Thanks. That was the most fun I've had in a long time."

"You're thanking me?" He laughed. "I know you were just doing charity, Mona, thank you."

"No, Sam, I wasn't doing charity," Mona said gently and sat down on the bed. "I like you. I'm a big girl and usually when I can get someone to sleep with me they make it clear that they think they are doing me some sort of favor. You like me, you were tender, and you cared how I felt. I think you need to understand that this was something I wanted as much if not more than you did. And now I'm going to go before Ally or Maggie catches us and asks a bunch of stupid questions." She kissed him on the lips again and started for the door.

"Mona, any man who gets you should count himself lucky."

"And thanks for helping me to believe that."

Tuesday had crawled into bed with them sometime in the night, and he was sleeping all over Ally's head. Maggie still had no idea why he did it or how he got there without waking Maggie up because as always Ally was wrapped all around her. So first she got out of Ally's grasp and then she took Tuesday off Ally's head and laid him beside her.

Ally was still sound asleep, so she was really out. Maggie got up and headed for the bathroom. She saw that the front door was open and hoped it hadn't been like that all night, but when she opened the door the rest of the way Sam had a trash bag and was cleaning up the front porch.

He turned to her and smiled. "It was a wonderful party, Maggie. Best party I've ever been to." He was picking up all the cans and bottles and sticking them in the same bag with the cigarette butts, but she wasn't about to bitch at him for not recycling. He wanted to help, and some recyclables in the regular trash weren't going to tip the scales of the environment into decline.

"Thanks, Sam," Maggie said. "And thanks for helping clean up. The smokers were up here and for some reason they always make the biggest mess."

"For one thing they think everything is an ash tray," Sam said, pulling a butt from one of Ally's hanging plants. Maggie realized it wasn't because he didn't know they recycled that he wasn't separating the trash. After all he had been all this time. No, he was throwing these cans and bottles away because they were full of butts. She started helping him pick up the mess. He started singing, of all things "Pretty Woman." He had a decent voice, too, and Maggie thought with a smile, *This is where Ally got it from—the singing when she's happy. I don't want to know, so I'm just not going to ask why he's so happy this morning.*

It was Friday and Ally, for one, was glad to be going home for the weekend. "I swear, baby, all I've done for the last two months is fix stuff I already built, and now it's hotter than two sticks of shit."

"Two sticks of shit!" Tuesday laughed from the back seat.

"Honey!" Maggie sighed, and Ally just shrugged.

"Well it is."

"Really, Ally? What degree of heat does two sticks of shit radiate?" Maggie asked, but not without a smile.

"A lot." Ally laughed. She stopped laughing when she pulled into the driveway and saw the door was ajar. Her dad had trouble getting it to latch, so why it made her blood run cold she didn't know. She turned the truck off. "Stay here."

Maggie nodded. Ally got out of the truck and ran up to the house. She opened the door and found her father lying in the middle of the living room floor. He looked up at her, and he'd obviously been crying.

"Dad!" She knelt beside him.

"I wet myself, dammit! I fell and pissed myself, and now I can't get up—just like that stupid-assed commercial. I'm so sorry."

"It's no big deal, Dad. We have a three year old and a pet rabbit; it's not the first time this floor has been peed on. How do you feel?"

"Old and useless, ashamed...."

"Shame is a useless emotion," Maggie said from the door.

"Maggie I told you...."

"It's hotter than two sticks of shit out there, Ally," Maggie reminded her, then walked Tuesday straight back to his room.

She came back from the bathroom with towels and Ally dried up the floor.

Maggie gently took hold of her dad's lower eyelid and pulled it down. "He's anemic again; he needs another iron treatment. I'll go get him some dry underwear and pants."

She took off down the hall.

"Help me sit up, Ally," her Dad near begged her, so she did.

"I want to change my own pants, Ally. I'll go to the hospital, but please let me change my own pants."

She nodded and moved him till he could lean against the sofa.

Maggie returned with the dry pants and underwear, and Ally handed him the dry towels, took hold of Maggie's arm, and led her from the living room to the bathroom. She started washing her hands.

"Ally, he needs help."

"He doesn't want it, Maggie. He's embarrassed as hell, and...." Ally couldn't help it. She started to cry then quickly splashed water in her face. Maggie handed her a dry towel. "He's dying. Is it too much to ask that he could do it with a little dignity?"

"Listen to me, please." Maggie put her hand on Ally's shoulder, and Ally looked down at her. "It's going to be what it is, and you aren't alone. I'm going to help you, and I'm going to help him. It's *you* he doesn't want help from because you're his child. *I'm* going to go help him. If he tells me not to, I'll go away, but otherwise I'm going to because I don't think he can undress or dress himself right now, and the frustration of trying is going to make him feel worse not better."

And Maggie knew what she was talking about because after all just taking her right to practice away didn't change the fact that she knew medicine.

"If you need my help."

"I won't. It will take me a couple of minutes, tops." Maggie left and three minutes later she was back. "Alright, let's get him in the truck and you can take him to the hospital."

He was so weak it took both of them to get him in the truck, too. Ally kissed Maggie good bye.

"Thanks, Maggie."

"Be careful, Ally. There is no reason to hurry. He's probably going to have to wait for the treatment anyway. I'll call ahead and tell them you're coming. I love you, Ally."

"I love you, too." Ally got in the truck and started for the hospital. Her dad was silent looking out the window.

"It'll be alright, Dad."

"I know," he said. Then he turned to her and smiled. "If I don't die tonight do you think we could go fishing in the morning?"

Ally laughed and shook her head. "Alright, Dad, but only if you don't die."

"Just you and me, Ally, alright? Just the two of us like old times. I love Maggie and Tuesday, but I'd just like to have you all to myself for a couple of hours if that's alright."

"Of course it's alright, Dad."

"And maybe when we get home you can grill us up some fish."

Sam wasn't too surprised when Mona met them in the waiting room. Ally had gone to fill out some paperwork and Mona sat down by him and took his hand. She smiled at him.

"You'd just do anything to be near me wouldn't you, Sam?"

"Well of course I would. You're one hot mama and I'm just dying to see you," he said with a smile. The truth was he'd seen her a couple of times since the night of the party. There was no weirdness between them; they were friends who had shared something special that brought them closer was all.

"How are you doing? Not with this, I know what's going on

with you medically. How are you handling the whole Parish going free thing?"

"I'm not going to lie, Mona, it isn't my favorite thing." Sam took a deep breath and let it out. "But Laban Parish isn't free. He's got a bracelet on his ankle and he's a registered sex offender. I'm a little worried about Ally, though. She doesn't look at or read the news, but she knows. I'd like to ask her if she's alright, but she's made it clear that she doesn't want to talk about it and she doesn't want anyone to know especially Maggie... But Mona there may come a time when Maggie needs to know. I trust you to know when or if that time comes."

Mona nodded.

"I don't want them to have to take care of me, Mona," Sam said, and fought his tears. "Your sister had to change my pants. I just want to die and get it over with."

"Sam, Medicare will pick up once you have to go to hospice. They won't have to take care of you for the worst of it. And you won't be alone because we'll all be able to come and see you."

"You are an amazing woman, Mona. I hope you get exactly what you want from life...."

"You know what, Sam? Save the speech for when you're really dying."

Maggie mopped up the living room floor with disinfectant then put Sam's clothes in the washer.

When she turned around Tuesday was standing there watching her, Jack in his arms. The rabbit was not a dwarf as the pet store sign had claimed. At this point the rabbit's feet sometimes dragged on the ground as Tuesday packed him around, but neither the rabbit nor her baby seemed to mind. Tuesday would sometimes play with the rabbit in his room for hours, and yet it rarely pissed or shit in the floor.

Maggie reached over and petted the rabbit's head then got down on one knee and looked at her son. "What's wrong, baby?"

"Is Sam dying now?"

"No, Honey, not now."

"I don't want him to die."

"None of us wants him to die, but it can't be helped."

Tuesday nodded and headed for his room and Maggie

went to the kitchen and called Ally.

"Your sister pulled some strings, so he's already on the drip now. They said I can take him home in a couple of hours."

"Good. Do you want me to make you something to eat when you get home, or...."

"Mona and I are eating in the cafeteria right now. You and Tuesday go ahead and eat dinner. I love you, Maggie."

"I love you, Ally. How are you?"

"I'm alright really."

"So..." Mona said looking across the table at her. "...are you really alright?"

"He's lost a bunch of weight just in the last couple of weeks. Even if I still felt the way I did about him when they stuck him on my front doorstep it wouldn't be easy to watch. It sort of sucks that I have a father again only to turn around and lose him, and now watching him die in stages is really hard, but I'm so happy that we got to fix things between us. I have Maggie and Tuesday; I'm not going to be alone. Karen is back from the brink of insanity. I'm in a place where I can handle it, and what's Maggie always saying? 'The universe won't give you more than you can handle'." Ally actually laughed then. "You know what the old fart wants to do tomorrow? Go fishing. I only recently realized why he so loved to fish... because it got him away from mother. All of my best childhood memories center on me and the old man with lines in the water which is no doubt why I also love to fish. I'm sure that's why he wants just me and him to go fishing. It's going to be hot, the bugs are going to be out, but he wants to go fishing because it reminds us both of a time when we really loved each other and there wasn't a bunch of crap between us. All our memories were good ones, and I wasn't afraid of anything because I always figured he would protect me."

"Are you going to take him fishing?"

"If he still wants to go in the morning and if he can get in the truck, you bet I am. If he died at the lake fishing... well that would be great, wouldn't it?" she pushed her plate away, the food wasn't bad at all but she was done eating.

"Ally, don't do anything crazy," Mona said.

"I'm not going to drown my dad, Mona."

"You said that a little too fast for it not to have crossed your mind." Mona reached across the table and patted her

hand, then she pointed right in Ally's face. "Don't think crazy
shit. He'll die when he's supposed to die."

Ally grinned at her. "Mona, did you give my old man a
little?"

"The woman who's banging my little sister doesn't get to
ask such a question."

Ally laughed. "That's what I thought."

Mona laughed loudly and smiled. "Everyone ought to have
a going-away present."

Ally had asked Mitch if she could use his boat. He said
sure so she'd loaded her Dad into the boat at the dock and
motored out to the middle of the lake. They put lines in the
water then sat down to wait. The boat had a pullout shade
awning, and away from the shore they neither had to deal
with the bugs nor were they as hot. Her dad had been mostly
silent till they put lines in the water which in her mind was
completely ass backwards.

"It was awful nice of Mitch to let us use his boat," he said.
"Bet this put him back about fifteen thousand bucks." And of
course he'd hit it right on the head because after all her dad
had run a bait and tackle shop for most of his life. "Thanks,
Ally. I know you'd rather spend the day with Maggie and
Tuesday."

"You know what Dad? Maggie, Tuesday and I are going to
have a whole lifetime to spend together." Ally grinned and
nudged him with her elbow. "Actually she seemed pretty
excited not to have to put up with me today."

Her dad got a bite and she had to help him get his fish
into the boat. It was a nice size fish, but the fact he couldn't
handle it on his own showed how weak he was. The doctor
said it would take a couple of days for the iron to give him
enough strength to be noticeable. He also said it was like
putting a bandage on a bullet wound.

Her dad watched her as she took her pole out of the stock
on the side of the boat and sat back down. She hadn't had so
much as a nibble; she was thinking about changing her bait.
"Did you ever notice how still the surface of the water gets
right before you get a strike?"

"Yeah," she said, but she really hadn't and today the
breeze was making the lake a bit choppy. It was also making
it a lot cooler than it had been the last couple of weeks so she

wasn't going to bitch about it. Obviously it wasn't bad enough to keep the fish from biting at least not for her old man.

"You're just sitting and nothing is happening and everything is still and then you can feel that things are about to change and then you have a fish, everything speeds up and nothing is still. Your blood pumps a little faster and when you land a fish there is this moment of triumph and then everything is still again."

"Yeah," and this time Ally knew just what he was talking about.

"Life is like that, Ally. Everything gets still and you think nothing is going to happen and then *boom* good or bad, everything is happening at once. When you get through whatever it was you feel a moment of triumph and then everything is still again, and... you know what we never really appreciate?"

"What, Dad?"

"The moments when everything is still."

"Dad," Ally laughed. "Do you listen to everything Maggie says?"

He smiled back at her. "She's very pretty, so of course I do." He looked out at the lake. "Most of fishing is sitting and waiting. People like you and me who get good at it are good at it because we learn to enjoy the sitting and waiting part. For us this is like that meditation that Maggie does or that Chechy googoo stuff she has you do with her in the mornings."

"Chi Gung, Dad." Ally laughed.

"Fishing is how we find that inner calm she's always talking about. Then we jump up and run around and get our fish off the line. Most of life is the sitting and waiting part; learn to enjoy the sitting and waiting part."

Ally didn't laugh at him because she knew what he was doing. He was dying and he wanted to tell her what he'd learned from life.

"And kids grow up too quick. People have kids and then they just can't wait for them to get through this, that, or the other thing. Then they're gone. The best time of my life was when you were a little kid, Ally."

Ally got a bite, so she snapped the pole and started reeling. It was a big fish and it had a lot of fight in it. She no sooner got it on deck than her dad caught another one and she had to help him get it in.

When they were still again, their lines back in the water, her Dad said to her, "And what's better, Ally, the catching or the sitting?"

"I like them both but neither without the other."

"Exactly."

"...because I want to plant the trees the way I want to plant them, and if Ally is here she will do them the way *she* thinks they should be done. Which will mean heavy equipment and following the plan to the letter," Maggie said, sticking the shovel into the earth. "But now it's hotter that two sticks of shit and the ground is hard, and I'm thinking I should have just let Ally do it."

"I really figured you'd use a day away from Ally to go to a yoga class or meditate." Mona looked at the hole Maggie was trying to dig. "Don't you need to find your center, rebuild your chi?"

"I meditate every evening before dinner and I do a set of Chi Gung with Ally every morning. The truth is I've never felt more centered or Chi filled in my life," Maggie said with a smile. "I'm a little worried about Ally, though."

"Why?"

"Something's bothering her. She's more twitchy then normal, and she's not singing as much as she was."

"Honey, her father is dying," Mona said. "She was at the hospital with him most of the night."

"And see this started before that, so I don't think that's it. Wednesday Mitch asked me if Ally and I were having trouble. I told him we weren't."

"Why would he think that?"

"Because Ally apparently laid into Billy Bob and Ray for— of all things—talking too much. When I asked her about it she didn't snap at me, but she didn't look happy, and she said she was just tired of them running their mouths all the time talking shit."

Tuesday came running over with the tot shovel Ally had bought him and wanted to help dig, so she stepped aside and let him have at it. He got bored in seconds and ran off to play on his big wheel on the deck.

Maggie remembered something she'd seen them do at the shop, and feeling a little stupid for not thinking of it till then she went and got a hose, stuck it in the small hole she'd made and turned it on.

"I think you actually have to plant the tree before you water it," Mona said.

"Ha ha. I just remembered that Ally and the guys will sometimes water the ground when it's hot and dry like this to make the holes easier to dig, or she uses an auger or back hoe. I'd kind of like to keep the heavy equipment use to a minimum."

"Why?" Mona said, making a painful sigh. "Is using heavy equipment going to single handedly cause global warming and sterility in our children?"

Maggie turned the hose off and left the water to soak in. She walked over to stand in the shade of the house where her sister was sitting. "Because I sort of want to enjoy the doing of it."

"And working in the heat and wearing blisters on your hands, is that enjoyable to you?"

Maggie smiled and nodded. "Yes. I like getting my hands in the dirt. I want to plant things and grow them. Raise food for my family, stuff that hasn't been sprayed with toxins and fertilized with chemicals."

"That does it! Mother dropped you on your head when you were a baby; there is no other answer that makes sense." Mona smiled as she watched Maggie peek around the corner to check on Tuesday on the deck. "So I notice the deck now has a gate. Your idea?"

"No, though I'm glad it's there. Tuesday ran his big wheel off the back deck and down all three steps. Scared the crap out of all of us but the worst that happened was he scraped up his knee. He's barely done crying, I hear Ally mumbling, and then she's on the back deck clomping around. When I walk out there she's dragged out all of her tools and an hour later there was a gate."

Maggie walked over and worked some more on the hole. It was considerably easier to dig now.

"Maggie, why don't you leave that for Ally? You know how anal she is. She's never going to be happy with the way you plant those trees."

Maggie grinned at her sister. "But she will never say jack because she won't want to hurt my feelings and I know how to plant a tree as well as she does. After all, the directions are on the bag on the root ball."

"What will happen is that she'll just dig it up and replant it when you aren't looking," Mona said.

"No she won't." Maggie laughed then stopped. "Will she?"

"You know she will," Mona said.

"I should just dig the holes and wait till she gets home to plant them anyway because she'll have fish and that means scales and fish guts and we can stick them in the bottom of the holes."

Mona rolled her eyes and her nose scrunched up.

"It's a super fertilizer."

"If you say so."

Maggie dug the holes, and when Ally got home she dug on them more. Then Ally cleaned and gutted the fish and "helped" Maggie plant the two apple trees she had bought which meant Ally had let Maggie push some dirt around them.

The whole time they were planting them every time Maggie glanced at Mona she was laughing. Maggie looked at Ally as she finished spreading the mulch.

"Seriously, Ally, I sort of wanted to do it myself."

"Why?" Ally asked, looking at her with a modicum of hurt.

"Because when you 'help' me do something it always turns into me helping you in much the same way as we let Tuesday help us—which means really not at all."

"I'm sorry," Ally said. Then she grinned. "Next time I'll sit on the deck, drink a hard cider and watch you work."

Maggie sighed. "Oh, don't I wish."

Sam sat on a chair on the lawn watching Ally and Maggie mostly playing grab ass as they pretended to be watching the fish on the grill. Tuesday and Jack were playing on the grass a few feet from him. The sun was mostly down and it was starting to cool off. Mona walked out of the kitchen, grabbed a lawn chair on her way across the deck and sat down across from him.

"And so I finished the potato salad. Be warned, Maggie will probably bitch at me about the contents as they are neither all organic nor particularly good for us."

"I can hardly wait."

"So did you have a good time fishing with Ally?"

"Yes."

"And did you tell her all about life the universe and

everything?"

He took a deep breath, sighed, then looked at her smiled and shrugged. "I tried. I don't know. I wanted to. I mostly wound up talking about fishing and how it related to life which when I think about it now just sounds like a bunch of psychobabble. I realized the greatest wisdom I could give her I didn't want to. You know, please don't live your life like I lived mine, in lies, regret and fear. And it's bothering her he's out, and I can tell it's bothering her, but she's just trying hard not to think about it. I think it would be easier for her to forget about it if I wasn't here."

"Well I don't know about that, but you're right. Ally's upset; Maggie said so. She doesn't know why because Ally's not saying. So I think we both know what's bothering her, but you know what? She's mostly dealing with it just fine, Sam."

"She shouldn't have to deal with it at all," Sam hissed. "No one should."

"For Christ's sake, Maggie, it's potato salad not the devil's own curds and whey," Mona said, slinging a spoon full of it at Maggie.

"Dammit, Mona," Maggie peeled the spoonful of potato salad off her blouse. She quickly spun on Tuesday. "Don't."

He turned the spoon around and stuck it in his mouth as if that was all he was planning on doing all along, and they all had a good laugh.

"Look, Mona, I know alright? I get it. It's delicious; everything you make is, but you have to find a new way of cooking that's healthy for you."

"And I have, Maggie. I swear I don't eat like this all the time but dammit when I'm cooking for other people I want it to taste the way I want it to taste."

"She's lost forty-five pounds," Sam defended her sister.

Maggie nodded. She knew she couldn't make Mona eat right because she'd tried for years. She could try to encourage her but if she pushed, Mona was likely to go the other way just to remind Maggie that she wasn't the boss of her. And Mona was doing better. For one thing she'd only eaten a small portion of the devil's own curds and whey, and had filled up mostly on grilled fish.

Sam's color was better but it was by no means good.

So as she sat there Maggie knew Mona really needed to

take better care of herself, Sam was dying, and Ally was in a funk. She was working hard at not being, but she was, and whatever it was she wasn't talking to Maggie about it, and that was worrying Maggie more than anything else. That Ally had some problem that she didn't feel like she could talk to her about.

"Maggie!" Mona yelled.

"Huh?" Maggie asked, showing a complete lack of intelligence.

"I said quit worrying. I'm not going to go off my diet. I'm going to keep doing the treadmill thing. I know I've said all that in the past, but I didn't nearly die before. I get it, alright?" Mona said.

"I'm sorry Mona, I just worry."

Maggie looked over at Ally briefly and she had the same blank look on her face she'd been getting for most of that week when she thought no one was looking. *And it's true I'm worried sick about Mona but what the hell is going on with you and why can't you talk to me about it?*

"Come on baby," Ally said, gently shoving Maggie off of her. "I'm tired."

"You're never *this* tired," Maggie said, her frustration immediate and evident because of course this was the third time she'd put her off this week. "What's wrong?"

"Nothing's wrong," Ally said, but it sounded like a lie even to her. It wasn't Maggie. Wasn't anything Maggie had done or said. It didn't make any sense and Ally hated it, but right then she just didn't feel like being touched. She'd spent the last couple of days with her dad reminiscing, and that bastard Parish was out of prison. She felt ten again, which wasn't a good place for her to be. But it wasn't Maggie's fault and she knew if she worked at it just a bit she could get it out of her head and once she did Maggie would fix everything. In fact if she let her Maggie could chase *all* of that crap out of her head.

When Maggie moved towards her again she didn't put her off she was, however, all top—which Maggie didn't seem to mind at all.

Later when she was holding Maggie and was almost asleep Maggie asked, "So can you tell me what's wrong?"

"Nothing," Ally said honestly. "Nothing at all is wrong."

Ally had to work later than Maggie on Monday and Tuesday, so they took both vehicles. But on Wednesday Ally wasn't going to have to work till dark, so they all went in the truck. Sam smiled as he watched them leave for work then he walked over to the table that stood by the door and picked up the penny.

Ally was wondering whether she was going to get to go home with Maggie and Tuesday or if she was going to have to have one of the guys bring her home after work. She was in waders in a ditch where a waterline feeding some huge fountain at the university hospital—nothing she had designed or built—had broken. She was covered in water and mud and was just beginning to make the actual repairs when her smart phone rang. She wiped the mud off her hand and pulled it from her pocket. It said the call was from the Monroe county court house.

"What the hell?" She answered it. "Hello."

"Hello Ally, listen this is your dad and this is my one phone call. I just killed Laban Parish. I've confessed and been arrested. Now I don't want you to worry because I have thought this all out."

Mitch came boiling out of his office with his cell phone in his hand. "Ray, don't let her leave the site. I'm sending Maggie."

Maggie jumped out of her chair. "What's going on?"

"I just saw something on the news. I need you not to ask questions just leave the boy with me and go get Ally."

"Is she alright?" Maggie got her purse and Ally's keys.

"She's fine but she's about to be very upset so just get over to the job site," Mitch said.

"Mitch what the hell..."

"Just go," he started pushing her towards the doorway.

"What the hell, Dad?" Ally yelled into the phone.

"Now Ally, I didn't call to upset you. I just didn't want you to worry."

"Don't worry! Dad, are you nuts? Why Dad, why?"

"You know why, Ally. I'm dying. What's the worst they can do to me? They just let him go. He ruined everything and they just let him go."

Ally watched as Maggie pulled up to the job site, stopped and all but jumped out of the truck. She came running down the incline, slipped in some mud and nearly fell on her ass.

"I'm coming to get you, Dad," Ally said.

"They aren't going to let me go. I shot a man in the head in broad daylight and confessed."

"Bullshit, Dad! Bullshit! You aren't a danger to the population. I'll talk to them and they'll see that."

"Now dammit, Ally, don't you ruin everything I've worked for. My time is up; I have to go." Her dad hung up as Maggie slid into the mud in front of her, looking panicked.

"What's going on?"

"I have to go to Monroe," Ally said, crawled out of the hole and put down a muddy hand to pull Maggie up after her.

"What the hell happened, Ally?" Ray asked, running up to her where she was walking towards her truck, dragging Maggie behind her.

"Well you ought to be happy; my dad just killed Laban Parish." Ally let go of Maggie, walked around the truck and dropped her waders. Then she got in the truck; Maggie was just standing there.

"Get in the truck, Maggie. I have to go."

Maggie got in the truck feeling numb. Ally took off but was driving like a normal human, and Maggie suddenly realized why Mitch had insisted Maggie go get Ally, because if Ally had gotten into one of the company trucks alone or even with one of the guys she would have driven like a bat out of hell. She never drove like that with Maggie or Tuesday in the vehicle.

"Why would your dad kill Parish?" Maggie asked.

"He was a bastard who preyed on kids, that's why," Ally said dismissively.

"You sound like you don't care that he killed a man."

"I only care because he's now probably going to spend what life he has left in jail."

"Ally, he took another person's life. He killed a man."

"That man was a fucking pedophile who molested kids who went to my Dad's fucked up church."

"Why would he do this horrible thing, and why are you condoning it? No one has the right to play judge, jury and executioner."

"Maggie, I don't really want to hear your bleeding-dove crap right now. My dad's in trouble."

"He's in trouble because he killed a man."

Then Ally made a sound Maggie had never heard before and hoped she never heard again because it sent a shiver down her spine. "I have killed more than one man. I know you know that because Helen knew and she told you everything. She didn't tell me everything, just you."

Maggie did know. She tried not to think about it but she knew. "But that's different, Ally. This was premeditated murder."

"Is it really? I think if you go to a country with a riffle with orders to hunt and kill people, that's pretty premeditated. Are you going to help me or just sit there and pass judgement?" Ally pulled into their driveway and stopped. She got out without saying another word and by the time Maggie got in the house Ally was already in the storm cellar. She came out slamming the door behind her. "He used my gun." She held up a piece of paper. "But he was nice enough to leave a note. Sorry I took your gun. Really, Dad really!"

"That damn gun, Ally, if you didn't have it he couldn't have done this."

"Really Maggie? Because I think that makes about as much sense as me saying to you that damn car—if you didn't have it he couldn't have done it." It was only then that Maggie realized her car wasn't in the driveway.

"I... I thought he couldn't drive," Maggie defended.

"No, he *shouldn't* drive; there's a big difference."

Maggie followed Ally in the bathroom where Ally took off her muddy shirt and started to wash up. "Could you get me a clean shirt, please?"

Maggie walked towards their bedroom and froze for a second. *I don't know her. Her father killed someone. The guy was a maggot, but no one deserves the death penalty. But clearly the only problem Ally has with this is that her father's going to be in trouble. I've been living with my son in a house with a man capable of murder and Ally is a killer, too.* Maggie had to make herself walk the rest of the way into the bedroom and go to the closet. She got Ally a clean T-shirt because when Ally wasn't at work she just always wore T-shirts. *I know everything about her that doesn't matter and nothing that does.* She took the shirt to Ally and handed it to her. *I love Ally but... well is this a deal breaker? The whole she doesn't really believe in the sanctity of life. That she has killed people that she's alright with what her dad did because after all the victim was scum.*

"What?" Ally asked of the look on Maggie's face.

"You really have no problem at all with your dad using your gun...."

"And your car."

"...to kill a living, breathing human being."

Ally pulled the T-shirt on and looked down at Maggie. She took a deep breath and let it out. "Don't make this a thing, Maggie."

"Don't make it a thing?" Maggie bellowed. "This isn't a *thing* Ally. Your dad took your gun and shot and killed another person with it, not in self-defense, not because he didn't have a choice."

"I have to go. I don't have time to fight with you, Maggie. Are you coming?" Ally started out of the house.

"No." Maggie felt like the word was being dragged out of her, and she started crying. "You need me to be someone I'm not right now, and I'm not sure I know you at all. This is a huge problem for us, Ally."

Ally stopped at the door and turned to look at her. "What do you mean, Maggie?"

"Maybe this with us is a mistake."

"Are you kidding me, Maggie?" Ally ran her hands down her face. "You're going to throw what we have away over fucking Laban Parish? You know what; if you can do that then *I* don't know *you* at all." She marched out the door without closing it, got in her truck and roared off.

"Why did you kill him?"

Sam was actually enjoying giving his statement to the police. It was sort of like crowing. "He was the worst kind of pervert. That bastard ruined my family and my life," Sam said. "I'm dying. I couldn't protect my family alive how could I do it when I was dead? And you think people get over the sort of thing Parish does but they don't—they never do. You know he raped my grandson Kyle because Parish told you that himself. It wasn't enough that he did it, no he had to make sure everyone knew he did it so that there would be nowhere the boy could go where everyone didn't know."

"I guess..." The cop slid the recorder a little closer to Sam. "...all we need to know is how you did it."

"During the tornado we all went down to the storm shelter. Afterwards Ally went out to look for survivors." He looked at the cop with pride. "My daughter was in the National Guard. She fought in Iraq. Now she works for a landscaping company, so she's a first responder. Well she kept her service pistol locked in a safe in her storm shelter. She unlocked it and pulled it out because apparently people's dogs get lose after a storm and some of them can get vicious." The cop nodded. "She keeps the key to the safe on her key ring, and she always keeps her keys on a table by the front door. I waited till she and Maggie were asleep last night and then I went down and got the gun. I waited for them to go to work this morning and Maggie left her car. Now Maggie broke the key off in her ignition switch a few months back, so all I needed was a penny to start it.

"I'm coming to the bitter end now. My health is fading fast and if I didn't kill him now I wasn't going to be able to later. Plus... I don't want Ally and Maggie to have to take care of me. Let some state employee wipe my ass and watch me disintegrate, roll me around and clean me up, not my kids. This way the government has to pay for everything, my hospice, my cremation; my kids don't have to deal with anything.

Monroe is close to Flint Town—only a thirty-minute drive and I just got an iron infusion this past weekend so I was feeling just about as good as I do these days. I took only a half dose of my pain killers, still the drive was the hardest part of it, and it wasn't that bad. Now you see I'm really good with the computer and he's a registered sex offender, so the GPS on my phone brought me right to his door. Then I just got out of the car, walked to the front door and rang the bell. He should have recognized me because we went to church together for over fifteen years, but since I wasn't a little kid when he looked out that peephole he didn't recognize me at all. He opened his door said, 'Hello can I help you?' I looked that evil fucker right in the eye and said just like Clint Eastwood might, 'You can die.' And I picked up Ally's pistol, put it right between the bastard's eyes and fired. Then when he fell backwards I waited till he landed and I stood right over the top of him and emptied that mother fucker into his face just to make sure he was good and dead. Then I dropped the gun, called you guys, and waited there for you to come and arrest me. I'm pretty sure that is first degree, premeditated murder, and you know what? It felt so damn good that if I make bail I'm going to go kill another sex offender and another and another, so you by God better keep me in jail."

Maggie had packed two bags, one for her and one for Tuesday. She was sitting on the front porch crying and waiting for Mona.

Mona pulled up and parked. Maggie picked up the bags and headed for Mona's car. Mona got out of the car shaking her head and walked right up to her. "What the hell is wrong with you? Do you just hate being happy?"

"I can't stay here, Mona."

"I'm not going to let you do this." Mona easily grabbed the bigger of the two suitcases out of Maggie's hand and started towards the house. "You aren't going to be able to leave Ally no matter what you think right now, and if you leave her right now there is just going to be this huge thing between you."

"Dammit, Mona, listen to me…"

"No you listen to me. *You are wrong.* Ally needs you right now, and you already flaked out on her. I'm not going to let you do this, too." Mona walked in, took the bag right to their bed room opened it and dumped the contents on the bed.

Maggie looked down at the smaller bag in her hand then set it on the end of the bed.

"Do you really want to leave Ally? I thought you loved her. Was that bullshit? Do you want to uproot Tuesday take him away from her and her from him?"

"No," Maggie cried and flopped on the bed. "But if I won't make a stand, I stand for nothing."

"Yes now is a great time to quote crap from some self-help book you read. If you're going to leave Ally over some matter of principle then I was wrong; you don't deserve to be happy. Stuff your crap back in the bag and I'll take you to a hotel…"

"A hotel? Why can't we stay with you?"

"Am I right that you're going to leave Ally because she doesn't have a problem with her dad killing Parish with her gun?"

Maggie nodded silently, tears streaming down her face.

"Then, Honey, you don't want to stay with me because I also don't have a problem with Sam killing Parish with Ally's gun."

"Mona!" Maggie cried in disbelief. "What are you saying?"

"That you need to get your dumb ass up and start putting your crap back where it belongs, call Ally up and apologize, because apparently no one but you and the ACLU wants to throw this fucking creep a parade."

"I don't want to throw him a parade, but... premeditated murder, Mona," Maggie said in disbelief, standing up.

"Of a blemish on the ass of humanity!"

"And is that the kind of world we want one where people just kill each other?"

"So is this really about Parish or is this because you finally remembered what you conveniently forgot—that Ally has killed people, too?" Mona asked. "Don't be a fucking hypocrite, Maggie. You're the one who always wants everyone to live in truth. If someone killed Tuesday's father in cold blood would you be damning them the way you are Sam and Ally right now?"

Maggie was so shocked by the question that she actually didn't answer right away. When she did her answer surprised her, "I... I don't know."

"Because you don't ever want Doug to show up and cause any trouble for your son. You don't want any other woman to go through what you went through." Mona went and got the empty hangers out of Maggie's side of the closet and started hanging Maggie's clothes on them. "This woman is crazy in love with you. She loves your kid. She separates her trash. She bought you a lot so you could build an organic garden. For God's sake she gets up with you in the morning and does a set of Chi Gung with a leg that looks like chopped meat. She paints and sings when she's happy. She satisfies your rather bizarre and very energetic sexual desires. She even eats tofu when you feed it to her without bitching. And you're going to let a little thing like her father killed some maggot get between you? Are you nuts?" She stopped putting the blouse on the hanger. "You know what? Go ahead and leave her. I'll learn to like girls and I'll take her. You go back to your sad, empty life...."

"My life wasn't sad and empty."

"Well mine is, so...."

"Mona this isn't some joke. Ally's dad killed someone with her gun and Ally doesn't care."

"Would you like her to pretend to be all choked up about it?" Mona said and went right back to putting Maggie's clothes on hangers. "Don't make me say it." Mona stopped doing what she was doing, looked at Maggie and sighed. "Maggie, you know people probably better than I do—at least when you're sober—does Sam seem like the kind of man who would just up and kill someone?"

"Ally said it was because Parish molested some kids from his church. But Mona we can't just go around..."

"Would you do anything to protect your son?"

"Yes," Maggie said without a second thought, "but no one was in danger...."

"Really? Because no repeat offender has ever slipped through the cracks and gone right on molesting kids. Maggie, Sam is dying—sooner rather than later. He feels like he screwed up everything that was important in his life, but the truth is he had help."

"What are you talking about, Mona?"

"Come on, Maggie. You aren't this dense. Think about it a minute, about the way Ally's been acting lately."

Maggie shrugged.

Mona sighed. "You huge dumbass. Sam said I might need to tell you, and I'm guessing it's because this was his plan all along and he knew you were going to be this stupid." Mona took a deep breath and let it out before she went on. "Maggie, Laban Parish molested two generations of Sam's family."

Maggie suddenly felt sick. She sat on the end of the bed and looked up at her sister. "Carol?" she asked hopefully, feeling her stomach twist in a knot.

"No, Honey, not Carol."

"Ally..." Maggie cried and put her face in her hands.

"And Sam's grandson, Kyle," Mona said.

"Still Mona murder..." Maggie choked out.

"He molested Ally, Maggie, not some stranger. Ally. Do you really not trust Ally?"

Maggie cried. "I trust Ally completely."

"Then what else really matters?"

Maggie got up, dried her face on her sleeve and started taking the clothes Mona had put on the hangers and putting them back in the closet where they belonged. "I'm not leaving. You're right about everything." She smiled at her sister, walked over and kissed her on the cheek. "Right now I am so happy that you think you have the right to run my life."

"I do a damn sight better job than you do." Mona threw down the last hangered item of clothing and turned to look at Maggie. "You can finish unpacking yourself. I'm going to go pick up Tuesday at Mitch and Karen's and take him home with me for the night. I think it would be a good idea for you and Ally to have a night alone. Don't waste it fighting about crap that doesn't really matter. Maggie, Ally never wanted you to know, so if you're smart you won't know. You will just tell her that you love her so much that even though you hate when people take the law into their own hands you're going to be there for her through this whole thing because she is the love of your life. She is, isn't she?"

Maggie nodded.

"Then can all your hippy 'love and peace' bullshit at least for now and be who she needs you to be—someone who loves her unconditionally."

Dad, what the hell? They've set your bail at a million dollars because you told them you'd kill again and again and again?" Ally whispered as she sat down across from him.

He reached across the table and wiped a tear from her cheek.

"Genius huh?" He smiled at her. "Look, when I fell in the living room floor... Ally, you and Maggie have been so good to me, and the end of my life has been so much better than the last twenty years without you have been. I don't want you to have to take care of me. This last week I could see that it bothered you that he was out, and Ally it wasn't just you. He molested Carol's son, Kyle, too. That's in the public record and you know how kids are, Ally.

"Your mother had me by the balls, but I let her ruin me. I never should have let her try to ruin you. I knew something was wrong with you but I didn't ask because I was sure I knew that it was that you were a lesbian and I just didn't want to know that. I was stupid then and I couldn't imagine anything worse. I plead ignorance, Ally. But I didn't kill that bastard for you or for Kyle. I killed him for me. I let him get away before, and he did the same thing to other families that he did to mine. Today I got my balls back. They can't do anything to me that the universe isn't already doing in spades, and I'm ready to die now because I did one thing right."

"Dammit, Dad, do you hear yourself?" Ally cried, though it wasn't really for her dad and he probably knew it when she said, "Dad, Maggie's probably going to leave me over this shit."

"That girl isn't going to leave you, Ally. She loves you."

"It sure sounded like she was going to leave me." Ally cried pretty hard then; she just didn't care.

The cop in the room with them actually looked at a wall.

"You need to marry that girl, Ally. You know because you can and you should, and adopt that baby…"

"Did you not hear me, Dad? Maggie said she's going to leave me."

"No she isn't; she was just mad. Why couldn't you just act shocked and appalled? Why did you have to be honest?" Then he grinned, knowing. "Because part of you wanted to do a little dance when I told you he was dead."

"Dammit, Dad." She laughed through her tears. "Yes, and she was so mad Dad, and why did you have to use my gun?"

"Where else was I going to get a gun? You know she wanted you to get rid of it anyway and now it's gone. You know—evidence of a murder and all. Tell her she can thank me later."

CHAPTER 10

If there is no prize in your cereal box you probably have more cereal.

The sheriff told Ally that her dad would spend his jail time in the infirmary and that she could visit him any time she wanted. He also assured her that when his time came he'd die in a normal hospital, and he hoped to swing it so that he could send him to Flint Town University Hospital under the guise of it having a bigger hospice wing. "By the time we can't handle him here he won't be ambulatory, so it's not like he could make good on his threats to kill more perverts. I don't think I'll have any trouble getting him into the hospital closer to you."

"Thanks, I appreciate it," Ally said.

He actually followed her out of the building and helped her past the wall of reporters firing questions at her that she didn't want to answer.

"Do you know why your father killed Laban Parish?"

"He molested a bunch of kids from my father's church. My dad's dying of cancer, so he decided to kill him. That's what he said; that's all I know."

As they fired more questions at her she ignored them, and the sheriff said, "That's enough. Now please let her leave. I will answer any questions you have when I return." When they were at her truck and away from anyone else he said, "I saw you on TV a while back after the tornado. You're a real hero, kid. Between you and me and that post over there, so's your old man. We'll make sure he gets good care."

"Thanks again." Ally got in her truck wondering if it was worth her time to go home or if she just needed to go to the bar, get shit-faced drunk and pray for death. She put her key in the ignition but didn't turn it. If Maggie and Tuesday weren't there when she got home she had no idea what she was going to do. Should she just go over to Mona's and order Maggie to get her ass in the truck and come home? No that wasn't a good idea. She could try crying—after all that's what she'd been doing most of the afternoon. Begging and pleading might work. Maybe her dad was right and she needed to pretend that it was an awful, terrible thing that he killed Parish.

That awful bastard, I'm just so happy he's dead. I had years of therapy and I wasn't a victim anymore and then he was everywhere in the news and they let him go. When they did I didn't feel quite as healthy. Now he's gone and there is no wondering where he might be or what he might be doing to whom. My dad he is so happy and I can go visit him after work talk to him and then go home. I don't have to worry that I'm going to come home and find him dead or have to take time off work to sit with him while he dies in stages. He really did think of everything. If only Maggie could be more reasonable about the whole killing thing she'd see that this is what's best for everyone.

That right there is why she's so mad at me, because apparently it's not right to think it's fine to kill people if they suck. But I killed people during the war, and I accidently killed Tuesday's dad—but no one needs to know that, least of all Maggie especially if she's this pissed about dad killing a baby raper.

Doug should have known better than to pick up that two by four because the minute he had a weapon in his hand my military training just kicked in and then... I hadn't done that kick with the brace and he moved. I was trying to hit him in the side of the head with my foot, but he moved and the brace hit his face and he was dead instantly. It scared the hell out of us, but I never had any guilt and I'm sure Mitch didn't because after all he didn't really kill the turd though it was his idea to grind him up and compost him.

Her phone rang and she jumped because of what she was thinking. She dug in her pocket, pulled it out and looked at it. When she saw it was Maggie she was afraid to answer but she did starting with, "Baby, I'm sorry please don't leave me." And she was crying again though it wasn't a plan.

"I'm not going anywhere and I'm so sorry I didn't go with you. Where are you? Do you need me to come meet you there?"

"No. I'm coming home. Dad didn't make bail—lots of reasons. No doubt because what he did was a horrible,

horrible, terrible thing."

"Probably because he sounded about as sincere as you just did." Maggie laughed and Ally quit crying.

Dad was right; she isn't going to leave me because she loves me.

"Please be careful coming home. I never should have let you drive over there alone. I'm sorry."

"So it's not something we can't work through, Maggie?" Ally asked carefully.

"No, Mona told me he molested your sister's son. I don't condone killing, but I think I understand why Sam thought he had to do it, and why it doesn't bother you," Maggie said. "And Ally I know you aren't a killer. I trust you. We don't agree on this, but it's not as big a deal as I thought it was. It's not like you're going to start a militia and go out and kill sex offenders."

"No, but that's basically what my dad told the court to make sure they wouldn't let him out on bail."

"What?"

"I'll tell you more when I get home. Please, Maggie don't leave. My life was empty and hollow without you and that baby in it...."

"I'm not going anywhere. For just a minute I forgot that it's more important to be happy than it is to be right."

It was dark when she pulled into the driveway, but the porch light was on. She got out and walked up the walkway suddenly feeling like she'd run a five-mile race, hit the wall and now had nothing left to give.

She walked in and threw her keys on the table. The light was on in the kitchen so she walked towards it hopeful that Maggie hadn't changed her mind and left. She was more worried because normally by now Tuesday would have already run down the hall to hug her. *I went from being all alone here to having a house full of people and now dad's gone and I can handle that because that was always going to happen, but I need Maggie and Tuesday or at the very least I want them.*

She heard noise coming from the kitchen and nearly ran the rest of the way through the house. Maggie greeted her halfway across the kitchen, and Ally grabbed her and held her tight.

"Oh, baby, I'm so sorry. You were upset and I made it worse." Maggie wrapped her arms around her and held her tight.

"I was so much more upset that you were going to leave me, Maggie. My dad is fine. Being in jail was part of his plan. But... I don't want you to leave me, Maggie." Ally was really mad at herself because she just couldn't seem to stop crying.

Maggie felt about two inches tall because she suddenly realized why her big, tough, butch woman was crying like a baby. Ally loved her, Maggie didn't doubt that at all, and Ally had already permanently lost a woman she loved. So for that matter had Maggie. So Maggie started crying again because she had made Ally cry and her crying just made Ally cry even harder.

"I'm so, so sorry, baby."

"Don't be sorry, Maggie just don't go. Don't ever go."

"I won't, baby, I won't. I couldn't, Ally. Even if I'd gone I couldn't have stayed away."

Ally sniffled then and seemed to be trying to quit crying. "That's what my dad said. I'm sorry, and I know what he did was wrong."

Maggie laughed and shook her head, drying her own tears on the back of her hand. "Ally Taggart, stop with the lying right now. We don't agree on this. I thought it was a huge thing, but my sister tells me I'm being a hypocrite."

"Where is our son?"

"Mona is keeping him for the night. She thought you and I needed some time alone."

"But..." Ally sniffled and smiled at her. "...we've never had that before. What will we do?"

"The same thing we always do except anywhere we want and we can make as much noise as we want." Maggie laughed. "I made us some dinner. It's ready if you feel like eating."

"I am starving; I didn't get lunch. Let me go wash my face and hands so that I can pretend that I haven't been crying."

Maggie washed her face in the kitchen sink, dried off with paper towels and put dinner on the table. When Ally came back she was wearing a clean T-shirt, no doubt because the other one was covered in snot. Ally sat down across from her and made a face.

"What?" Maggie asked.

"It's too quiet." Ally smiled at her. "After dinner we should see what we can do about all the quiet."

And so they did—in the shower, then on the couch in the living room and finally in bed. And with every caress, every kiss, every orgasm, Maggie was more and more grateful that she hadn't gone anywhere, and she really was enjoying having Ally all to herself.

"You know we should do this more often," Maggie said.

"I think we do it enough," Ally said, still trying to catch her breath.

Maggie laughed rolled over and kissed Ally's shoulder. "I meant let someone watch Tuesday so that we can actually be alone."

"Really? Because I was wondering if it was too late to go get him from your sister's house."

Maggie laughed at her. "Are you the same woman who told me that everything you know about kids could be written on a tick tack box?"

"With room left over," Ally reminded. "I love him, Maggie. I talked myself into being alright with a kid because Helen wanted one so bad, but I was never really sure it was something I wanted, which is no doubt why the eggs just sit frozen. But your kid... Maggie, the first time I realized he actually cared about me, that he trusted me; I just fell completely in love with him. When Helen died I thought I'd never feel joy again but I am so blessed to have you and him. I don't want this to get between us. When I thought there was a chance...."

Maggie put her finger over Ally's lips, and then she moved her finger and kissed her. "There was never a chance. I was wrong today; I didn't think I just reacted. Let's face it, it's not every day your girlfriend's dad kills someone. It was a lot to process and you didn't react the way I wanted you to and I certainly didn't react the way you wanted me to. This can only get between us if we let it, and we just won't let it. I never could have left you. I know why you thought I would because I thought I would, too, but I never could so don't say it again because I feel bad enough."

"Is it too late to get Tuesday?"

"Yes."

It was the second day working on the water feed for that stinking hospital fountain, and Ally had changed her mind. *Alright I was wrong. I'd rather work on stuff we built that broke because at least then everything makes sense. Whoever installed this didn't know anything about... well, anything.*

She had her ear buds in blasting music because she just didn't want to hear it, any of it. She didn't want them asking her questions about it. She didn't want to hear them saying her dad was a hero—none of it. Especially since the kind of crap they were saying was the reason Maggie nearly left her.

She and Maggie had picked Tuesday up on the way into work.

"I thought Mitch and Karen were going to cry when I came to get him," Mona had told them. "They really wanted him to stay the night with them"

He ran right to Ally and she picked him up and hugged him tighter than normal and he rubbed her head and said, "I missed you Allybaba," and Ally had nearly cried again. She was really emotional and that was another reason she didn't want to hear any of their crap. Parish was dead. She was glad, but Maggie wasn't, so she needed to keep it to herself which was hard with everyone she worked with crowing like roosters as if they had shot him themselves. And Parish being dead didn't undo what he'd done. It didn't magically fix all his victims. She would be glad when it was old news and people just stopped talking about it because when they weren't talking about it she didn't think about it at all. She couldn't really blame them for wanting to ask her a billion questions. Her dad killed Parish; it was the biggest news item since the tornado. They wanted inside info, and she guessed in their position she would have been curious, too. Except she mostly minded her own damn business and she sure as hell didn't bother any of them when it was obvious they were in a mood.

And maybe at the end of the day that was what separated her from the boys.

It was one before they finally got the damn thing fixed right and got it all put back together. Chuck, Ray and Billy Bob got in the truck with her and of course Billy Bob couldn't help himself.

"So why did your dad kill him?"

"I told you assholes I don't want to talk about this shit. My dad's going to die in jail now, and that doesn't make me happy, so just shut the fuck up!" Ally was driving.

"Come on, Ally," Ray started. And somewhere inside the little cable just snapped. She pulled the truck over and turned to look at Ray in the back seat.

"What about 'shut up' do you fuckers not understand? None of you is this fucking stupid, do the God-damned math. Why do you think he killed him? Why do you think I don't want to talk about it!? Do I look for your weak spot and then get a stick and poke at it? I said shut up!" She turned around and pulled the truck back onto the road.

"I'm sorry, Ally, I didn't know…"

"Shut up, Ray. For the love of God, shut the fuck up!"

When Ally walked in the front door of Taggart's, Mitch was talking to Maggie, so she didn't interrupt but she wanted to because now she had to tell Maggie, and she just wanted it all over with at once.

"Allybaba!" Tuesday jumped up from where he'd been playing and ran over. Ally picked him up and held him.

"Honey, are you okay?" Maggie asked.

"I'm fine." She forced a smile and walked into the break room with Tuesday. She sat down and set him on the table in front of her. "What have you been doing today?"

"I drew a picture of something I want you to build and I helped Mom. I played with my cars. What have you been doing?" He started picking at a mud clod on Ally's face.

"Getting dirty fixing a mess some dumbass made."

"Mom said dumbass isn't a nice thing to call people," he said.

"No it isn't," and Ally for once was glad the dumbasses she worked with had decided to go to the café across the street for lunch instead of eating in the break room. She set Tuesday on the floor. "Tuesday could you go get my lunch out of the fridge?" He ran over to the door, opened it, and then they started playing his favorite game, "Is it this one?"

Mitch had just finished telling her she could send the invoices out after Ally finished lunch when Ray came to the front door and without walking in motioned for Mitch to follow him outside. Mitch headed for the door and Maggie followed him. "Not you," Ray said, in a hissed whisper.

"Is it about Ally?" Mitch asked, also in a whisper.

Ray nodded.

"If it's about Ally then Helen...." He caught himself and took a deep breath. He looked at Maggie. "I'm sorry, Maggie."

Maggie smiled at him, got on her tip toes and kissed his cheek. "Ally has done the same thing and at much more inappropriate times, I don't mind at all. And if it's important Ally will tell me later."

She glared at Ray. "I told you dill holes to shut up about it." Maggie walked away and into the break room. Seeing what Tuesday was doing she said, "Quit farting around and bring Ally her lunch."

Tuesday grabbed the bag with Ally's name on it and brought it to her. Ally mock snarled at him, "You mean you know exactly which lunch is mine?"

He laughed and pointed. "It has your name on it."

"I thought you couldn't read."

"I can't but I know what your name looks like."

Maggie kissed the top of Ally's head and sat down across from her. She had already eaten her lunch. "So... they just couldn't leave you alone?" she asked gently.

"No and I didn't want anyone to know, least of all you, and now I need to tell you before one of them do...."

"I already know, Ally. I'm not stupid; I can do the math." She didn't see any reason to tell Ally that Sam had told Mona or that Mona had told her. All things considered it really was obvious. "You can talk about it if and when you want to."

"I've worked it all out, Maggie. I just need them all to shut up."

"And they will, Ally."

"But now they're all going to be tip-toeing around me like I'm damaged and I'm not, not about this, not about anything."

"The problem is they are basically all nice guys, Ally. They love you so now they all feel like jackasses, but give it a couple of days and everything will get back to normal. You know, them treating you like crap."

"I feel like one giant, raw nerve, Maggie."

"You know what? When we get off work let's go fishing. Didn't you tell me that your Dad said that's how you meditate?"

"Yes." Ally smiled at her. "But you don't like to fish."

"But I like to eat fish and I love to watch you fish. So how about we take our son and go to the lake?"

Sam looked at Tuesday as he jumped around on the foot of

Sam's bed on his knees. "I caught a huge fish, huge, Sam." He held his arms out as far as he could stretch, and when Sam looked over at Ally she held her hands up about a foot apart and grinned. "Mom made us stop and get another tree so we could feed it fish guts. Do you think trees like fish guts?" He made a face and Sam laughed.

"I have heard that they do."

"You weren't in the clink long," Ally said.

Just a week really. Though there wasn't much difference between the infirmary in the jail and the hospice room he was in now. This room had a better view was about it. "Nope, I'm afraid without all the good food Maggie was feeding me and the vitamins I'm going downhill fast."

"I could bring your vitamins," Maggie said. It was the first time she'd spoken to him. She didn't like what he'd done, but she still loved him.

He looked from Maggie's hand to Ally with meaning.

Ally's brow scrunched all up saying she had no idea what he was thinking, so he looked from Maggie's ringless finger to Ally again, and Ally quickly walked to the window and looked out.

"There is that fucking fountain I worked on for two days how's that for fate, Dad?" Ally asked.

"I want to see." Tuesday jumped off the bed and ran over to Ally. Ally picked him up and showed him and then they were busy talking.

"At least he didn't say fucking fountain," Maggie said in a whisper to Sam.

"I'm sorry, Maggie. They say you can have your car back when they have finished processing it."

"That car would be no great loss," Maggie said.

"I'm sorry that I made you mad at Ally. It wasn't Ally's fault, Maggie."

"I just think it's wrong to kill people, but...." She looked over at where Ally was holding her son telling him all about what a pain in the ass the fountain had been to fix. "...I understand why you did it. More I think than I want to. If anyone hurt one of them... I don't know what I might do. I'm not going to judge you; I love you Sam. We all miss you."

"And I love you, dear girl," Sam couldn't stop his tears from falling. He hurt like a bitch and they were giving him so much dope he had no control of his emotions. "You'll take good care of her for me won't you?"

"You know I will, Sam." Soft-hearted Maggie was just crying like a baby then, so Ally put Tuesday down and came over and held her, patting her back as Maggie cried on her shoulder.

Sam looked at Maggie's back with meaning then mouthed the words. "You marry that girl, Ally."

"We can't hear you, Sam," Tuesday said.

"There is a reason for that, Sport," Sam laughed.

Tuesday sighed. "Sam, how many times do I have to tell you my name isn't Sport, it's Tuesday."

"Come over here for a minute." The boy trotted over and Sam reached out and took the boys hand and looked in his eyes. "Do you know why I call you Sport?"

Tuesday shook his head no.

"Because that's what I used to call Allybaba when she was little. I called her sport."

"Because you couldn't remember her name, either?"

Sam laughed and let go of the boy's hand. "I could remember her name, just like I know your name is Tuesday."

The door opened and Carol walked in with Kyle. The minute Kyle saw Sam he started to cry.

"We better go," Ally said, and pushed Maggie gently away from her. She handed Maggie some tissues out of the box on his bedside table and then handed him some, too. "I'll see you later Dad." She kissed him on the forehead.

"Do it, Ally," he said. "Do it for all the right reasons, and do it because you can." He watched as Ally looked over at Maggie who had Tuesday by the hand.

"I will, Dad. I will." She whispered in his ear, "I love you Dad."

"And I love you, Ally." Ally took Maggie's hand and started to leave.

"Wait a minute."

Ally stopped and turned to face him, and there were tears in her eyes.

"This is your nephew Kyle who is sixteen, and who you have never met. Kyle, this is your Aunt Ally and her family, Maggie and Tuesday. Carol and Ally, you're sisters, can you not just for a minute act like sisters and at least say hello to each other?"

He watched as his not-so-grown daughters looked at one

another and begrudgingly said, "Hello."

"Weak," Sam said, and Kyle giggled walked over and hugged his neck. Then he walked right up to Ally and Maggie and held out his hand. Ally shook his hand, but good ole Maggie grabbed the boy and hugged him. Kyle shook Tuesday's hand.

"And now we'd better go. We don't want to get too much of our gayness on Carol's son," Ally said, giving Sam a wink. Carol almost said something but stopped herself, so maybe there was some hope for her yet.

Sam watched as Ally took Maggie's hand again and left the room.

"How do you feel, Dad?" Carol asked, and in that minute he knew why his wife was able to love Carol when she couldn't love anyone else but herself. *Carol is just like her mother. Jenny could love Carol because she saw her as an extension of herself. But Ally? Ally was too much like me. Jenny wasn't always a bitch, but every time she got too far away from it she went right back like she was always afraid to just be nice. And poor Carol got that from her, too. She will never change because she loves herself just fine the way she is and any change she might make would just be admitting she wasn't right all along. Yet part of her has to know she's not right; why does she fight that part? For the same reason I did. She's afraid of change. She asks how I feel, but she doesn't care any more than she cares about how Kyle feels. This is all just part of the show. I resented her, but now I just feel sorry for her because she lives on the world and not in it.*

"How do you think I feel, Carol? I feel like crap physically and I know I'm dying—which believe it or not is a bit of a downer. But I've just had the best five months of my entire life! I got to get to know Ally and her family and now realize that love, real love, comes in all sorts of packages. That God doesn't sit around and judge us; instead he watches us and hopes we'll figure it all out. God talks to us all, but most of us never hear. There is no hell except the one we make for ourselves right here. I wouldn't have known any of that if I'd stayed in your house.

"I even got laid, and all because you kicked me out of my own house. Thank you, Carol. Thank you for being so self-serving that you just have to keep your loveless, sexless marriage to that spineless jelly fish of a husband going so that all your worthless, bible-thumping friends will think you have it all. If you weren't just like your mean-ass mother I would have died there doing nothing, but thanks to your true failure to learn even one tiny thing from your parent's mistakes, I've lived more in the last few months than I have the whole rest of my life. And now, Carol, quit pretending to care and kindly leave for a few minutes so that I can talk to my grandson man to man." She obviously wasn't so sure it was safe to leave her son with him, no doubt because he was beyond the point of lies, and the truth hurt. She finally left saying she'd be right back, in case either of them might get too comfortable. Sam pointed at the chair sitting next to his bed and Kyle sat down. "So how are you doing really? Did they get you any real help?"

Kyle shook his head but smiled and said, "It helps you killed him."

"Twern't nothin'," Sam said and laughed. Then he frowned and shook his head. "It won't make it go away, Kyle. It still happened and you still have to deal with it. You need help, real help. Maggie said there are councilors at school that you can talk to, but you need to talk to someone. What about the drugs?"

"They did put me in a real rehab and at least for now I'm sober, but it's hard. They make it hard; they fight all the time. I think they really hate each other but I don't think they'll ever split up. They stay together for us but we'd all be better off if they weren't together." He shrugged. "Did you mean it, Grandpa? Did he molest Alice, too?"

"She goes by Ally now, and yes he did." Sam took a deep breath. The oxygen they had running in a tube up his nose burned. "She got help and you need to, too. I found twelve-step support groups online for teens. It's all loaded on my lap top. I don't need the computer anymore, so take it with you when you go. It's in that closet over there. Check it out. You have to know the drugs aren't going to help. I loaded some victim support groups, too. If they won't get you any help that's better than nothing and... you don't have to use your real name. They don't really know you; you don't know them."

He nodded. "I love you, Grandpa." Kyle started to cry. "I don't want you to die."

Sam laughed. "Well I sort of have to now or I have to go to jail."

"My dad said he's going to sell the bait and tackle shop." Kyle dried his eyes on the back of his hand. "I like the shop; I don't know why he's selling it."

"Because it's not his dream it was mine. I'm glad he's selling it," Sam said. He had lots of reasons but he told Kyle, "I'd rather someone had it who really cares about it."

"I miss being with you. I always loved it when you would take me to the lake and we would go fishing, just you and me."

"We did have some good times. I love you, Kyle and... well you just have to be alright."

"So, Grandpa, did you really get laid?"

Sam laughed. "Oh fuck, yeah, and by a hot young woman who turned my old ass every way but loose. Let me catch you up on what I've been doing. Because you see Kyle I forgot how to live and I remembered and now I'm ready to go."

So he told Kyle all about the fishing and the party and the tornado and Maggie, Ally and Tuesday, Mitch, Karen and Helen, and Ray and George and Mona. How Maggie used her gift to find survivors and Ally chain sawed them out. He told him about Maggie and Ally buying the lot next door and about the present he'd gotten Ally that still wasn't there. About Ally singing all the time and painting Tuesday's room and all about Jack. How he served coffee and sandwiches off the porch to the tornado refugees and just exactly how he killed Laban Parish. Till Carol came in and then he told exactly the same stories because well he was on heavy drugs and since he was dying, Carol didn't try to shut him up. Though she did gasp a couple of times.

Carol said she couldn't stay and so Kyle couldn't either. Sam was just as glad because the next three days he could all but feel the life draining from him, and he had plenty of visitors. The police who had arrested him all came by, and all the people he had served coffee and sandwiches to. Mona came by three or four times a day, and he could talk freely about the fact he was dying and just exactly how he felt. She neither broke down nor tried to shut him up. Mitch and Karen sent him flowers and a card, but they didn't come by. Mona said they hadn't really been in a hospital since their daughter died. He couldn't say that he blamed them.

Ally was there three times a day and in the evenings

Maggie and Tuesday had come with her... till tonight. He knew why. He could hardly talk today, and when Ally had come to see him at lunch she must have known it was the end. When she walked in that evening she was alone.

Sam looked up at her and in a voice he hardly recognized as his own asked, "So chicken shit, did you ask that girl to marry you yet?"

Ally laughed finished walking in the room walked over and kissed him on the forehead. She stood up and looked down at him. "Not yet, but if it will shut you up..." She dug in her pocket pulled out a box and opened it.

He looked at the ring with the small but pretty emerald setting then looked up at her and grinned. "It will look good with her eyes."

"She told me it was her favorite gem stone. I'm sort of nervous, Dad. You know Maggie; I'm not sure she's going to want a bunch of paperwork and such. She might say no."

"No, she won't say no." He coughed and couldn't stop for a minute. He'd been doing that all day. He blamed the oxygen. When he finally stopped he said, "I'm glad you didn't bring them. If you can... I don't want to be alone, Ally."

"You won't be, Dad."

His care nurse motioned for Ally to meet her in the hall and she did. "Last time I tried to get his blood pressure I barely got any reading. He should leave us some time in the next few hours."

Ally wondered why no one ever seemed to be able to just say he's going to die. Did the nurse think Ally thought her dad was going to check himself out get dressed and go get a coffee and a doughnut?

"Could you undo him from all the crap? He hates that fucking oxygen tube stuck up his nose, and the IV—can you quit giving him drugs in the IV line every ten seconds? Just get rid of the whole thing. He has a DNR. Can you just take it all off of him and let him go with some semblance of peace?"

"We can. I'll go get the papers for you to sign." She took off and Ally went back to her father's side.

"Dad, I'm going to have them pull all this crap out of you."

"Thank God," he said.

"Do you want me to call Carol?"

"No. I had twenty years with her that I didn't have with

you. Can you hold my hand, Ally?"

She took his hand; there wasn't much left of it. She took a deep breath then said, "Mona told me I should tell you that you can go whenever you want to."

"Try to find her a good man, Ally."

"I will," Ally said, although where she was going to do that she had no idea. All the guys she knew were married or dumbasses—and most were both.

The nurse came in with the paperwork and told Ally where to sign. Ally let go of her dad's hand just long enough to do it then took his hand again and another nurse joined the first one and started unhooking him.

When they had finished and left the room he actually sighed. "I love you, Ally."

"I know," Ally said, and then he was out. Not dead yet but out.

Ally walked over and was happy to see the window opened. She unlatched it, opened it, and she could hear that accursed water fountain. All of the sudden it seemed like that whole job was for this moment, when the sounds of the hospital at least for a moment were over-powered by the sound of running water. She took a deep breath, let it out, and went back to her father's side. She took his hand she could still see his chest rising and falling.

"Dad, let me tell you about all the fishing trips I remember with you...." She told him everything she remembered: every lure, every catch, every boat, river, stream or lake, the big ones they caught, the even bigger ones that got away. The whole time she watched his chest rise and fall, gradually slowing as his life eased gracefully from him...

"And we were fishing on Mitch's boat and remember you were trying to impart wisdom by tying it to fishing and...."

His chest stopped moving and when she looked at the monitor his heart had stopped. There was a ringing and the nurses came in with the doctor and they were checking for a pulse and filling out paperwork. She let go of his lifeless hand, walked over to the window and closed it. He was gone and all that was left was a husk.

She walked into the hallway and—of all people—there stood Chuck. She wiped the tears she only now realized were running down her face away with her fist and looked at him.

"Chuck, what are you..."

He took her in a huge bear hug, just held her, and started crying and patting her back. She hugged him back and just let go, crying all over him.

"Dad said he just couldn't be here, and I think we both know Mom can't. He brought me to get you because he didn't want you to drive alone."

Ally took in a breath and sniffled. "But of course I have to drive."

"Well of course." He laughed and pushed away from her. "You still have a Dad, you know."

"Yes, and I have a brother. You're a royal pain in my ass on most days, but I still love you." She got on her tip toes and kissed his cheek. "Come on; let's get the hell out of here."

Sam had no idea where he was going but he wasn't afraid, he wasn't in pain, and he was blissfully happy. He could just go; he didn't have to hang around like Helen had because he had finished everything he needed to do. Helen met him leaving even as he was coming or going he wasn't sure.

"Where are you going?" Sam asked.

"The same place you are, where I belong. Thanks for everything, Sam."

"Thank you." Then Sam went were he belonged and he didn't remember being Sam anymore, but he was still happy.

Mona had been sitting with her in the living room pretending to watch TV. It was after nine, and Tuesday was already down for the night. Maggie heard the truck in the driveway and got up. What she heard as she made her way to the door was all wrong because she knew Sam was dead. Ally was laughing, so was Chuck, and she hoped they hadn't stopped by a bar and gotten drunk on their way from the hospital. She opened the door and it was obvious neither of them was inebriated, which was good because there were only the two of them so there wouldn't have been a designated driver, and she would have had to kill them both.

"I'm alright, Maggie," Ally said, and took her in her arms. "He died peacefully; he was happy. I had my cry and I'm fine. Come on in, Chuck. You want a beer?"

"You mean you don't just have those girly apple crap things you drink?" Chuck came in taking off his Taggart cap and sticking it in his back pocket, waving at both her and Mona.

"Of course I have beer. Why would I give the good stuff to dumbasses like you?" Maggie watched as Chuck and Ally walked to the kitchen talking crap and laughing.

"Don't you lose serious butch points because you don't drink beer?" Chuck asked.

"Probably, but I don't care. It tastes like piss to me," Ally said. "Plus I fought in a fucking war, so if I drank something pink with a parasol in it I'd still be more butch than you."

Maggie looked over at Mona, "Denial?"

"I don't think so," Mona said. She got up to follow Maggie to the kitchen. "You know, Maggie, Ally's pretty honest. It's a relief when someone as sick as Sam was dies."

Maggie nodded. That did sound like Ally. When Maggie walked in Ally had already pulled a beer out and handed it to Chuck. "Honey, Mona, do you want something?"

"I'd take a beer," Mona said and flopped down at the table.

"A cider," Maggie said. "Are you sure you're all right, Ally?"

"Yes."

Ally handed Mona a beer and handed her a cider then got one for herself and sat down at the table. Chuck and Maggie sat down, too. Ally read the look on Maggie's face.

"Baby, I have cried more in the last few months than I have since Helen died, and I'm just done now. Honestly I was telling Chuck on the way home. It may sound crazy, but right now I'm really happy. One of the things that's making me happy is that I know later on I'm going to miss him. My mother died, and I flat do not care and never will. I got a chance to reconnect with my dad. He's dead and I will remember him fondly. That's wonderful.

"Maggie ever since we have been together he's been here, dying. There was a killer tornado and then he killed Parish. His death means that—at least for the right now—for the first time since we've been together there is nothing for us to worry about. It's over."

"And he went out with a bang," Chuck said. Then he and Ally were laughing in that way that told Maggie that this was the horrible joke they'd been laughing at when she met them at the door. She decided to let it slide and not make it a thing.

"And in more ways than one unless I'm wrong right, Mona?" Maggie said, giving her sister a wink.

"I'll tell you what I told Ally, everyone deserves a going away present," Mona said with a grin.

"How much weight have you lost?" Chuck asked Mona.

"Fifty pounds."

"I've got to lose at least forty. Doctor said my cholesterol is through the roof...."

"The happiest day of your life," Ally teased.

"Very funny, jackass. The list of crap he told me I couldn't eat... I might as well be eating Maggie's cooking."

"Maggie's a good cook," Ally protested, and of course Maggie—like everyone else—didn't really care what Chuck thought.

"Of course you think so, Ally. You ate the cardboard, burnt crap my sister fed you with a freaking smile on your face," Chuck said. He looked at the beer bottle and frowned. "And see? From the crappy taste I knew without looking this was a light beer. This is my life now. Fat free this and lite that."

"But you get to be sick which is your favorite thing," Ally said.

"Fuck you, Ally, fuck you," Chuck spat towards Ally.

"And he thinks that's oral sex which is why he never ever gets laid," Ally said with a shrug.

"You know what, asshole...." Chuck started to get up, and Ally grabbed his arm and dragged him back into his chair.

"I'm sorry," Ally said.

"Everyone's always riding my ass," Chuck grumbled. And they did, too, because he was such an easy target.

Maggie grinned and rubbed Ally's knee under the table. Ally grinned back and Maggie realized... *She really is alright. She's not all torn up and just putting up a front. She was with him when he died. She knows he was happy, then he was gone and now she can relax. So she's happy.*

"You know what douche? If I didn't love you I wouldn't ride your ass."

"You could love me less," Chuck said with a grin.

"I really don't think I could. I barely love you as it is," Ally said. Then she got serious. "Dude you are thirty-eight years old and you have high cholesterol. You'd better quit eating crap, get some actual exercise..."

"I work..."

"Oh is that what you young people are calling it these days?" Ally said with a huge grin, "Masturbating is not a workout program."

"You are such an incredible asshole," Chuck said but laughed.

"If you don't start taking care of yourself now you're going to end up like me," Mona said with meaning. "Getting a quadruple bypass in your forties. It's not fun and then you more or less have to eat the healthy crap or admit you have a death wish."

"Christ, Mona, don't tell him shit like that. Now he'll be having a heart attack every three days," Ally said.

Mona ignored her. "The truth is after you eat healthy for a while the other stuff doesn't taste right to you anyway, and the better you feel the more you can do. I'd rather have all the energy I have and feel as good as I do now than eat the crap I used to."

"Tell the truth, Chuck. Maggie's a good cook right?" Ally said.

"Yes," Chuck said grudgingly. He looked at the light beer in his hand took a swig and said, "Yum, yum." They all laughed. He finished the beer and stood up. "Now take me home, asshole."

"I can run you home," Mona said, which made sense. After all she lived right next door to him because he didn't *still* live with his parents, but he was living with them again. After the tornado he'd moved back in with his parents not because he had lost his place in the storm but because they had a shelter and now he was scared to stay in his apartment building.

"Thanks, Mona."

Maggie stood up and hugged her sister and whispered in her ear, "Yes, thanks Mona."

"Any time, kiddo," Mona kissed her on the cheek. "I'm going to miss that old man. He was a great listener."

"I'm always here for you, Mona, you know that," Maggie said and followed them to the front door. "Thanks Chuck."

He grinned at her. "You know me. I only do what Pop tells me, right?"

"But you don't have to, so thanks."

She watched them go then went back inside and locked the door behind her. When she turned around Ally was down on her knees on the floor in front of her. "Ally, what are you doing?"

"I tried, but I couldn't do one knee."

Maggie took a deep breath and held it then said, "Ally, are you doing what I think you're doing?"

"Probably. I can't read your mind." Ally looked nervous and so when she started digging in her pocket Maggie was sure she knew. "I know what you're going to say, that my timing sucks but... Right now we don't have anything to worry about and you never know how long that's going to last. It was the last thing my dad asked me to do."

Ally pulled a box out of her pocket opened it and held it up so Maggie could see it. It was beautiful.

"Maggie, will you marry me?"

Maggie had never for a moment thought that she would ever get married. She wasn't one of those girls who made books and had dreams of white weddings and fancy cakes and bridesmaids and dresses. She didn't pick a play list and flowers and such at twelve. She honestly had never even considered that she might marry anyone let alone Ally, or that Ally might want to marry her. She was silent and didn't move to take the ring, and Ally took Maggie's absolute shock for rejection.

"Look, Maggie, I know you probably hate the whole idea of a piece of paper and legal crap and all, but I love you. I want to marry you for all the right reasons, because I love you, I want to spend the rest of my life with you, and because we can. I want us to have the same rights that other couples take for granted. I want to adopt Tuesday, and...."

"Give me that ring and get out off the floor." Maggie grabbed the ring, box and all, then helped Ally get out of the floor. She looked at the ring and then at Ally. "Are you sure this is what you want, Ally?"

"It's all I want." Ally took the ring from the box and looked at her expectantly.

Maggie held out her hand and Ally slipped the ring on it; it fit perfectly.

"So are you just taking my jewelry or are you going to marry me?"

"Yes, yes I will." How could something she didn't even know she wanted till ten seconds ago make her so happy?

Ally seemed to start breathing again then she was hugging her and Maggie was hugging her back.

"So where are we going?" because of course though it was legal at a federal level, it still wasn't legal to marry in their state.

"You know what, Maggie, check it out online, find out where it's legal, and pick the place you'd most like to go."

"You know I've never really been anywhere, baby, so why don't we just go where it's going to be cheapest?"

"See I knew you were perfect."

Ally was silent for a minute then said, "When Tuesday asks—and he will someday—can we tell him that you decided to have him. That he's a product of artificial insemination? Is that any bigger a lie than you writing on his birth certificate that you don't know who his father is? That way he'll just be ours, Maggie, and that's the truth."

Maggie thought about it only a minute. "You're right; the truth is that he's our son."

When Ally woke up the next morning she felt almost hung over from the emotional roller coaster of the day before. She looked at where Maggie was wrapped up in her arms and at the ring on her finger. Tuesday walked up to the foot of their bed rubbing his eyes.

"Someone's at the door."

Ally heard the doorbell. She untangled herself from Maggie who hardly moved, got up and threw on her robe. She looked at the clock; it was eight.

"So my guess is we aren't going to work today."

"Mitch said take the day off," Maggie said, stretching.

Tuesday crawled into bed beside Maggie and Ally headed for the front door.

"Where are you going?"

Ally didn't have to answer because Tuesday did. "Someone's at the door."

Ally opened the door and a truck driver was standing there with a clipboard in his hand. She looked past him and his truck was holding something huge. She couldn't make out what it was without walking out on the porch. Trucks had been pulling in and out for months now with building materials. After all most of the houses in their neighborhood had been flattened or badly damaged and there was a lot of building going on.

"Who ya looking for?" she asked, because this wasn't the first time a truck had stopped to ask for directions. Her dad had told them where to go till he wasn't there anymore. She had a momentary lump in her throat when she remembered he was dead.

"Ally Taggart," the trucker said reading it off the manifest.

"There must be some mistake; I didn't order anything."

"The pool was custom made, ordered and paid for by a..." He looked down at the clip board. "...Sam Boyd."

"What is it?" Maggie asked, walking up behind her fully dressed and still causing the trucker to smile and move to get a better view.

Ally just grinned. He could look all he wanted.

"I almost forgot. Dad told me he got me a birthday present. It's weird it came today; he died yesterday," Ally told the truck driver.

"I'm sorry for your loss," the trucker said, and stopped ogling Maggie no doubt out of respect for the dead.

"It's alright. He had cancer and he killed someone, so if he didn't die he would have had to go back to jail anyway." The guy looked at her like she'd grown another head but she just shrugged and turned to Maggie.

"Dad bought us a pool."

Not just any pool, either. It was just the size she'd talked about—eight by sixteen, three feet deep at one end and five at the other—and it was the oddest shape she'd ever seen.

"What is it?" Maggie asked, looking at the shape of it as the guy unloaded it onto their vacant lot where Ally directed him.

Surprises like this were pretty inconvenient when you thought about it. After all if she'd known it was coming she would have excavated the hole, done all the plumbing, and they could just set it in it.

"I'm sure I don't know. It's got a very natural shape to it, and he had it custom made, so it's got to be something but... I just don't know what."

The truck driver walked over for her to sign that the pool was delivered without any damage or cracks in it.

"Do you know what it is?" she asked him.

He shook his head and handed her a rough sketch of the shape. On a piece of paper at the bottom it said *for Ally* in her dad's handwriting.

"Where did he get the money for this?" Maggie asked.

"I'm sure I don't know," Ally said. She knew it cost at least five thousand dollars, and God only knew what the delivery cost.

"From his room," Tuesday said.

"What, Honey?" Maggie asked.

"Come on; I'll show you." He took Ally's hand and led her into the house and to the guest bedroom. Ally had a momentary sense of loss when she walked in. She had been in here since her dad left and knew he'd made the bed, cleaned, vacuumed the floor and taken all of his things with him, but she hadn't bothered to look in any drawers. Tuesday lead her over to one and pointed. When she opened it she didn't find money, but she did find her dad's photo album. When she opened it to where it bulged in the middle there was a whole stack of cash. The note on top said, "For when you and Maggie get married."

In the several thousand dollars in cash was the paperwork from where he had cashed in an IRA two months earlier. She handed both the note and the paperwork to Maggie.

"That's where he got the money."

It wasn't enough money for him to have stayed even two months in a nursing home and besides she was glad he had stayed with them... before he went to jail.

Maggie picked up the money flipped it in the air and said, "And now I'm thinking we go to Hawaii to get married."

"We're getting a pool and we're getting married?" Tuesday asked excitedly jumping up and down, though Ally wasn't sure he even knew what "married" meant.

Maggie must have been thinking the same thing because she got down to his level and asked, "Do you know what married means?"

He looked thoughtful then said, "Like Mitch and Karen and Kathy and Ray."

"Well I hope not like Kathy and Ray," Ally mumbled. Maggie shot her a look and she shrugged.

"And Ally and I are going to get married," Maggie said. She smiled and looked up at Ally.

Ally smiled back; she was happy. Her dad had died the day before and she was ecstatic and something told her he was happy, too. Or she was just telling herself that to keep from having guilt to go with the money and her new pool.

"If it's alright with you of course," Ally said to Tuesday.

"Is anything going to change?"

"We're going to have a new pool," Ally said with a grin.

Maggie cut her a look and she shrugged really nothing was going to change except.... "We'll be legal, Tuesday. It means we can take care of each other and no one can say we can't."

"And I will really be your son?"

"You already *are* really my son; now there will just be paperwork to prove it."

The mortuary called two days later and Ally went to pick up her dad's ashes. They were in a plastic bag in a cardboard box that was taped shut. His name was on the side and so was a big stamp that said Human Remains. It felt sort of weird carrying that box knowing that was all that was left of a human body. But it was sort of tidy, too, not like the whole body in a coffin thing. Mitch and Karen had insisted Helen be buried, and for years when she lay awake unable to sleep and morbid thoughts toyed with her brain, she would get an all-too-vivid picture of Helen's body rotting in the ground. Then something would remind her maybe Helen's spirit— she liked to think it was—that thing in the ground wasn't Helen at all any more than this box of ashes was her father. She wound up setting them on the dresser in the guest bedroom till she could make a decision about where to put them.

Maggie assured her it would come to Ally in time and that it wasn't unusual for people to hang onto the ashes for a while as part of the grieving process. Ally had grieved before and she wasn't sure that was what she was doing now.

The day after she picked up her father's ashes she was at work again when the police department called to say she could have her service revolver back. She told them to just let it be melted, which made Maggie happy. Then they gave Maggie's car back which didn't make Maggie so happy.

Carol called to invite her—alone of course—to come to the memorial her dad's church was having for him. Part of her really wanted to go just to show her whole entire ass, but in the end she declined. Her sister asked her about his ashes and Ally lied and told her she had already spread them. She didn't want some stupid-assed custody battle over a box of ashes and knew Carol would plant him by their mother which was the one place he had said he specifically didn't want to be.

They soon learned that getting the paperwork to make

Tuesday legally Ally's and Maggie's was going to take every bit of the money Sam had left in the dresser. So they decided to go to Iowa to get married. Of course the only day Maggie could get them a date was a Tuesday. Mona was going with them as one witness, and as luck would have it the only other person Ally could find that could go with them on a week day had been Chuck. They all loaded into Mona's car because it was the best for the trip, but of course Mitch made Ally promise she would drive. Ally was sure the trip would be a true test of her and Maggie's love and commitment because... three adults, a three-year-old, and Chuck on an eight-hour road trip there and eight hours back.

They rented one room with a king for themselves and one with two queens for Chuck and Mona and Tuesday to share. For a change Chuck didn't whine or bitch at all, and he only claimed to feel sick once, so the trip wound up being a blast. The marriage ceremony itself was brief but very nice, and of course Mona, Maggie and Chuck all cried.

Frankly Ally had never gotten the crying when you're happy thing, and Tuesday had looked up at her confused and said, "I thought they wanted to get married."

Ally wanted to marry Maggie mostly for legal reasons, and she really thought it wouldn't change the way she felt, but there was a feeling of affirmation that she couldn't deny. The joy of having something she never thought she would have. Since they'd gotten back from Iowa Ally had called Maggie her wife so much that she was sure she was annoying the crap out of the guys she worked with. She didn't expect straight people to understand what a huge deal it was that they were actually and factually legally married. It was *huge*.

Of course they weren't married a week when Carol and Jimmy sold the bait and tackle shop, and because it had still been in her father's name Ally got half the money from the sale which was thirty-thousand bucks. So Ally's first thought was if they had waited a week they could have gone to Hawaii to get married. She was sure that her sister and her husband hadn't realized that they would have to hand half the money over to her. It made it all that much sweeter that it must have chapped Carol's ass raw.

Her father hadn't left a will, and he'd already legally signed over the house, so there was no way Ally could get any part of that. But because they had kept the store in her father's name—to dodge taxes—when they sold it by law they had to give her half. All things considered she had no guilt taking it. As good Christian folk her sister and brother-in-law should have known better than to lie to Uncle Sam.

She was able to pay off their house and their new lot. They could afford to put the pool in the way they wanted and still have enough money left over to have a serious honeymoon, or maybe a huge party and wedding ceremony at home. They knew what they really wanted to do, but their family and friends were pushing for the big party so they were having a little trouble making up their minds. There was no pressure to make a decision right away so they didn't. Maggie said if they gave it time the universe would tell them what they should do, and Ally was just fine with that.

Ally finished the rock work on their waterfall. Of course their pool was completely finished just in time for it to be too cold to use it, but they did any way.

"Come on in the water's fine, my ass," Maggie said, shaking like a leaf as she started to dry off.

"But it's not cold, it's not." Tuesday didn't want to get out, but his teeth were chattering and his lips were nearly blue.

"Yes, oh yes it is," Ally said and grabbed him.

It was as she was getting out of the pool carrying their son and they were all freezing their asses off that she knew just exactly where to put her father's ashes. Why she knew she didn't have any idea but she guessed Maggie was right and the universe was telling her.

That weekend she loaded the truck with her fish and tackle, grabbed her wife, her kid, and her dad in the box and headed for White Horse Lake.

"So," Maggie said with a smile as they started down the road. "We're going to dump your dad's ashes and then we're going to go fishing?"

"Yes. Well two things, baby. First, my dad would come back to haunt us if we went to the lake and didn't throw a line in the water. Second it's basically illegal to dump human remains in a public waterway, so fishing is our excuse for being there."

"And if we get caught?"

"You show some cleavage and we say we didn't know any better." Ally laughed.

The whole drive she felt an uneasy feeling in her stomach that had nothing to do with what she planned to do or even a fear of getting caught doing it, and everything to do with going back to a place where she was everyone's whipping boy. A place where she had no real friends, no one ever had her back, and she had been bullied, harassed and beaten until she left.

It was a place she was glad she left and really had never had any desire to go back to.

But Maggie and Tuesday were with her, there were a host of people who had her back now, and just before her dad died he was one of them. She was legally married; she had rights. The closed-minded fuckers of Wicker Falls would never embrace her, but it didn't matter because Wicker Falls was her past, and she didn't, couldn't, wouldn't live in her past. Besides she wasn't going to the school or that God-forsaken church, she was going to the lake. Ally had always felt safe and at peace on White Horse Lake.

So had her dad.

When they went past her father's bait and tackle shop she pointed it out. The lights in the windows were too bright, and the sign was some gaudy back-lit plastic piece of shit, but she had no way of knowing if that was something Carol's husband had done or if it was the new owners. She didn't stop; she'd brought her own bait and gear. She drove through town towards the lake.

"It's beautiful," Maggie said, as they turned a corner and suddenly there was the lake. "It's huge."

It was. You could have put three Flint Rock Lakes in it. There weren't a lot of people at the park, no doubt because the kids had gone back to school and the wind had a little bit of bite in it. She drove around till she found a spot way off the beaten track where they had to hike through a small section of woods to get to the water. It was, without a doubt, her father's favorite fishing spot.

She had put the box with his ashes in it into a cooler. She grabbed her poles and the cooler and let Maggie handle the tackle box.

"Let's do this and get it over with," Ally said as she set the cooler down. Maggie nodded and Ally pulled the box out. She tried to rip the tape off but couldn't find the end, and ripping it open didn't work either. Giving up she opened the tackle box and dug around till she found her pocket knife. Her hands were shaking and she was extra twitchy, but she couldn't have told you in that moment if it was because she was messing with her father's ashes or because she was afraid of getting caught.

She took the knife and went to cut through the tape. Of course when she did the knife slipped and she cut into the bag on the inside and little bits of her dad fell on the ground which she quickly decided was alright since there wasn't a damn thing she could do about it. She finished opening the box and dragged the bag out making sure the small hole was on the top. She quickly walked to the water's edge. "Dad, you always loved this place, and I hope you rest in peace."

Then Ally very unceremoniously dumped the ashes in the water. They sort of heaped up right there in the shallows.

Maggie handed her a twisted stick.

"What's this for, some mystic thing?"

"I was thinking you could stir the ash up so that it would dissipate," Maggie said.

"Oh, good idea." Ally stirred. "Do you want to say something Maggie, Tuesday?"

"Goodbye Sam and thanks... you know for not sleeping on the couch," Maggie said.

Ally smiled.

Tuesday looked thoughtful then said, "That doesn't look like Sam."

"No it doesn't, because it's not," Ally said. She stuffed the box and plastic bag back into the cooler and sat on the lid. She watched as the ashes started to drift in the water. It wasn't happening quickly; it was taking some time. "Ah... let's get the hell out of here."

They hauled their crap back to the truck and drove back to the front of the park because of course the minute there wasn't a crapper in sight Tuesday had to make number two.

Ally used the bathroom then waited outside for Maggie and Tuesday. She sat on a bench and looked at the lake. She smiled.

I know this is where he'd want to be. I miss him, and that feels good. Love the pool, Dad. Don't know what the hell it is, but... Then she remembered what her Dad had said when he told her he had bought her something for her birthday. He said, "Remember how much fun we had there." *It's White*

Horse Lake it has to be. She walked around the building looking for and finally finding a topographical map, and when she saw the lake on the map and the shape of it she smiled.

Maggie walked up behind her and Ally pointed to the map.

"That's our pool," Tuesday said, jumping up and down.

Ally picked him up so that he could see it better.

"Oh Ally." Maggie put her arms around her and rested her head on her back. "That's wonderful."

"Now I love it even more," Ally said. "Come on; in Dad's memory let's go throw some lines in the water."

"Just be still, dork," Ally said, watching Chuck jump around as Karen tried to tie his tie for the sixth time. She finally finished and moved on to Ally's

"Why couldn't they have given us normal ties?" Chuck said.

"You mean with clips on the back?" Ally teased.

Karen laughed and finished tying her tie.

"Fuck you, Ally," Chuck snipped.

"Chill out, Chuck," Ally said. "You'd think you were the one getting married... Oh that's right, you are."

"I said fuck you, Ally."

"And still not oral sex." Ally laughed.

"I know how to do oral sex, asshole."

"Well not there," Ally said, making a face.

"Kids really," Karen said, patting them both on the shoulders. "Is that any way for family to talk to each other?"

"Mona... you look amazing," Maggie said, and fixed Tuesday's hair for the third time.

"Am I making a huge mistake?" Mona asked.

"Do you love him?"

"Yes, but he's such a doofus, he's twelve years younger than I am, and we've only been dating for six months... and he's a doofus."

"You said that already."

"But at the end of the day, Maggie, that's what bothers me most."

"You let Mother get in your head. I told you—didn't I tell you—not to invite her. Don't pick today to start listening to her. Chuck's a good guy and he's crazy about you. He has a good job and at least your lawn will always get mowed."

When Mona had first told her she was dating Chuck, Maggie had to admit she was not quite ready for Chuckona. But Mona—who had already raised two kids—knew just how to make Chuck toe the line, which was what he needed. She also knew when to give him a hug which he also badly needed. He was a hypochondriac; she was a nurse. It was sort of a match made in heaven.

Together they had both lost weight and were in much better health which was too bad for Chuck, except Maggie noticed that now that Chuck was happy he didn't enjoy being sick as much. Mona made Chuck happy. More importantly for Maggie, Chuck made Mona happy because he made her feel special. Turned out dumbass Chuck was the kind of man who brought his girlfriend flowers, wrote her poetry, opened doors, and pulled out chairs. He wanted to go dancing all the time so he could show her off. He told her every day how much he loved her, and in return Mona loved him.

After the wedding Mitch grabbed Maggie away from Ally and started dancing with her. Maggie grinned at him. She could tell he was three sheets to the wind.

"We should have done this for you and Ally. You know, a big fancy wedding," Mitch said.

"We decided we'd rather go to Hawaii, remember? Besides it wasn't legal in this state till last week," Maggie said. They were already legal federally when the Supreme Court decided it was legal in all fifty states. It was huge, but the truth was even if she had it to do all over again she'd still rather spend a week alone in Hawaii with Ally than have some big, huge wedding. If they had spent their money on that it wouldn't have been for them; it would have been for everyone else.

"So we have officially joined the Muntz sisters to the Taggarts, and we are legally one big, happy family."

Maggie watched as Ally swooped in and saved Chuck from Agnes, only to start leading. Chuck just sighed in relief and let her as they danced across the floor looking goofy as shit.

"Just so you know, neither Mona nor I expect you to include Mother in the family," Maggie said, grinning.

"Have you and Ally made a decision yet, Maggie?"

She started to pretend like she didn't know what he was talking about, but knew that wouldn't shut him up. "Well I had my tubes tied after I had Tuesday, which sort of seems like a waste now, but maybe it's meant to be because my uterus is just fine and it sort of makes me the perfect candidate," Maggie said. Karen and Mitch wanted a grand baby. That was something they weren't going to get from Mona and Chuck, but of course Ally still had Helen's eggs on ice.

"Does that mean yes, Maggie?" She'd expected Mitch to pressure her much more than Ally had.

"Like I said, I had my tubes tied and we want another baby. We both loved her and Helen had to have some reason for wanting a baby so much. Who knows, maybe this baby is going to save the world or cure cancer. We're going to do it, though Ally says it means we're going to wind up on Jerry Springer for sure. But I'm just having one, and you're paying for the implantation because it's super expensive. Mostly you have to promise me you'll still treat Tuesday the same."

"Honey, Tuesday's always going to be my grandson."

After his ring bearer part was over, Ally had run Tuesday over to Frances so they had to swing by and pick him up before they could go home. Frances opened the door looking rumpled and half asleep. She pointed towards the couch where Tuesday was sleeping on Laurie's head. Laurie had recently been thrown out of the newest girlfriend's house and was crashing with Frances. This was just one of the many reasons Ally loved Maggie.

Ally walked over, picked him up, and carted him out to the truck where she had a fight with the damn car seat belts as she held the sleeping boy's head up because Maggie was about half drunk.

"Thanks, Frances," Maggie said.

"Twern't nothing. I can see why you guys want another one. That one's pretty special."

"Thanks, while your kid on the other hand…." Ally threw up her hands with a grin.

"I have to get a life so that I have nowhere to put her," Frances said.

"But she has to be a total bitch like me," Maggie said.

"Oh, Honey," Frances said, leaning on the open window of the truck. "I will take a bitch like you any day."

As Ally pulled into the driveway she could plainly see someone sitting on the porch.

"Stay here."

Ally got out of the truck and locked the door as she shut it. She walked slowly up wishing she'd thought to leave the porch light on. "Hello, can I help you?"

"Ally?"

She recognized his voice mostly because he sounded so much like her dad. "Kyle?"

"Yeah."

"What the hell are you doing here?"

"My parents kicked me out of the house. I didn't know where else to go."

"Are you gay?" Ally asked carefully.

"Maybe." He shrugged. "I really don't know. I surely don't think there is anything wrong with it. They got mad because I wouldn't tell them one way or the other, but they mostly kicked me out because I told them I didn't believe any of the fucked-up stuff they believe. That I didn't believe in heaven or hell and wasn't sure I believed in God, but I sure didn't believe in the devil. That people did evil because they wanted to not because the devil made them do it. But I guess the kicker was that they ordered me to tell them if I was gay, and I told them it shouldn't matter and hadn't they learned a damn thing."

"How did you get here?"

"I've been working and I had saved some money. I got a bus ticket. I walked here from the bus depot." Which was at least five miles away. "I know I don't know you and you don't know me, and you have no reason to take me in, but you took Grandpa in and you had no reason at all to do that. I'd like to get to know you. I wouldn't be any trouble I promise."

Maggie had gotten out of the truck. She walked up behind Ally and put her hand on her shoulder. "He needs some place to stay, Ally."

And of course Kyle was the exact same age she had been when her parents threw her out of the house.

"Are you clean? I won't have any drugs in my house with my family."

"I am sober for over a year now, I promise. I'll take a drug test if you want. I only need to crash here till I start college in the fall. I've got a scholarship that includes a dorm room.

And I can work. I thought maybe you could get me a job at your company, you know Taggart's Landscaping."

"I don't own the company, but I can probably get you a job. However if you screw up I am the one that will shit can your ass."

Ally looked at Maggie and Maggie nodded and said, "He can stay."

She turned to Kyle. "We don't have a lot of rules. No drugs, and please don't kill anyone while you're living under our roof."

Ally laughed, handed her keys to Maggie and went to get Tuesday out of the truck as Maggie fumbled with the keys trying to get the door open.

Ally carried Tuesday past Kyle and when she did their eye's met. "You look just like Dad." She nodded her head towards the open door. "Grab your bags and come in."

He followed her in, closing the door behind him.

"Just let me lay my son down and check to see where my wife's at. I'll be right back."

He nodded.

She laid Tuesday down and found Maggie waiting there. Maggie started taking off his clothes and putting him in his pajamas, and Ally helped her.

"Is this such a good idea, Maggie?"

"His energy is fine. He's scared, but who wouldn't be?" Maggie kissed her on the cheek.

"But you're drunk, Maggie, and you know your wuju doesn't work when you're drunk," Ally said in near panic.

"I'm nowhere near drunk. I'm a little tipsy. He's fine." She sighed. "Though I must admit that I hate sharing our one bathroom with a man again."

Ally nodded; she knew just what she meant.

"We need our own bathroom. I have no idea where we'd put it, but we need one."

"Well I'm going to go get a bath, so whatever he needs to do will just have to wait."

Ally nodded and went back to the living room. She found Kyle looking at some of her paintings. "Did you do all of these?"

"Yes."

"I draw."

"Good." She picked up one of his bags and led him to the guest room. "I used to have a studio of sorts, but now it's a little boy's room. I'm thinking of building one in the yard."

They walked in and she put the bags on the bed. "The TV is hooked up to cable, there is a plug in behind the dresser and one in the closet... Don't ask me, it was like that when I bought the house. Maggie lied; there are actually a lot of rules here, but we can touch on those in the morning. No smoking."

"I don't smoke," he said. He unzipped his bag and pulled out a sketch pad, and that's when she saw it. He had a fishing pole packed in his bag.

She smiled as she took the sketch pad he handed her. She pointed at the fishing pole.

"We'll have to go fishing."

"I love to fish," he said.

"Me, too." Ally opened the sketch pad took a deep breath and then sat down on the bed. He was good—at least as good as she was—but that wasn't why she had to swallow her tears. It was a picture of her dad fishing in his favorite spot.

"Kyle, this is really good, and this is right where I put his ashes."

"Really? That was his favorite place to fish."

Then they looked at each other and said at the same time, "Which means it was his favorite place." They laughed and he proceeded to show her his drawings.

Maggie looked in and saw them talking and looking at a sketch pad. For a second she could see the shadow of Sam's spirit hover over the boy's face. The old man had moved on, but he hadn't gone far.

ABOUT THE AUTHOR

I started writing at twelve as an escape. The situations I have lived through are the stuff of which my fiction is born. My relationships with the many and varied people I have come into contact with over the years is a catalogue of characters from which I pull.

I am Jewish but consider myself spiritual not religious. I have studied every form of spirituality and try to live a spiritual life. I don't always succeed, but I do try.

My wife of nearly twenty-four years and I own a small farm where I raise milk goats, rabbits, chickens and a garden. I raise—depending on the weather and bugs—between forty and sixty percent of our food mostly organically. By "mostly" I mean if it looks like I will lose an animal I will do what I think is necessary. We make no trash; we use or recycle everything.

I lived for fourteen years of my life without electricity or running water. I had my only son naturally with no drugs. Though I was married off at sixteen (in an attempt to keep me from being gay) to a thirty-four-year-old man who immediately took me to New York and stuck me in a drug den for a month, I have smoked a total of five joints in my life. I have never done any other drugs. My son was a prescription drug addict for nine years.

I have worked every shit job you can imagine from pulling car parts in a junk yard and cleaning rich people's houses to home health care. I ran an industrial plane and have logged timber using a team of mules. I have worked at saw mills, framed houses, and poured slabs. I am a carpenter and a rock mason. I can run (install) electricity, and I can plumb (I hate plumbing). I have also built more than one house using only hand tools and a chain saw. I like to hike and cave, and I love the ocean.

I fought heavy weapons (and trained other fighters) with the SCA for about twelve years. During that time I broke several bones, and I have a seven-inch plate and eight screws in my left arm as a result of a bastard sword blow. Elizabeth

Moon talked me into fencing many years ago and I still do that, but I sold all my armor and heavy weapons last year. Erin Grey talked me into trying Tai Chi to help with my CFS, so I have now been doing do a mixture of Tai Chi and Chi Gung every day for the last five years.

Mercedes Lackey helped me get my first short story sale in Marion Zimmer Bradley's magazine. That sale opened the door for others to MZB, one of which was included in a German-language anthology, and the royalties came in steadily for many years.

CJ Cherryh line edited the first two chapters of *Chains of Freedom* and taught me more about writing doing that than I had learned to that point.

I'm not just name-dropping here; I'm giving credit to people who helped me who certainly didn't have to. Over the years I've come to know many very famous people, and here's what I know for sure—we are ALL the same.

In the writing community the person who is the most famous and makes the most money is often the least talented or deserving—not always, but often. In our business who makes it and who doesn't is often determined by nothing in the world but dumb-ass luck. That being the case, the near worship we see of the "famous" is something I just don't get at all.

The truth is I always think bios are sort of a waste. Anyone who reads my work knows more about the real me than I could ever put in a bio. If you want to talk to me, find me on Facebook. If you see me somewhere, come right up and talk to me. I am just like you. Luckily, I have a job I love, and the reason I have this great job is that people like you let me.

ABOUT THE COVER ARTIST

Melanie Fletcher is an expatriate Chicagoan who currently lives in North Dallas with her husband the Bodacious Brit™ and their five fabulous furbags JJ, Jessica, Jeremy, Jemma, and Jasmine (yes, they were following a theme, moving along now). When not herding cats, she turns into SF Writer Girl, and has the SFWA membership card to prove it. Her recent SF sales include "The Lark Ascending" (serialized in **Gearhearts Steampunk Glamour Review**) and "Le Gardien" (*Tales from a Lone Star: A Future Classics Anthology*, Belaurient Press). She also writes paranormal erotic romance under the name Nicola Cameron, and her second novel *Two to Tango* was just released in June from Evernight Publishing.

Yard Dog Press Titles As Of This Print Date

A Bubba in Time Saves None, Edited by Selina Rosen

A Man, A Plan, (yet lacking) A Canal, Panama, Linda Donahue

Adventures of the Irish Ninja, Selina Rosen

The Alamo and Zombies, Jean Stuntz

All the Marbles, Dusty Rainbolt

Almost Human, Gary Moreau

Ancient Enemy, Lee Killouth

The Anthology From Hell: Humorous Tales From WAY Down Under, Edited by Julia S. Mandala

Ard Magister, Laura J. Underwood

Assassins Inc., Phillip Drayer Duncan

Bad City, Selina Rosen & Laura J. Underwood

Bad Lands, Selina Rosen & Laura J. Underwood

Black Rage, Selina Rosen

Blackrose Avenue, Mark Shepherd

The Boat Man, Selina Rosen

Bobby's Troll, John Lance

Bride of Tranquility, Tracy S. Morris

Bruce and Roxanne from Start to Finnish, Rie Sheridan Rose

Bubba Fables, Sue P. Sinor

The Bubba Chronicles, Selina Rosen

Bubbas Of the Apocalypse, Edited by Selina Rosen

The Burden of the Crown, Selina Rosen

Chains of Redemption, Selina Rosen

Checking On Culture, Lee Killough

Chronicles of the Last War, Laura J. Underwood

Dadgum Martians Invade the Lucky Nickel Saloon, Ken Rand

Dark and Stormy Nights, Bradley H. Sinor

Deja Doo, Edited by Selina Rosen

Dracula's Lawyer, Julia S. Mandala

The Essence of Stone, Beverly A. Hale

Fairy BrewHaHa at the Lucky Nickel Saloon, Ken Rand

The Fantastikon: Tales of Wonder, Robin Wayne Bailey

Fire & Ice, Selina Rosen

Flush Fiction, Volume I: Stories To Be Read In One Sitting, Edited by Selina Rosen

The Four Bubbas of the Apocalypse: Flatulence, Halitosis, Incest, and... Ned, Edited by Selina Rosen

The Four Redheads: Apocalypse Now!, Linda L. Donahue, Rhonda Eudaly, Julia S. Mandala, & Dusty Rainbolt

The Four Redheads of the Apocalypse, Linda L. Donahue, Rhonda Eudaly, Julia S. Mandala, & Dusty Rainbolt

The Garden In Bloom, Jeffrey Turner

The Geometries of Love: Poetry by Robin Wayne Bailey

The Golems Of Laramie County, Ken Rand

The Green Women, Laura J. Underwood

The Guardians, Lynn Abbey

Hammer Town, Selina Rosen

The Happiness Box, Beverly A. Hale

The Host Series: The Host, Fright Eater, Gang Approval, Selina Rosen

Houston, We've Got Bubbas!, Edited by Selina Rosen

How I Spent the Apocolypse, Selina Rosen

I Didn't Quite Make It To Oz, Edited by Selina Rosen

I Should Have Stayed In Oz, Edited by Selina Rosen

In the Shadows, Bradley H. Sinor

International House of Bubbas, Edited by Selina Rosen

It's the Great Bumpkin, Cletus Brown!, Katherine A. Turski

The Killswitch Review, Steven-Elliot Altman & Diane DeKelb-Rittenhouse

The Leopard's Daughter, Lee Killough

The Lightning Horse, John Moore

The Logic of Departure, Mark W. Tiedemann

The Long, Cold Walk To Mars, Jeffrey Turner

Marking the Signs and Other Tales Of Mischief, Laura J. Underwood

Material Things, Selina Rosen

Medieval Misfits: Renaissance Rejects, Tracy S. Morris

Mirror Images, Susan Satterfield

Mirror, Mirror and Other Reflections, James K. Burk

More Stories That Won't Make Your Parents Hurl, Edited by Selina Rosen

Music for Four Hands, Louis Antonelli & Edward Morris

My Life with Geeks and Freaks, Claudia Christian

The Necronomicrap: A Guide To Your Horoooscope, Tim Frayser

Playing With Secrets, Bradley H & Sue P. Sinor

Redheads In Love, Linda L. Donahue, Rhonda Eudaly, Julia S. Mandala, & Dusty Rainbolt

Reruns, Selina Rosen

Rock 'n' Roll Universe, Ken Rand

Shadows In Green, Richard Dansky

Stories That Won't Make Your Parents Hurl, Edited by Selina Rosen

Tales from Keltora, Laura J. Underwood

Tales Of the Lucky Nickel Saloon, Second Ave., Laramie, Wyoming, U S of A, Ken Rand

Tarbox Station, Rhonda Eudaly

Texistani: Indo-Pak Food From A Texas Kitchen, Beverly A. Hale

That's All Folks, J. F. Gonzalez

Through Wyoming Eyes, Ken Rand

Turn Left to Tomorrow, Robin Wayne Bailey

The Twins, Selina Rosen

Wandering Lark, Laura J. Underwood
Wings of Morning, Katharine Eliska Kimbriel
Zombies In Oz and Other Undead Musings, Robin Wayne Bailey

Just Cause
(A YDP Imprint):

The Bitter End
Selina Rosen

Double Dog
(A YDP Imprint):

#1:
Of Stars & Shadows, Mark W. Tiedemann
This Instance Of Me, Jeffrey Turner

Death Under the Crescent Moon
Dusty Rainbolt

The Ghost Writer
Selina Rosen

It's Not Rocket Science: Spirituality for the Working-Class Soul
Selina Rosen

#2:
Gods and Other Children, Bill D. Allen
Tranquility, Tracy Morris

Meditations of a Hoarder
Melinda LaFevers

Not My Life
Selina Rosen

#3:
Home Is the Hunter, James K. Burk
Farstep Station, Lazette Gifford

The Pit
Selina Rosen

Plots and Protagonists: A Reference Guide for Writers
Mel. White

#4:
Sabre Dance, Melanie Fletcher
The Lunari Mask, Laura J. Underwood

Vanishing Fame
Selina Rosen

Non-YDP titles we distribute:

#5:
House of Doors, Julia Mandala
Jaguar Moon, Linda A. Donahue

Chains of Freedom
Chains of Destruction
Jabone's Sword
Queen of Denial
Recycled
Strange Robby
Sword Masters
Selina Rosen

Three Ways to Order:

1. Write us a letter telling us what you want, then send it along with your check or money order (made payable to Yard Dog Press) to: Yard Dog Press, 710 W. Redbud Lane, Alma, AR   72921-7247

2. Use selinarosen@cox.net or lynnstran@cox.net to contact us and place your order. Then send your check or money order to the address above. *This has the advantage of allowing you to check on the availability of short-stock items such as T-shirts and back-issues of Yard Dog Comics.*

3. Contact us as in #1 or #2 above and pay with a credit card or by debit from your checking account. Either give us the credit card information in your letter/Email/phone call, or go to our website and use our shopping carts. If you send us your information, please include your name as it appears on the card, your credit card number, the expiration date, and the 3 or 4-digit security code after your signature on the back (CVV). Please remember that we will include media rate (minimum $3.00) S/H for mailing in the lower 48 states.

*Watch our website at
www.yarddogpress.com
for news of upcoming projects
and new titles!!*

A Note to Our Readers

We at Yard Dog Press understand that many people buy used books because they simply can't afford new ones. That said, and understanding that not everyone is made of money, we'd like you to know something that you may not have realized. Writers only make money on new books that sell. At the big houses a writer's entire future can hinge on the number of books they sell. While this isn't the case at Yard Dog Press, the honest truth is that when you sell or trade your book or let many people read it, the writer and the publishing house aren't making any money.

As much as we'd all like to believe that we can exist on love and sweet potato pie, the truth is we all need money to buy the things essential to our daily lives. Writers and publishers are no different.

We realize that these "freebies" and cheap books often turn people on to new writers and books that they wouldn't otherwise read. However we hope that you will reconsider selling your copy, and that if you trade it or let your friends borrow it, you also pass on the information that if they really like the author's work they should consider buying one of their books at full price sometime so that the writer can afford to continue to write work that entertains you.

We appreciate all our readers and *depend* upon their support.

Thanks,
The Editorial Staff
Yard Dog Press

PS – Please note that "used" books without covers have, in most cases, been stolen. Neither the author nor the publisher has made any money on these books because they were supposed to be pulped for lack of sales.

Please do not purchase books without covers.